Every Bride Has Her Day

LYNNETTE AUSTIN

Published by Sourcebooks Casablanca, an imprint of Sourcebooks, Inc.
P.O. Box 4410, Naperville, Illinois 60567-4410
(630) 961-3900
Fax: (630) 961-2168
www.sourcebooks.com

Printed and bound in Canada.
MBP 10 9 8 7 6 5 4 3 2 1

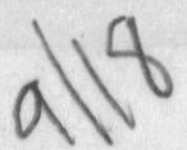

Chapter 1

Sam DeLuca had never run away from a fight. Until now. And look where it had landed him.

Smack-dab in the middle of nowhere.

"This has to be the stupidest idea I've ever had."

He'd forgotten how dark country nights could be. A thin moon scuttled from cloud to cloud and only a rare star twinkled in the inky sky. His Harley's single headlight cut a narrow swath through the darkness.

Not a solitary light shone from the windows of any of the houses he passed. Was every single person in Misty Bottoms, Georgia, asleep?

He checked his GPS. He was close. As he approached an intersection, he slowed, watching for a street sign. And then he spotted it. Frog Pond Road. Thank God.

Eighteen years had passed since he'd last stepped foot in this town, and he'd been all of twelve. Sitting at the crossroads, he couldn't remember if he was supposed to turn right or left. *Well, roll the dice and pick one.* He could always turn around if his choice proved to be wrong. Traffic sure wasn't a problem.

The clock on his instrument panel read a little after one a.m. He'd expected to get here while it was still daylight. But between his late start and all the hold-ups due to interstate construction, well, it was what it was.

His already-sour mood took a further dip when he

caught sight of his great-aunt Gertie's house. Hell, his house now. Or what remained of it.

Sam pulled up in front of the deserted building and sat on the motorcycle, legs spread, studying it in the nearly nonexistent light. No street lamps. No porch lights. He cursed small towns and rundown houses as the Harley idled smoothly beneath him.

He backed up and turned the motorcycle so that he sat perpendicular to the house, his headlight bathing the tumble-down two-story.

"Nope, not a very well-thought-out plan, bud."

Muttering a curse, he wondered if he shouldn't book a room at some little motel for the night—if he shouldn't pull a U-ey right here and head north, back to the city.

A person would have to be crazy to even consider doing anything with this place. But then he was crazy, wasn't he? Why else would he be here?

Maybe it was karma, and he was meant to move into this dump, which looked as broken-down as he felt. Maybe the two of them could nurse each other back to health or at least some semblance of sanity.

Squinting, he studied the place once more before setting his kickstand and climbing off the Harley. Nah. Who was he kidding? He and the house had both passed the point of no return.

Hands on his hips, he stood at the curb, sizing up the place the way he would a suspect and deciding on his approach.

The weeds and overgrown yard made it nearly impossible to even see the house itself. Tree branches, long overdue for a trimming, scraped against the siding, sending a chill along his spine. Damned if some film producer couldn't walk right in and shoot a horror movie here.

A New York City detective, he'd charged into many a dark alley, faced more than one drawn gun aimed at him by some badass high on meth or cocaine or simply the thrill. Yet the idea of wading through that waist-deep grass in the pitch-black had him sweating. Who knew what hid in those weeds?

From the time he was eight till he'd turned twelve and become obsessed with Little League baseball, he'd spent two weeks every summer here with Great-Aunt Gertrude. That was plenty long enough to learn that snakes lived in this stuff. Gertie had insisted they were more afraid of him than he was of them. Guess he'd have to take her word on that because if it were true, he sure as heck was safe. There wouldn't be any reptiles within twenty miles. They'd all have turned tail and slithered away.

And now here he was back in Misty Bottoms. Gertie was gone, but because of the bond they'd forged, she'd left this place to him when she'd passed two years ago. Some Southern lawyer had mailed him the deed and a key. At the time, Sam had sworn he'd never step foot in the house again. He'd had every intention of putting it up for sale.

But he hadn't, and now he needed a hidey-hole, a place to take stock of his life, to heal physically and emotionally. This place had seemed as good as any other. Until he'd seen it again, anyway.

Still, why was he hesitating? For Pete's sake, it couldn't be worse than those dark alleys of New York, could it? But then, hadn't one of those alleys betrayed him? Hadn't he ended up facedown on the rough pavement in a pool of his own blood, the stench of garbage permeating the air?

Not for the first time, the idea that the department had missed someone, that one of Nikolai Federoff's men was still out there set on revenge, wrapped him in a stranglehold. Fighting off the bleak memories, he shoved the paranoia into his back pocket and waded in.

Halfway to the house, an owl hooted, and he automatically reached for his shoulder-holstered gun, the gun that wasn't there anymore. His rueful laugh sounded loud in the once-again silent night.

Sam unlocked the door and winced as it creaked open. When he flipped the light switch, nothing happened. Mentally, he kicked himself. Of course he had no electricity or air-conditioning. Other than the taxes and insurance, he hadn't paid any bills or contacted anyone. After all this time, the electric company was bound to have shut off service. He wouldn't have water, either, and that was something he should have factored in, but because he'd been in such a hurry to get away, he hadn't.

Some insurance agent had sure been ripping him off because there was no way this place was worth the stated valuation. But he'd worry about that later, in the light of day.

A spider's web brushed his cheek, and he swiped at it. The flashlight on his cell played over the wallpaper in the hallway and up the stairs. Years of sitting empty hadn't been kind to the house. A neighbor had closed it up after Gertie passed. Sam himself had been undercover and hadn't made it back, then or since.

His nose wrinkling at the musty smell, he pried open

the two living room windows. "Got to get some air in here," he mumbled. "Some circulation. Tomorrow I'll see about having the place fumigated."

Neither window had been locked despite the house having been closed up for so long, yet no one seemed to have been inside. No graffiti. No garbage. No used needles or beer cans and no whiskey bottles. Small town Misty Bottoms, so very different than the city he was used to.

Thankfully, both windows had screens that seemed to be intact. Hopefully they'd keep out whatever insects hadn't already made their way into the house. A moth had come through the door with him and fluttered around the edge of his phone. He swatted at it, and it darted away.

As his flashlight's beam swept the room, he swore again. Coming here had been as bad an idea as booking passage on the *Titanic*. He'd pretty much run out of options, though. After he grabbed some much-needed shut-eye, he'd see about making the place habitable. Right now, four- and six-legged varmints were about the only things that could have been comfortable in this house.

That said…

Sam waded back out to his bike, relieved to breathe clean, fresh air. He opened one of his saddlebags and removed a bottle of water, then grabbed the package that held his brand-new sleeping bag. In the other pouch, beneath his all-weather gear, he dug out a change of clothes. He'd crash on the living room floor tonight. Even Bill Gates couldn't pay him enough to venture up to the second story in the dark.

Back inside, he guzzled the water and wondered vaguely about the house's plumbing. *Que será, será.* With a shrug, he stripped off his jeans and shirt and slid into the bag.

Hot, road-dirty, and bone-tired, he hoped to sleep long and hard. His imagination, however, had different ideas. The thought of what might be keeping him company had him on full alert. When he did finally drop off, it was a light, uneasy sleep.

Bang, bang, bang!

What the hell? Sam sat bolt upright and glared at the weak stream of sunlight that stole around the edges of tattered drapes.

Rubbing sleep from his eyes, he tried to remember where he was. Aunt Gertie's. His gaze traveled over the room, which looked even worse than it had in the dark.

But none of Federoff's goons would announce themselves, so he cursed, flopped back down, and tugged the sleeping bag over his head.

The banging started up again.

Somebody'd better be in the middle of a life-or-death crisis. Throwing the bag open, he sat up again. Who in the hell would come barging in on a total stranger at practically daybreak? He glanced at his watch. Nine o'clock. Okay, slightly past daybreak. It didn't matter.

He'd ridden hard yesterday and God only knew when he'd finally actually fallen asleep. Hauling on his jeans, his fly half-zipped, he staggered shirtless to the door, where the banging continued.

When he threw it open, a furious woman stood there

in baggy clothes, her short, choppy blond hair framing a pixie face. She yanked a slim phone from the pocket of her oversized, olive-drab cotton pants. "I'm callin' the sheriff. You're trespassing."

Raking fingers through his hair, he closed his eyes and counted to ten. God save him from do-gooder neighbors.

"Good idea. See if he delivers coffee."

"What?" Storm-colored eyes widened.

He made to shut the door, but she crammed a sneakered foot in it.

"Oh no, you don't. Who are you?"

"The big bad wolf," he growled. "And I eat little girls like you for breakfast. Go on home to your mother."

She sputtered. "My mother? For your information, I—"

"I don't want any information. I want sleep. Move your foot."

"No, I won't. Who are you?"

"I already answered that question."

She simply raised a brow, and her foot stayed in his door.

Sam squinted. The bright morning sun behind this infuriating stranger hurt his road-weary eyes. Her hair looked like she'd stuck her head in a blender. Kind of. Snipped short at the top and in front, it hung just past her jaw on the sides. He'd never seen anything like it. Yet, now that he looked closer, that blond, blond hair with its darker roots framed one heck of a face. And those winter-storm eyes? Whew!

She smelled like fresh rain and sunshine. And wildflowers.

He didn't care. It didn't matter what she smelled like or what her face looked like as long as she removed it from his sight.

When he attempted to close the door again, she wedged her body against the doorjamb.

"What is wrong with you? You're not welcome. Go away."

"Who are you?"

On an exasperated sigh, he gave in. "Sam. Your name?"

"Cricket."

"Like the bug?"

She ignored that. "What are you doin' here?"

"I own the place."

"You do not. Ms. Gertie owns it."

A sense of sadness and loss pinched at his heart, and his voice softened. "Gertie died."

"I know." She raised the hand that still held her phone and hit a number.

He groaned.

The woman had absolutely no street smarts. Sam stood close enough that he could have plucked the phone from her hand if he'd wanted to, then dragged her inside and had his way with her. Was her naïveté the product of rural America rather than the worldliness of the cosmopolitan he usually dealt with, or was it only her? Could things really be that different here?

He heard a male voice answer and strained to catch his words.

"Hey, Cuz, did Ms. Gertie leave her house to some guy—"

"Her great-nephew," Sam snarled.

"Some guy named Sam." Her eyes traveled over him. "Dark, kind of surly. Claims he's her great-nephew."

"Yep." The answer, short and clipped, carried to Sam.

"Okay, thanks." Without so much as a good-bye, she ended the call and studied him again. "Your eyes are bloodshot. Have you been drinkin'?"

"Any law against that?"

"No, I guess not, since you're not behind the wheel of a car or a motorcycle." She glanced contemptuously over her shoulder at his Harley. "Still, it seems kind of early."

"See, there's the thing. You hit it right on the head. It *is* early considering what time I got to bed. And I *was* driving the Harley. For sixteen hours straight yesterday. I need sleep—which is exactly what I was doing till you started banging on my damn door."

She ignored that, her eyes narrowing. "So maybe I won't call the cops."

"I am the cops."

She snorted. "That's what they all say, Sam."

He toyed with the idea of badging her, then decided against it. She wasn't worth the bother. Besides, his badge wouldn't carry any weight here in Georgia, and he doubted it would even faze this woman.

"You don't know me from Adam, yet you come tromping over here pummeling my door, assuming I've broken into the house and am a squatter. No weapon, no defense at all."

"This is Misty Bottoms."

"So?"

"So it's safe here. Where are you from?"

"Not Misty Bottoms, that's for damn sure." Again, he

closed his eyes momentarily, then opened them to meet hers. "Look, the fact remains that I could be a serial killer. Don't you have any survival skills, any sense of self-preservation?"

"I certainly do," she drawled. "And they're tellin' me to walk away from you. Think I'll run on home and fix myself a nice big stack of pancakes. I don't need your negative vibes."

"My negative—"

But she'd already made it down the rickety front-porch steps and was picking her way along the weed-choked sidewalk.

He started to slam the door but instead leaned against it and watched her cross the road, her pale blond hair shining.

Nothing, absolutely nothing about her matched his ideal woman, the type he found attractive. Still, there was something. Those eyes. Oh, yeah. And that mouth and sexy Southern drawl. She'd smelled good amid the decay of this house.

Speaking of smelling. Now that she'd mentioned them, darned if he couldn't all but smell a stack of warm, golden pancakes, swimming in syrup and melted butter.

His stomach growled, and he patted it absently.

There had to be somewhere in this flyspeck on the map where he could get a decent breakfast—without any of the complications a meal with Cricket would surely entail.

Slowly, he closed the door.

Talk about starting off on the wrong foot. But that was actually a positive, wasn't it? He didn't want to be a good neighbor, didn't want to get involved in anybody else's mess. He had a big enough one of his own.

He'd come to Misty Bottoms, to Gertie's, for solitude. He'd come to be left alone.

To get away from suspicion, betrayal, and lies. Away from sympathy and pity.

Cricket slammed into her kitchen. Holy Toledo! The man was hot! And rude.

So okay, she'd jumped the gun. In his place maybe, just maybe, she'd have been a little put out, too. She'd wakened him from a deep sleep and insinuated he'd broken in. The red eyes? He'd been telling the truth. She hadn't smelled any alcohol on him, so no doubt the bloodshot eyes were the result of long hours on that big motorcycle, like he'd said.

She moved to the kitchen window and fingered back the curtain over the sink. The big, black bike hunkered down at the curb. How had she not heard him roaring up the street on that last night? Had she really slept that soundly?

When he'd yanked that door open, her heart leaped into her throat. He looked for all the world like some dark god standing there, jeans half-zipped and bare chest with that trail of hair leading to—well, to the unsnapped waistband of those well-worn jeans. And he'd made not a single move to cover himself or make himself presentable.

Yep, the big, bad wolf incarnate.

She fanned herself. Best not go any further.

A nasty, fairly new scar marred that otherwise perfect chest. A story there?

None of her business.

Reaching into the cupboard, she pulled out a mixing bowl and the O'Malley family's secret pancake recipe, then dug around for the ingredients she needed.

Did he actually intend to live in that house? She'd caught a glimpse of it when she'd planted herself halfway inside. What a disaster. And the smell. Stale with an underlayment of… She didn't want to think about it. Yuck!

Sam must be hurting for money. Why else would anybody in his right mind even consider staying there? She'd noticed the sleeping bag spread on the floor. That couldn't be comfortable.

Watching out the window, she saw not a sign of life in the house. He'd apparently gone back to sleep. What a waste of a beautiful day. Well, his loss.

She turned up her stereo and did a few hip swivels to Miranda Lambert's gritty, empowered-woman lyrics. That lady always made her feel good.

Half an hour later, her resolve to ignore her neighbor had evaporated. She could at least feed him. From the way his jeans drooped at the waist, she guessed he'd lost some weight recently. Of course, it could simply have been that he hadn't bothered to button them before answering the door.

Whatever. She crossed the street once more, this time with a plate of warm pancakes drenched in melting butter and maple syrup in one hand and a cup of freshly brewed coffee in the other. Now if she could navigate the cracked, uneven walk of weeds again, she'd be good.

The steps were rickety, and she held her breath as she tiptoed across the porch, certain it would give way beneath her any minute. Hands full, she bumped the peeling front door with her elbow. Once, twice, three times.

The door flew open, and she almost tumbled inside.

"You again!"

"Yep, and I come bearing gifts."

He eyed the plate hungrily. "Damn Trojan horse."

"Nope." She shook her head. "Nothin' hidden here. What you see is what you get."

"Oh yeah?" Shamelessly, he allowed his gaze to travel the length of her. Those damn baggy clothes kept him from catching so much as a hint at what lay beneath them.

A smudge of flour streaked across one cheek, and his hand lifted to wipe it away. Fortunately, he caught himself and lowered it back to his side.

"I don't know if you take cream or sugar in your coffee." She held it out to him.

He couldn't resist. Against his better judgment, he reached for it. "Black." The scent of it tickled his nose, and he took that first sip. Manna. Whatever else this woman did or didn't do, she made a mean cup of coffee.

"You're welcome," she said.

"I didn't thank you."

"I noticed."

"Pretty darn cheeky, aren't you?"

"You're pretty darn rude."

Despite himself, he laughed out loud. It almost startled him, it had been so long. "Thank you."

Without a word, she held out the plate, silverware, and an actual cloth napkin.

Juggling the coffee, he took them. "Thanks."

He nodded toward the living room. "I'd, ah, invite you in, but this place is in seriously bad shape. It's filthy and stinks to high heaven."

"Why don't we sit on the steps?"

"You think they're safe?" he mumbled, eyeing them. A few spots of paint hung tenaciously to the otherwise bare wood, and they leaned crookedly to one side.

"They've held so far."

He dropped to the top step and she moved down a couple, leaning on a banister that tilted precariously.

Hungrily, he wolfed down the cakes. He doubted even his last meal at Delmonico's had tasted as good. His new, temporary neighbor reminded him of the cheerleaders in high school, all perky, fresh, and outgoing.

He hadn't been very nice to her earlier. Catching himself, he almost laughed at the understatement. He'd been in-your-face rude, yet here she was feeding him. What was up with that?

"I don't know what shape your bathrooms are in or if you even have any water." She nodded at his house. "I thought after you eat, you might want to come over and take a nice, hot shower. If you really did travel as long as you said—"

"I did," he answered around a mouthful of pancake. "I have a lot of faults, Bug, but lying isn't one of them."

He thought of his last undercover assignment. But that wasn't actually lying. That had been doing the job, a job that nearly got him killed.

"Bug?"

"Yeah, you said that was your name."

"I did not."

"Did too."

"My name's Cricket."

"Cricket. Bug. Same thing." He shrugged.

With a small sound of annoyance, she grabbed for the not-quite-empty plate. "Maybe I'll take these back home with me. Feed them to the birds."

He moved the pancakes just out of her reach. "You wouldn't."

"Want to test me?"

"Not this morning." He speared the last couple bites before she could carry through on her threat. "Not sure why you fed me after I about bit your head off, but thanks. These are some of the best pancakes I've ever eaten." He held up his coffee cup. "This, too."

"You can have another cup while you shower."

He narrowed his eyes. "Why are you being nice to me?"

"Because we're neighbors. Here in the South, we watch out for each other."

"You don't think I'm from the South?"

"New York would be my guess."

He leaned back, resting on his elbows. "Really?"

She nodded. "Despite sleeping half the day away, I doubt you sit much. You've got a restless edge about you."

Damned if she wasn't right. He'd have to keep an eye on her. She read people too easily, and he didn't want her stumbling on the nightmare of his life, didn't want her catching even a glimpse of that reality.

But he'd accept her hospitality once more. Yesterday's ride, coupled with last night in that filthy house, left him desperate for some soap and shampoo.

"Besides," she said, "you've got a New York plate on that big motorcycle of yours."

He barked a laugh. "Got me." He paused. "You serious about that shower?"

"Yes. But I need to head into town pretty soon. My new shop's grand opening is set for next Friday, and I still have a ton of things to do."

"I'll make it fast. What kind of a shop?" he asked as he headed inside for his clean clothes.

"A flower shop. There were, um, some problems with the last owner."

"Oh?" He stuck his head out the door, clothes bundled under one arm. Considering, he shut the door but decided locking it would be the ultimate in foolishness. Nobody else would head in there without a hazmat suit and a darn good reason. "So you're from here?" he asked as they crossed to her house. Then he kicked himself. *Don't ask questions. Don't get involved. You're not here to make friends*. Still, something about this woman tugged at him.

"I was born here, but I've been away now for, oh gosh, twenty years. So I guess you could say I'm new in town, too. I have family here, though."

"Yeah, I gathered that."

Her forehead creased.

"Your cousin. The one you called when you wanted to have me thrown in jail."

She mock grimaced. "Sorry about that. That was Beck Elliot. He and his family are practically the backbone of the town, along with the Beaumonts. Beck's family owns the lumberyard, and he runs a construction company."

Sam rubbed a hand over the stubble on his jaw. "Good to know. My guess is I'll be on a first-name basis with Cousin Beck if I decide to do anything with Gertie's place."

"Ms. Gertie taught my mom in Sunday school, and they kept in touch. Gertie was old school and still believed in letter writing."

"Yeah, she wrote to me, too."

What a difference, he thought, as he neared Cricket's house. Night and day from his, everything was all neat and tidy, including a fresh coat of white paint with deep-green trim. Some kind of flowering plant arched over a trellis.

He fingered one of the sweet-smelling flowers. "What is this?"

"Wisteria, Yankee boy. One of the South's treasures."

"Uh-huh." More flowers hung from the porch while others lined a white picket fence. The porch, one step up from sidewalk level, held still more plants in colorful pots. He guessed it made sense since she owned a flower shop. Colorful Adirondack chairs waited for someone to sit and take a load off. All in all, the house was homey. Nice.

She obviously sensed his interest. "I brought some things with me, but a lot of my furniture is donations and hand-me-downs. Mrs. Michaels wanted to move to Wyoming to live with her daughter and grandkids, so I got the house dirt cheap. It still needs some work, so don't expect too much."

He shook his head. "You're wrong. This is cozy. I could sit right here with a cup of coffee and a good book all day."

"Somehow I doubt that. You feel like a bundle of nervous energy to me."

"I'm working to lose that. It's part of the reason I'm here." Damn. He hadn't meant to let that spill. What was wrong with him? Where was his cop training? This woman made it way too easy to talk.

She swung the door open, and he grinned.

The kitchen smelled of pancakes and coffee. A pot of sunflowers sat on the counter beside fresh produce. He chuckled. Whatever else Cricket was, "tidy chef" would never earn a spot on her résumé. Bowls, spoons, measuring cups, and spilled flour cluttered the counter and farmer's sink. She added his dish and cup to the mix.

"Sorry." She ran her fingers through that choppy, blond hair, standing pieces on end. "I wanted to get your cakes to you while they were still warm."

"And I and my stomach thank you. I'll help you clean up since the cook shouldn't have to. That was always the rule at my house."

"I like that rule, but I've got it today. Why don't you grab your shower?"

"You sure?"

"Absolutely."

She led him down the hallway, a country song echoing through the house.

"You a country music fan?"

"You bet I am. You?"

"No, not so much."

He caught a glimpse of her living room and a spare bedroom. The door to the master hung open, giving him a view of strewn clothes and an unmade bed. Cricket was a free spirit from the word go, no doubt about it. Guess she'd rather play in the dirt than do housework. Though to give her her due, take away the clutter and the house was squeaky clean.

"The towel is fresh, and there's a new bar of soap in the shower. Feel free to use the shampoo."

"Thank you. I can't tell you how much I appreciate this." He closed the door, turned on the water, and stripped. The water was hot and plentiful, and he almost whimpered as it rained down on him, rinsing away the road grime and the tension of the past few weeks.

He poured shampoo in the palm of his hand and smelled Cricket—light, floral, and woodsy. He'd either have to pick up something a little more masculine in town or be prepared to turn in his man card.

And when he bought the shampoo, he needed to load up on garbage bags. Lots of garbage bags. Gertie's house—*his* house, he reminded himself—needed a thorough cleaning out regardless of how long he stayed. The time had come to quit straddling the fence. The house needed to go on the market—if it could be salvaged.

As he lathered his hair, he found himself hoping he could save the place. Gertie had lived a good life in that house and, for five years, had shared a few happy weeks of summer vacation with him there. He'd hate to see it crumble beneath a wrecking ball. He owed Gertie more than that.

Chapter 2

THE SHOWER DID ITS JOB, AND SAM LEFT THE BATHROOM a new man. "Cricket?"

When he got no answer, he assumed she'd stepped outside. He finger-combed his wet hair and headed for the kitchen. Like so many other things, a haircut hadn't been high on his priority list, and he was more than a few weeks past a trip to the barber's.

Peeking around the corner into the kitchen, he spotted a glass of iced tea, along with a note, in the center of the neon-green table.

Sam,

I'm off to work. If you're still hungry, check the fridge. Don't worry about locking up when you leave. Nobody will bother anything.

You can return the glass later.

Welcome to Misty Bottoms,
Cricket

Disbelief, followed by temper, chased through him. She'd gone to work and left him, a stranger, in her home? Didn't she watch TV? Read the paper? Listen to the news?

He knew she was safe with him, but she had absolutely no way to know that. This lady needed a keeper, but he sure as hell didn't intend to sign up for the job. No, sir. Living alone out here, though, she'd darned well better wise up, and fast.

But that was her problem, wasn't it?

His? Taking care of the utilities. Until he had running water and electricity, Gertie's house would remain uninhabitable.

While he downed the tea, he took a closer look at Cricket's surroundings. He'd like to think it was the cop in him, but honesty demanded he acknowledge it for what it was—curiosity, plain and simple. He wouldn't open any drawers or closets, but he needed more than the fast glimpse he'd caught on his way to the bathroom.

The kitchen itself was homey and comfortable, and the counters now devoid of dirty mixing bowls and spilled flour. Obviously, Cricket had been busy. Open shelves held an almost obsessively organized arrangement of dishes and glassware along with a couple funky, multicolored roosters.

Herbs flourished on the windowsill above the farmer's sink, and no curtains filtered the Georgia spring sunshine.

The neon-green pedestal table and chairs, along with more open shelving, were tucked into an eating nook. Books fought for space on already-crammed shelves, and he ran a finger over the spines. Romance, suspense, and true crime. Several recipe books mixed with tomes on plants. No surprise on that last considering her occupation.

Moving to the doorway, he grinned. Her living room was sparse, furnished with a white slipcovered sofa and a comfy, overstuffed, tomato-red chair. A distressed-looking teal trunk served as a coffee table. But it was the wall behind the sofa that caught his attention. A giant bulletin board had been hung there, chock-full of children's artwork. The vivid colors splashed life into the room. Moving closer, he saw several had been signed to "Aunt Cricket." So the bug wasn't an only child. Seemed Andy and Mindy, in addition to being exceedingly prolific artists, were fond of crayons, watercolors, and Aunt Cricket.

Sam sighed and rubbed the back of his neck. This sure as heck beat the decor in Gertie's house, even, he knew, once he chipped away the grime.

He turned back to the kitchen, refusing to peek into her bedroom. That was way too personal and totally off-limits. He'd had that quick glimpse earlier and had seen enough to know the bedroom was indeed her personal sanctuary.

Cricket. An interesting character.

Hands stuffed in his jeans pockets, he turned a three sixty. The place fit her. If he were a betting man, he'd have gone all in that the white walls and flooring were left over from Mrs. Michaels. But the funky roosters, the neon-green table, and bright red chair? The teal trunk? Definitely Cricket's taste.

It might have been fun getting to know her—if he'd come to Misty Bottoms to socialize. But he hadn't. He didn't need or want anybody poking around in his life—or into his psyche—right now. As if to remind him, a sharp pain shot through his shoulder. He rubbed it absently as he headed across the street to his own place. It galled him to leave her door unlocked.

Fed and showered, he couldn't put off the inevitable. First on his to-do list had to be a ride into town to take care of the utilities. And, unless he wanted to run a load of laundry every day, he'd have to buy another pair or two of jeans along with a couple T-shirts. While Gertie had a washer, she'd never bothered with a dryer. He'd found the clothesline he remembered from his visits sagging between two metal poles in the backyard, but no way in hell did he intend to hang his boxers out there in front of God and country.

While he was in town, he'd keep a lookout for a laundromat. It was so much simpler at home. He simply dropped his stuff off once a week at Lenny's Cleaners and picked it up the next day washed, ironed, and folded.

Even though he had nothing of value of his own in the house, unlike Cricket, he locked up this time since he was doing more than running across the street. The cop or the cynic? Whatever. It didn't matter. Crime made no exceptions based on zip code.

He hopped on his Harley, turned the key, and felt the healthy thrum of the engine beneath him. Tugging on his helmet and dropping his dark glasses in place, he headed toward the bustling metropolis of Misty Bottoms, population five thousand and ten.

In last night's inky darkness, he hadn't seen much. He'd missed the towering oaks with their drapes of Spanish moss and the splotches of color from well-tended flower beds. Yards were newly mowed, hedges trimmed, and houses well maintained. People here obviously took pride in their homes.

His? A blight on the neighborhood. Shame jabbed at him. Well, he couldn't undo these past two years, but he was here now, wasn't he? He'd take care of it. Then it would be up to the new owners to maintain it.

In town, he turned down Anderson's Alley. More than once, he found his gaze traveling to the side-view mirror as a niggling feeling of being followed skimmed up his back. Nah, he wasn't in New York anymore, wasn't wearing his badge. Those troubles had been left hundreds of miles away.

Bumping along the cobblestones, he said a prayer of thanks it wasn't raining. These suckers would be slippery when wet.

Kitty's Kakes and Bakery looked exactly as he remembered it. Gertie had taken him in for a treat once in a while, and coming from a family of five kids, that was a big deal. Even a trip to the Golden Arches nearly bankrupted his dad, so the whole crew rarely went out to eat.

But when he was here with his aunt, there was no sharing or clamoring for attention. He'd had her all to himself.

A pink-and-green awning shaded the front window and welcomed him. Trays of pies, doughnuts, and golden breads lured in passersby. Pulling to the curb, he set his kickstand. Maybe he'd grab another cup of coffee and chat up the server for some information.

Even though he had no intention of mingling with the locals, he needed to know the lay of the land. Where better to get it than from one of their own? He might be able to drag the latest gossip and happenings around town from the person working the counter. After all, hadn't he spent his career investigating and doing undercover work? This was just more of the same, really.

But all that had been BI. Before Ingrid. Before he'd nearly died. Before something essential in him *had* died. Hands on his hips, he stared up at the colorful awning.

Maybe the time had come to resuscitate that spark, that enthusiasm for life—if that was possible.

He swung through the door and the cheerful little bell overhead tinkled merrily. Personally, he'd like to rip down every single one of the annoying chimes.

But maybe that was just him. Somebody must like them.

Then he grinned, his bad mood evaporating.

No barista here. Kitty herself leaned on the counter. She'd put on a few pounds and earned some wrinkles, but he'd have known her anywhere.

"Can I help you?" She wiped her hands on a frosting-smeared apron.

"I think you can, Kitty. My great-aunt left me a house—"

The baker's hands flew to her cheeks. "Sammy? Sammy? Gertie's little nephew! All grown up. Look at you!"

He cringed. Nobody—not one single person—had called him Sammy since he'd turned thirteen and announced his name was Sam. His oldest sister had goaded him with the nickname once, but he'd gotten her good for it, and that had been that.

He cleared his throat. "Yeah, well, it's Sam now, ma'am."

"Of course it is." She sighed. "Gertie certainly enjoyed your visits. That's all we heard about for weeks before you came and weeks after you'd left." Her eyes grew sad. "I sure do miss her. We all do. Your aunt was truly one of the good ones."

He nodded, not sure what to say. But he'd had his fill of sadness and pity. "Yeah, well." He rubbed the back of his neck. "I'm staying at her place for a bit."

Kitty made a face. "It's a mess, isn't it? Darn shame it's been let go like that." Heat colored her cheeks. "Oh, I didn't mean—"

"Nope. It's okay. I'm the one who neglected it. The fault lies right here." He jerked a thumb at himself. "Came in to get the utilities turned on. Don't suppose you can tell me where I go to make that happen?"

"Sure can. Wait till you see the Taj Mahal the electric company built for itself. Then they have the nerve to charge us eighteen dollars a month to pay for it. Customer service charge." Kitty humphed, then picked up an order pad and flipped it to the back. "We're here." She marked a star. Then she went on, pinpointing the utility offices as she drew a map. "You tell them I said to take good care of you."

He smiled at her and tucked the paper in his pocket. "Will do. Before I go, though, I could sure use a cup of coffee. Black." He peered into the doughnut case. "And even though I already had a good breakfast, I think I'll have a bear claw. It's been a long time."

"For here or to go?"

"For here."

Even as Kitty reached inside for his treat, she asked, "You eat at the diner this mornin'?"

Sam did a mental eye roll. How long would it take before he remembered he wasn't in the city anymore? Small towns had a way of knowing everything about a person almost before they knew it themselves.

"Ah, no, actually. My neighbor fixed me some pancakes this morning."

"Your neighbor?" Her forehead creased, then cleared. "Oh, y'all must be talkin' about Beck's cousin, Cricket.

She moved in about a week ago. Cute little thing, isn't she? Took over the flower shop from that horrid woman who was there before. She'd named the place *Bella Fiore*. Pretty uppity for here."

Sam reached into his shirt pocket and dug out the little map. "Could you mark the flower shop on here? I'd like to stop by and thank Cricket again for breakfast."

"You bet." She marked an *x* on the map. "You won't have any trouble findin' it."

"Great. Thanks, Kitty."

She scooped his bear claw out of the case and plated it. "Sure do miss Brenda Sue. She ran that shop for next to forever. Didn't figure that city gal who took it over would last long. She—well, I'm not even goin' there."

Hmmm. Another person who didn't look favorably on the last florist. He'd have to make it his business to find out what happened there. Maybe. Then again, maybe not. It really didn't affect him one way or the other, did it?

"Did you hear that Jenni Beth Beaumont started up a wedding venue out at Magnolia House?"

"No." Who the heck was Jenni Beth Beaumont, and what was Magnolia House? Cricket had mentioned the Beaumonts, too.

"I haven't really kept up on things here," he admitted. "Gertie used to write me, or we'd talk on the phone, but since she passed, I really haven't had any connection to Misty Bottoms."

"Jenni Beth's new business is the most excitin' thing to hit Misty Bottoms since…well, probably since the War of Northern Aggression." Again, she colored.

No doubt she'd remembered he was one of those with Northern aggressor's ancestors. A damned Yankee.

Clearing her throat, she covered with, "Her first bride and groom? Bikers." Kitty set his pastry and coffee on one of the small tables, indicating for him to join her.

He figured the nod amounted to the same as a royal edict, so he did. The first bite of the bear claw had him sighing with pleasure.

"These are to die for, Kitty."

"Thanks, honey. Anyway, her first couple had themselves big old Harleys." She nodded toward the window. "Lot like that one of yours. The bride rode down the aisle on hers."

"Different." He didn't know what else to say.

Kitty sighed. "Jenni Beth is probably the most beautiful thing on two feet. She's absolutely gorgeous—but doesn't act it. Which, in my opinion, makes her all that much prettier."

Sam nodded and thought of his next-door neighbor. Not so bad looking herself but annoying as all get-out.

"So you're movin' in to Gertie's, I'd guess, if you're wantin' electricity and such."

"Not permanently," he corrected quickly. "It's temporary. Kind of a time-out."

"Oh, really?" Curiosity burned in her eyes.

He shut his mouth. Oh yeah, he'd developed a severe case of foot-in-mouth. He'd lost his touch in just the couple months he'd been off the streets. But he would *not* broadcast that he was NYPD. Not yet anyway. So much for flying under the radar, though.

He said nothing while he folded his napkin in half, then half again.

"Here, let me fetch you some more coffee." She grabbed his nearly empty cup and moved behind the counter to fill it. She glanced over her shoulder. "Are you actually stayin' in that old house?"

"Yes, ma'am. Got in late last night and put my sleeping bag to good use." He tossed her a small smile. "I didn't realize it was so run-down."

"It is now, but accordin' to Gertie, you helped maintain that place for her. Because of you, Sam, and the money you sent, she was still in her home at the end. Thank you for that."

Uncomfortable, he squirmed in his chair. He took a big bite of his bear claw, then sipped the scalding coffee she set down and was rewarded with scorched taste buds.

He didn't want gratitude. He'd helped financially, but he hadn't visited. He hadn't even made it to her funeral, though he had, at least, arranged for flowers…as if that made up for his neglect.

But he'd been deep undercover when she'd gotten sick. Lousy job. It had cost him, and the people he loved, a lot. Too much.

Following Kitty's hastily drawn map, he made quick work of the utilities. A little info, more than a little money for deposits, back charges, and the customer service fee Kitty had warned about, and he was good to go. The falling-down house on Frog Pond Road had running water and lights once again.

The better to see you, my dear, he thought. *Cracked plaster, spiders, and all.*

Time he headed back and rolled up his sleeves. Still, would it hurt to take five minutes to run past Cricket's flower shop? Curiosity ate at him and would, he knew, till he scratched that itch.

Glancing at Kitty's map, he realized he was close. Old Church Street.

As he swerved to miss a pothole, he understood where the "old" came from. The street was old as sin. He slowed to a crawl as he spotted her place. Son of a gun if Cricket's shop wasn't a repurposed railroad car. It had been connected to another small building in the back. Clever. And, again, it suited her.

The door opened and a guy stepped out. Blond and rugged, he looked like he ate nails for breakfast. Sam decelerated as Cricket stepped out behind Blondie, a huge grin on her face. She followed him down the short flight of stairs, the expression on her face announcing Christmas had come early.

Once on the sidewalk, Cricket stepped closer, and the guy wrapped his arms around her, dwarfing her. When he gave her a cheek kiss, she laughed and kissed him back.

Better scratch little miss florist off his list of interesting things to do while in town. Obviously she had a connection here. Or…considering her invitation to breakfast, maybe she was just friendly with all the guys. Kind of like Ingrid.

Before he could turn around, she spotted him and waved. He drove by as though he hadn't seen her. And he could live with that.

Chapter 3

Guilt and excitement mixed in Cricket's system. She had so much to do, yet she'd left boxes sitting in the middle of the shop and locked up way earlier than she'd originally planned. Thus, the guilt.

A horn tooted out front, and she ran outside just as Beck hopped out of his monster truck. And there was the reason for the excitement. When he'd dropped by her shop yesterday, he'd promised to take her to meet Jenni Beth this afternoon.

Jenni Beth and Magnolia House, weddings, and bridal bouquets—a dream come true.

"Hey, Cuz." He slid his sunglasses up to rest on top of all that thick, blond hair. "See your neighbor's keepin' an eye on you."

Sure enough, she followed his gaze and spotted Sam at the window. The curtain drifted back into place, and he was gone.

"What do you know about this guy? Should I be worried?" He paused. "Didn't he ride past the flower shop?"

"He did. Mr. Nose in the Air. What do I know about him?" She tapped a fingertip on her lips. "Let's see. His name's Sam. He rides a Harley, claims he's Gertie Taylor's great-nephew, doesn't like country music all that much, and he's lost quite a bit of weight recently. Oh, and he might be a cop."

Beck's brows shot up. "A cop?"

She made a face. "He kind of threw that out there, and I couldn't tell if he was kiddin' or not."

"Okay. Maybe I should have a talk with Jimmy Don. Have him check out this Sam. You're kind of isolated here, and—"

"I'm fine, Beck. Believe me, if he meant to do me harm, he would have yesterday morning when I banged on his door and woke him after a very short night's sleep."

Now her cousin's eyes narrowed. "Why'd he have a short night's sleep, and exactly how do you know that?"

She waggled her brows, a mischievous grin curving one side of her mouth. "It had nothing to do with me. Girl Scout's honor. He'd ridden sixteen hours on that motorcycle to get here."

"Where'd he come from?"

"Jeez, how would I know? I didn't ask for his life history, but he's got New York plates." She rested a fist at her waist. "You're worse than my brother, and that's going some."

He held up his hands in surrender. "I'll drive, then drop you off back here. Jenni Beth's excited to finally meet you."

"I'm nervous," Cricket admitted.

"Don't be. You won't meet a nicer person anywhere. The fact that she took back that rascal Cole Bryson proves it."

"I don't know. Cole sounds pretty dreamy to me. When she and I spoke on the phone, she sounded over the moon about him."

"Yeah, well, that road goes both ways, believe me. Cole figures he's the luckiest guy this side of Saturn. And I was just kiddin'. Cole's one of my best friends."

"They're lucky, aren't they?"

Beck's jaw tightened. "Guess so. If that's what you're lookin' for. Me, I'm single and happy about it."

Cricket detected sadness behind those words and more than a little anger. Some woman had done Beck wrong. For that, she was prepared to hate her on sight. Maybe Jenni Beth would fill her in.

"You ready?"

"I am."

As Beck opened the truck's door for her, Sam stepped out of his own house, bounded down the rickety front stairs, and headed into the backyard.

"Friendly cuss, isn't he?" Beck muttered.

"I think he's havin' a tough time right now."

"Oh, Pollyanna, what am I gonna do with you and those rose-colored glasses?"

"Let me keep wearin' them?"

Beck said nothing, simply shook his head.

Cricket buckled up, then rolled her shoulders. The morning, spent unpacking and placing inventory, had been a physical one, but she couldn't remember the last time she'd been so excited. It was like buying a new notebook for the beginning of the school year. Nothing had been written in it yet, no mistakes made. The pages waited to be filled.

"I owe you so much, Beck. A month ago, I was out of work and fast running out of hope. One phone call from you changed all that."

He sent her a sideways glance. "It's good to have you back in the Low Country."

"It's wonderful to be back." As she spoke the words, she realized how true they were. She'd lived in Misty

Bottoms the first five years of her life, then her folks had packed up and moved to Blue Ridge in Georgia's northern mountains.

When Beck turned his big truck off the two-lane road and onto the winding drive that led to Magnolia House, Cricket's mouth popped open but no words came out.

Through the live oaks that lined the lane, she could see the house. Shades of *Gone With the Wind*! This was Jenni Beth's home? She'd seen pictures, yes, but they sure as heck hadn't prepared her for the real deal.

It was like stepping back in time.

To the right of the main house, tucked in amid magnolias and roses and stately oak trees, sat a beautiful redbrick carriage house. A wrought-iron arm held a beautifully engraved sign that read *Magnolia Brides* in a flowing script. Magnolia blossoms dotted the *i*'s.

Very elegant, very, very romantic, and absolutely perfect.

The white sheers in the windows, the buckets of colorful flowers on the stoop, the red French doors. Wow!

"Has someone dropped me into the middle of a fairy tale?" she whispered.

Beck laughed and slowed down to give her time to take it all in. "I suppose, seein' it for the first time, it might be a little overwhelmin'."

"Thank you again." She turned to him. "You've given me the best gift ever."

"No gift, sugar. It's a job. At first glance, Jenni Beth Beaumont is pure Southern belle. Underneath? One of those steel magnolias we're famous for down here. She's gonna make you work and work hard, believe me."

"That's a good thing."

"Yeah, I believe you're right about that." He pulled up in front of the small brick building.

Those incredible red doors opened and out stepped one of the most beautiful women Cricket had ever seen. Long, blond hair tumbled past her shoulders. Dressed in white shorts and a slate-blue top that matched her eyes, she had a phone to her ear and held up a just-a-minute finger.

"Everything will be fine. You'll see," she said into the phone. "I'll call you tomorrow. Bye now." She disconnected and ran through the grass to meet them. "I'm so sorry about that."

"No problem." Beck hopped out and caught her in his arms. "Hey, gorgeous. That man of yours around?"

She laughed and gave him a smacking kiss. "Nope. He's in Savannah tending business." Turning to Cricket, she said, "And you must be the cousin from Blue Ridge, the woman who's going to save my bacon and help me put Magnolia Brides on the map."

"I sure hope so."

"Well, welcome to Misty Bottoms, the second time around." Jenni Beth gave her a welcoming embrace. "Is Beck bein' good to you?"

Hugging her back, Cricket nodded. "He is. He not only helped me become the new owner of the cutest little flower shop in all of Georgia, but he also found me the perfect house."

"Mrs. Michael's little white house on Frog Pond Road, right?"

"Yes."

"A darn shame you have to live with that mess across

the street," she said. "Somebody needs to do somethin' about that."

Beck and Cricket exchanged a quick glance.

"Actually, somebody is," Cricket said.

"Seriously? Who?"

"Sam."

"Sam who?"

Cricket shrugged.

"Gertie Taylor's nephew," Beck explained. "Great-nephew, maybe. If I remember right, he and Cole hung out a bit when he visited her during summer vacations. That's been, I don't know, probably fifteen, twenty years ago."

"After all this time, he's back?"

"Yep. I got up yesterday morning, and there he was, Harley and all. Guess he got in really late," Cricket said. "He's not exactly the friendly type."

"He inherited the place," Beck said.

"I'd heard she'd left it to a great-nephew, but I wonder why he's neglected it. Wouldn't you think he'd want to sell it if he doesn't intend to live here?"

"Who knows?" Beck asked. "Could be any number of reasons. Maybe he didn't realize what was happenin' to it. Or he didn't have the money to keep it up or hasn't been able to get here before now."

"Two years?" Jenni Beth sounded skeptical.

"He drove past the flower shop yesterday and totally ignored Cricket—even after she'd fed him breakfast."

Jenni Beth laughed. "Sounds like a story there."

"A boring one and one that won't have a sequel," Cricket said. "Anyway, enough about Sam. I can't wait to see your home."

"Okay then. Let's start right here at my office, where

I meet clients, have initial consultations and whatnot. My attic bedroom is where I do most of the real work." She laughed again. "It's where I make a mess and don't have to worry about anybody walking in on it. I haven't decided what I'll do after Cole and I get married."

"Soon?"

"Oh yeah. I'm not one for long engagements. Why wait when dessert's right there in front of you?" She laughed, then started to open her office door.

"He's got this great old barn on his parents' property that he converted into his living space with lots of unique pieces from his architectural salvage shop in Savannah. You'll have to stop by and take a peek at it. Anyway, we'll live there, but I think I'll probably still use the attic for my workroom. That way, I'll be here on-site during the day. It'll be good for work, and, well, I'll be here for my mom and dad." As Jenni Beth opened the doors, she put a hand on Beck's arm. "Beck, I—"

Cricket felt her cousin go ramrod straight beside her.

A beautiful redhead stood by the fireplace, hesitant, Caribbean-colored eyes in a pale face. She was an inch or two taller than Jenni Beth and rail thin.

"Think I'll wait outside." Beck turned on his heel.

"No, Beck, please." The redhead moved toward them. "Don't leave on account of me. I have to go anyway. My mom's waitin' for me."

"You don't have to go," Jenni Beth said.

"Yes, I do."

As she hugged Jenni Beth, Cricket wondered what had happened between her cousin and this gorgeous redhead to drive the ever-affable Beck into such a deep freeze. Was she the one who'd hurt him?

Hand extended, the redhead stepped to where Cricket still stood at the threshold. “My name’s Tansy. Tansy Forbes, and you must be Cricket.”

“I am.” She took Tansy’s hand in her own, shocked at how cold it was. From nerves? “Very nice to meet you.”

“Welcome to Misty Bottoms. I don’t live here anymore, but I’m sure we’ll be seeing each other again.” She stepped outside. “Beck.”

He stuffed his hands in his pockets and actually turned his back.

Cricket was appalled. The three stood silent as Tansy started the car parked off to the side and headed down the drive.

“That went well,” Jenni Beth said.

Cricket’s mouth dropped open, and Beck mumbled an obscenity.

“Beck!”

“Don’t expect an apology.” He glared at Jenni Beth. “You blindsided me.”

“I’m sorry,” she said. “I had no idea Tansy was in town or that she’d stop by today. You know I would never have done this deliberately.”

“Yeah,” Beck said. “I hear you.”

“But you don’t believe me.” Her slate-blue eyes held hurt.

He met her gaze with cold eyes. “Let’s just pretend I do and leave it at that.”

A ripple of heat radiated from the previously laid-back Jenni Beth. “Don’t you honestly think it’s time to get over this?”

“Don’t you think it’s time to show Cricket around?”

“Fine.” Two red spots bloomed on Jenni Beth’s

cheeks. "Cricket, I really am sorry you had to witness this. Not our finest hour."

Her drawl was heavier than it had been earlier, a sure sign of her distress.

"Come on in and see what I've managed to create with the help of my *friends*." She stressed the last word, her gaze shifting to Beck, who was sprawled in an easy chair, legs straight out in front of him.

"This is phenomenal." Cricket sighed, then moved to the center of the room to stare up at the small chandelier. Dozens of dripping crystals surrounded a small cherub, his chubby arms and legs wrapped around the base. "Gorgeous."

"It is, isn't it?" Jenni Beth wore a goofy grin. "Cole found it."

Oh yeah, Cricket thought. *The man loves her, and she him.*

She ignored Beck, who remained sullen in the flowery chair. She would not let him spoil this for her.

The office oozed femininity, but not so much so as to scare a groom away. A mannequin wearing a bridal gown posed in front of a gilt-edged mirror.

Cricket ran a hand along its edge.

"My grandmother's," Jenni Beth said.

"You're fortunate to have all this history."

Jenni Beth smiled crookedly. "Most of the time, yes. I don't know how much Beck has told you, but my family's rich on heritage, poor in the financial realm. The Beaumonts of Misty Bottoms—held captive by our legacy, one that's sucked up the remains of my folks' dwindling bank balance. I practically had to sell my soul for the money to keep the house from fallin' down around our ears. I might have lost it if not for Cole and Beck." She shook her head. "My ranting about your neighbor letting Gertie's place go to ruin was a little like calling the kettle black."

"But this place is amazing."

"Now," Beck muttered. "If you'd seen it a few months ago..." He shrugged.

Cricket wandered the room, noted the chintz easy chair, the gleaming mantel with antique pewter candleholders. She stopped beside the African violet on the little table.

"Ms. Hattie gave me that. I'll take you to meet her one day. Amazingly enough, the plant's thriving." Jenni Beth led Cricket into the small bath. "Look at these incredible faucets. Dinky Tubbs had tossed them in a wooden crate at his architectural salvage place. A little polish, and I think they're perfect."

"I'd have to agree." Cricket found herself enthralled with both Jenni Beth and the office.

When they stepped outside, Beck surprised her by tagging along.

"Over your pout?" Cricket asked.

"I don't pout."

"Could have fooled me."

Magnolia House didn't disappoint her. From the bridal suite to the wide sweep of stairs that absolutely begged a bride to descend them to her waiting groom, to the parlor, with its impressive fireplace, the house stunned with its beauty and grandeur.

When she saw the gardens, the florist in her wanted to weep with joy.

Back inside, Beck headed to the kitchen to talk

Charlotte, the Beaumonts' housekeeper, into a snack and a glass of sweet tea.

"Come upstairs," Jenni Beth said, "and I'll show you where the real work happens."

Her fingers trailing along the mahogany handrail, Cricket stopped in front of two portraits. One was Jenni Beth, the other a handsome young man with twinkling eyes of the same slate blue.

"Your brother?"

"Yes." Jenni Beth stopped. "We lost him in the war."

"Beck told me. I'm so sorry." She squeezed Jenni Beth's hand. "I have an older brother and can't even begin to imagine how awful this must be for you and your family."

"Thank you."

It hit home for Cricket, the discrepancy between her house and Jenni Beth's, between her life and Jenni Beth's. On the surface, Jenni Beth seemed to have so much more. Not so. Jenni Beth had lost her brother, while Cricket still had hers. From Cricket's perspective, that put her way, way ahead. Her heart hurt for her new friend.

When they reached the third floor, Jenni Beth spread her arms. "Here it is. My kingdom."

"Wow. And might I just say wow again." Cricket started toward the work corner. "May I?"

"Absolutely. If you've decided on your shop's name, I'll include it in my new pamphlets."

"The Enchanted Florist." The name alone made Cricket smile.

"I love that!"

"Better than Bella Fiore, right?"

"Boy, you can say that again. Misty Bottomers didn't much care for that—or for Pia. I can't tell you how happy I am to be working with you. Pia and I, well, let's say we had different tastes."

Cricket rolled her eyes. "Tell me about it. I inherited her leftovers, most of which, I'm happy to say, have now been donated to a women's shelter outside of Savannah."

Jenni Beth dropped onto the edge of her bed. "I hate to ask this..."

"What?"

"I know you're not settled in yet, either at home or at the shop, and when I booked my events, I took that into account. But that phone call I was on when you came?"

"Yes?"

"It was one of my brides. She wants to move up her wedding. To next weekend."

"Whew."

"Whew is right. It turns out they've started their family a little sooner than they'd planned, and she's afraid if she waits, she won't fit into her gown."

Cricket nodded.

"She insists the invitations are no problem, that she and her groom will simply call everyone. Kitty already has the cake topper, and I think I can handle everything else." She paused. "Except the flowers."

"Ah, I see." Cricket chewed at her bottom lip. "I have most of the basics, and I've already lined up my fresh flower suppliers. Do you know what she wants?"

"Yes, I do!" Jenni Beth slipped a file from her desk and thumbed through it to the flower sheet. "Holly's decided on a Victorian-themed wedding. The ceremony will be in the rose garden, and her dress—Wait till you see it. Tons of lace and oh-so-romantic. Her colors are deep blues and whites."

"Victorian," Cricket mused. "The bouquet should be a nosegay with white roses, deep-blue hyacinths, and some stephanotis. If it's Victorian, we have to include orange blossoms."

Jenni Beth smiled. "I think I love you."

Cricket grinned. "This will be a piece of cake." She rubbed her hands together. "How about white roses and sprigs of lavender for the tables?"

Within minutes, they were elbow deep in wedding plans.

Chapter 4

After Beck dropped her off, Cricket took a few minutes to detox, threw together a peanut butter sandwich, then jumped into her vehicle and headed back to her shop. Today's trip had been a real eye-opener in more ways than one.

Cricket had seen a side of Beck she hadn't guessed existed. Despite his black mood, though, he'd officially moved up in rank to her number-one favorite cousin! Curiosity about what had happened between him and Tansy Forbes ate at her, but she didn't intend to ask Beck about it.

And Magnolia House? Absolutely stunning, as was its owner. Jenni Beth Beaumont was a gal with credentials. Her family had actually founded the town of Misty Bottoms, yet she'd transformed their large, antebellum plantation home into a wedding venue pretty much on her own. She'd worked hard.

And speaking of hard work, Cricket forced herself back to the moment.

The minute she hit her shop, she grabbed a sketchbook. Ideas came fast and furiously for Holly's bouquet, the bridesmaids' flowers, and the centerpieces. Finished, she scanned and emailed them to Jenni Beth for the bride's approval. As soon as she had that, she'd get in touch with her supplier.

Her first bride! Her first collaboration with Jenni

Beth! She toasted herself with a Coke from her tiny fridge.

That done, she picked up her box opener and got back to the business of unpacking. While she unwrapped vases, she glanced at the photo tacked on a small bulletin board beside her computer, the one Jenni Beth had sent her of Magnolia House's first bride. Stella Reinhardt looked both beautiful and blissfully happy as she rode down the grassy aisle on the back of a monstrous Harley. Why anybody would voluntarily climb onto a machine like that was beyond her. She'd never ever been on one and had no intention of breaking that streak.

She yawned and arched her back to stretch the kinks from it. Today had been extremely productive, but it was time to call it a day.

Errands taken care of and a few essential groceries stowed in her vehicle, Cricket decided on an iced coffee. Nobody made them better than Kitty.

"Saw your new neighbor yesterday," Kitty said in greeting.

"Oh?"

"Nice havin' two young people move to Misty Bottoms. And right across the street from each other."

Uh-oh. Cricket heard the matchmaking wheels grinding. "I don't think he plans to stay for long."

"Maybe. Maybe not. You know, he spent a few summers here with his great-aunt Gertie. She's the one who left him that house."

"He told me that."

"Seemed to me the boy was happy here." Kitty straightened the doughnuts on one of her trays. "Appears wound a little tight right now."

"He certainly does." Cricket ordered her coffee.

"Maybe he's come searchin' for a little happy again."

Cricket made a noncommittal sound.

"You goin' straight home?"

"Yes."

"Why don't I make another of these? You can take it to him. My treat."

Cricket opened her mouth to object, but Kitty was already putting Sam's coffee together, adding frozen coffee cubes to keep it from diluting.

"Give him this, too." She scooped up a bear claw. "His favorite. It'll be too old to sell tomorrow. I'll throw one in for you if you'd like."

She started to say no, then changed her mind. By darned, she deserved a pastry more than Sam.

Kitty waved away her offer to pay, and Cricket headed to her car, loaded down with goodies for herself and Sam. Woohoo. Guess that meant she'd have to talk to him again.

After he'd snubbed her. Twice.

Cricket backed into her drive, turned off the engine, and then, smiling, rolled down her window, unable to think of a single reason not to simply sit there a few minutes and take in the view. Sam, who still chose to ignore her, was hard at work in the front yard. Shirtless.

Chris Hemsworth, Hugh Jackman, eat your hearts out. She'd have to be very careful around Sam, though, because this man played by a different set of rules, with sophisticated, cosmopolitan women.

A radio blared hard rock, making her almost sorry he'd managed to have the electricity restored. Music with an edge. Much like the man himself.

Even over the music, he had to have heard her as she'd driven down the street, but he didn't even look up. Fine. She'd deliver Kitty's goodies, then take her own iced coffee out to her back patio, where she wouldn't have to think about her new neighbor.

As she started up his walk, she spied a nasty scar on his left shoulder, one that looked fairly new, still pink and puckered—one that matched the scar on his upper chest. Did those scars have something to do with his weight loss?

Despite the scars, the man looked yummy enough to eat. It was like being in a candy store and told no tasting or being in a fabric shop full of silks and cashmere and not being allowed to touch.

If she trailed her fingers down his back right now, it would be hot and sweaty. Jeez, was that drool on her chin?

Muscles rippled when he hefted a huge branch as though it weighed no more than a feather. *Jiminy Cricket, a body like that should be illegal.* The man was making her very, very hungry. Would an afternoon snack—something other than Kitty's bear claw—be so bad?

He must have felt her staring because he finally turned. His eyes were hidden behind dark glasses, but the set of his jaw warned "No trespassing."

Aloof and chilly, yet that body screamed "smokin' hot."

He wore old sneakers, work gloves, and tattered jeans. A smattering of dark hair trailed into the waistband, and her mouth watered again.

Oh yeah. Coming or going, this man made her motor run.

Rude. He's rude, she reminded herself.

So? Her naughty angel sighed. *Who cares?*

Cricket blushed. If Sam had any idea of the thoughts bouncing around in her head right now…

Harley, sexy six-pack, nice butt, her bad angel continued. *He's a certifiable bad boy. Come on! You know you want one. Step over that line, Cricket, just this once. Look at that mouth, the dark stubble on his rugged jaw. Go get him, girlfriend.*

He did look as though he'd jumped straight off the pages of a romance novel. Her feet, on their own, took one step toward him, then another.

"Don't happen to have a saw, do you?"

Pop. Her bubble burst.

She blinked. "What?"

"A saw." He pointed across the street. "I noticed a storage shed in your backyard yesterday when I showered."

Oh, would she ever again be able to get naked in her own shower without thinking of him there, butt naked?

He snapped his fingers, and she blinked again.

"You okay?"

"I'm fine. I come bearing iced coffee and a bear claw for you." She held up the bag. "Compliments of Kitty."

"Set it on the porch."

"You're welcome," she said primly.

"Yeah, thanks." He shot her a glance. "Figured I'd try to at least clear a pathway to the front door. But I need a saw, and I hate to buy one if I don't have to."

"Oh. Sure. I don't know if there's one in there or not." She deposited the coffee and pastry on the top step.

"I have a key to the shed. Why don't you look inside? I've been meaning to but haven't gotten around to it."

"Speaking of keys," he said. "Do you have a brain inside that head of yours?"

"Excuse me?"

"I can't believe you left me, a perfect stranger, alone in your house yesterday, then wrote a note to say I should leave it unlocked for the day."

"Why shouldn't I?"

"Why—honey, the reasons are too many to list. Misty Bottoms might be a small town, but the world has some pretty nasty people in it. Everywhere."

"Not here."

He planted his hands on his hips, and her eyes followed. His jeans rode low. She swallowed. Hard.

"You don't know me from Adam. I could have been waiting in your house when you came home. I could have attacked you."

She shook her head. "No, you're rude and disagreeable, but you wouldn't hurt me."

"Rude and—" He made a sound deep in his throat. "Tell me you at least lock up at night."

"Okay." She threw him a saucy smile. "I lock up at night."

"But you don't, do you?"

Frustration fairly poured from him. His problem, Cricket decided. She didn't bother to answer. "Why don't I get you that key to the shed?"

Sam sighed, then took a long, greedy drink of his iced coffee and followed her.

After he unlocked the outbuilding, he stood in the doorway, trying to get his bearings. Cricket could stand his world on end without breaking a sweat. He'd never in his life met anyone like her.

He'd been working hard, but that wasn't what had him short of breath. This quirky, totally unpredictable woman affected him.

When he'd turned and saw her standing there, it was either ask for a tool or throw her down in the tall grass and weeds and have his way with her. Since the latter went against everything his mother had ever taught him and against everything he believed in, here he stood, in the cramped, hotter-than-Hades metal shed.

What had he told her he needed?

A hammer?

No. A saw. And solitude, he reminded himself. He'd come to Misty Bottoms, Georgia, to get away. To heal.

Bad luck sexy little Cricket lived right across the street.

"Did you get the inside of your house cleaned up?"

He jumped and damned Ingrid all over again. Would he ever shake the jitters that continued to sneak up on him? Regain his confidence?

He cleared his throat and bought himself a few seconds before answering. "No. I didn't think to check before I rode into town, but all Gertie's supplies are worthless. I meant to head back in today to pick up fresh, but…"

"You can't sleep there again, Sam. Not with it like that."

"It'll be okay. I've opened all the windows and aired out the place. I'll get what I need tomorrow."

"Don't be stupid." She marched off, leaving him scratching his head.

Since he saw no sign of life, reptilian or otherwise,

in the shed, he plowed into the heat. Gertie'd had an old wooden one she'd let him use as his private hangout. In there, he could be anything he wanted—a pirate, a fireman, a cowboy, or a villainous fugitive hiding from the law. He'd actually slept in it one night, armed with a flashlight and a box of Little Debbies.

The shed was still standing. He'd seen it earlier, but the kudzu had practically covered it. Kudzu, the vine that ate the South.

A few minutes later, saw in hand, he walked around to the front to find Cricket resting in one of her Adirondack chairs, a broom in one hand, a mop in the other. A basket of cleaning supplies sat at her feet, and a bag perched on the porch railing.

"Grab that." She nodded at the basket and tucked the bag under her arm. Patting it, she said, "Clean sheets. I'll tackle the bedroom while you hit the bath. For tonight, that'll do."

"You always this pushy? Poking your nose in where you're not wanted?"

She thought about it for a few seconds. "Occasionally. I can give you today, but that's it. I'm only home now because I finished unpacking my new inventory. Tomorrow, another shipment will arrive, and I'll be at work all day."

"I didn't ask for your help."

"No, you didn't, you grumpy old man."

"I'm not—"

"I'm assuming," she said, interrupting him, "that since the radio works, you managed to get the utilities up and runnin'."

"I did. Electric, water, and gas. The essentials of life."

"Groceries?"

"No." He shook his head vehemently. "I'm not about to bring food into that place yet. I want to chase the varmints out, not feed them. And while I might not be the neatest person in the world, that house's hygiene registers way off my scale of acceptable. I'm surprised the county didn't condemn it."

"Good point." She scrunched her nose. "I could feed you tonight, I suppose."

"Nope. You made breakfast for me yesterday. My turn to feed you."

"But you just said—"

"I did. I'm willing to deal, though—if you help me clean up enough that I can sleep here tonight."

The light in her eyes matched the heat in his belly. Dangerous ground. Ground he'd best avoid.

"I'll take you to Dee-Ann's. My treat for helping."

"Deal."

"Come on then. The sooner we get started, the sooner we're done."

"Jeez, you sound like my mother."

"Really? She's a baritone, too?"

A quick laugh escaped her. "Is that a smile on your face, Sam?" Her eyes narrowed. "Or a trick of the light?"

"Ha-ha. Very funny."

"You ready?"

He grabbed the basket and followed her across the street. He was starting to think of the stripe down the center of the road as the Mason-Dixon line, the demarcation between North and South, at least in this neighborhood.

~

Cricket stood in the middle of the hallway and turned in a full circle. "An antique dealer would have an orgasm just walking in here."

Sam choked back a surprised laugh.

"What?"

"Nothing. You do have a way with words."

"I tell it like I see it. There's some great stuff here." She faced the stairway, her hand over her mouth. "Except…ouch. That wallpaper."

"Ass ugly, isn't it?"

"Yes." She chuckled. "I'm sorry, but it might be the worst I've ever seen."

As far as he knew, the dark green paper nearly smothered beneath huge, white magnolias had been there forever. It curled at the seams and pulled away from both the ceiling molding and the baseboards. The stuff had to come down. But did he want to tackle it, or could he leave it for whoever bought the place?

"Wait'll you see the walls in the bedrooms."

"They can't be worse."

He simply raised his eyebrows.

She groaned. "This is a big a job for one person. You should have some help."

"I'll manage. One room at a time."

"Okay." Cricket drew out the word and splayed her hands on her shapely hips. "I've changed my mind on how best to tackle this place. Clean the windows first and get some light in here, while I take the top layer of grime off the kitchen. After you finish the windows, you can tackle the downstairs bath and I'll hit one of the bedrooms."

He saluted her. “Yes, sir.”

She picked up the bottle of window cleaner from the coffee table and handed it to him. “You know, this whole rude, sarcastic attitude you’re wearin’? It’s not scaring me, so you might as well put it away.”

“It’s not an act. It’s who I am, Bug.”

“That’s BS, and you and I both know it.”

“There’s the thing,” he said. “You don’t know anything about me, who I really am, what kind of demons hide inside me.”

Those dark gray eyes of hers widened. Good. He was getting through to her. Maybe if he was obnoxious enough, Ms. Goody Two-shoes would go away and leave him alone to wallow in his pathetic life.

Instead, she swept the toe of a shoe over the grimy linoleum. “Don’t call me ‘Bug.’ They’re disgusting creatures.”

“No, they’re not. They’re cute. Sort of,” he said. “Especially when they stay away from me and I can view them long distance.”

“Point taken.”

“I didn’t mean you.” Or did he? he wondered. Now wasn’t the time to dissect it. There was a lot of work to be done to make the place habitable. He refused to sleep another night in filth.

“There are three bedrooms upstairs. Gertie’s and two smaller ones. I’ll bunk in the room that overlooks the backyard. It’s my room—well, the room I used when I visited.”

Those gray eyes turned on him, made him feel far too vulnerable.

“Stop looking at me like that. Nothing sentimental

about it." He shrugged. "I don't feel right intruding on Gertie's private space."

"I didn't say a word."

"You didn't have to. Those eyes of yours say it all."

"I'll start up there then." She nodded and headed to the stairs. Halfway up, she stopped, pivoted toward him. "Why didn't you wave back at me in front of the shop yesterday? You saw me. I know you did."

He decided to play it straight with her. "Okay, yeah, I saw you. And I saw the guy you were with. I don't believe in horning in."

"Hornin' in?" She stared at him, incredulous. "It was a wave. I wasn't propositioning you, for heaven's sake." She wiggled her fingers at him. "That's all. A simple wave."

"Your boyfriend might not have seen it that way."

"My—you mean Beck? He's my cousin, you lunkhead."

"The one you called when you were contemplating siccing the cops on me, hoping they'd take me away in handcuffs?"

"Yep."

He shrugged. "Doesn't matter one way or the other."

"I wonder."

"Don't." He paused. "You know, he reminded me of somebody. Seems I should know him."

"Dierks Bentley."

"Dierks." He snapped his fingers. "That's it. I'm not all that into country music, but him I know. I've seen photos of him riding his Harley at some charity fund-raiser for hospitalized kids."

"That's him."

Sam nodded, then mumbled, "Cleaning these

windows? A huge waste of time." Still, he grabbed the rest of what he needed from the basket, found a step stool in the kitchen, and went to work on years' worth of grime.

When he'd finished the last of the living room windows, he stood back and admired them. Damned if Cricket hadn't been right. The glass fairly sparkled, and sunlight flooded the room. Even though an inch of dust covered everything, the space felt better.

Before he tackled the dining room or kitchen windows, though, he'd best hit the bathroom. When he finished for the day, he'd need a shower, and he would not take his next one at Cricket's. That had been too strange, too intimate somehow. He wanted his own.

After a quick peek inside the room, he had second thoughts. It might have been better to hire a wrecking company after all. He could have them level the house, then sell the land.

For reasons he couldn't put into words, he understood that wasn't an option. Gertie had entrusted this house, her past, to him. Time he stepped up to the plate.

But he was honest enough to admit that had it not been for his injury, for Ingrid and her betrayal, he wouldn't have returned. The house, eventually, would have collapsed in on itself because he'd never have come back to this rinky-dink town.

Misty Bottoms wasn't for him. He was city through and through.

"How are you doing down there?" Cricket called.

"All done. I'm sitting down to a little beluga caviar and a flute of chilled Dom Pérignon."

"Yeah, well, save some for me."

He snorted.

Ignoring the pain in his shoulder, he set to work on the bath. As he scrubbed the tub, sink, and toilet, he heard Cricket moving around upstairs. The scent of lemon polish drifted down and made him think of his mother and cleaning day at home, of the threats she'd made to him and his sisters if they dared make a mess.

Growing up in a big Italian family had been a blessing—even with four sisters. Sandwiched in the middle, he'd taken full advantage as the only son. He'd used it shamelessly to get out of chores and sticky spots. His sisters should have hated him. Strangely enough, they didn't.

He swept the small space, then ran a mop over the floor, changed the water, and mopped again. Not bad. It didn't exactly sparkle, and he sincerely doubted it would pass any white-glove test or his sister Sally's scrutiny, but he wasn't likely to catch anything from showering here.

Cricket came back downstairs and did the kitchen windows while he cleaned the ones in the dining room.

"Have you been upstairs yet?" she asked.

"No. After what I saw down here, I figured I was better off not knowing what it looked like up there."

"When you go up tonight, take some time to check out the pictures. There're a lot of you and Gertie."

He stopped swiping at the glass to turn to her. "Really?"

"I'd say she treasured her time with you."

More guilt.

"Yeah, well, she didn't have any kids of her own. Her husband died young in some kind of an accident, and she never remarried."

He went back to his windows, finding it easier to rub away the dirt than dig through the emotions that nagged at him. Hadn't he in a sense betrayed his great-aunt? Not intentionally and certainly without Ingrid's malevolence, but he'd hurt her all the same.

Amazingly enough, Gertie hadn't held it against him, had instead forgiven him. Well, he wouldn't be forgiving Ingrid anytime soon. Anytime, period. He wasn't Gertie; he wasn't his sisters. And his improprieties hadn't been purposefully malicious. He'd been inconsiderate, but he hadn't meant any harm.

"The ugly wallpaper still there?" he asked.

"Oh, yes. I gave Gertie's room a quick run-through, too," Cricket said. "Not an award-winning cleaning, but it'll do till you get to it. The third—"

"What?"

"From the looks of it, she used it as a storage room."

He groaned.

"Lots of stuff stacked in there. You'll want to go through it, see if there's anything worth keepin'. Anything your family might want—a parent, a sibling, an ex maybe."

"You fishing?"

"If you mean would I like to know somethin' about you, then, yes, I would."

"Okay, here's the scoop. My mom and dad are both still alive, thank God, and still married. I have four sisters, two older, two younger."

"Seriously?"

"Seriously."

"Brothers?"

He shook his head. "Dad and I used to barricade

ourselves in the basement when it was that time of the month for two or more of them at the same time. Things could get downright ugly in the DeLuca household."

A pretty blush rouged her cheeks.

He wanted to run a fingertip over them and barely resisted the urge.

"As far as an ex goes? There aren't any. No Mrs. DeLuca former or present, no little DeLucas. Anything else?"

"Nope."

They finished their windows together. Reaching for a bottle of water he'd set on the counter, he stopped short.

"Would you look at this?" He tapped his finger against the trim of the basement door.

"What?" Cricket crowded in behind him.

Five short pencil marks and five scrawled names—Adriana, Beatrice, Sam, Sally, and Ysabelle.

"Gertie measured us the one summer we were all here. Had us back up to the door, then she marked our heights on the wall." He shook his head. "All this time, and she never cleaned them off, never painted over them."

A rush of emotion flooded him, making him uncomfortable. Of one thing, he was certain. After all these years, he damn well wouldn't be the one to remove those marks.

Rather than meet Cricket's eyes, he tossed her a bottle of water and grabbed one for himself. "I didn't get a chance to slop out the fridge yet, so they're not cold, but they are wet. Why don't we take them outside? Maybe catch a breeze."

They sat together on the front steps, neither talking.

That shaggy hair of hers stuck out in a couple places,

but unlike most of the women he knew, she didn't fuss with it. And despite having worked like a dog, she smelled good.

"You'll have a much cleaner place to sleep tonight," she said.

As Cricket talked, she stood, grabbed a stick, and raised an arm to knock down a spider web. The first time he'd seen her, she'd been dressed in clothes so baggy they'd practically swallowed her. Today? That stretch hiked up her fitted top to show more than a few inches of bare skin between its hem and the skimpy, second-skin shorts that rode low on her hips. Smooth, exposed skin drew his gaze. But it was the tiny jewel winking in her belly button that practically had his tongue hanging out.

He wanted to kiss it, to run his tongue over it.

What in the hell was wrong with him?

He let out a big breath as heat rushed through him. Who'd have thought the pesky neighbor who'd shown up on his doorstep would turn out to be such a sexy little thing? She'd done one heck of a job camouflaging that sweet body since he'd met her. He stood quickly. "Hey, appreciate your help. I'd intended to flop on the floor again tonight, but thanks to you, I'll have a bed with clean sheets." Facing the house, he said, "Think I'll try out that shower."

"Okay." If she was surprised at the suddenness of his retreat, she didn't question it.

One hand on the screen door, he turned back. "We still on for dinner?"

"You bet." She twisted the cap on her water. "If you *want* to go to the diner, that's fine with me. We do, actually, have a couple other choices, though."

"Such as?"

"Mama's Pizza and Wings and Fat Baby's Barbecue. Fat Baby's serves steaks, too. I haven't eaten at either place, so I can't vouch for them. When I joined the Chamber of Commerce, they provided me with a list of businesses in town."

"You like pizza?"

"I do."

"Me too. Mama's for sure won't be as good as *my* mom's, but then nobody's is."

"That's a nice thing to say."

"It's the truth. Will an hour give you enough time to get ready? I'm starved."

"Absolutely. It doesn't take me long."

"I should have had you around to give my sisters lessons. My dad and I barely saw the insides of our bathrooms." One foot across the jamb, he said, "Dress casual. We'll take the bike."

"But I don't—"

"It's my only transportation."

"I could drive."

The look he threw her ended that discussion. Italian males didn't ride in the passenger seat—except under extreme duress.

Chapter 5

Cricket started down Sam's weed-covered walk and heard the screen door close behind him. What a whirlwind this afternoon had been. Sam had worked tirelessly despite the fact that more than once she'd caught him wincing, reaching around to rub the scar on his shoulder. Car accident? Motorcycle wreck? Or something else?

What happened, Sam? No doubt she'd have to work it out of him in bits and pieces because this man had definitely shut in on himself.

It might be fun to unwrap him. She thought about that body of his again. *Yeah, that way, too.*

She checked her watch and decided she'd better kick it into gear. He'd given her an hour, and she doubted her new neighbor would tolerate being kept waiting. Everything about him said restless.

Common sense warned her not to go with him, that this was a bad idea. Still, she wanted pizza. With Sam. Cleaning house had made her hungry. Watching those muscles of his bunch and flex had made her even hungrier.

In case he watched, she kept her pace easy till she got inside, then she practically ran to the bathroom. Shedding her clothes, she stepped into the shower, grabbed the soap Sam had used, and rid herself of the accumulated dirt and dust from Gertie's. Her sweaty hair stuck to her head; she scrubbed it vigorously, using her best shampoo. And, yes, she shaved her legs.

In less than ten minutes she was toweling off and smoothing wisteria body lotion all over. She'd already driven past the pizza place, so she knew casual would work fine. Even so, deciding what to wear turned out to be a problem. She didn't want to look like she'd tried too hard or given it too much thought. On the other hand, she did *not* want to look thrown together.

It was hot, so she prayed Mama's Pizza would have their air conditioner running full blast. That in and of itself added a problem, though. Did she dress for the heat and risk frostbite from an overactive cooling system, or did she go for cool, assuming the restaurant would be ungodly warm from the pizza ovens?

And she was definitely overcomplicating this, wasn't she? Layers. With layers, she'd be ready for anything.

With that in mind, she dug through her closet. If she was riding on the back of a Harley—and didn't that give her a major case of nerves all by itself?—she had to wear pants…or shorts…or capris. Argh. She pulled out a pair of white shorts, then stopped. What if they wrecked? There'd be nothing between her skin and the pavement. She groaned and smacked her forehead. Overthinking again. Nothing she owned would soften a spill. Well, maybe her black leather pants, but it was way too hot for them.

She finally settled on capri-length black leggings and a bright red, flowing cotton top. The thing weighed less than nothing and would be perfect. She grabbed a short-sleeved black sweater. It would roll up and fit in her bag, one she could sling over her chest for the ride. Black strappy sandals would have to do for footwear.

Dressed at last—and wasn't that a miracle?—Cricket

headed back to the bathroom, dried her short, choppy hair, and added a touch of blush, mascara, and a hint of lip gloss. She decided to wear her new garnet earrings. They'd been her celebratory splurge—the morning she'd signed her life away at the bank for this house and the railroad car.

As she threaded the silver wires through her ears, her thoughts drifted back to Sam. The man was a mystery, very complex and very moody. She was still on the fence as to whether or not she wanted to even try to figure him out.

Well, she'd approach tonight as a reconnaissance mission. They'd worked together on the house much of the afternoon, but with them on separate floors most of the time, there'd been pathetically little chatter. He'd kept his radio on, too, which had pretty much squelched any get-to-know-each-other talk even when they were in the same room. A deliberate move on his part because the man was *not* a talker.

His taste in music didn't speak all that well of him as far as she was concerned. She'd heard him go out back at one point and had sneaked downstairs, switching the station to her favorite country one. Her bliss had lasted all of five minutes, just one and a half songs.

The screen had slammed again, and within seconds, Lady Antebellum was gone and rock was back. One more con to add to the growing list.

That sweaty back, though, with those rippling muscles. His stubble-darkened jaw. The pain flickering in those black eyes. His comment about his mama's cooking. She sighed. Yep, he definitely had some items on the plus side, too.

She eyed the bear claw on her counter. She hadn't

had time to eat it earlier and probably shouldn't now. Reaching into the fridge, she found a stalk of celery and crunched on it. Lunch had been too many cobwebs and dirty windows ago. She really needed some fuel and hoped Sam wasn't one of those guys who thought a woman should pick at her food. What was the sense in that? If you paid for it, why not eat it?

Exactly fifty-nine minutes after she'd left Sam's, she heard the throaty thrum of the Harley as it started. Her stomach did a quick, nervous rumba. Ten seconds later he pulled into the drive behind her practical little red Chevy SUV. She wanted a sports car; she needed something to deliver flowers. Since she could only afford one vehicle, she'd gone with the SUV.

One peek out the kitchen window and a kaleidoscope of butterflies took flight in her belly. Hadn't she sworn she'd never get on one of those just that morning? She stared at the Harley as though approaching a fire-breathing dragon.

"Come on." Sam tipped his head. "I'm starving. You do know how to get to Mama's, don't you?"

She nodded.

"What's wrong?"

"That's a, um, pretty big motorcycle."

"Yeah." He ran a hand over the gas tank. "She's a beauty, isn't she?" Then he glanced up and saw her round eyes, her pale face. "You afraid of bikes?"

She chewed her lower lip. "I've never ridden one."

"You're kidding."

"No." She studied the grass at her feet as though it held the answers to all the questions in the universe.

"So you're a virgin."

Her head jerked up. "What?"

"You're a virgin." At her outraged expression, one side of his mouth lifted in what could have been a smile. "A motorcycle virgin."

Her mouth opened and closed, and the laugh he'd been holding back escaped.

"Honey, you're the most transparent person I've ever met. Right now, you look as nervous as a perp in a lineup."

He hopped off the bike and unsnapped an open-faced helmet from the back. Walking up to her, he placed it over her head and snapped the chin strap. "We don't want you getting hurt, and we sure don't want to break the law."

She made a face. "It feels kind of claustrophobic."

"You'll get used to it." Holding her hand, he led her to the bike. "I'll steady the beast. Just throw one leg over and hop on."

She approached the Harley the way another woman might sneak up on a coiled rattler. "This is a death trap."

"Not with me driving. I don't take stupid chances."

"Other drivers—"

"I'll keep an eye on them," he promised. "You really are scared, aren't you?"

"No. I'm cautious."

"You're afraid. Admit it. I figured you'd be game for almost anything."

Her expression changed, and he fought back the grin that threatened. Oh, he'd found the right button…and pushed it. He'd issued a challenge.

"Fine." Her brow rose and she stared at him icily.

"Fine," he agreed. "One time. Come on, you can do this."

She held on to the handlebars to support herself. "Whew, okay, I'll admit it. I'm nervous."

"Understood. The first time's always the hardest." His coal-black eyes met hers. "And the most memorable."

Heat coursed through her. Okay, now he had her heart racing and her breath ragged. He knew it, too. A cat playing with a mouse.

Cautiously, she climbed on, the handlebars still clenched between her fingers.

"Good job, Bug. Unless you're planning to drive us to dinner, though, you're going to want to slide back a little so I can hop on."

"Oh!" She did, her hands grasping the sides of the seat.

He settled in front of her. "You'll need to hold on to me." He watched her in one of the side-view mirrors.

When she put her hands on his shoulders and gripped till her knuckles turned white, he winced and she pulled away.

"I hurt you."

"Don't worry about it. I'm fine." He moved her hands, one at a time, to his waist. "You'll do better holding on here. You might even want to wrap those arms right around my midsection."

"Are you joshin' me?"

"Nope. I wouldn't do that, since this is your first motorcycle ride and all."

She kept her hands right where they were—until he revved the bike's engine. The second they moved, so did her arms. They came up to wrap around his neck in a near stranglehold.

He stopped the bike, braced his feet to steady them.

"A little lower. I have to breathe."

"Lower? How much lower?" She put her hands on his biceps, wrapped her fingers partway around them. "Mmmm, nice. Strong."

"Lower." His voice sounded husky, even to himself. Now they played a more dangerous game, and they both knew it.

Okay, he enjoyed games. He zipped out of the driveway and down the road, grinning at her surprised squeal.

Cricket wrapped her arms around Sam's midsection and leaned forward, practically melting into him. Despite the mind-numbing fear, she enjoyed the feel of him.

He slowed as they went down Frog Pond Road. "Which way?"

"Left. You'll go about a mile, then turn right. The road follows the river. It's actually a pretty ride."

Without another word, Sam turned, and they were off.

For the first few minutes, Cricket didn't move a muscle for fear she'd unbalance them. Then, the warm spring air blowing across her face, caressing her skin, she gave in to the beauty of the Low Country, of the evening, of Sam and her first motorcycle ride.

By the time they reached the restaurant, she was tempted to tell him to just keep driving, but her stomach growled. Definitely time to eat.

Sam unsnapped his helmet, raked fingers through his gorgeous dark hair, then offered her his hand. "I'd say you're a pro at this already. The first few minutes were touch and go, but once you relaxed, I think you actually enjoyed it."

She removed her own helmet and handed it to him. She, too, finger-combed her hair, thankful for her carefree cut. "I absolutely loved it! It's so liberating!"

"It is that." He tipped back his head and sniffed the air. "If the smell's anything to go by, this place is a keeper." He nodded toward another Harley in the parking lot. "Guess we've got another biker, huh?"

They walked inside, Sam behind Cricket, both careful now not to touch.

The hostess wound her way between tables, heading toward the back of the restaurant, and they followed. The smells coming from the kitchen reminded Sam of Sunday dinners with the family back in New York City.

"Cricket?" Someone spoke from one of the side booths.

"Jenni Beth?" Cricket stopped, and Sam nearly plowed into her. He reached out, put a hand at her waist to steady himself.

He glanced at the woman who'd called out to Cricket. So that was Jenni Beth Beaumont, the destination wedding planner. Kitty had been right. Jenni Beth was, indeed, a true Southern beauty. Everything about her shouted class and wealth. Yet, for all her looks, he felt nothing. The zing that slapped at him when he got anywhere near Cricket was nonexistent when he looked at Jenni Beth.

Across from her, a dark-haired man with hazel eyes glanced at him.

A faint sense of recognition crossed his face. Sam looked at him again. "Cole Bryson?"

"That would be me." Those hazel eyes moved over him again. "Sammy? Gertie's nephew?"

"One and the same."

Cole stood, and the two men exchanged back slaps.

"It's been years," Cole said.

"Yes, it's been a long time since I've been to Misty Bottoms."

Cole held out a hand to the woman beside him. "Jenni Beth, this is Sammy. You'll have to forgive me. I can't remember your last name."

"DeLuca. Sam DeLuca."

The hostess waited beside them, tapping the menus on her palm. She shot a look toward the door where a lone man stood waiting to be seated.

"Sorry, darlin'. We're tyin' you up here," Cole said. "Hey, why don't you two join us?"

"Yes, do." Jenni Beth stood and moved to sit by Cole, her small hand slipping into his. "We haven't ordered yet."

Sam noticed the big rock on Jenni Beth's left hand and hoped Cole knew what he was getting into.

"Cole and Jenni Beth are newly engaged," Cricket said as she slid onto the bench.

"I noticed." Sam slid in beside her, his hip bumping Cricket's. He pulled away slightly, then thought, *What the heck?* and nudged till he felt her heat again through those sexy little leggings that fit her like a second skin and hid none of her curves.

When she'd stepped out of the house in them, he'd had a few seconds of insanity where he'd nearly given in and kissed those full, pouty lips. Instead, he'd given her her first ride and enjoyed the feel of her pressed against him, her touch as she'd held on for dear life.

Slowly, she'd relaxed and sighed with pleasure. All in all, he was looking forward to their ride home in the dark.

Their waitress, a brunette with purple and green streaks in her hair, barely looked old enough to drive. According to her green plastic tag, her name was Hannah.

"Hi, guys." She gave Jenni Beth a hug. "Ain't seen you in a while." Her attention swung to Cricket. "And you must be Beck's cousin."

Cricket smiled. "I am."

"Beck told me all about your plans for the flower shop."

"My grand opening is next Friday. Hope you can stop by."

"I will. And who's this good-lookin' guy? Your boyfriend?"

While Cricket sputtered, Sam extended his hand. "Sam DeLuca."

"Gertie's nephew." Blushing, Hannah took his hand.

Jeez, Sam thought. *What did these people do? Broadcast everybody's comings and goings over some secret network? Text? Internet? Smoke signals?*

"What'll you have to drink? We've got Coors on tap."

"No beer for me," Sam said. "Not when I'm driving the bike."

"Sweet tea?" Hannah suggested.

"I don't know."

"You ever try it?" their waitress asked.

He shook his head. "Nah."

"You're in Dixie now, Sam," Cricket chided. "I swear our mamas fed it to us in our bottles. Gertie didn't introduce you to it when you stayed with her?"

"Nope. She enjoyed it by the pitcherful but made me drink milk. Claimed that's what growing boys needed."

"Well, you've probably reached your full height. You're a big boy now. Besides, how are you goin' to fit in if you don't drink sweet tea?"

"I don't plan to fit in. I'm not going to be around that long. I'm short term, Bug."

The laughter died in her eyes, and Sam could have kicked himself. Just because he was miserable didn't mean he had to drag others down with him.

"You've got a motorcycle?" Cole asked.

"A Harley," Cricket answered for him. "Tonight's the first I've ever ridden one."

"Enjoy it?"

"I did." Cricket's gaze drifted to Sam. "I tried something new." Her brow lifted. "Your turn."

"You're going to shame me into it, aren't you?" Sam asked.

"Yep."

"Okay." He sighed. "Make mine a sweet tea."

The others followed suit.

"We came on Cole's Harley," Jenni Beth said.

"That's yours out there?" Sam folded his napkin.

And they were off, chatting about their hogs and agreeing they needed to head out for a ride together.

Cricket and Jenni Beth discussed business and Beck.

Talk moved to Sam's summers with Gertie, the time he and Cole had sneaked away and gone swimming in the river, and the scolding they'd endured when his aunt and Cole's parents had found out about it.

"So what are you doing now, Sam?"

Cricket's ears perked up. He could have sworn they actually waggled, straining to hear better. Boggy ground here. Not that he was hiding anything, but he didn't want to talk about the past few months. Nor did he want to admit he'd come to Misty Bottoms to lick his wounds—both physical and mental.

He noticed, too, the man who'd come in after them had laid down his book. He doubted they'd be overheard, however... Was he part of the Misty Bottoms Communication Network, sent here to spy on him, then spread the word? It wouldn't have surprised him.

Still, Cole needed an answer. Sam cleared his throat and took a sip of sweet tea. Not bad. "Right now I'm on vacation. Thought I'd fix up the old house a bit."

"It needs it." Cole apparently picked up on his reticence and didn't push. "Did Cricket tell you about the renovations Jenni Beth's been doin' at Magnolia House? It's incredible. You need anything, let me know. I can help you find doorknobs, moldings, faucets, hinges, you name it."

And they were off and running again, like four old friends with a shared background.

Jenni Beth and Cole touched often and shared intimate glances. *Oh yeah, these two have it bad*, Sam thought. They could hardly keep their hands off each other. And that was fine—for them. He didn't need it.

The food was great, the conversation even better. When he checked his watch, he was shocked to see that nearly three hours had passed since he'd picked up Cricket. It had been a long time since he'd pushed aside the shooting and simply enjoyed himself.

"You're tired." Cricket caught his time check. "You worked your butt off today."

"I'd say that makes two of us," he said easily. "You worked today, then helped me put the house to rights."

"For which you bought me dinner."

He shook his head. "Cheap labor. But you're right, I am tired."

The men took care of the tab while the ladies hit the restroom. Then, together, the four of them stepped out into the balmy spring night.

It had grown dark while they ate, and the fog had crept in, dense and wet.

"Jeez," he said. "This stuff is thick enough to spoon."

Jenni Beth laughed. "This, Mr. DeLuca, is why the town is named Misty Bottoms."

The ride home was eerie, like being swallowed by the moist, low-hanging clouds. It was as if the rest of the world had disappeared. Both the dampness and Cricket clung to him.

"You warm enough?"

"Yes, but I'm glad I brought a sweater along."

His single headlight cut through the fog and turned the mist into a shimmering curtain. When he pulled into Cricket's drive, he felt a tad off center. The night had been a good one. Still, it had unsettled him.

He walked her to the door careful not to touch, figuring it was safer that way for both of them.

"Good night, Cricket."

"Night, Sam, and thanks again."

"Right back at you."

Hell with it. Before he could second-guess himself, he leaned in for a quick, light kiss. Her lips parted, and he lingered longer than he'd meant to. When he pulled away, he stumbled over his words. Did he thank her or apologize?

Before he could do either, she laid a hand on his cheek, rose to her tiptoes, and gave him another, shorter kiss. Then, without a word, she turned away.

Returning to his bike, he watched by the hazy glow from her porch light as she disappeared inside. He saw a light blink on. He listened for the click of a lock and swore under his breath when he didn't hear it.

Not his business.

~

In bed half an hour later, with clean sheets beneath him, he couldn't get Cricket out of his head. He imagined her smoothing these sheets, imagined her here beside him, the two of them entangled in the soft cotton. He replayed their kisses, so innocent, so hot.

Kisses that shouldn't have happened.

He flopped onto his belly and dragged a pillow over his head to block out the weak moonlight. Time to put some distance between himself and his sexy neighbor.

Tomorrow, he'd patch up the leaks his personal wall had sprung today.

The night was too damn quiet. No sirens, no cars driving by. No music from the apartment next door. Just him, the big, old house, and Mother Nature. The hoot of an owl, no doubt the one that had scared the bejeezus out of him two nights ago, was the last sound he heard before he drifted off to sleep.

Chapter 6

A CHOPPER THRUMMED OVERHEAD. *WHUP, WHUP, WHUP*. The shrill cry of a siren cut through the night. Sam's own breathing sounded ragged over the pounding of his heart.

Something was off.

And then he was falling, his alarm clock bleating.

No. The phone. His eyes searched the darkness for the clock even as his hand reached for his cell—2:15 a.m.

"Yeah?"

"Sam, it's me. Ingrid."

He erupted from the bed, fumbling for a light.

"What's wrong?"

He heard a man's garbled voice in the background but couldn't make out the words.

"He's got me, Sam."

A muffled scream followed, and Sam's stomach twisted into knots.

"Who has you, Ingrid? Who?"

"That man." She cried some more. "The one you've been hunting."

"Nikolai Federoff?"

"Yeah," a man growled into the phone. "You want to keep your lover alive, you've got exactly fifteen minutes to get here. Alone. Every minute you're late, the lady loses a finger. When the fingers are gone, so's she." He spit out an address.

Sam heard Ingrid's sobbing protests in the background,

registered that even on a good day with no traffic, he'd have trouble making that timeline.

The phone went dead.

Shit! Already dragging on pants, he berated himself. This was his fault. He'd made Ingrid a target by hooking up with her. He tugged on a shirt and jammed his feet into a pair of shoes.

He hit the door at a run, snapping his shoulder harness. Starting his car, he called his partner.

"Come on, Torres, pick up. Pick up!"

This time of night, even the streets of New York were fairly empty. He ran every light, broke every traffic law in the book.

"This better be good." His partner, Rico Torres, sounded groggy.

"I need you to meet me." Sam rattled off the address. "Federoff's got Ingrid."

"What?"

"He gave me fifteen minutes to get there before he starts cutting off fingers. I'm to go alone, so no sirens."

"Already on my way." No sleep in Rico's voice now. The man might have been rousted from a deep sleep, but the cop was wide-awake.

"When you're a minute out, Rico, phone this in. That should give me time to take care of things. If not, you'll need help. Nikolai is one mean bastard—and chances are he won't be alone. Do not go in solo, you hear me? Be careful, partner."

"You too, Sam. Don't do anything foolish. Follow your own advice. Wait for me!"

Sam hung up without answering and took the next corner on two wheels. Six minutes left. He swore a blue streak. He seriously doubted he'd make it in time, and he sure as hell couldn't wait for backup.

Ingrid. Shit! What had he done?

He and Rico had been dogging the drug lord for months, but every time they got close, he had disappeared. Why had he made a move tonight? What did he gain by taking Ingrid?

Self-loathing churned in Sam's stomach. It didn't take a genius to figure that one out. Federoff would rid himself of the cop who'd been hounding him, the cop who'd sworn to take him down.

Sam swiped a hand over his eyes and squealed to the curb. He glanced at his dashboard clock. Two minutes and counting. Heart in his throat, he turned off the car's overhead light and slid out, closing the door with barely a sound. The street looked deserted. Anybody in his right mind was home in bed. Unease skipped up and down his spine. Even the greenest rookie knew to call this in. Now. He was breaking the most fundamental of rules.

Yet he couldn't call for backup. Rico would do that. Soon.

So here he was, alone in one of the worst sections of the city with half the streetlights out, headed into an even darker alley and praying to all that was holy Ingrid would be there. Alive…and whole.

He sprinted the last couple blocks, staying in the shadows. He'd go in low.

As he covered the distance, his mind, on an adrenaline high, tried to make sense of it all. Had he wanted Federoff too badly? Should he have seen this coming?

Ingrid, of the pale, pale skin and midnight-black hair,

alone in a dark alley with that monster. He stopped, held his breath, and listened. He heard nothing.

Sweat broke out on his brow. If he arrived too late…

Low clouds scuttled across the sky, blocking what little light the moon might provide. Both a blessing and a curse, he guessed.

He pulled out his phone and sent his partner a text.

Where are you?

A few seconds later, his response came.

2 minutes out. Wait for me.

Another text came in. Ingrid.

Hurry Sam. Time is up. Scared.

Drawing his gun, Sam stepped past the edge of the building. His eyes adjusted to the inky darkness, and he saw her. What little moonlight there was caught on Ingrid's hair and turned it to shining jet. She stood halfway down the alley, hands bound in front of her, feet tethered.

Beside her stood Federoff, pointing a big, ugly gun at her head.

"We meet at last," he said, his speech heavy with a Russian accent. "Glad you could make it."

"Let her go," Sam ordered, his gun aimed straight at the bastard's head. "She's not part of this. Let her go, and we'll talk."

"Talk?" Nikolai laughed gutturally. "The only thing

you want to talk about is how many years you're gonna send me away for. Not gonna happen."

"Help me, Sam." Ingrid's voice sounded small. Her eyes widened. "Look out! Behind you!"

As Sam turned, the world exploded. Fire sliced through him, and he dropped to the pavement. His ears rang from the reverberation of the gunshot in the narrow space.

He managed to roll over but couldn't get up. Flat on his back, he stared up at the few stars overhead. The stench of rotten garbage assaulted his nose. Warmth spread beneath him like a comfortable blanket. But it wasn't a blanket. It was his own blood pooling around him. He was dying.

Ingrid's voice rang out sharply in the dark alley. "Untie me, Nikolai. These damn ropes are cutting into my skin. I told you they were too tight. But did you care? No. Now I'm gonna have bruises."

"I'll buy you a diamond bracelet to cover the marks."

Through the spreading gray haze, Sam fought to process what he was hearing.

"Or maybe not," Nikolai crooned.

Sam rose up on one elbow, the pain so intense his vision dimmed. He tried to find his gun but couldn't seem to make his arm move.

Federoff's gun came up again, and one more shot rang out.

The world went dark.

Sam woke with a jerk. Sweat slicked his body. His breath wheezing in and out, heart rate off the charts, he tossed the covers aside and sat on the edge of the old double bed, head low, fighting for a shred of sanity.

He hadn't had the nightmare for a couple of nights now and had dared to hope the department's shrink had been right, that a change of environment might help. That he wouldn't wake up every night of his life battling these memories.

The cold, hard facts? Ingrid had set him up right from the get-go. It turned out she'd been working for the drug lord the night Sam met her in the bar. Federoff had planted the sultry beauty there for him to find.

For nearly two months, they'd tangled the sheets, yet he'd meant less than nothing to her. She'd left his bed and gone straight to Nikolai's. He was a trained professional, a member of the Narcotics Division, and he'd been played for a fool. She'd asked questions, and he'd been too sex-drunk not to answer.

Sam pulled on a pair of jeans and ran a hand through his tousled hair. One thing was for sure: he wasn't about to go back to sleep anytime soon. He headed downstairs, steps creaking beneath his bare feet and the night of the shooting continuing to play on the film loop in his mind.

He'd regained consciousness to find his partner leaning over him.

"Officer down," Rico shouted into his radio. "Officer down!"

Never good words to hear and even worse when you were that downed officer.

Rico told him later he'd found Ingrid dead when he'd arrived on the scene and Federoff nowhere around. But fellow officers had collared him at the airport as he brazenly walked up to the ticket line, passport in one hand, a suitcase filled with hundred dollar bills in the other.

Ingrid had willingly acted as bait to lure him in for the kill. The betrayal went deep.

Sam wondered if he'd ever again be able to trust his own judgment. Until he knew, he wouldn't walk the streets of New York carrying a badge and a gun. The city's people deserved better.

Downstairs, he headed to the kitchen and pulled a cold beer from the now-sparkling-clean fridge. He popped the top and headed outside. Dropping to the top porch step, he looked up at the twinkling sky. It was darker here, the stars brighter since they didn't have to compete with the city lights.

Sprawled on the steps, he took a long drink. The cold beer felt good on his parched throat.

He ran a hand through his hair. Because of these dreams, he'd come to hate the night. But here on Gertie's porch, in this serene setting, he felt calmer. His heart rate slowed and his breathing evened out. He took another sip and leaned back on his elbows to study the inky-black sky even as the world around him came alive with the sounds of the cicadas. When he'd been a kid, he'd been fascinated by them. He smiled, remembering the nights he and Gertie sat around a small fire listening to them and eating burned marshmallow. Those had been carefree times.

A tree limb scraped against the house's siding. Tonight, the night sounds actually soothed him.

Over and over again, he'd asked himself what he could have done differently that night. Time after time, he went through other scenarios and cursed himself for not smelling a rat.

Ingrid paid for her duplicity with her life. He'd gotten off lucky.

At least that's what everybody kept telling him. The shot through the back of his left shoulder had torn muscle and bone but missed his heart by a fraction of an inch. The bigger problem? That bullet had blown an even larger hole in his psyche, in his confidence and peace of mind. And no surgeon on earth, no matter how skillful, could repair that.

He'd been suckered in by a pretty face and a hot body.

It wouldn't happen again.

His head jerked up when, across the street, a light went on. Speaking of pretty faces and hot bodies. It seemed Cricket was awake, too.

"What keeps you up in the middle of the night, Bug?"

Whatever it was wasn't his concern, and he'd do well to remember that.

The badge, his gun, and women. Right now, all of them were off-limits.

So why the nightmare tonight? Because he'd kissed Cricket?

He didn't think so.

He tipped back his head and swallowed the last of his beer. As he crushed the can in his hand, he remembered the man at the table beside them tonight. He'd had a beer, too. Sam had seen the man somewhere before. But where?

Had he triggered tonight's nightmare?

That niggling feeling of being followed returned, and the night lost its friendliness.

He glanced at the wisteria-covered house across the street. Tomorrow he and Cricket would have another chat about those locks.

Chapter 7

Cricket sat in the middle of the chaotic mess of the shop and experimented with bows for Holly's lavender-and-rose bouquets. White or lavender ribbon?

A sharp rap sounded on the door, and, startled, she covered her racing heart with a hand.

"Cricket? I didn't mean to scare you." Jenni Beth opened the door and peeked around it. "Can I come in?"

"Absolutely. I'm glad you're here. You can help me decide." She picked up the three centerpieces she'd been playing with.

"They're perfect, Cricket. Simple and classy. Super romantic." She leaned close. "And they smell like heaven."

Cricket chewed at her lip. "You think Holly will like them?"

"She'll love them."

"Not too simple?"

"No."

"Which color for the bow?"

"Oh, boy, they all look great."

Cricket gave her an eye roll. "That's not what I asked."

"The lavender."

"Okay." She took a good look at the always-immaculate, pulled-together Jenni Beth. Today, her new friend's hair was mussed and she had an almost frantic air about her. "What's wrong?"

"I can't believe I'm doing this. You're not even open for business yet."

"And?"

"I have an emergency." She pointed to the centerpieces. "Another emergency. Oh God, three emergencies actually." Waving a handful of file folders, she dropped into a small chair by the door. "And I'm going to ask you to bail me out. I'm sorry."

Cricket mentally made a list of today's have-to-get-dones, then nudged them aside. After all, wasn't this what the business was all about? Taking care of customers and creating the perfect day for Magnolia House brides?

"First, can I ask you something?"

"Sure," Jenni Beth said.

"What's with Beck and Tansy?" Cricket held up a hand. "I don't need all the dirty little details, just enough to understand."

Jenni Beth nodded. "Everybody in town knows, so it's not like I'm telling tales. All through school, Tansy and Beck were a couple. Even after she left for college, they stayed together. Then, out of the blue, a month or so after her dad passed away, she was pregnant with another guy's baby and married him. No warning, nothing."

"Seriously?"

"Seriously. Personally, I think it was a huge mistake. She still loves Beck."

"Hmmmm." A lot to think about here, but she'd table it for later. "Okay, so talk to me about your emergencies." She grabbed a notebook and a pencil.

"What have I done to deserve you?" Jenni Beth picked up a folder. "Okay, first, I have a bridal shower in two days. The friends who are throwing it insisted they'd make the centerpieces and didn't need any flowers."

"Let me guess. They've changed their minds?"

Jenni Beth nodded.

"Two days doesn't give us much time."

"I know." She groaned. "I'm ashamed to dump this on you."

Cricket smiled at her. "I'm the florist, remember? This is what I do. So what do they want? Theme? Colors?"

"They want fun. Bold, bright, and quirky. This bride's a little out of the box, and her friends want to celebrate that. The plates, napkins, and table runners are striped in red, orange, and fuchsia."

"Hmm." Cricket tapped her pencil on the notepad, then she jumped up and plucked a replica of an old-fashioned milk bottle from one of the shelves. "How about this? We half-fill it with red, orange, pink, and yellow jelly beans. Then we add gerbera daisies in the same colors with water tubes."

"Oh, you're good."

"Yes, I am. I'm humble, too." She laughed. "Hit me with crisis number two."

Jenni Beth did. "Number two is a Virginia bride, while three is a Georgia bride. Both need rush jobs, and, since I'm not scheduled tight yet, I can fit them in."

Dogwood went into the Virginia bride's proposed bouquet, along with white lilacs and jasmine. For the Georgia bride, Cricket suggested fruited peach branches, apricot roses, a few heirloom mermaid roses, and pom-pom dahlias. She promised to draw up sketches for both brides that afternoon, and the world was once again in alignment.

"You saved me, friend." Jenni Beth collected her folders. "Last night was fun, wasn't it? You and Sam—"

Cricket felt the color flood her cheeks.

Those slate-blue eyes narrowed. "Anything you want to share?"

She shook her head. "No. Nothing. It's just… Well, Sam—"

The door opened, and the man himself walked in.

"Hey, Sam, I was just leaving." Jenni Beth gave Cricket a quick hug. "Enjoy."

Sam watched her go, a bemused expression on his face. "Was it something I said?"

"No. We'd just finished up some work. She had a couple problems with brides and their friends. Minds change, blah, blah, blah." Cricket rubbed the back of her neck. "But it's all fixed now."

"Good."

"Did you need something?"

"Actually, yeah." He scanned her shop. "You're busy. This can wait till you get home."

"Consider it doing me a favor. You're giving me a breather."

Now that he was here, he wasn't quite sure how to go about it.

"Are you worried about something?"

"Yes, I am."

"Before we get into that, can I try something, Sam?"

His brow creased. "Sure."

Before he could react, she stepped closer to him. With a hand on either side of his face, she pulled him in and touched her lips to his. A small sound of pleasure escaped.

Caught totally off guard, Sam hesitated, then thought, *What the hell?* and went for it. He slipped his arm around her waist and brought her body solidly against his as he angled his lips to go deeper. Explosive! One single kiss from this woman sent his libido flying off the charts.

"Cricket—" He drew away.

Her eyes had gone winter-storm gray, deep and smoldering, her lips moist and red from their kiss.

She sighed. "I had to know."

"Know what?"

"If I'd imagined how good that felt last night."

"You're killing me." He rested his forehead against hers. "You're killing me."

She laughed, then stepped back. "Now, what did you want to talk about?"

He stared at her. "What?"

"You came to see me about something."

Yes, he had. Something important. That kiss, though, had wiped his mind blank. He could only stare at her.

"You said you were worried."

And then he remembered. The locks. He had to get her to promise to lock up at night without scaring her and without sharing too much of his story. After all, it had been a woman who—

No. Cricket wasn't Ingrid. He wouldn't paint her with the same brush.

"Look, I know you have an aversion to locks although the why of that escapes me." He paused, unsure how to approach this without scaring her. "Thing is, I'd feel a whole lot better if you'd lock up when you leave your house and at nighttime."

"You drove into town to tell me this?"

"Yes. No. I came in to get a few supplies, then figured as long as I was here, I'd stop by."

"Okay, thanks. I'll keep it in mind."

He pinched the bridge of his nose. This quirky neighbor of his had absolutely no intention of locking her doors. "I'd sleep better if you locked up."

"Did you stay awake last night worrying about me, Sam?"

Oh yeah, he had. But he wasn't about to admit that or discuss the thoughts or the nightmares that had kept him awake last night.

"I lock my shop."

"Why?"

"Why? Because…because I don't want someone coming in and taking anything."

"Good thinking. But it doesn't matter if somebody goes into your home?"

"Well, sure it does."

"But not enough to lock up." He gestured. "The stuff in here's worth more than what you've got at home?"

"No, of course not. This is my business, though."

"Do me a favor. Lock up both places. Protect your possessions and yourself."

Before she could say anything else, he walked out, unsatisfied with their talk and with himself. Her kiss had left him rattled.

This whole solitary thing wasn't working very well.

Chapter 8

THE CAN OF CHICKEN NOODLE SOUP DROPPED TO THE floor and rolled toward the hideous velveteen flowered sofa. Sam groaned and rubbed at his shoulder. Without a gym or weights, the soup he'd bought for lunch had to pull double duty.

Although with the way he'd worked the last few days around here, both inside and out, he probably didn't need any more exercise. Still, he grabbed the can and finished the series his physical therapist had prescribed. The sooner he was back in top shape, the sooner he could move on and get back to work.

He would put the nightmares to rest and let the past slide into the past.

A car door slammed, and Cricket's SUV started up across the street.

Pumping the soup can, Sam wandered to the window and watched as she backed out of the driveway, headed off to her shop, no doubt.

He hadn't talked to her in two days. He had, in fact, gone out of his way to avoid her after that last kiss.

Remembering he hadn't had breakfast yet, he wandered into the kitchen. When he opened the fridge, he found a couple swallows of milk, a wedge of cheese, a nearly empty container of deli macaroni salad, and one rather sad-looking apple. Time for a Bi-Lo run.

Country living was harder than city living. No delis, no subway or buses. No grocery delivery.

Most of all, there was no mom a few blocks away to invite him for Sunday dinner, then send him home with enough leftovers to last into the middle of the week.

He pulled out a loaf of bread and the jar of peanut butter he'd picked up. Resting a hip against the counter, he wished for a pork gyro. If wishes were fishes… One bite in, his back screen door bumped.

Straightening, Sam went on instant alert. An animal of some sort? But was it a two- or four-legged one?

Listening, he heard snuffling, then scratching. Definitely four-legged, he decided. What lived around here? Bears? Wild boars? He had no idea.

Dumping his sandwich on a paper plate, he picked up the soup can, holding it like a baseball, and inched toward the door. What he saw on his porch stopped him cold.

A dog—burrs in his dull, matted coat, ribs showing—stared up at him with sad, bottomless blue eyes. It had to have been days since the animal had eaten.

"Who do you belong to, boy?" Sam backtracked into the kitchen and picked up his sandwich. "Hungry, aren't you? You like peanut butter? Hmmm?"

He opened the door and stepped onto the badly-in-need-of-paint back porch. The boards creaked beneath him. It should probably be his next project.

The dog may have been half-starved, but he had manners. He waited politely till Sam knelt and laid the food down in front of him to sniff at it.

"Go ahead, pal. Eat up. I'll make myself another one."

The dog had no collar, no tags, and desperately needed a bath.

Sam went back inside and slapped together two more sandwiches. Rooting around, he found an old pie tin, filled it with water, and carried it outside. He set the water and another sandwich in front of the dog, then sat down on an old wooden rocker and ate the other himself.

Finished with breakfast, the dog dropped down beside the chair, his head on the toe of Sam's old boot. The pads on his paws were worn slick. He'd obviously been doing a lot of walking—and very little eating.

"Sure do wish you could talk, fella. You look about as worn-down as I feel. Quite a pair, aren't we?"

The dog gave a quick bark in answer.

"Let's hose you down." Sam stepped off the porch, the dog at his heels. The faded green hose he'd found yesterday was no doubt rotten in places, but it would do the trick.

Would the dog have fleas? Probably. He held up a finger. "Hold on a minute."

Shooting back inside, he headed for the bath and grabbed the bottle of shampoo he'd picked up. Hopefully the dog would appreciate its manly smell. The screen door slammed behind him, and the old dog jumped.

"Sorry about that." He patted the dog's head and was rewarded with a warm tongue on his hand. He grinned and petted the dog again. He'd never had a real pet growing up. With five kids to feed, his parents insisted the budget couldn't stretch to cover an animal. One year, tired of his whining, his mom had bought him a goldfish. Theodore had lived one week to the day, and that had been that.

Two of his sisters had dogs now, and Ysabelle, the youngest, had three cats. Himself? He'd never wanted the responsibility. His hours were too erratic, and, maybe, he was a bit too self-centered. He wanted to do what he wanted to do when he wanted to do it.

But now, with those wise, heart-rending eyes studying him… No, he still didn't want or need an animal or the responsibility that went with it. Besides, he was only temporary here in Misty Bottoms. His postage-stamp-sized place in New York couldn't accommodate an animal.

The dog sat patiently while Sam wet him down, lathered, and rinsed him. Then he had Sam backing away quickly when he shook to dry himself off.

"What are we going to do with you, boy? Hmmm? Some kid's probably bawling his eyes out, missing you."

He pulled his cell from his shirt pocket. A quick search showed no animal shelters in the area. Okay, on to plan B. He'd give the local sheriff a buzz. Stray animals probably weren't high on his priority list, but who knew?

The phone rang only once before it was answered.

"Sheriff Jimmy Don Belcher here. What can I do for ya?"

"This is Sam DeLuca. I—"

"Ah, Gertie Taylor's great-nephew. Heard you were in town."

Ten seconds of complete silence followed.

"DeLuca? You still there?"

"Yeah, yeah, I am. How'd you know who I am?"

Jimmy Don laughed. "Kitty, over at the bakery, said you'd been in."

When Sam said nothing, Jimmy Don went on. "Couple things you should probably understand, DeLuca. You're in Misty Bottoms now. Think you'll find you have very few secrets while you're here. All part of small-town life."

Sam sighed. "Well, then, you should be able to help me out. Somebody in town's missing his dog. An older brown-and-white mutt with the ice-blue eyes of a husky. But he's much smaller than that breed. He has a white face and brown fur on top of his head that forms kind of a widow's peak."

"How do you know all this?"

"Because he's at my house."

"Haven't heard of anyone huntin' for a lost dog," Jimmy Don said. "Fact is, we don't have a shelter here. Can't afford one. But tell you what I can do. I'll call them over in the next county and have them come pick him up."

Sam looked at the old boy. Battered and worn, he was plain tuckered out, yet his tail thumped when he met Sam's gaze. Chances of this guy getting adopted? Somewhere between slim and none.

A ride to the shelter would be a one-way trip. The old dog would never run the fields again or eat any more peanut butter sandwiches on a sun-warmed back porch. And wasn't he waxing poetic?

Gertie's house could provide refuge for one more lost soul, couldn't it? Temporarily.

"Tell you what, Sheriff. Think I'll keep him here with me for now."

"Your choice."

While he had the sheriff on the phone, should he tell him about… What exactly? That a guy who sat beside them at the pizza parlor looked vaguely familiar? In a town this size, a person probably saw a third of the population daily. Everybody'd look familiar.

Hadn't his therapist warned him about this? About intensified suspicion and seeing danger everywhere? Sam could call Dr. Phelps, but he wasn't sure if the danger was real or imagined. If it was real, he needed more than a therapist.

If it wasn't, and he cried wolf, they'd think he was bonkers.

Still, his gut told him something was off.

Yeah, his gut.

When he ignored it—well, his instincts had been off for a while. Ingrid was proof enough of that.

He was a New York City detective, for hell's sake. What did he expect this Mayberry sheriff to do?

For now, he'd stay quiet, keep his eyes open, and watch out for Cricket. He didn't want her tangled in this nasty web just because she happened to be his neighbor.

Because he'd kissed her, and she'd kissed him.

Sam thanked Jimmy Don and slipped his phone back into his pocket. "How about we finish piling those tree limbs I cut down this morning, dog? Tomorrow will be soon enough to decide what to do with them. And you."

The job took longer than it should have since the dog had a penchant for chasing sticks. Sam would haul a big limb away, and the dog would find a smaller one, drop it at Sam's feet, and wait patiently for him to toss it.

"Your feet have to hurt, pal." Sam slapped the stick against his leg and sent the dog into a delirium of joy. "Okay, ready?"

He tossed the hunk of wood and watched the dog race after it. Two sweaty hours later, man and dog were both tired, the branches formed a crazy, lopsided tower, and he'd made a start on a few other projects.

"I need a shower." Sam walked up the steps and into the house, his new friend trailing in his wake.

The day's grime removed, Sam slid into clean clothes and glanced at the dog, who now snored softly on a tattered throw rug next to his bed.

"Hey." Sam prodded him gently with a bare toe. "We both need food. I'll make a quick trip into town and see what I can find. If you're still here when I get back, you old hobo, I'll have something for you besides a peanut butter sandwich."

The old dog opened one eye, then slowly stood, shaking himself. Downstairs, he lapped up some water from the bowl in the kitchen before following Sam to the end of the sidewalk.

When the motorcycle started up, the dog yelped and ran cowering onto the front porch. Okay, Sam thought, so he wasn't a biker dog. That was okay.

As he swung into the heart of Misty Bottoms, the town no longer felt foreign to him. Instead, he had an odd sense of belonging. That, of course, was an illusion, he reminded himself. He didn't belong here. He didn't fit in and never would.

He stopped at Dee-Ann's Diner, with its red-and-white awning. Flowers and ferns scattered over the sidewalk, its bricks buckled with age and worn smooth over the years.

"Hey, Sam, good to see you," the owner called out as he walked in.

"Thanks, Dee-Ann. You've got a starving man on your hands."

"Well, lucky for you, we've got plenty of food in the kitchen. Sit anywhere you want. Coffee?"

"Please. A gallon or two at least."

Before he could slide into a booth, the sheriff, in full uniform, signaled him over. Resigned, Sam headed his way. As a cop himself, he understood that it made sense for the man to want to know who'd come into town.

"Have a seat." The sheriff, who looked like he'd downed more than his share of Krispy Kreme doughnuts, thrust out a meaty hand. "Jimmy Don Belcher."

As Sam shook it, Jimmy Don said, "You must be Sam DeLuca. We talked this mornin'. D'ya find the dog's owner?"

"No, sir, I didn't. Think I'll hold on to him and fatten him up till we can find who he belongs to."

"Might have yourself a dog permanently."

"Not going to happen. I'm not here permanently, and I can't take him with me when I head home."

"Where's home?"

Yep. A cop to the bone. It didn't much matter what state issued the badge he wore. "New York."

"State or the city?"

"The city."

"What d'ya do there? Gertie told me you were a cop."

Okay. So much for believing he could keep his background a secret. "You heard right. I'm with the NYPD. Detective with narcotics."

Jimmy Don's eyes narrowed. "What are you doin'

in our little borough? Got a professional interest here? Anything I should know about?"

Dee-Ann saved him when she set down his coffee and a menu. "You need this?" She threw Jimmy Don a glare. "Or is he on the menu? Grilled Sam."

"Don't you have somethin' burnin' in the kitchen?"

"Nope." Dee-Ann crossed her arms over her ample bosom.

"I like you, Dee-Ann," Sam said. "You're a stand-up woman."

"You bet I am. You decide what you want?"

"I'll have your meatloaf special and a piece of that cherry pie." He pointed to the display case.

"You got it." She hustled away.

Sam threaded his thumb, index, and middle fingers through the mug's handle and unconsciously twisted the cup back and forth. "Look, Sheriff, I'm, ah, not advertising any of what we just talked about."

"Got ya. You undercover?"

"No, not now."

"Takin' some time off?"

"Yeah, something like that."

Jimmy Don's eyes drilled into him. "That can be a good thing."

"I sure hope so." Sam took a sip of his still-scalding coffee.

"You let me know if you need anything."

"Will do." Before Jimmy Don could bombard him with questions again, Sam asked, "Actually, maybe there is something you can do. Know anybody with a truck for sale? Something older and dirt cheap?"

Jimmy Don's radio crackled, and he drained his

coffee cup. "Gotta run." He tossed a *Penny Shopper* guide at Sam. "I think old man Gilmore's tryin' to sell his. Page five. We'll talk some more later."

Sam watched him go and wondered how different the sheriff's job was from the one he did in New York. He doubted Jimmy Don had ever stared down the wrong end of a gun barrel, ever held a twelve-year-old gang member who'd been shot during a drive-by, ever gone undercover to nail a drug lord. Wasn't that what Sam had wanted, though? That adrenaline rush from wading into a pile of shit?

"Here you go." Dee-Ann set the heaping plate in front of him. "Dig in."

Sam looked up, past Dee-Ann, and straight into the eyes of the same man he'd seen last night. He stood across the street, leaning against a tree. Sam half rose from his chair.

"What's wrong?"

Sam glanced at her. "Who's that guy across the street?"

She looked up. "Who? I don't see anybody."

"What?" He looked outside. There was nobody there. Was he losing his mind? Was it playing tricks on him?

When he sat unmoving, she said, "You look lost in thought, Sam. Listen, if it's Jimmy Don, don't pay him no never mind. He's a good guy."

"No, I've got no problem with Jimmy Don." Sam nodded at his plate. "This meatloaf looks great. Thanks."

Not quite as hungry as he'd been a couple minutes ago, he picked at his food. He swore he'd seen the man somewhere else. Before Misty Bottoms.

Ten minutes later, Dee-Ann stopped by his table. "You want a go box for that?"

"No, I'm good." Folding back the page in the *Penny Shopper*, he showed her the ad for the pickup. "What do you think?"

"You gonna go look at it?"

"Might buy it if it's any good."

"It doesn't actually look like that anymore." She pointed at the grainy black-and-white photo. "It's seen some wear, but Lem still brings it into town once in a while, so..." She shrugged and gave him directions.

A quick stop at the grocery store netted Sam a small bag of dog food. He figured it might make one, maybe two meals for the beast at his house, but until he got a different vehicle, he had no way of hauling a larger one home. A couple steaks, two potatoes, an onion, and some eggs stowed safely in his second saddlebag, and he was good to go.

With one eye on his side-view mirror, he left town. Maybe having a dog at the house wasn't such a bad idea. Temporarily.

After only two wrong turns, Sam swerved onto the gravel path that led to an old, white farmhouse. An older model truck sat in the side yard, a "For Sale" sign displayed on the front windshield.

A faded green-and-rust truck. Not rust-colored, but rust-rust. The entire front quarter looked in serious danger of falling off.

He pulled the *Penny Shopper* out of his back pocket and glanced at the ad again. Then he squinted at the truck in front of him. Dee-Ann had been right. This picture had to have been taken a good many years ago.

"May you rust in peace," he mumbled.

A screen door slammed, and Sam set his kickstand.

"Hey, young fellow, you lookin' for a good truck?"

"Yes, sir, I am. The sheriff told me you had one for sale."

"Name's Lemuel Gilmore." He stuck out a hand.

"Mr. Gilmore." Sam shook. "Sam. Sam DeLuca."

"Folks call me Lem. Mr. Gilmore was my daddy."

The stooped man wore bib overalls and a ball cap and was about as bowlegged as they came. His bewhiskered face split into a grin. "Old Betsy here is a doozy, son." He slapped an arthritic hand on the top of the tailgate.

"Does she run?"

"Like the wind."

"Mind if I take it for a short drive?"

"Nope. Keys are in her. Never take them out."

You and Cricket, Sam thought. *Far too trusting*. But he said nothing, simply walked around to the driver's side and hopped in.

"Mind if I come along?" Lem's question was rhetorical as he'd already hobbled around the truck and opened the passenger door.

"Not at all." Sam turned the key and registered surprise at the sweet-sounding engine. Old Betsy sounded a heck of a lot better than she looked.

As he headed down the drive, Lem said, "Glad you came by, boy. Wife's drivin' me nuts today. She decided to clean out the bedroom closet. Humph. The woman wanted to throw out my favorite fishin' shirt 'cause it's a little tattered. Tried to tell her that meant it was broken in is all."

Sam nodded. "Understood. I grew up in a house with five females. My mom and four sisters are all pros when it comes to being annoying."

"But you love 'em anyway."

He grinned. "Yeah, you do."

~

Parked back at Lem's house, Sam had second thoughts. He could rent a truck—if Misty Bottoms had a car rental. But then he'd have to worry about scratching it up hauling things.

He kicked a tire. Didn't buying this seem un-temporary, though?

On a sigh, he decided he'd think of it as an investment. Rent a truck? Kiss the money good-bye. Purchase it? He could recoup his investment. Maybe.

He peered at the rust bucket over the top of his sunglasses. There must be another sucker somewhere in Misty Bottoms besides him.

Sam bought the truck.

After they'd hammered out the details and Sam paid him, Lem asked, "You won't mind haulin' a few things for me once in a while, will you?"

Sam's head swiveled to him. "What?"

"Well, I don't have a truck no more." Lemuel pulled off his ragged Atlanta Braves ball cap and scratched his head, the wisps of gray hair standing on end. "What am I gonna do for haulin' stuff I need hauled?"

With a sinking feeling, Sam understood he was doomed. "Sure. Give me a call if you need anything hauled."

"Every Tuesday I cart a load out to the local dump. Ain't no way I'm payin' somebody to carry my garbage away for me."

"Every Tuesday?"

"Yep. Like clockwork. Lyda Mae, that's the wife, depends on it."

Sam rubbed at the nagging pain between his eyes. "Any special time on Tuesday?"

"Best if you get there at ten. Not as busy then."

Resigned, he said, "All right. I'll see you Tuesday at ten."

"No." Lem shook his head.

"No?"

"Nope." He swiped a hand over his chin. "If we're gonna be there at ten, you'll want to come about twenty minutes before that, so's we have time to load up and drive there."

We. Sam's stomach dropped. Maybe he should give the old man his truck back, tell him to keep the money if it came to that.

"We could go into town and have ourselves a cup of coffee on the way home. Chew a little fat."

With those words, Sam understood he had lost his second battle of the day. First the dog, now Lem Gilmore.

He gave in graciously. "Sure thing. Look, Lem, I have a small problem." He nodded at his Harley, then at the pickup. "Two vehicles to get home. Would you mind following me there in the truck? I'll drive you right back."

The old man squinted toward the sun and rubbed at his chin stubble again. "Don't think that'll work. *Jeopardy*'s gonna be on in fifteen minutes or so. The wife and I never miss it."

"I can have you back in less than twenty minutes."

"You miss the categories, you might as well not watch any of it," Lem explained.

Sam closed his eyes and counted to ten. He couldn't think of a single argument to toss back at Mr. Gilmore. "All right. I'll leave the truck here for now and be back in a day or so to pick it up."

"Thought you needed it now."

He bit his tongue. "I do, but I can't drive two vehicles at once."

An unholy gleam came into the man's pale blue eyes. "You could leave that bike of yours with me. I'd take good care of it."

"Bet you would," Sam mumbled. "I'll be back for the truck."

Sam drove away on his Harley the new owner of a rusty, old pickup truck named Betsy. And a nine forty garbage-run date on Tuesday with Lemuel Gilmore.

On top of that, he had a tail. Whoever it was wasn't very competent. Either that or he wanted Sam to sweat.

Wasn't there some story about a blond chick who fell into a rabbit hole and everything got all screwed up? Maybe he'd fallen into that same hole.

He sighed.

As long as he was so close to town, he might as well take another few minutes to stop at Elliot's Lumberyard and talk to somebody about his backyard. He'd actually accomplished a couple things today—in addition to acquiring a dog and a truck.

While he'd been outside cutting back branches, he'd studied the old wooden storage shed in the far west corner. Kudzu vines had pretty much blanketed it, but that didn't surprise him. He figured if he stood still for more than fifteen minutes, the fast-growing, insidious vine would shroud him, too.

Cricket had called the wisteria that twined around her porch railing one of the South's treasures. Kudzu? Not so much.

He'd used one of Gertie's butcher knives to hack his way through enough of the greenery to pry open the door. Inside, he'd found the now-rusted, secondhand bike Gertie had bought him. After they'd cleaned it up, she'd spent hours running behind him, steadying him as he learned to ride it.

Both tires were flat now and the rubber rotted.

Gertie had been a good woman, and he'd been lucky to have shared time with her.

Now, once again she was helping him by providing a place of refuge when he needed it most. Unable to heal in New York City, he'd run away to hide, to lick his wounds like any other animal.

Beside the bike, he'd unearthed an old lawn mower. Sweating and swearing, he'd untangled it from years' worth of discarded lawn implements, then dragged it outside to study it. Sad to say, he'd never in his life used one. City kid.

After fussing with it for a good half hour, he gave up. The thing wouldn't start. Sam guessed the gas was too old and the plugs were gummed up. He declared the machine DOA. Either that or he just didn't know what the hell he was doing.

The old mower was no match for the jungle anyway. He'd need something bigger. Since he couldn't tackle the yard, he'd found pruning shears and a pair of leather work gloves and worked on the shrubbery.

Spotting the lumberyard, Sam pulled into the unpaved lot and parked his Harley before heading inside.

A skinny little guy walked up to him. "How can I help you today?" His name tag read "Jeeters."

Sam explained his dilemma.

"You need a scythe." Jeeters scratched his head. "Or you might hire Harlan Griggs. He's got a big old Bush Hog and can knock that yard down with no problem."

Heavy footsteps came up behind them, and Sam, on full alert, swiveled on his heel. It wasn't the guy from the street but the blond he'd seen with Cricket the other day. Her cousin.

Sam held out a hand. "Sam DeLuca, and you must be Beck Elliot, the one who kept Cricket from calling the law on me the other day."

"Yep. She can be a little high-strung sometimes."

"No kidding."

Beck flashed a quick grin. "Tryin' to get that lawn in shape, huh?"

Sam blew out a resigned breath. "Yeah. Big job."

"I mowed Ms. Gertie's lawn when I was in high school. Did a couple others, too. Earned some money on Saturday, then spent it on…my date that night. If I know Gertie, the mower you found is probably the same one I used."

Sam decided he liked Beck. The guy seemed open and down-to-earth, and if his scuffed and worn boots were any indication, he was no stranger to hard work.

"Jeeters is right. You're gonna want to knock it down some before you use that mower. Get yourself one of these." He pulled a scythe off a wall rack.

"Yeah, well, I can't get the mower to work."

"It sat too long," Beck said. "Bring it in, and I'll have one of my guys go through it for you."

"Appreciate that." Sam pointed at the scythe. "I can't take that home with me today. Maybe tomorrow if I'm lucky." When Beck threw him a questioning look, he said, "I'm riding a Harley, and I don't think that'll fit in my saddlebag. I bought a truck about half an hour ago. Lem Gilmore's."

"That rust bucket?"

"That would be the one. Betsy's my rust bucket now." Sam scrubbed his foot across the floor. "Surprisingly enough, it actually runs great, and I don't need anything pretty. Thing is, I couldn't drive both home, and apparently, it was time for *Jeopardy*."

Beck laughed. "Got ya. Lem and Lyda Mae can be pretty rigid—and they never ever miss *Jeopardy.* I'd be glad to shuttle one of the vehicles for you, but I'm right in the middle of a project."

"That's okay. I'll figure something out."

"Stop by tomorrow, and I'll make time. Promise."

"I just might do that. Unless I can talk Lem into helping—after I make a garbage run for him at nine forty. On the dot."

A slow smile spread over Beck's face. "So you bought his truck and now you have to do his haulin'."

"Looks like it."

"Welcome to Misty Bottoms, Sam."

Chapter 9

CRICKET HELD HER BREATH AS SHE TURNED ONTO Frog Pond Road. Sam had shown up in Misty Bottoms with no warning. Every day she worried he'd disappear the same way, that he'd simply pack his bags and leave without telling her. Had their kisses scared him off? The first had been impulsive on his part. The others? She didn't regret them a bit.

She hadn't seen hide nor hair of him the last couple days, yet the yard was starting to look better. A lot of the brush had been cut back and removed. Apparently he didn't shy away from hard work—just people.

The house itself stood proud again. It needed paint in the worst way, but the roses, now visible, twining over the porch railing almost made her forget that.

And what do you know? Sam was still there, his Harley parked in the gravel drive. Late last night, she'd opened her bedroom window and heard his music, the throbbing bass. What kept him up till two a.m. when most of the world slept?

Sliding from her car, she groaned as the oppressive heat and humidity hit her. She leaned in to fish her purse from the backseat, then tipped her head. Did she hear barking? And was that laughter? A man's laughter?

Sam's?

Curious, she slipped across the street, rounded the corner of the house, and stopped. Sam tossed a stick toward the back of the yard in a throw that would have made any quarterback green with envy.

A shaggy, brown-and-white dog chased it, his tongue lolling out. Retrieving the stick, he raced back toward Sam, caught sight of Cricket, and veered in her direction.

Surprised, Sam turned to stare behind him.

"You have a dog!" Cricket dropped to her knees and sent the dog into ecstasy when she rubbed his head, then scratched behind his ears. "Aren't you a pretty boy?"

She laid her forehead against the dog's.

"Boys aren't pretty," Sam grumbled. "He's handsome. And he's not mine. He showed up on the back porch, a little worse for wear."

"You didn't just send him away?"

"No." Sam looked affronted. "I shared my peanut butter sandwich with him. Poor guy looked like he could use a safe haven."

Just like you? she wondered. But she kept that thought to herself.

"You want him?" Sam asked.

The dog stared up at him with those soulful eyes.

"Uh-uh. He's yours. He loves you."

Sam snorted.

"He does."

"I fed him, so right now, I'm his meal ticket. The minute I stop, that look of adoration will evaporate. But here's the thing." He jammed his hands in his pockets. "And you already know this because I've said it before. I'm not staying in Misty Bottoms, Bug. I can't have a dog. Take him."

"I'm not takin' him. He's yours. He chose you."

Sam shook his head. “First, we’ve already established the dog doesn’t love me. He loves food in his belly and will put up with any sucker who’s willing to provide it. Second, he didn’t choose me. He ended up on my porch. It could as easily have been your back door he scratched at. Third, and this is a repeat, I’m not staying. Misty Bottoms is temporary.”

“I disagree with the first argument, and the second? Kismet. The third? What difference does it make where you live?”

“I can’t take a dog back to my cramped apartment in New York City.”

“Hmmm. New York City. So I was right. Not many grassy yards, but still, you’ve got parks. Lots of them.”

“Exactly how do I get him there on my Harley?”

“You could figure it out if you wanted to.”

He threw up his hands in frustration. “Forget it.”

“Fine.” She turned to go.

Sam’s hand caught hers. “Wait.”

She almost squealed from the heat, the zing of that simple touch. The man had some powerful mojo.

“I have a favor to ask.” He told her about the old truck he’d purchased.

“You bought a truck so you and your dog can go for rides!”

“No,” he answered emphatically. “I bought one so I could drag around what I’ll need to fix up this place.” He nodded toward the house. “I need it to haul away junk and to transport supplies and tools, not dogs. And, again, the mutt’s not mine.”

Instead of answering, Cricket knelt and cupped the dog’s muzzle in her hands. “You like to go for rides? Huh?”

The dog's tail started swinging like a whirligig.

Sam stood patiently, trying to ignore their antics. With a pained expression on his face, he said, "I really hate to ask, but would you mind driving me to pick it up?"

"The truck?"

"Yeah." Before she could answer, he added, "If you can't, Beck said he'd help me tomorrow."

"You've met Beck?"

"I stopped at the lumberyard for advice about cutting down this grass. The mower I found in the shed won't start."

"It wouldn't work for this anyway," she said. "You need a scythe—or somebody to come in with a Bush Hog and knock it down for you."

His brow crinkled. "That's what Beck and Jeeters told me."

"There you go. I'm a country girl, Sam. I know these things."

"You worked all day and want to get off those feet. I understand. I'm tired, too. It was late when I went to bed, and I was up before the sun. Normally, I wouldn't ask, but..."

"I get it. You're new in town. Me too, but having family here helps. A lot." She slung her purse over her shoulder. "You want to go now?"

"You don't mind?"

"Not at all. We'll take my car, though. I'm not driving the old truck back."

"Fine." He started across the street.

"Aren't you taking the dog?"

"Why would I?"

"Dogs like to go for rides, don't you, beautiful?" She knelt again, and the dog gave her a kiss. "See?"

"All I see is a grown woman making a fool of herself, talking baby talk to a mutt."

Cricket put her hands over the dog's ears. "You'll hurt his feelings."

"Oh, for—" Sam rolled his eyes.

"What's his name?"

"Whose?"

"The dog's."

"I don't know. Hobo, I guess, since that's what he is. Here today, gone tomorrow. He's not my dog."

"Sure. Come on, Hobo. Let's go for a ride."

The dog was in the car before Sam could get there and acting for all the world like the front passenger seat belonged to him. Sam pointed toward the back, and Hobo reluctantly crawled over the console.

Once on the road to Lem's, Cricket lowered the back windows halfway. The dog stuck his snout out, ears flapping, a big grin on his face.

"Hobo would be a heck of a lot happier with you," Sam said.

"I don't think so. He showed up at your door. You two were meant to be."

At Lem's, Sam pulled the keys from his pocket and walked over to the truck.

"Since we have to drive right past the Dairy Queen, why don't we stop for ice cream?" Cricket asked. "I'll let you buy me a cone."

That surprised a chuckle from him. "Oh, will you? That's nice of you."

"I know. I'm a nice person." She stuck her head

in the car window. “You want to ride with me or Daddy, Hobo?”

“For the love of Mike.”

“Hey, hey, hey. You’ll hurt Hobo’s feelings.”

“I wouldn’t think of it.” He opened the door, and the dog jumped out of Cricket’s vehicle and hopped into Sam’s. Hobo moved to the right side, and Sam slid behind the wheel of his new truck. And wasn’t that using the term loosely?

Cricket took in the trio—the dog, the truck, and Sam. In some odd way, they fit. They belonged together. All three of them broken-down wrecks but still vital and worthwhile.

Sam cranked the key, and the purr when the engine kicked in surprised her, another reminder that appearances could be deceiving.

“Follow me,” Cricket said.

Five minutes later, they stood at the Dairy Queen’s order window.

“What do you want, Hobo?”

“He doesn’t need anything, Bug. He’s fine. He had dinner.”

“You aren’t going to buy him anything?”

“I bought him five pounds of dog food this afternoon.”

“That’s sustenance,” she countered. “Dairy Queen is a treat.”

When the teenaged boy popped into the window, Cricket threw him her best smile. “We’ll have a vanilla cone and a medium dish of vanilla. What do you want, Sam?”

“Remind me not to waste my breath arguing with you anymore,” he grumbled.

"I will." She tossed him her megawatt smile.

He shook his head, then ordered a large hot fudge sundae.

A couple minutes later, they sat at one of the small outside tables, Hobo sprawled on the grass between them, lapping up his ice cream. She could have sworn Hobo sent her a quick grin of thanks.

"So, how's your shop coming along, Cricket? You going to make your opening?"

"Come hell or high water. Jenni Beth had some emergencies come up, so I'm already busy with weddings and bridal showers. That's put me behind a little, but, oh gosh, it's so worth it."

She watched him swirl his spoon through the dark fudge topping. Maybe she'd get one of those next time.

"You have everything you need?"

"For the most part. I'm still waitin' on one shipment of plants and prayin' it'll make it in time. I want to plant them around the outside for a pop of color. I can make do with some pots if I need to, but I'd rather not. The rest of my inventory is all here and accounted for. Most of it's unpacked and arranged. Martha, at Bi-Lo, is puttin' together a couple deli trays for me, and Kitty's makin' a cake. I've even put together a special playlist for opening day."

"You've been busy."

"Yes, I have. But Beck and Cole have both pitched in. They helped Jenni Beth with her renovations, and now they've done the same for me. Beck, well, he's Mr. Handyman, and Cole, in addition to volunteering sweat and hard work, found some great fixtures and lights for me at his architectural salvage shop."

"Yeah, he finds new homes for all the old things he gathers."

Cricket nodded. "He rescues things, too." She reached down and rubbed Hobo's head.

"I didn't rescue the dog. He's temporary," Sam growled.

"Just like you."

"Yeah, just like me."

"I'll keep that in mind." Cricket sent him a quick smile. The man was bound and determined to be argumentative. Guess he figured if he said something often enough, it would be true. For now, she'd let him get away with it.

"Anyway," she continued, "without their help, I'm not sure I could have pulled all this off."

She licked a trail of melted ice cream and saw Sam's eyes darken. Good. Her fledgling business might keep her awake, but so did this new neighbor of hers. He was too sexy by far. Only fair that he was bothered, too, although she didn't think he slept well, regardless. Something was eating at him, and sooner or later she'd get to the bottom of it. She loved picking at things.

They finished their treats and headed for the vehicles. "Come on, Hobo," Sam said. "Let's go home."

He walked her to her SUV and held the door open.

"Thank you, Sam."

"You're more than welcome. We Yankees have manners, too. Sometimes, anyway. I appreciate your help tonight. It really simplified things for me. And I enjoyed the Dairy Queen stop. It's been a long time since I sat in the twilight eating ice cream."

"I'm even happier we stopped, then. You ought to ice that shoulder tonight," she said. "You're favorin' it."

"It's fine."

She shot him a look that cried, *Liar, liar.*

"I could use a little PT, a little horizontal exercise." The instant the words popped out, he regretted them. It was that pouty little mouth of hers, watching her eat that ice cream. "God, that was absolutely, totally out of line. My mother would box my ears if she'd heard me…and rightfully so. I apologize."

"What happened, Sam? Who hurt you?"

He rolled his eyes, but not before she'd seen the truth in them. He read the knowledge in her own eyes but kept it light. "You've been watching too many soap operas, Bug."

"How would you know anything about soap operas?"

A laugh erupted from him. "You might be surprised. My mom and sisters love those things and watch them 24-7. Sunday dinners? We rehash who's sleeping with whom, who's having their best friend's baby ad nauseam."

When she grinned, he blessed her for the ease with which she'd handled his incredible faux pas. The night could have turned ugly because of his stupidity. Where were his filters?

"Growing up in a house of females, I've seen more than my share of chick flicks, too. Meg Ryan and Tom Hanks practically camped out at our place. And my nieces? Watch out. They're into *Frozen*, *Mulan*, *Tangled*, all those Disney movies." He frowned. "I don't get it, though. Somewhere along the line, the roles have reversed. It used to be the princess waiting for the prince to ride in and rescue her. Now, it's the gal who rescues the guy."

"Why shouldn't she?"

"Why not indeed?" Sam asked. "You planning to rescue me, Cricket?"

"If you need rescuin'. But, then, with you, nobody'd know. You keep everything locked inside."

His eyes shuttered.

"Yep. Just like that." She stood on tiptoe and kissed his cheek. "Thanks again for my ice cream."

Without a word, he opened his truck's door and Hobo hopped in.

He didn't need rescuing. End of story.

Sam unlocked the door and walked into his decrepit house, the dog at his heels.

"What am I supposed to do with you, Hobo?"

Those big, sad eyes met his, and he gave it up for a lost cause for now. He had a bag of kibble in his kitchen, an old, rusted-out truck in his drive, and a dog.

Oh, and a date to take Lem's garbage—and probably Lem—to the dump tomorrow.

How the hell had all that happened in a single day of minding his own business?

He'd topped it off by sitting at a picnic table, eating ice cream with one of the most interesting and unique women he'd ever met. One who'd crawled into his head.

Not a good thing. He'd come to Misty Bottoms to escape and do nothing. He wanted no responsibilities and no schedule. He wanted to eat what he wanted, when he wanted. To sleep, read, watch old Clint Eastwood movies, and listen to loud music.

And now, walk his dog and toss a slobbery stick for him. Wasn't that, in and of itself, a responsibility?

Then add in his house. Instead of the golden goose, his inheritance had turned out to be an ugly duckling desperately in need of a makeover.

Outside, dusk settled in. He opened the kitchen window and felt a warm breeze play over his face. Out back, he could see the newly uncovered wooden shed with its tin roof. It looked good. Rustic, peaceful, and a little lopsided. He'd have to shore it up.

Grabbing a beer from the fridge, he decided to sit on the front porch steps for a bit. Hobo followed him out, dropping down heavily beside him, his head on Sam's lap. Within minutes, the dog was out cold, sighing every once in a while.

Ten minutes turned to twenty, half an hour to an hour.

He thought about Federoff, about the stranger who kept popping up.

The dark didn't scare him. It was the nightmares in his own head that had turned the night against him and made it his enemy. Rather than fade away, the dreams came more often now, even with the sweet scent of the flowers he'd cut from Gertie's rosebush filling the room.

Across the road, the bedroom shade opened a crack, and Cricket stood in the window, backlit by a soft lamp. He told himself to look away.

He didn't.

Feeling exposed, Sam drew back farther into the shadows. Did she know he sat watching her? She wasn't beautiful in the classical sense. That short, choppy blond hair, those storm-cloud eyes, and her little, pointed chin shouldn't add up to attractive. They did.

The sizzle he felt for her was purely physical, he reminded himself. It had been a while since he'd been with a woman. Would be a long time till he wanted to again. The betrayal, the shooting, the hospital and physical therapy had all exacted a huge toll.

Now, here he sat in the dark, on the outskirts of a Podunk town in Southern Georgia, alone with his thoughts and an annoying neighbor. One who looked like sin on two legs as she stood at her bedroom window in a skimpy little nightgown.

Sam swallowed a pain pill he'd tucked in his shirt pocket, then took one last look toward Cricket's. He told himself it was the cop thing, the need to protect. He sure as hell hoped that's all it was because, otherwise, he was turning into one sick puppy.

Speaking of pups. He nudged the old dog. "Hey, Hobo, bedtime. Run out in the yard and take your last tinkle for the night."

With a bark, the mutt hopped up.

Restless, Cricket sighed and closed her blinds. Not a single light on across the street.

Still, she could have sworn earlier—

She shook her head. Her magnetic draw toward Sam DeLuca was silly, with more than a touch of loneliness thrown into the mix. But, oh, her girly parts tingled when the man was around. The man was GORGEOUS in capital letters.

Black hair and eyes, all that dark stubble, and oh-so-male. Torn, tight jeans and a T-shirt that hugged his muscles. And she'd seen earlier what that shirt hid. Ooh, boy. No wonder she couldn't sleep.

She slipped out the back door and hit a switch. Strings

of tiny white lights twinkled throughout the garden. Mrs. Michaels had planted a moon garden, and the night blooming jasmine, the Annabelle hydrangea, and white angel's trumpet shone beside the lamb's ears and dusty millers, even in the slim moon's glow.

Barefoot, she crossed to the small fountain and sat down on an ornate stone bench. The evening dew moistened her nightgown and hair. A fairy's kiss.

And still, Sam filled her mind.

Why couldn't she look like Jenni Beth Beaumont? Why was it that every time her hair started to grow, she whacked it off with her manicure scissors? Next time she needed a haircut, she'd go to the beauty shop. Pinky promise. After all, she owned her own business now and needed to look professional.

Yeah right. Like that was gonna happen.

And then, all hell broke loose.

The most pitiful howls and cries she'd ever heard erupted out front. Hobo? Had Sam hurt him? No! Had something happened to Sam? She raced through the yard, mindless of her bare feet.

"What the hell are you doing?" Sam's outraged voice lifted over Hobo's distress.

Relief rushed through her. Sam was all right, but he definitely wasn't happy.

Hobo sat in the middle of the road, howling pathetically.

"What's wrong with him?"

"I have no idea."

Cricket walked toward them, and Hobo greeted her with a bark and a leg nudge.

"He seems okay now," she said.

Sam raked his fingers through his hair. "Yeah, he does."

His gaze traveled over her, making her aware of how thin her gown was, how short it was.

He grinned. "Nice look."

Her eyes drifted down the length of him. He, too, was shoeless, and his jeans hung low. "I might say the same."

"Cricket." He raised his hands. "I'm sorry he woke you."

"He didn't. I was actually in the backyard."

"You should get some sleep. Come on, Hobo."

Sam started toward his house, and Cricket did the same.

Hobo dropped back onto the pavement and, again, filled the night with long, mournful cries.

"I don't get it." Sam eyed the dog. "See, this is why I don't need a dog. What's up with him?"

Cricket crouched beside Hobo and ran her hands over his body. "He doesn't seem to be hurt."

"He isn't. He was fine till I tried to take him inside for the night. Hell, I don't care if he sleeps outside, but he can't lay here in the middle of the road, and he absolutely cannot keep howling like that."

Sam took another step toward his house, and the dog's yelps grew louder.

"He thinks you're abandoning him."

"What? He ran away from me. He's the one who decided the middle of the road was the perfect spot to pitch a fit." Hands on his hips, Sam studied the dog.

Cricket moved closer.

Hobo stopped baying.

"Maybe he just wanted to wish you good night." Sam pulled Cricket into him.

She could barely breathe. In the moonlight, Sam looked like some pagan god, the soft, silver light glinting off that dark, dark hair. His body, so hard and warm, lit a fire deep inside her.

Their lips touched, tongues danced, and she went weak kneed. When he broke the kiss, only his warm hands on her arms kept her from falling.

"Good night, Bug."

"Night, Sam."

Hobo got to his feet, shook, then quietly stood beside Sam, watching her. Turning, she moved toward her house. At the door, she stopped and waved.

"Lock your door," Sam called.

"Consider it done."

With a smile, she watched the man and his dog cross the street and walk inside.

GLENDALE LIBRARY, ARTS & CULTURE

CHECKOUT RECEIPT

Library Connection @ Adams Square

03/24/2018 1.12 PM

BARCODE: ***********992

TITLE: Every bride has her day /

BARCODE: 39010055765956

DUE DATE: 04-14-18

TOTAL ITEMS: 7

RENEWAL OPTIONS

1) http://www.glendalelac.org/

Click on "My Account"

or

2) By phone @ 818-548-8010

Chapter 10

Sam stretched and yawned hugely. Damned if he didn't feel good. Since the shooting, he hadn't slept well. Strangely enough, Hobo's soft snoring had actually soothed him the last couple of nights, kind of like a lullaby. It was nice to have a warm body of any kind in his bedroom.

And how pathetic was that?

Still, he'd slept all night, two nights in a row, with no nightmares.

He hadn't seen Cricket yesterday. She'd left early, before either he or the dog woke, and she'd been late getting home. He'd seen the lights go on, her silhouette on the shades as she moved around the house, and, later, he'd watched again as the last light went out. Secretly, he'd hoped Hobo would kick up a fuss again till Cricket came out and kissed him good night. It hadn't happened.

Sam's first thought when the dog had started baying had been that the man who'd been dogging him was at Cricket's, that she was in danger. Then she'd come racing around the side of the house, the moon backlighting her and shining through that thin cotton, and all rational thought had deserted him.

Hobo, the matchmaking dog. That might make a good Disney movie, except, with Cricket, Sam wanted an X-rated ending.

Lots of luck with that.

Parting the slats at the living room window, he saw her car still in the drive. Good. He hoped she was sleeping. The lady put in some long hours. He took another sip of his coffee, then headed toward the bathroom and a shower. Hobo plodded along behind him.

"Hey, guy, you my new bodyguard? Huh?" He bent to scratch behind the old dog's ears. This kind of loyalty was rare. Rico, his partner, had his back like this. Every time.

And it had saved his life.

What was his partner doing today? The few times Sam had talked to him, he'd been less than happy, paired up with a rookie straight out of the academy. Maybe he'd give Rico a buzz later today.

New York and his life there felt far away and long ago, like he'd done all that in another life. But he knew that once he returned to the city, his time in rural America would be nothing more than a respite, exactly what he'd meant it to be.

Sam turned on the spray, stripped off his boxers, and stepped into the antiquated shower. Lifting his head, he let the water and his thoughts flow freely.

He wondered if Lem Gilmore and his wife had any other family. He'd guess not. Otherwise they'd have stepped up to help, right?

Yesterday had been—interesting. At exactly nine forty, he'd pulled the old Chevy pickup into Lem's driveway. Together, they'd loaded the Gilmores' garbage into the back along with some of his own debris from the cleanup at Gertie's.

"Why don't I ride along?" Lem already had the passenger door open.

Since he'd dropped some pretty broad hints the night before, Sam had been prepared for a passenger. With Hobo squeezed between them, he'd followed Lem's directions to the county dump, half an ear tuned in to the old man's nonstop monologue and half his mind wondering if dogs should wear a seat belt.

"Next week we need to pick up Martha Crosby's garbage. I told her you'd be happy to take it in for her. She's a widow and needs a little help now and again."

"Next week?"

"Sure. Gotta do this every week, you know."

"Right." He guessed that, along with the other hats he'd acquired lately as handyman, landscaper, dog owner, and new neighbor, he'd also become the town garbage man. Small-town life was kind of like a riptide. It sucked you in, tumbled you around, and refused to spit you out.

When he was ready to leave Misty Bottoms, though, he'd break free.

At the dump, Sam dug out his wallet when Lem got otherwise preoccupied. He paid for both his and Lem's bags. Guess there'd been hidden charges on the Chevy truck the old man had forgotten to mention.

As he tossed the last bag on the conveyor belt, Lem suggested they stop at the diner for coffee and a bite of breakfast. It had been well after noon before he'd dropped Lem off and turned onto Frog Pond Road, headed home, his wallet lighter from the dump costs and the price of two breakfasts.

But that was yesterday. Right now, he was awake, showered, and bored. Even though a Mack truck and its trailer could still get lost in the overgrown jumble out back, yard work held no interest. Neither did stripping ugly-ass wallpaper.

He wandered into Gertie's bedroom and picked up a framed photo from the old bureau of the two of them roasting hot dogs over an open fire. Another picture showed Gertie pushing him on an old rope-and-tire swing they'd hung in the backyard.

He regretted he hadn't come to visit her once he'd grown up. They'd kept in touch, her through letters, he through phone calls. She'd even bought a laptop, and they'd used it for a bit of FaceTime, but she wasn't much for what she called "this newfangled stuff."

Gertie had been a feisty old lady, and he missed her.

In a strange mood, he decided he'd work later. Right now, he needed to get away for a bit. In the kitchen he pulled the bag of dog food from the pantry. Hobo, tuned in to the sound of the rattling paper, nearly knocked Sam over when he came barreling in from his post in the living room.

"Behave yourself." Sam filled the bathtub-sized food bowl he'd pilfered from one of Gertie's cabinets. "You're fed, and you're watered. I won't be gone all that long, but I'll give you the run of the yard rather than locking you inside, just in case you have somewhere else to go."

Sam couldn't believe how badly he hoped that wasn't true. He'd miss the mutt if he left, and that surprised him. He swore he wanted no ties and no obligations. Still, when Hobo leaned into him, he rubbed the furry head a little longer than he meant to.

With the sunrise little more than a pink promise to the east and fog wrapping the world in a soft and eerie cocoon, Sam set out on his bike to explore his temporary home. He left one very unhappy, loudly protesting Hobo in the driveway. He'd take the dog for a ride later, but this morning was for himself.

As Tommy's Texaco came into view, Sam grinned. All the lights were on. It seemed Tommy—or one of his employees—was an early riser, too. He swerved into a parking space in front of the gas station.

The door opened and a man in his mid-fifties stepped out. Dressed in well-worn jeans and a blue denim shirt, a mass of copper-hued hair bushing out from beneath a ball cap, he nodded toward Sam. "Name's Tommy. Guess you must be Sam."

He blinked. "I am."

"Heard you'd come to town, fixin' up Ms. Gertie's place. Heard, too, you had yourself one right nice Harley. Glad to see the gossip mill has the facts straight. Mind if I take a peek?"

"Not at all." Sam set his kickstand and slid off the bike. "Mind if I grab a cup of coffee?"

"Help yourself. Fresh ten minutes ago."

While Tommy inspected the bike, Sam dug his dented Stanley thermos from a saddlebag and went inside to fill it. He'd barely stepped through the door when the rich smell of ham and biscuits had his stomach growling.

"Oh yeah." He reached inside the self-serve cabinet.

"Wife makes those," Tommy said, coming back inside. "Best biscuits in Misty Bottoms."

Even before he paid for it, Sam had the sandwich unwrapped. After the first bite, he had to agree. These biscuits might actually be the best in the Western Hemisphere.

"Lard's the secret." Tommy stuffed his hands in the back pockets of his denims. "Can't make a decent biscuit without it."

Sam nearly choked and could have sworn he heard his arteries screaming. He took another bite and smiled. New York City had some fine restaurants, but standing here at the counter, literally chewing the fat with Tommy? Not too shabby. He could actually get used to this. Maybe.

And maybe he could chalk it up to the strange mood that had driven him out of the house so early.

Didn't he have his favorite hangouts in the city? The coffee shop on the corner, Luigi's little deli that carried meatballs second only to his mother's. The newspaper stand where he got his daily news fix—and a PayDay candy bar. Hell, the street corner vendor where he got his dirty water hot dogs.

Funny, he hadn't even thought about any of them till that moment. He didn't miss them, didn't miss reading the *New York Times* or watching the nightly news. He had his music, his dog, and his truck. He'd just made a new friend in Tommy and discovered he liked ham biscuits.

"Been out to Magnolia House?"

"No, but I've heard about it," Sam answered.

"All kinds of brides descending on the town. Misty Bottomers can't quite make up their minds how they feel about it all."

"Oh?"

"You know, some are happy, some not. Town's busier than it's been in a long time."

"I'd think that would be a good thing."

"It is. Don't get me wrong. There's a lot goin' on. Which is also the problem. A lot goin' on means lots of strangers here in our little town, and that worries some folks."

Strangers. Like the man who kept popping up. He refused to let that ruin his morning, though, so he simply said, "Change can be scary."

"Yep."

Popping the last bite in his mouth, he paid Tommy, walked outside, and saddled up. He drove around town, listening to a talk show through his helmet speakers, and trying to reacquaint himself with Misty Bottoms. A few new places, but for the most part it was pretty much the way he remembered it.

The town looked a little down at the heels, and he sure didn't remember so many empty storefronts. Then again, maybe that was adult eyes versus a young boy's perspective. He doubted an empty store or two would have registered on his ten-year-old radar.

Scattered among the storefronts, though, he noticed a few fairly new-looking businesses. Hopefully, Magnolia House and its brides would give the town's economy the boost it needed, despite the naysayers.

It was still early, and most of the businesses hadn't opened for the day. Curiosity had him turning onto Old Church Street. Would Cricket be at work yet, or was she still sleeping?

He drew closer and saw her.

She knelt in front of the old railroad car, digging in the dirt. Bright new flowers sat in rows, like tin soldiers, on the sidewalk. One by one, she scooped them up and planted them, forming clusters of color.

At the Texaco station, when he'd mentally listed the good things he had here in Misty Bottoms, he hadn't added this neighbor of his. But he should have—even if she did churn him up. Without her, the place would have been—lifeless.

In return? More often than not, he'd acted like a jerk.

Well, today he wouldn't.

She turned at the throaty growl of the Harley, and he pulled his bike to the curb. "Morning, Cricket."

A huge grin spread across her face. "Hey, neighbor! Isn't it beautiful?" She waved her arms, the gesture encompassing the shop.

"It is." He nodded at the plants. "I see your flowers came in."

"They came late yesterday afternoon. Thought I'd get them in the ground this mornin'. When I have my grand opening next Friday, I want my baby to shine."

"It will." He swung a leg over the bike and dismounted. "It used to be green and yellow, didn't it?"

She nodded. "Beck and Cole helped me paint it."

"The color's a big improvement. Gives it a punch of energy. And the white trim really sets it off."

"Thanks. I worried the periwinkle blue might be too much, but I like it. I'd hoped to get my new sign hung by today, but I'm still waitin' for it."

"That would make it official, wouldn't it?"

"Yes. I don't want to open with a handwritten sign."

"You've still got plenty of time."

She nodded, and he watched her face fall. Nothing he could do about the sign.

"The building behind yours, too?" he asked.

"It is. The train car is a great attention grabber and

good for display, but it's not big enough by itself. I'm going to use the other building for my nursery and yard tools, hoses, extra inventory, whatever. Eventually, I'd like to expand the shop into it. Right now, though, it's pretty crammed with boxes. The last owner—well, she left town in a hurry, and most of her stock wasn't really my taste, so, for now, it's stored in there."

"I think this calls for a toast."

She sent him a puzzled look, then settled another plant in the red earth. Sam grabbed his thermos, poured half his coffee into another cup from his saddle bag, and handed it to her.

"Ah, coffee." Her smile dazzled him. "Thank you!"

"What's your shop's name?"

"The Enchanted Florist."

He raised his cup, tapped it to hers. "Here's to the Enchanted Florist, to its success."

She smiled even bigger, sipped, and closed her eyes. "This is good. I grabbed a fast coffee this mornin' but have been seriously missin' that second cup. I didn't stop for one, though, because I wanted to get this plantin' done before the temperature spikes."

"Yeah, it's hotter than Hades here by noon, isn't it?"

She nodded. "And humid. You do your outside work as early as possible."

"I've learned that the hard way. I swear I've sweat a river the last couple days."

She packed dirt around a geranium, then rested on her haunches.

Sam swigged the last of his coffee and set the cup on the seat of his bike. "What can I do to help?"

"Seriously?"

"Seriously. Consider it payment for breakfast and a hot shower. For welcoming a stranger into the neighborhood."

"You already bought me dinner."

"You turning down free labor?"

"Okay, but remember, you asked for this."

"So noted."

For the next hour, he hauled boxes and dug holes. And the entire time, he asked himself why he was really there. Why was he helping her? It wasn't payback for a meal or for putting up with a grouchy neighbor.

It sure as heck wasn't because he wanted to get to know her better. He didn't. He didn't want to get involved with her or anyone else in Misty Bottoms.

He was bored, he told himself, and working through the mess that passed as his life at present. That was all.

When he rubbed at his shoulder, Cricket came up behind him. "You're workin' too hard."

"It's good therapy."

"What happened, Sam?"

"Long story, Bug. One that would make your eyes glaze over." He finished mounding the dirt around a small shrub. "These need water."

Without another word, he moved to the hose.

Okay, she thought, *that subject is off-limits*.

While he busied himself watering the new plants, a FedEx truck pulled up. The driver hopped out with a large, flat package tucked under his arm.

"Cricket O'Malley?"

"That's me."

"If you'll sign here."

Sneaking a peek at the address label, she clapped her hands. "My new sign!"

Sam stood. "Ah, the long-awaited package."

"Yes!" She scrawled her name on the form and took the parcel. "Thank you so much."

The FedEx delivery man tipped his hat. "You're welcome. Y'all have a great day now."

"I will."

"If you're done playing in the dirt," Sam said, "why don't you wash up? We'll hang this sign, then grab a late breakfast at the diner." He'd more than worked off the ham biscuit from Tommy's.

"Dressed like this?"

"Why not? You look exactly right for you."

"Meaning I'm a slob. Nobody expects anything more."

He laughed. "Meaning you work with plants, with flowers, with the earth. You're going to have a little bit of it on you once in a while."

She shook her head. "I'm afraid I'm startin' to like you, Sam."

"Uh-oh," he said. "Careful there. You're stepping to the dark side."

They both laughed, but Sam knew it wasn't a joke. He *was* the dark side. Cricket would be far better off not liking him because he really was that rude dude who'd shut the door in her face the first time they'd met. And the thing was he'd do it again, the second she got too close.

In the meantime, though, he'd help her with the sign. He understood its significance. Naming the shop made her dream real.

"Where's your ladder?"

She pointed to the other building. “In there. I’m not sure exactly where, though.”

“I’ll find it.”

He did, buried behind boxes of silk magnolia garlands. Thousands and thousands of feet of the stuff. Cricket and Jenni Beth could drape the entire plantation house in it and still have some left over.

He dragged the ladder outside, then lugged it to the front of the railroad car, careful not to mangle any of her new plants. Beck had already drilled holes and installed hooks, so all the tedious work had been done.

Together, they hung the sign. *The Enchanted Florist.* Blue and lavender flowers wove together with green vines to form the words against a white backdrop.

Cricket centered her camera on the old railroad car with its new paint and new sign, clicked, and sent the photo to her parents via Facebook.

Sam nodded approvingly. “So much better than the ugly I’m used to on my job.”

“It’s beautiful, isn’t it?” Cricket threw her arms around his neck and kissed him.

Without thinking, he deepened the kiss, taking it to a new level. Tongue touched tongue and did a lazy little dance.

When they stepped away from each other, her mouth dropped open. She stared at him, and he quirked a brow.

“I promised myself that wouldn’t happen again,” she said. “I’m sorry. I’m impulsive, and I do stupid stuff like that all the time.”

“Really?” One hand on the back of her neck, Sam drew her in and all but devoured her. Pulling away, he said, "Don't expect an apology for that because I'm not the least bit sorry."

He watched as a fingertip traced her lips where his had been only seconds before. Her gray eyes widened, and her breath hitched.

"Let's go find that breakfast," he said. "I'm hungry."

She nodded. "Okay."

Since he didn't have a second helmet with him, they decided they'd each drive to Dee-Ann's in their own vehicle. He arrived before she did and waited outside, studying the street. No one seemed out of place.

Cricket pulled up, and they walked in together.

Jimmy Don nodded to them, and a couple older women stared. With a hand at Cricket's back, Sam greeted them all and guided her to a table in the corner. Cricket figured the gossip would start the minute they left the diner. It would be all over town that the new guy in town had breakfast with their new florist. There'd be speculation over whether or not they'd spent the night together.

And if anybody had seen them outside her shop? Seen that kiss? Heck, kisses plural. Mind-blowing kisses. What in heaven had she been thinking? She honestly didn't know, but she sure knew what she was thinking now—that Sam DeLuca just might be the hottest thing on two legs. The man could kiss!

Over steaming cups of coffee, they talked about nothing and everything. Sam told her about his day with Lem.

"I honestly considered giving the truck back and just letting him keep the money."

Cricket laughed.

Sam shook his head. "It just didn't seem right

somehow, though. Obviously, Mr. Gilmore needed some social time. Tell the truth, I probably did, too. Next week, we're picking up Widow Crosby's garbage."

"What have you gotten yourself into?"

His eyes met hers. "I don't know."

She almost forgot to breathe.

Their food came, and he set to the task of drowning his pancakes and eggs in warm maple syrup. She watched as he studied the bowl of grits Dee-Ann set in front of him.

"I haven't had these since Gertie fixed them for me." He grinned. "She put cheese in hers."

"Food of the gods."

"The Southern gods," he said.

"Hey, I need some coffee over here, Dee-Ann," Jimmy Don called.

"Keep your britches on. I'll be right there." She turned back to Sam and pointed at his bowl. "Enjoy."

"I intend to."

Cricket sat, silently watching the interplay between the two. After Dee-Ann ambled over to fill Jimmy Don's cup, she asked, "So, what's up with you, Sam? Why so secretive? You're not runnin' from the law, are you?"

He choked on the coffee he'd just sipped. When he finally caught his breath, he said, "No, I most certainly am not."

"You're sure? I'm not aiding and abetting?"

"I'm absolutely positive." He scooped up some pancake and egg.

"You mentioned New York City. Is that where you're really from?"

"Yes."

"All your life?"

"Yep."

"So you really are a city slicker."

He laughed. "Through and through. It took all the courage I could muster to wade into that tall grass the night I got here."

"Why?"

"Some things a man likes to keep to himself, but you're a persistent devil. If I don't answer, you'll just keep digging, won't you?"

"You got that right."

Taking a sip of his coffee, he looked at her over the rim. "Here's the thing. Snakes live in that grass. They slither around on their bellies and hide out. Me? I like to be able to spot my enemy before he sees me."

Strange way to put it, she thought.

He set down his mug. "Opening that creaky front door, wondering how many mice, coons, and, yes, bugs might be in residence? I consider myself a pretty brave man. I've done some things that take guts, but..."

She shook her head. "Huh-uh. You're a city slicker."

"You keep saying that like it's a bad thing."

She shrugged, a smug expression on her face.

"City slickers can be brave. They can be very heroic."

"But not when it comes to snakes and bugs."

"Not so much."

"So I have to wonder, Sam, why didn't you plan your trip so you arrived in the daylight?"

"That would have been smart, wouldn't it?"

She nodded.

"Actually, I did. But it took longer than I thought to

wrap up all the last-minute stuff—close up my apartment and do some banking. Unwisely, I decided to stop off at my parents' place for a ten-minute visit which turned into two hours and a big meal." He waved a hand. "I think you get the picture."

"A late start," she provided.

"A day late. I ended up sleeping on my folks' sofa and left the next morning. *After* the breakfast Mom insisted on making." He grimaced.

"Still—" Cricket started.

"I ran into detours and delays the whole day." He shrugged. "It became a very long trip. And I've turned a simple answer into a long story, haven't I?

"Arriving after the midnight hour wasn't on my agenda. I considered a motel, but that seemed dumb. Hindsight? I should have. I didn't exactly get a great night's sleep. Then somebody"—he arched his brow—"came pounding on my door at daybreak."

"It was after nine o'clock," she said.

"That's what I said. Daybreak."

Dee-Ann came over and held up the pot. "Yes, please." Sam pushed his cup toward her.

So did Cricket. "Thanks."

"So how about you, Bug?"

"When I was five we moved to Blue Ridge, where my folks own a little shop—Books, Wines, and Coffee Beans. But my people are from Misty Bottoms, and in the South, that's of the utmost importance. I'm hopin' the good people of Misty Bottoms will accept me back and do business with me."

"One look at that face…how could they do otherwise?"

Coffee cup halfway to her lips, she stopped. "Why, Sam DeLuca, is that a compliment?"

"Whatever." Looking uncomfortable, Sam picked up his cup and drained it. "You ready?" He dug in his pocket and tossed money for the bill and tip on the table.

"I guess so."

"You've got lots to do at your shop, and I'd better get home, make sure Hobo didn't destroy the house." He shrugged. "As if it could get any worse."

"Thanks for breakfast," she said. "And for your help this mornin'."

"I didn't do much, and I enjoyed breakfast."

The man was an enigma, and if there was one thing she loved as much as digging in the dirt, it was solving puzzles and sifting through others' secrets. Sam had been right. She *was* a persistent devil!

Sam knew he'd been abrupt to the point of rudeness, but he'd forgotten momentarily his purpose for coming to Misty Bottoms. While he'd enjoyed his neighbor's company, it was time to take a step back.

Those kisses that morning… Whew. The first couple had been good—very, very good. That morning's had been potent. She tasted sweet and vibrant, and it threw him off stride and made him want more. Made him want to run for the hills. At breakfast, their sharing had suddenly felt all too intimate.

Good manners, though, dictated he walk with her to her SUV.

Again, he scanned the streets. Whoever was following him didn't plan to hurt him, or he'd have done it by now. He'd had plenty of chances to take him out. So what *did* he want?

"Who's that?" He tipped his head toward a lanky teenaged boy hard at work in the center island that divided the two sides of Main Street. According to the signs, the Ladies' Garden Club had been responsible for turning the space into a little park. Beautiful trees and flowers mixed with benches and small sculptures.

Several stores—including a gift shop with a little white picket fence and a porch full of colorful rockers, along with the diner and Henderson's Pharmacy—faced the green area.

He liked the setup. It gave the town real character.

"That's Jeremy Stuckey. He's part of the reason I'm now the owner of the Enchanted Florist."

"That kid is?"

"In a way." She leaned against her fender. "He got kind of a raw deal."

"I'm guessing there's a story here."

"You want the abridged version?"

"Please."

"Okay, so when Jenni Beth decided to turn her home into a wedding destination, she needed money to make it happen. She owned a piece of bottomland and, after some arm-twisting, used it for collateral. Her backers wanted the land badly. Badly enough, in fact, to make sure she failed. To help that along, one of them hired Jeremy to destroy Magnolia House's rose garden just before Jenni Beth's first wedding."

"Ouch."

"Ouch is right. Anyway, the kid made a mess and got caught." She glanced toward him. "Now he's paying the price. Rather than sticking him in some juvy place, the judge ordered community service. Taking care of the park seemed fitting. So this is how he gets to spend his Saturdays."

"Today's not Saturday."

She frowned at him. "No, but since it's a teacher planning day, the kids are off. My guess is that he's banking a day to finish his hours ahead of schedule."

He tipped his head toward Jeremy again. "Has the kid been in any other trouble?"

"Not according to Beck and Jenni Beth. His dad left him and his mom, and I think he got caught up in a bad situation."

"It happens."

Sam narrowed his eyes and studied the kid.

Right there in front of him might be the answer to one of his own problems. Maybe he could use the boy to help with his yard work. The job was way more than he could handle on his own, and he was big enough to admit it. No matter how much he did, he didn't appear to be making much headway. Another set of hands would come in handy.

Chances were good that he'd be able to talk the court into counting some of the kid's time against his court-ordered sentence. He'd check into that.

But not right now. He'd socialized all he intended for today. More than he'd intended. And the remark about Cricket's looks? That was the kind of thing that got a man in trouble, that had a woman expecting…more.

Definitely time to go home. He sent Cricket a curt nod, hopped on his bike, and headed down Main Street without looking back.

He'd been doing way too much of that lately. Nothing was gained by looking back. You couldn't change what had already happened. Even more important than repairing the house, he needed to fix himself—if he could only figure out how to do that.

Ironic that Cricket had asked if he'd run away from the cops. He'd denied it, but in a twisted sense, wasn't that exactly what he was doing? He'd been sorry he'd just taken a big swig of coffee because he'd almost spit it across the table at her. She'd have to be blind to have missed that bobble.

He kept crossing that boundary he'd set for himself. Time to draw it tight and stay inside it. Starting now.

Chapter 11

Cricket sat in front of the Enchanted Florist in the pretty little garden she and Sam had planted. Before the kiss. And she needed to put that away. It had been an anomaly, and one that would not be repeated. End of story.

Today was Mother's Day. She missed her own but had already spoken to her on the phone. And speaking of… She'd promised to send more pictures.

Edging over to the curb, she snapped several photos of the shop, her new sign, the sweet filigreed table she'd picked up for a song from Traditions, Cole's company. She'd painted it siren red.

The iced sugar cookies she'd baked in the shape of hearts and teacups looked scrumptious, and the vase of pink and red roses popped against the table's white lace cloth. A pretty crystal pitcher, drops of condensation trailing along its sides, held ice-cold sweet tea.

Today was her gift to the moms of Misty Bottoms.

In the hour she'd been here, she'd already met more of the townspeople than she had in the couple weeks prior. She hoped they wouldn't hold it against her if she didn't remember all their names. Faces, yes, she didn't forget faces. But names? Not always her strong suit.

She heard him before she saw him.

Sam.

A smile teased her lips.

Her grouchy, chip-on-his-shoulder neighbor pulled up to the curb in that weather-beaten truck he'd bought. And beside him? One very happy dog.

His arm resting on the open window, Sam said, "You're losin' money."

"Maybe short-term. But, fingers crossed, next year everybody who stops by today will buy Mom's flowers right here from me."

"Ah, yes, you and that half-full glass of yours. Your optimism is amazing."

She held up her disposable paper cup, stared down into it, and threw him a cheeky smile. "Actually, it's a little more than half-full, thank you very much."

"I've got to say the neighborhood sure smelled good last night."

"My cookies?"

"I swear you left that kitchen window open to tease us. Hobo and I sat on the front porch steps salivating."

"You should have come over. I'd have shared."

"Would you?"

"You bet. It's the rule."

"Ahh, those pesky rules." She held out the plate, and he opened the truck door and got out. "Don't mind if I do. Thanks."

Taking one, he broke off a corner and carried it over to Hobo. "I'm going to let you out, but you have to promise to behave."

Hobo's tail thumped enthusiastically, and the second the door opened, he jumped out and devoured his share of the cookie.

She smiled, glad to see the two of them. She'd worried when Sam left so quickly the other day, but maybe the morning they'd spent together hadn't been a total bust after all. They'd had a good time, a good talk. Right up until the instant he'd turned tail and run.

An interesting man, Sam DeLuca. There was so much she didn't know about him, and so much he wasn't willing to share.

Hobo let out a howl.

Startled, Cricket hurried over to the dog. "You're sure nothing's wrong with him?"

Hobo nudged her a step closer to Sam.

"I've checked him all over. Maybe it's time to take him to a vet."

Hobo whined.

"He probably needs his shots updated anyway."

Hobo fell to the ground, his head buried between his paws.

Cricket arched a brow. "White-coat syndrome?"

"In a dog?"

Hobo's tail wagged, and Sam shook his head. "Oh, for pity's sake."

The dog crawled through the grass to him, then howled mournfully, stood, and nudged him toward Cricket.

"This is going to sound strange"—Sam sent her a wicked grin—"I think he wants you to kiss me again."

"Oh, really?" She couldn't hold back her own slow smile.

"Let's take a walk around back where it's private and test my theory."

"Mr. DeLuca, if I didn't know better, I'd think you were tryin' to take advantage of me."

Managing to keep a straight face, he said, "It's for Hobo."

"Right."

Still, she put her hand in his outstretched one and took that walk.

Another kiss from Sam, she thought, her heart racing. *If he'd come over last night for a cookie*... He pulled her in for a kiss, and her mind short-circuited. Long and lingering, she simply melted into the kiss, into him. His hand slipped beneath the back of her blouse and those oh-so-capable fingers trailed along her skin, traced down her spine.

She sighed, then nearly whimpered when he stepped away, breaking contact.

"Whew." He let out a long breath. "Your kisses set me on fire, Cricket."

She felt the hot blush creep up her chest and across her face.

A finger beneath her chin, he lifted her face so their eyes met. "Thank you."

Then he nodded toward the dog, who'd dropped into the grass beside them, grinning, she swore, like a lunatic.

"I think Hobo approves, don't you, boy?" Sam rubbed the top of the dog's head.

The dog gave a sharp bark of approval.

"Guess that proves my theory."

"Right." Cricket laughed. "And I'd better get back to my station."

Sam took her hand again while they walked to the front of the shop.

"I sent some pictures to my mom so she can kind of be with me today." She thumbed through her phone, showing them to him.

He stopped her. "Can I see that?"

"Sure." With a puzzled frown, she handed him

her phone, then watched as he backed up to one and enlarged it.

"Can I send this to my phone?"

"Of course. Why?"

"For now, let's just say because I like it, okay?"

"But that's not the truth."

"I'll tell you later. Right now, you've got customers." He slapped his thigh to call his dog. "Come on, you old matchmaker. I think you've earned yourself a treat."

A family of four, who'd obviously just been to church, wandered down the sidewalk. Cricket stood, hand out, a beautiful red rose in it. "Hi, I'm Cricket O'Malley. Welcome to the Enchanted Florist."

"Thank you." Mom buried her nose in the bloom, then held it down so her two young children could sniff it. "When are you opening?"

"This coming Friday."

Sam waved as he headed for his truck, and she waved back, more puzzled than ever. Even as she made small talk with the family, her mind stayed on him as he drove away. That wasn't a good thing. Misty Bottoms was her new home. Sam was merely passing through.

She shouldn't get too used to looking out her bedroom window to see if he sat on his front steps because one of these nights the house would be empty, and he'd be gone. That was a fact of life. But in the meantime, couldn't she enjoy him, enjoy his kisses?

Why had he wanted that picture? During a lull, she pulled out her phone and studied it. Nothing exciting, not to anyone else at least. To her, the unofficial opening meant a lot. To Sam? She couldn't see it.

Unless… She enlarged it. A man had stepped into

the corner of the frame. Was that what had caught Sam's attention?

Several hours and nearly five dozen roses later, Cricket swore she should have been smiled out. But she wasn't. She'd had fun meeting so many Misty Bottomers. And she'd been right to follow her gut. When they needed flowers, these people would be back. The Enchanted Florist would be their go-to flower shop.

In the meantime, she had one more stop before she headed home. Packing up the last of the cookies and her last dozen and a half roses, she loaded them into her SUV and headed to the nursing home on the outskirts of town.

Maybe she could spread a little more cheer.

Sam waved at some boys playing ball in an empty lot on the lazy spring day. What he wouldn't give to be that age again.

Another mile down the road, he pulled off and forwarded the picture to Rico. Maybe his partner could ID the guy. If he was really lucky, there'd be a picture on file to match.

He'd almost swallowed his tongue when he'd caught a glimpse of the man as Cricket scrolled through her photos. This was the guy who'd been following him—maybe. Maybe they'd just landed at the same place at the same time. Was it simple coincidence that had him walking down Old Church Street this morning?

Damn! He hated this.

His phone rang. Rico.

"Hey, partner," Sam answered. "Did you get my message?"

"Sure did."

"Think you'll be able to find out anything?"

"I've got a name for you."

"Already?"

"What do you want with this guy?"

"I think he's following me."

Silence followed—an uncomfortable silence.

"Are you still having the nightmares, Sam?"

Sam felt his jaws clench. His therapist and Rico were the only two who know about his dreams. "That has nothing to do with this."

"I think it might because this guy's not going to cause you any trouble, believe me."

"Who is he?"

"Carter Scott."

"Who?"

Rico groaned. "You need to get out more, bro."

"So fill me in. You're sure it's him?"

"Yeah, I am, and I didn't need to run his picture. His face is plastered on half the books in my mom's bookcase. The guy's an author. A huge author. His books have all been made into movies."

"What's he write?"

"True crime."

Son of a— A bad feeling coiled in the pit of Sam's stomach. He and Carter had shown up in town at the same time. Coincidence? He thought not. "Any idea why he'd be in Misty Bottoms, Georgia?"

"Can't answer that."

Neither could Sam, and that bothered him.

He'd done some research on Carter Scott, and Rico was right on all accounts. The guy was an award-winning *USA Today* bestseller. So why was he here? Why had he come to this small town? And why did Sam keep looking up to find Scott watching him? Pure chance? He doubted that. His years on the force had taught him that.

Even though he didn't have all the answers, Sam could breathe easier. Scott definitely wasn't one of Federoff's boys, come to town for a revenge kill.

Carter Scott wouldn't hurt him, at least not physically. An author's weapon of choice was words. While they might occasionally hurt, they weren't lethal. More than anything else, Cricket was safe. He didn't even want to think about how much that mattered or why.

Bottom line—he and Mr. Scott needed to have themselves a little chat.

In the meantime, he'd spent the past three days focused on the inside of the house and had boxed up some things to donate. He'd ask Cricket about a women's shelter that was close. For being here such a short time, she sure had her finger on the town's pulse.

She'd do well. She loved people, loved chatting with them. The woman, despite all she still had to do, never seemed flustered or too busy to make time for someone else, including Jenni Beth's bridezillas.

Him? Everybody, himself included, was better off if he isolated himself. The nightmares still haunted him. He couldn't count the times he'd woke in a cold sweat the last few nights, unable to get back to sleep.

Hard work should have helped, but it didn't seem to be doing the job.

His only venture away from the house had been his Tuesday garbage run with Lem—and that had taken half a day by the time they'd gone to the dump, had breakfast, and made a stop at the post office for Lyda Mae, Lem's wife. Then the old guy had wanted to take a drive down by the river—just to look.

Sam figured Lem was lonely, so he'd gone that way without any argument.

Actually, it had been a nice hour. They'd sat on the riverbank, watched some fishermen, and talked. Lem Gilmore was an interesting guy.

Right now, though, Sam needed some caffeine. He dug in the fridge for the last remaining soda, then checked the updated calendar he'd hung on the still-papered wall.

Thursday.

Tomorrow, Cricket opened her shop. With one finger, he drew aside the curtain over the sink. Her vehicle was gone. No surprise. She was still leaving early and coming home late.

Today would be the last hard push before she opened.

He poured a serving of kibble for Hobo and patted the dog's side when he gave a quick, sharp bark of thanks before diving into the bowl.

"What do you say, dog? Since we're up so early, why don't we head into town and lend a hand?"

Hobo brushed his head against Sam's leg, and he decided to take that for a yes.

What kind of help would she need today? Arranging flowers? Not in his wheelhouse. Tying fancy bows? Fussing with little doodads? Nope.

But if she needed cabinets or shelves moved, curtains hung or nails hammered, he was her man. He'd been doing that kind of thing for years for his mom and sisters. The longer he tossed the idea around in his mind, the better it sounded. An added bonus would be putting their relationship back on the right footing. They were neighbors. Friends.

No more scorching kisses. No more of that hot body pressed against his.

Sexually, Cricket O'Malley was off-limits. She'd helped him, though, when he'd first arrived, and the least he could do was give her a hand now. But first, he needed a shower. Rubbing a hand over his chin, he figured a quick shave might be called for, too.

Twenty minutes later, dressed in well-worn but clean jeans and his favorite black T-shirt, hair still wet, chin whisker free, he opened the back door for an ecstatic Hobo.

"Take a run, boy. I've decided to leave you here. One swipe of that tail, and half of Cricket's inventory could be history."

Hobo dropped a stick at his feet. Sam's first instinct was that he didn't have time to play. Then he figured what the heck. Hadn't he, half an hour ago, been thinking that Cricket made time for these little things while he felt compelled to keep moving, keep busy regardless of what he actually wanted to do?

So he threw a spit-covered stick around the yard for the next ten minutes. It was peaceful; he relaxed. A couple birds called to each other from the crepe myrtles in the yard, and a light fog misted the air. The sun fought its way through in bursts of light.

All in all, not a bad way to start the day. Maybe this, right here, was his path to recovery, shutting things down a bit and making time for the small joys. Remembering to breathe.

"That's it, guy. You're on your own for a few hours. It's going to be hot, so I'll leave you inside, but don't you dare eat the sofa while I'm gone. As ugly as it is, it's all we've got." He ruffled the dog's head. "Be a good boy."

Fifteen minutes later, he pulled up outside Kitty's bakery and parked what he still thought of as Lem's truck. Eight o'clock and she was behind the counter, a smile on her face, her display case loaded with fresh doughnuts, pastries, and breads.

A welcoming note of fresh-brewed coffee laced the air and made him almost glad he hadn't bothered making a pot at Gertie's. What a miserable job. The only pot at her house was one of those old metal ones you perked on the stove. He swore a person could die of caffeine deprivation in the time it took that thing to turn water into coffee. He'd update it today before he headed home. Come this time tomorrow, he'd be the proud owner of a single-cup brewer like the one at his apartment in New York. Maybe. If he could find one in Misty Bottoms.

"Hey, handsome. You're up early this morning." Kitty tossed him a smile, her cherubic cheeks bright pink. "Been back in that kitchen, and it's twenty degrees hotter with the ovens goin'." She fanned herself with her apron.

He studied the array spread before him. "You've been busy."

"I have. In addition to all this, I'm makin' cupcakes for a bridal shower at Jenni Beth's tomorrow. Came in a little early so I could play with a couple designs I have in mind."

"They'll be beautiful." He threw her a hangdog look. "Don't suppose you could spare a couple cups of that coffee?"

"Sure can." She moved to her industrial-sized maker and tossed him a glance over her shoulder. "One of these wouldn't be for Cricket, would it?"

"It would."

"She takes cream in hers."

He grinned. "Good to know. I fed her black the other day. Guess I'll have to apologize for that."

"Don't think she minded. You'll hear no whinin' from her. And she's a darned hard worker. She and Jenni Beth will make a go of Magnolia Brides, you mark my words."

He nodded.

"S'pose you'll be wantin' a bear claw to go with that."

His grin grew. "You'd be right again."

"Cricket prefers pecan rolls."

"Then I'll have one of those, too."

So much to do! In addition to all the finishing touches for her grand opening, Cricket needed to put together eight floral arrangements for Jenni Beth, and she wanted them to be perfect.

She wanted to impress Jenni Beth and, at the same time, knock the socks off the shower attendees. Every single one was a prospective customer. No, make that a *future* customer.

Misty Bottoms' Main Street still slept. Most of the

stores didn't open till nine or ten o'clock. In the short time she'd been there, she'd grown to love the small town.

Driving to work this morning, she couldn't hold back the grin. Even the fog made her happy. Part of it was undoubtedly the blasé response that came with familiarity of the mountains versus the newness of Misty Bottoms, yet something about the Low Country grabbed her and drew her in. She couldn't quite put her finger on that intangible something, but it was strong.

This was where she wanted to be.

This was where she wanted to live and grow her business.

This was where she wanted to settle in, maybe raise a family. When Sam's image popped into her head, she groaned and gave herself a light forehead slap.

So not going to happen.

Sam, by his own admission, was temporary. Misty Bottoms was nothing more than a whistle-stop on his journey. And even if it wasn't, even if he intended to stay there till the twelfth of forever, why would she choose to spend her life with him? Why tie herself to Sam with all his heavy baggage when so many good-natured, happy men roamed the earth?

Her and Sam? Never.

With that, she shoved Sam into a small closet at the back of her mind and locked the door.

Cricket turned onto Old Church Street, and her grin bloomed. The Enchanted Florist was hers, all hers! She gave a little squeal of delight as she pulled to the curb. Then she simply sat in her SUV, Tim McGraw singing on the radio, and the sun peeking through the clouds.

But this wasn't getting things done, was it?

The instant she stepped through the door, the sweet scent of flowers greeted her. Grounded her. Oh, yes.

Time to roll up her sleeves—if she'd been wearing any—stop daydreaming, and hit it hard. In addition to everything else, she had to produce the most magnificent nosegay she'd ever created for the cake topper at Susan Dougherty's shower. That would be the centerpiece, and she intended to bedazzle Misty Bottoms with her creation.

Tomorrow, she'd open her doors and welcome the entire town to the Enchanted Florist. "No pressure," she mumbled. "No pressure at all."

In the meantime, she had one more day to herself in her pretty little store. Her intent had been to create a magic-garden feeling, to keep it light and airy and full of soft fragrance. She'd chosen background music of pan pipes and wind whistles to add to the ambience.

By her measure, she'd pulled it off. The red and gold the former owner had used, the heavy velvet and brocade—all gone. Cricket used filmy gauze, pastel netting, and wispy silk ribbon.

She did a happy dance, blew a stray strand of hair from her cheek, and wished she'd remembered to buy another bag of coffee beans. Later today, the store would have her order for tomorrow ready, so she'd have plenty of coffee then. But that didn't help right now.

Oh well. Dreams sometimes called for sacrifices. She stretched to reach some ribbon she'd placed on the top shelf.

The knock on the window of her door startled her, and she jumped. Turning, she saw Sam, grinning like the Cheshire Cat and holding a Kitty's Kakes and

Bakery bag in one hand, a tray of—could it be?—coffee in the other.

Oh, yeah. She truly might be falling in love, and wouldn't that be the pits? Hurrying down the narrow path between displays, she opened the door, happiness winning out. "You are definitely my hero, Sam. Do you read minds?"

"Majored in it in college." Dimples winked at his cheeks as he held out the tray. "The one closest to you is polluted with cream."

"How'd you—"

"Mind reader. Remember?"

She threw him a sardonic look.

"Okay, Kitty told me. Seems you have a preference for her pecan sticky rolls, too."

"They make my eyes cross, they're so good."

He jiggled the bag. "Why don't we take five outside, then I'll help in here. Although I have to say, things look pretty darned good exactly the way they are."

The sun wasn't high enough yet for them to bake, the humidity still low enough to be bearable.

She'd moved the red filigree table and chairs beside a fountain, into the shade of the one dwarf magnolia tree left on the property. The rest of her meager space had been used for plant display.

"You've turned this into a magical spot, Bug. I like it."

"Thanks." She accepted the sticky bun he handed her. "Mmm. I have an unhealthy attachment to these."

"Here's my downfall." He held up the bear claw, then bit into it. "You've created your own little fairy tale." He shot her a look. "You the princess? Waiting for someone to come carry you away?"

"No." She shook her head slowly. "I don't want carried away. I'm happy right here. And I'm definitely not sitting on my butt waiting for my prince."

A bit of a bite crawled into her last words.

"I didn't say you were." Sam eyed her carefully.

"You intimated it."

He frowned. "Did not."

"Did too." She picked up a pecan that had escaped the gooey roll and popped it into her mouth. "While we're at it, I should probably make this clear, too. I'm not looking for…" She shrugged, felt the heat rush across her face, but plowed on anyway. "I'm not looking for a friends-with-benefits type thing."

She couldn't quite bring herself to meet his eyes.

"Good."

Her gaze flew to his. "Good?"

He kicked out his legs, crossed his ankles, and took a drink of his coffee. "Yes, good, because neither am I."

"Oh. Okay. That was easy. Not that I really thought you—that is, that I—" She waved a hand back and forth several times.

He caught her hand. "Understood. And relationships—friendly relationships—can be easy. It only gets complicated if you let it."

He grabbed the bakery bag and wadded it up into a tight ball. "You done?"

"Yes. Except with this." She held up her cup. "I'll take it in with me."

Within five minutes, Sam was sorting her office supplies and arranging them in her desk. No doubt she'd redo it all at some point, but it would work till she could get to it.

While he did that, she sketched out her design for the shower centerpieces. For Susan, she'd wanted something different. She'd ordered hot-pink gift bags that looked exactly like cute purses. Using pale pink and white sweetheart roses, she'd add a couple calla lilies to each arrangement. Since Susan was marrying Sean Murphy, the finishing touch would be a few green sprigs of Bells of Ireland.

With a name like Cricket O'Malley, she'd always assumed she'd have some of those in her own bridal bouquet—if she ever found a groom to walk down the aisle with her. Not that she was looking.

No time for that now. That would come later. A lot later.

To keep the bouquets hydrated, she'd arrange the flowers in a clear vase inside the bags, with the blooms fountaining out of them. Then she'd drape strands of pearls over the front of the bags. No good Southern girl got married without her mama's pearls.

Sam checked his watch when he pulled away from the Enchanted Florist and decided to stop in at the diner before heading home. It should be about time for Sheriff Jimmy Don Belcher to take his coffee break, and they had some things to discuss.

He'd been right. When he swung through the door, he saw the lawman at a corner table. He nodded at Sam, who decided that was enough of an invitation to join him.

Whether or not Carter Scott was in town because of him, Sam wanted to share the info he had with Jimmy Don. He also wanted to know a little more about Jeremy Stuckey. He needed some help, but God knew he didn't need some punk who'd steal him blind the second he got a chance.

The sheriff used a foot to push out the chair across from him. "Take a load off, boy. You been helpin' Cricket all day?"

Sam hid his surprise. Jimmy Don might appear laid-back and small town, but in reality, the man knew all, saw all.

"Yeah, pretty much. Tomorrow's her grand opening. On top of that, she's been putting together some arrangements for a shower at Jenni Beth's place."

"Good for you for pitchin' in. I'd think you'd have enough of your own work to do to keep you busy."

"Funny you should mention that. It's one of the reasons I stopped by. First, though, I need to tell you about something that seems a little off to me."

"Okay. Spill."

Without going into his whole sad story, Sam gave just the facts about New York, the shooting, and Federoff.

"Jeez, boy, you've dealt with a heap full of heavy, haven't you?"

"It's the job."

Jimmy Don nodded.

"Have you heard of Carter Scott?"

The sheriff leaned back against his chair. "The true crime author?"

"Guess everybody but me has read his stuff."

"The guy's good. He gets in there and digs, produces

a tight read." Jimmy Don narrowed his eyes. "You're from New York, Sam. Ever met him?"

"Nope, can't say that I have, but according to my partner, Carter likes to do his own research. Anything here for him?"

"Not that I know of, but I've had a few people insist they've seen him. Lots of whisperin' going on about him. Big deal when a celebrity like that comes to town—if it's him." His eyes stayed focused on Sam's.

"It's him." Sam filled the sheriff in on his own sightings. "I kept thinking I knew him from somewhere. In the middle of the night last night, it came to me. He was outside my parents' when I left to come down here. He looked different, though, and he had a poodle with him."

"You think he's tailin' you?"

"Might be."

"Any particular reason he'd be doin' that? Could it be tied to the Federoff case?"

"I don't know," Sam admitted. "To be honest, when I first spotted him, I suspected he was one of Nikolai's men. Someone hired to take me out."

"And you didn't come to me?" Both affronted and more than a little pissed, Jimmy Don's voice rose.

"I'm a cop, trained to do the job same as you. And I'm coming to you now."

Jimmy Don's expression relaxed, but his eyes didn't. "Could be he's simply on vacation and stayin' in Savannah. Might have come here for a day trip. Or maybe he's holed up writing."

"Maybe."

"But you don't think so?"

Sam shook his head. "I've seen him too many times

for day-tripping. And if he's writing, he'd have his butt in the chair doing exactly that. The man's got an agenda."

"Here's the thing." Jimmy Don tapped a finger on the tabletop. "Misty Bottoms is a small town. My town. When somebody new comes in, I like to know about it, like to know why they're here." He shrugged. "Just the way it is. So when I kept hearing Carter's name, I got curious and did a quick and dirty check of the hotels around. He's not checked in at any of them."

"Maybe he's using an alias."

"Nope. Showed them the cover picture from his last book." Jimmy Don eyed him. "What do you want me to do?"

"Nothing yet. He hasn't caused any trouble or broken any laws. Hell, maybe he is just trying to fly below the radar and catch some private time."

"But you don't believe that."

"No, I don't." Sam took a sip of the coffee Dee-Ann had placed in front of him.

"So for now, we'll keep an eye on things and see how they go."

"All we can do."

"You said Carter was one of the reasons you wanted to talk. What else is on your mind?"

Sam explained that he needed help setting Gertie's place to rights. He'd bit off more than he could chew in the time he had left in Misty Bottoms.

"I saw Jeremy Stuckey working in the median flower beds the other day. Cricket explained what she knew of the situation, and I thought maybe the boy would be interested in helping me."

"But you want to know what you'd be gettin' into."

Dee-Ann placed a generous slice of cherry pie à la mode in front of Sam and refilled both men's coffee. "You ask me, that kid should have had a pass. I know what he did to Jenni Beth's roses was a dirty shame, but it's the guy who hired him who should be out there breakin' his back, not Jeremy."

"Dee-Ann, it's a cheap lesson," Jimmy Don said. "He'll think twice before he does anything like that again."

She set her jaw. "The boy needs his daddy. That's what he needs."

Jimmy Don squared off with the diner's owner. "Understood. But there are consequences for breakin' the law. Have to be."

"Humph. Richard Thorndike is the one who put Jeremy up to it. Richard's in some white-collar jail and that wife of his? Up to her neck in it, too, and where's she? Back in New Jersey livin' the high life. And the boy's left here workin'. More misery for him and his mother." In a huff, she took her coffeepot and turned back to the counter.

Jimmy Don ran a hand over his thinning hair. "That tell you what you need to know?"

"Yeah. Yeah, it does. Don't suppose some of the time he spends working with me, a law enforcement officer, might count against the time he owes the county?"

"Might. I can put in a word with the judge."

"Appreciate that." Sam popped a bite of pie and ice cream in his mouth. "*Mmmm.* This sure is good."

"You know, Sam, you ever decide you want to leave big-city life behind, you let me know. Sure could use you here in Misty Bottoms."

"You offering me a job, Jimmy Don?"

The sheriff rubbed his clean-shaven double chin. "Yep, I believe I am. Tyrell Parker decided he wanted to go back to college, and while that's a real good thing for him, it's left me shorthanded."

"I'll keep it in mind."

The sheriff picked up his hat from the chair beside him. "Gotta go. Time for my rounds. Good talkin' to you."

"Same goes," Sam said.

He finished his pie in silence, refusing another cup of coffee.

Two desserts today. Well, he'd work it off.

When he walked out the door, he wondered what in the hell he'd do in Misty Bottoms on a permanent basis. Inside a week, he'd be itching to escape.

His mind drifted to his across-the-street neighbor.

Maybe he could find plenty to do. Might be fun to poke a little deeper into that complex psyche.

Nope. The department's shrink had warned him about that, about the need for things to return to exactly as they'd been before the "incident"—or for them to be totally different.

Since he'd been warned, he was prepared. He recognized it for what it was.

Reaction. Compensation.

Nothing more.

Chapter 12

Sam swore he hadn't been watching for Cricket, hadn't been waiting for her to come home. Yet there he was, right out front on his old, splintery wooden ladder when she pulled into her drive. She'd added a magnetic sign, identical to the one on her shop, to her red SUV's door panel.

Because the mutant, out-of-control shrub he'd decided to tackle still stood higher than Mount Everest, she didn't see him, which gave him the chance to look his fill.

She slid from behind the wheel, stretched, and had him catching his breath. Then, while he stared, transfixed, she undid the bottom few buttons on her shirt and tied it in a loose knot. Her pants rode low on her hips, and that shiny belly button jewel winked at him again.

Did the world really stop spinning or had he simply stopped breathing?

He should make some noise. Cough. Call attention to himself. Anything to let her know he was here.

He didn't, and the reasons were complicated.

Because of a nearly overwhelming need to deal with Ingrid's betrayal and death on his own terms, in his own time, he'd run away from home. From friends and family.

So here he was, isolated, in Georgia's Low Country. His choice.

And how was that working? Not so well.

Truth? He was tired of being alone in his falling-down house. Although, to be honest, beneath all the layers of "stuff," it really wasn't all that decrepit, just old and neglected.

Neglected by him.

He needed more company tonight than Hobo provided, and, right there, standing in the driveway across the street, was that company.

Would he have preferred a couple of the guys from his station in New York or one of his buds from school? Sure. Any of them would have been glad to share a few beers in front of the TV and cheer on the Yankees while they creamed some other team. They'd ask no questions, give no unsolicited advice.

They weren't here, though, were they?

Cricket O'Malley of the stormy eyes and bejeweled navel was. As simple as that. That was the only reason he'd invite her over, or so he told himself.

"Hey! New neighbor," he called out. "Want to come to my place for dinner?"

"Are you talkin' to me?" she asked.

"See any other new neighbors around?"

"Not really." She narrowed her eyes. "I'm not sure my food poisoning vaccine is up-to-date."

"Ha-ha. It's too nice a day to be such a smart-ass."

"Really?" She feigned surprise. "I didn't know nice days existed in your world."

Meant to be sarcastic, the words arrowed straight to the truth. His world lately had been dark and depressing. Today? Well, it was looking up. He'd enjoyed the morning in her shop, his chats with Kitty, with Dee-Ann and Jimmy Don.

But any change had to come from him. The words of the shrink the department had forced him to see floated into his head. He had to own his moods.

Today had been better. Not because of this neighbor of his, though. Definitely not because she'd pulled into her drive and showed him that belly button sparkle.

Absolutely not. Positive Polly tired him out and made his teeth ache from all her sweetness. Yet this evening he found himself wanting to spend time with her, do something for her. It wouldn't hurt him to treat her to a home-cooked meal.

Well, home-cooked might be stretching it a bit, but…

"Nothing fancy," he warned. "I'll grill some steaks."

She threw a hand over her heart. "You cook?"

"I grill. There's a difference." He shrugged. "I have a little barbecue on my postage-stamp-sized balcony in New York."

"You drink a cold Bud or Coors while you cook?"

"Sometimes, but make it Michelob." The corner of his lips turned up. "Why?"

She tapped her forehead. "Such a macho picture. A man, his grill, and his beer."

He laughed. "I also make a mean antipasto salad. And my spaghetti and meatballs? They'll make you weep."

"That's to be expected, isn't it? I mean DeLuca, right? I've always figured the stuff that pours out of a good Italian is red sauce, not blood."

Remembered pain shot through his shoulder, and he felt his face pale. All that blood in the alley. Both Ingrid's and his. What flowed from him sure as hell had been real enough that night.

With an effort, he shook it off.

Cricket studied him but said nothing.

"Yeah, you're probably right. It's in the genes."

"All kinds of good things in there, aren't there?" she said.

When her eyes moved from his face to his tattered jeans, damned if he didn't blush.

"Tell you what," she said. "How about I add some corn puddin' to the mix? My aunt stopped by the shop this afternoon and dropped a bowl of it off. I'll share."

"Corn pudding?"

"You'll love it."

"I'll keep an open mind. Sweet tea and corn pudding. My list of new foods continues to grow."

"We'll make a true Southerner out of you before you know what hit you, Sam."

"I doubt that. Won't be here long enough."

He wasn't the staying kind. Get in, get out. That was Sam DeLuca. A cop like him, with the hours and the risks, was a fool to give the white-picket-fence life a try. It rarely worked out.

It sure hadn't with Ingrid or, he admitted honestly, with any of the others before her. Settling down and having kids? That would be his sisters, not him.

"You want to change first? I'll start the grill."

"A quick shower and fresh clothes would be great. I feel like I've been in this outfit for forty-eight hours straight."

He laughed. "You don't look it. Think I'll grab a shower, too. Been a busy day."

Cricket O'Malley was a welcome surprise. The woman headed back across the street toward his house before he'd pulled the better of his T-shirts from his closet. If that had been any one of his four sisters or any of the women he'd dated, they'd still have an hour or more before they'd be good to go.

And Cricket was certainly good to go. He whistled long and low. She'd changed into a tiny little sundress that showed off a spectacular pair of legs. The soft cotton swirled around those legs, and the pale blue made her storm-cloud eyes even darker. Bigger. When she got to the front of his house, she picked her way through the yard.

He held his breath. As much as those strappy little sandals added to the sex appeal, he worried about stray nails or pieces of wood or metal hiding in the grass—right beside those snakes. Nothing put a damper on an evening like a trip to the emergency room.

Opening the front upstairs window, he said, "Cricket, be careful. Those sandals of yours don't provide much protection."

"From what?"

He shrugged. "God only knows what's lurking in the grass."

"Snake phobia again, Sam?"

"Nope, not this time. Right now it's a fear of nails, shards of metal and glass, splinters of wood—"

"I'm watchin' where I step." She sighed. "It'll be nice when this is all done." She sat down on the front stairs. "Better? I made it through safely."

"Oh yeah." From where he stood, the woman was all tanned legs and pretty pink toenails.

"I brought us a bottle of wine." She held it up.

"Great, I'll pour you a glass." He bounded down the

stairs and opened the front door, tugging his T-shirt over his head. "Come on in."

She walked halfway into the front room and turned in a circle. "You've been busy."

"Mostly clearing out and boxing up. I need to find a place to donate some of Gertie's things. They're good, but I have no use for them."

"I'll check around for you."

"Appreciate that." He took the wine and followed her into the kitchen. Reaching into a cupboard, he pulled out a wineglass.

"Just one?" she asked. "You're not havin' any?"

"Think I'll stick to iced tea. I've been working out in the heat and feel a little dehydrated."

He didn't miss her scrutiny, but it couldn't be helped. With all the meds and painkillers he'd been on lately, he'd cut back severely on the booze, and he'd already had a beer today.

If she hadn't already seen him with a drink, she'd no doubt have figured him for a recovering alcoholic. That was okay, too. If he'd stayed in New York much longer, he probably would have been. Minus the recovering bit. Despite the meds, he'd given alcohol the old college try for a while.

It hadn't helped, and he'd ended up with some hellish headaches to add to the rest of his pain.

He tapped his iced tea glass to her wine. "To summer nights."

"To late spring nights," she corrected.

"Feels like summer," he growled.

"It does. It heats up fast down here." Then she waved her glass toward a coatrack by the door. "You know, you might want to think on it before you wear that around town."

"What? My hat?" He yanked it off the rack and jammed it on his head. "My team. The New York Yankees."

"Yeah, well, where you come from it's probably okay, but here in the Deep South?" She grimaced. "Not so good."

He took it off and hung it up. "I'm not ashamed of it."

"Nor should you be. But there're still some, shall we say, unresolved feelings around here about Yankees of any kind."

Right then and there, Sam decided that next time he went into town, he'd damn well be wearing that hat.

"I tossed a couple potatoes in the oven before I went up to shower." He reached in the fridge and pulled out a package of steaks. "This should be enough to feed a family of four."

"Yeah." She stared at it. "What in the world did you plan to do with all that?"

"Eat it. Cook once, eat for days. That's my motto." He pulled out the cutting board and neatly trimmed off some of the fat.

As they stepped outside, he noticed the sun sliding low over the trees. Any doubts he'd had about asking Cricket to dinner disappeared. It was a perfect night. Be a real shame not to share it.

He slid a sidelong glance at her. His neighbor was some looker. Thinking about her, remembering the taste of her lips, imagining the body beneath that little dress, could keep a man awake on a hot night—and keep him steaming hot on a cold winter's one.

Her dress was kind of a throwback to an earlier time.

Not old-fashioned but vintage. Adriana, his oldest sister, would love her style and tended toward it herself. But where Adriana leaned toward bright colors and sharp lines, Bug wore soft colors and even softer fabrics. Everything seemed to move around her and with her. No matter what she wore, though, with the exception of those baggy pants he'd first seen her in, a man knew a killer body hid beneath the fabric.

"Hold on a sec." He raised a finger and headed back inside. Grabbing the small radio he'd found tucked inside a closet, he placed it on the ledge above the sink, dialed up a station that played a lot of Frank Sinatra, and opened the window. The music drifted into the twilight.

In another cupboard, he found a stub of a candle in a squat holder. Gertie'd probably kept it in case of a power outage. It would do. He lit it and stepped outside to find her curled up on the back porch swing, Hobo at her feet.

"So you decided to come home," he said to the dog. "You've been gone half the day."

In answer, Hobo thumped his tail on the porch.

"Yeah, I know. You heard steak was on the menu for dinner."

The tail thumped harder, and Cricket laughed, a warm, sultry sound.

Sam set the candle on a small side table, his system on high alert.

Cricket O'Malley. The girl next door meets sex goddess.

He didn't understand it, but that didn't seem to matter. Chemistry fairly sizzled between them.

He cleared his throat, then leaned down beside the

fire pit. After he got a nice little blaze started, he pulled an old bench close. "I know we don't need the heat—" He broke off. No, they sure didn't. If they got within ten miles of each other, they generated enough of their own. "I mean, uh, I thought it might add a little ambience."

"Nothing I enjoy more than sittin' around a campfire."

"Good, good. Why don't you move over here, and I'll start the steaks."

He felt like a tongue-tied schoolboy.

The coals in Gertie's old barbecue had burned down nicely and were glowing embers. After he tossed the steaks on the grill, he inched down beside Cricket.

The woman smelled like heaven. Or sin. He couldn't decide which and slung an arm over the bench back. Hobo jumped up beside him.

Sam slid closer to Cricket to give the dog more room.

Hobo took it and more.

"You're crowding me, boy."

Those big eyes stared up at him, then Hobo threw his head back in an ear-piercing howl.

"Stop that!"

The dog answered with another mournful cry.

"Oh, for Pete's sake." He tried to move the dog off the bench, but he'd become a boneless, dead weight.

Cricket laughed. "I think we both know what he wants."

Sam let out a half laugh. "You up for it?"

"I think I can handle it if you can."

"Oh yeah, I'm up for it." He rolled his eyes. "Wrong way to put that, but—"

He broke off as she laid a hand on the side of his face, leaned into him, and gave him a taste of heaven.

"Not enough," he muttered, pulling her closer,

dipping his lips again and angling them to take more. He trailed kisses along her neck, then moved back to her mouth. His hands moved down her arms, brushed the sides of her breasts.

A log dropped and sent up a loud *pop* and a shower of sparks.

He drew back and laid his forehead against hers, noticed—thank you, God—her ragged breathing matched his own. "Cricket—"

"Shhh." She laid a finger over his lips. "Let's just accept that for what it was."

"What was it?"

"Darned if I know." She laughed. "But Hobo's quiet."

Sam looked at the dog who, job done, had hopped off the bench and rested in the grass. "I'm liking that dog more every day."

"Me too," she whispered. Tipping her head to hear the music better, she asked, "You like the Sinatra era?"

"I do. My mom listened to him all the time. My dad? He loved the Three Tenors. Me? I'm kind of a blend."

"With an edge toward hard rock."

He grinned. "Yeah, when I'm by myself or working, I tend to go there. The Sinatra is for when I'm with a beautiful woman in the moonlight. Not bothering you with my rock music, am I, country girl?"

"Nope."

"You're more Blake Shelton, Carrie Underwood, and whoever else fits those boots."

"I am. So what do you do in the big city, hotshot? Financial advisor on Wall Street? A dot-commer? Hotel manager? Bouncer at an after-midnight club?"

He shook his head and made a bleating, you're-wrong

sound after each guess. Since he'd already shared with Jimmy Don, hard telling how many others the sheriff had already told. Besides, it wasn't a dirty secret, just something he'd have preferred to keep to himself for a bit longer.

"I was—am—a cop. A detective."

Her mouth dropped open. "You weren't kidding?"

"Nope."

"A cop as in dealin' with dead bodies?"

Again, an image of Ingrid flashed through his mind. Her bound hands and feet. The blood splashed across the front of her dress. That paler-than-pale skin.

"Sam? You okay?"

"Yeah." He let out a deep breath. "I'm okay. Yes, sometimes I have to deal with dead bodies. I don't work homicide as a general rule, but I'm with the narcotics department, and sometimes that means people get hurt."

"Any gang stuff?"

"They get involved sometimes."

"Mafia? Mobsters?"

"You're a bloodthirsty little thing, aren't you?"

"Curious."

"Uh-huh. Yes, Ms. Elvira, sometimes the mob." He raised a brow. "And drug lords. You forgot them."

She turned on the bench to see him better. "And snakes scare you?" The words were almost whispered.

He chuckled. "Yeah."

"You're a complex man, Sam DeLuca."

"I suppose so."

In the distance, a bird called to its mate. Hobo, who'd fallen asleep beside the fire, whimpered and raised his head. One eye opened. Then, with a sigh, he dropped his head and fell back asleep.

"Guess he didn't figure the noise was anything he needed to investigate." Sam stood, turned the steaks, then went back to the bench. "They'll be done in a few minutes. So will the potatoes. Here are our choices. We can clear a spot and eat in the house, or we can juggle our plates on our laps out here. Neither is ideal, but it's all I've got."

"Let's keep it simple. Let's juggle."

They did. The steak was tender, the potatoes perfectly done. And Cricket's Aunt Judy's corn pudding? Extraordinary. He'd have to get the recipe for his mother.

Hobo dined on little pieces of meat they both sneaked to him, then dragged a bone into the grass to gnaw on in peace.

"I have no dessert."

"It doesn't matter." She poured another glass of wine, then held it up to him.

He shook his head, and she didn't press it.

"What do your folks think about you renovatin' Gertie's place?"

He gave her points for the easy segue. Rattling the ice in his glass, he said, "It's not exactly a renovation. More a shoring up of the place. And my parents?" He pulled a face. "They don't know."

"You didn't tell them you were doing this?"

"No."

"Do they know you're here?"

"No, again. I neglected to tell them much about my trip."

"Sam—"

"Looks like we need some more fuel." He walked to his brush pile, selected a couple more pieces of wood, and tossed them on the fire. Flames shot into the air, their blue, yellow, and red tendrils lighting the yard for a few seconds.

While he did that, Cricket carried their dishes into the kitchen. When he sat down, she came back out and silently slid closer to him. He raised an arm, wrapped it around her, and tucked her into his side.

"See?" he said. "Sinatra's music is just right for holding a beautiful woman close."

She didn't bite. "I take it you don't want to talk about the reason you're in Misty Bottoms or the reason you've kept your family in the dark."

"Not right now, no."

"Okay. Are you here because of your work?" she asked quietly.

He tensed. "I'm here to see if I can salvage Gertie's house."

"I don't think so." Her voice was soft, but something in it let Sam understand she wasn't giving up on it. "The fact that you had this house to come to, to shelter you, is why you're actually here, but I don't think that's why you left New York City."

He didn't say anything.

"It's about work, isn't it? It has somethin' to do with that scar on your back."

Staring into the fire, he remained silent.

"What happened, Sam?"

He opened his mouth, prepared to hand her the pat answer, but the words stuck in his throat. Easy wouldn't work tonight. Not with Cricket.

So he told her the whole story. Once he started, he couldn't stop. He told her about his relationship with Ingrid, her perfidy, and her death, along with his own close brush with it.

As the ugly story spilled, fireflies winked on and off in the yard, a neighbor's dog barked, and Hobo answered. The fire snapped and crackled.

When he finished, they sat in the firelight for a long time, neither speaking. Then Cricket slipped her hand into his and brought it to her lips. She dropped a light kiss onto the back of his fingers.

"I as much as killed her."

"You're wrong," Cricket said. "Ingrid didn't die because of anything you did or didn't do. She died because she, quite literally, crawled into bed with the devil. And he destroyed her."

"Yeah, I guess."

"No guessing about it, Sam. I'm glad you're here," she whispered. "Gertie's house has been waiting for you. You'll be able to heal in Misty Bottoms, inside and out."

He didn't answer her. He couldn't. Tears, hot and painful, burned his eyelids, and he fought them back. He hadn't shed a single one, not through all those days and nights in the hospital. Not when he'd written the report, reliving Ingrid's death and her betrayal. And he wouldn't now, nearly three months later. But it was a battle. This sprite of a woman got to him.

He'd handed his family a whitewashed version of the whole hideous event, had downplayed Ingrid's role. They'd known he and Ingrid had dated but hadn't a clue about the extent of their relationship.

Relationship? What a joke. He'd been set up, their relationship a sham.

"Just so you know, I didn't love Ingrid, and, obviously, she didn't love me. Neither of us ever pretended otherwise. We enjoyed each other—or so I thought. There were no promises, no hints of a happy ever after. I'm not the marrying kind, and I've always been upfront about that."

"Understood."

He shot a sideways glance at her, concerned he'd hurt her, but she looked fine.

Strangely enough, he felt better. Opening up to Cricket had been a lot like lancing an angry wound. Telling her had actually put things into perspective.

With his arm around her, they watched the stars come alive. He counted as one became ten, ten became thirty. The city skyline was beautiful at night. The country sky? Amazing.

From somewhere in the back of his mind came memories of sitting in the window seat, listening to Gertie downstairs tidying up for the night, and marveling at this same sight.

"I need to go to bed."

The blood rushed from Sam's head. "What?" His voice cracked like a prepubescent boy's.

Cricket laughed and patted his knee. "Don't get all worked up. I have a big day tomorrow. I need to go home and get some sleep."

"Oh. Sure." He nodded vigorously. "Sure."

He stood.

"No, stay put. Enjoy the fire. I can see myself home."

"You sure?"

"Absolutely." She leaned down to kiss Hobo's head. "Night, big guy. You take care of Sam here. I think the two of you were meant to find each other."

Then, catching Sam off guard, she leaned in and gave him a gentle kiss. Her lips were so soft, her smell so clean and feminine. Sam bit back the groan and forced himself not to deepen the kiss.

When she straightened, he caught her hand. "Thanks, Bug. You're a good listener."

"I'm good at lots of things." She threw him a saucy grin, her gray eyes dancing in the firelight. "Sleep well. And, Hobo, he's had his kiss, so no howling tonight."

With that she walked into the night and disappeared.

Sam released his breath. "Hobo, that woman could put a serious hurting on a man if he let her."

For a few seconds there when she'd mentioned bed, he'd thought… And wouldn't that have been the worst possible turn of events? That would be an unequivocal yes. It would have been disastrous. Still, a man could dream, couldn't he?

Kicking back on the old bench, he stretched his legs out in front of him and did exactly what she'd told him to do. He relaxed. The purging had been good for him, but he didn't fool himself. It wasn't finished. He'd still beat himself up over what had happened, and a chat with Carter Scott lay on the horizon. But right now, in this moment, he felt peaceful for the first time in way too long.

He wasn't a nature boy by a long shot but found he really liked watching the stars, watching the moon pass through its phases as the days went by, listening to the insects and night birds.

And right now, it felt kind of nice to be awake while the rest of the world slept.

He'd spilled his guts tonight. Maybe now the wound could heal.

Lifting his glass of iced tea, he toasted Hobo. "Here's to you and me, boy, and to more evenings like this."

Hobo sighed deeply, stared up into Sam's eyes, then, with a huge doggie rumble, dropped his head onto Sam's shoes. His tail beat time to some music only he heard.

An ugly toad hopped out of the grass and splatted onto the seat beside Sam. Tea sloshed as he jerked away. Another leap and the damn thing landed on his leg. Big, bad detective that he was, he jumped to his feet and nearly fell over Hobo. *Shit!*

Gingerly, he flicked a finger at the disgusting amphibian that clung to him. After the third time, the thing hopped off, disappearing in the grass. Hobo barked as though he'd single-handedly routed the enemy.

Sam grimaced and looked around, peering into the darkness. He'd been less than heroic in that battle. "Hope to hell there aren't any security cameras around. I'd hate to see that clip show up on YouTube tomorrow."

He threw another glance at the stars, at the fire that had burned itself down to glowing coals. So much for the idyllic romance of a starry country night.

"Come on, Hobo, let's call it a day. Time this city slicker put some distance between himself and the great outdoors."

Chapter 13

Nerves did a skip-to-my-Lou in Cricket's belly. In a few short hours, the Enchanted Florist would no longer be merely wishful thinking but reality. The day she'd dreamed of for so long had finally arrived.

Yet a part of her brain remained on Sam. The man dragged around a lot of baggage. She thought of the first time she'd met him and understood better his gruff dismissal, the barrier he'd erected. Like any wounded animal, he'd run away to lick his wounds, and she'd wandered into his hidey-hole. It made sense he'd tried to drive her away.

But it hadn't worked.

And last night? She'd kissed him. Again. He'd tasted so masculine. So…dangerous. And ever so slightly of moonlight and mystery.

She wanted…more. So much more.

Not smart. Her sense of preservation warned her to draw a large, impenetrable circle around Sam with her on the outside. He had a brooding side, a side he needed to deal with before anyone could get close. And she knew to her very marrow that a fling with Sam would never be enough for her. With him, it would be all or nothing. He wasn't ready for all; she wouldn't settle for less. So nothing it would have to be.

What a shame.

She'd arrived a little early last night and caught him

minutes out of the shower. Him and those damned unbuttoned jeans. When he'd called to her from the upstairs window wearing them and nothing else, Cricket's mouth had gone Death-Valley dry. If the wine in her hand had been uncorked, she'd have stood on his porch and taken a huge swig.

That was last night. Today? She had too much to do to dwell on Sam and his problems. On Sam and her lust for him.

Shake it off, girl.

First, a shower and coffee. Then she could finally break out that new outfit she'd splurged on. Opening the closet, she reached inside and withdrew the loose-fitting jersey dress with its little spaghetti straps and modest V-neck. The charcoal-gray fabric nearly matched the color of her eyes. Simple and fun, it was long enough to be easy to work in, short enough for a little pizzazz. A smile split her face.

With it, she'd wear a silver necklace with a single dangling pearl. One pearl, one dream come true.

Oh, today would be fun.

On the drive into town, Lady Antebellum serenaded her. Before she could settle in at her store, she needed to pick up the arrangements for that day's bridal shower and deliver them to Magnolia House.

It was official. She and Jenni Beth were in business together.

She glanced longingly at Kitty's Bakery as she passed, practically salivating when she thought of the pastries inside. But not today. No time.

Parking at the curb in front of the Enchanted Florist, she took two seconds to just breathe it all in. To take in the day. The moment.

On an exhale, she hopped out and opened the rear hatch on her SUV. Practically running to the shop's door, she unlocked it. The perfume from a host of flowers rained over her.

Hers! All hers!

She rubbed her hands together in glee, then did a little happy dance a foot inside the door. One more deep breath and she hurried to her cooler. Sweetness! The little pink purses bursting with sweetheart roses, calla lilies, Bells of Ireland, and strands of pearls made the hottest bridal shower arrangements she'd ever seen if she did say so herself. And she did.

Very carefully, she placed the flowers in a cut-off box, then carried them to the back of her vehicle, giving thanks she'd thought to wear her flats. Once she had the arrangements set up at Magnolia House, she'd rush back here to the shop and do one final check that everything was in place. Then? She grinned. Then, she'd change into her heels and open the Enchanted Florist's door to the public!

She ran back inside, grabbed the little lace doilies that went beneath each of the bouquets, locked up, and headed for Magnolia House.

Cricket's breath caught as she turned onto the lane to Magnolia House. Sunlight filtered through the avenue of live oaks hanging heavy with Spanish moss and formed a pattern every bit as intricate as the one on the lace doilies she had packed in the backseat.

It would have been a sin to let this house tumble in on itself.

Jenni Beth had decided that in addition to weddings, she'd open it to showers and birthday and anniversary parties. That was a good thing. From what Cricket had gleaned from Beck, Magnolia House hadn't seen much joy lately. She prayed this new venture would help the Beaumont family in its quest for healing.

She rapped on the open front door.

The family's housekeeper shuffled toward her, a huge smile on her face.

"Well, Ms. Cricket, sure is good to see you. We've got a lot goin' on here today, let me tell you. Jenni Beth is mighty happy to have you takin' care of the flowers." She swung the door wide. "You got them with you?"

"I do." Cricket gave the older woman a big hug. "How are you today, Ms. Charlotte, other than busy?"

"Enjoyin' my girls. Ms. Tansy drove in this mornin'. Does my heart good to see those two together."

Cricket's smile faded. Tansy. The woman who'd broken Beck's heart.

Before she could say anything, Jenni Beth stuck her head around the dining room door. "You're here! I can't wait to see what you've done."

Another head popped around the doorway, and Tansy, dressed straight off the runway, stepped into the room. Not over the top but classy. Expensive but simple. It didn't take more than that to understand Beck fell short in the financial column compared to the man she'd married.

Although she and Tansy had only met once, very briefly, Cricket would have recognized her anywhere.

That wildly curling, shoulder-length auburn hair and those huge, turquoise eyes.

"Hey, Cricket."

Cricket wanted to hate her out of family loyalty, but she couldn't. Tansy radiated warmth. But, more than that, deep in those incredible blue-green eyes, Cricket saw sadness. The same bone-deep sorrow she read in Sam DeLuca's in unguarded moments. It seemed Sam and Tansy shared something.

What Cricket wouldn't give for a magic wand, one with the power to remove hurt and pain. The closest she had to that was her flowers. Helping out at the flower shop in Blue Ridge, she'd watched her deliveries bring a smile in the saddest of moments and add to some of the happiest.

Maybe they would today, even if only momentarily.

"Did you come to help?" Cricket asked.

"No, actually, the bride is a classmate of ours." She waved a hand toward Jenni Beth. "So when I received an invitation, I thought why not? I brought Gracie, my daughter, along for some Grandma time."

"Are you spending the night at your mom's?"

Tansy's smile evaporated. "No. I'll drive home tonight after the shower."

"Emerson doesn't like her to stay over," Jenni Beth said.

Cricket swore she heard censure in the simple sentence. There were undercurrents here she didn't understand.

Tansy paled.

"I'm sorry. That was mean." Jenni Beth laid a hand on her arm.

"No! I'm not driving home because of Emerson

tonight," she blurted. "I'm signing divorce papers Monday."

A flush bloomed up her neck and splotched her cheeks.

"What?" Jenni Beth stood rooted to the spot.

Cricket's head swiveled from one to the other.

"I didn't say anything before because, well, call me superstitious, but I didn't want to jinx it."

A tear trickled down Tansy's cheek, and Cricket wondered if she should leave. When she took a backward step, though, Jenni Beth gave her head an almost imperceptible shake.

"Are you safe?"

"Yes." Tansy sniffed. "I'd never put Gracie in harm's way."

"Does Beck know?" Cricket asked.

"No!" She turned, wide-eyed, and looked from Cricket to Jenni Beth. "Don't tell him. Please! Don't tell anybody. You two and my mom are the only ones who know."

"What are you going to do?"

"I'm movin' back to Misty Bottoms." Stress intensified her soft drawl.

Oh boy, Beck would go through the roof, Cricket thought.

At the same time, Jenni Beth squealed, then looked contrite. "I'm sorry, Tanz. A divorce. That's nothing to celebrate."

"This one is." Tansy reached out and took Cricket's hand. "Our second meetin', and I dump this on you. I can only imagine—"

"It's okay. Sometimes, when you're carryin' a load like that, you have to set it down."

"Yes." Tears clouded those big eyes again. "Thank you." She swiped at her tears. "Enough of that. I can't wait to see your incredible arrangements."

Cricket exchanged a sidelong glance with Jenni Beth, then said, "Incredible? I hope so! After you take a peek, we'll see what you think."

"Are the flowers in the car?" Jenni Beth was already headed outside.

"Yes." She followed her out and opened the SUV's rear hatch.

When both women squealed in delight, Cricket let out the breath she'd been holding. She felt as though she were on probation. Self-doubt had always nagged at her, and now was no different.

"You like?"

"Oh my gosh. Tansy hit it on the nose. Incredible!" Jenni Beth threw her arms around Cricket. "Together we are going to make people weep, girl."

Tansy picked up one of the bags, placing a hand beneath it to support the weight. "This is really clever. The flower mix is stunning." She smiled and her whole face changed, became softer. "And the pearls. Oh! Susan will absolutely love these. What are you doin' for her wedding bouquet?"

"We're still discussin' that. The bride is havin' a tough time makin' up her mind."

"I'll bet she jumped on these." Tansy lowered her face to smell the bouquet.

"She hasn't seen them yet. After an hour of tossin' ideas around, she told me to do whatever I wanted, so..."

"She needs to do the same with the rest," Jenni Beth said.

"That would be nice, I think." Cricket rolled her eyes. "On the other hand, it's kind of scary to be the one makin' all the decisions. It can be risky."

"Amen to that. I've been up since five this morning," Jenni Beth said.

"You're almost as bad as Sam," Cricket said. "That Yankee moves too fast, talks too fast, and has the worst time relaxin'. Give him a good front porch for sittin' and a cool drink, and before you can say Robert E. Lee, he's rippin' that porch apart to fix something about it."

Jenni Beth laughed. "He's got a lot to do there."

"He does." Cricket ran the toe of her shoe through the drive's gravel. "What does Cole say about Sam? I mean, they played together as kids."

Jenni Beth tipped her head. "Nothing really."

"Oh, come on, Jenni Beth. He had to have said something."

Her new friend gave Cricket a long, hard stare. "Anything I need to know?"

"No, nothing." She shrugged. "I was just curious."

"Want me to pass Cole a note later today when he stops by? Ask him to give you some juicy tidbits about ten-year-old Sam?"

"Of course not!" She reconsidered. "Actually, yes, I do. Maybe not the note part, but—"

Jenni Beth and Tansy both laughed.

"I'll see what I can coerce out of him," Jenni Beth said. "For now, though, come on inside. I'll show you what we've done for today's shower."

Cricket checked her watch. "Okay, but I'm on a tight schedule. Today's opening day."

"I know. Promise to have you in and out in five."

And she did.

~

Driving back to town, Cricket's thoughts vacillated between Tansy's news and her own upcoming debut. She had to keep Tansy's secret, no question there, but Beck would suffer because of it. And he'd be really angry if—no, make that when—he found out she'd known and hadn't told him. She couldn't, though. Girl code.

And she wouldn't dwell on it. She'd cross that bridge later.

Today's bridal shower would be a smashing success, and that would lead to another and another. Jenni Beth had a real knack for organizing, for putting a special sparkle into an event.

The table, the decor, and the house itself were nothing short of a fairy tale. Any bride would consider herself lucky to start her happy ever after there.

She'd have loved to stay for the event itself, but since she'd not yet figured out how to be in two places at once, she couldn't. Maybe, if things at the shop went well, in a few weeks or a few months, she could afford to hire someone to cover while she attended a few events at Magnolia House. Time would tell on that.

She owed Beck for nudging her into this move. Tansy's secret wiggled into her mind again. Tansy Calhoun Forbes wasn't at all what Cricket had expected. No devil's horns, no artifice, not a single thing she could fault. Instead, she'd seemed like someone Cricket could be best friends with given the opportunity.

Argh! And that made her feel insanely guilty. She owed it to Beck to hate the woman.

She couldn't.

What a bombshell she'd dropped. If Beck started asking questions…

Why would he? She wouldn't mention running into her. Even that, though, seemed wrong. But that was something to worry about tomorrow or the day after. As she drove along Old Church Street, Cricket fairly vibrated with excitement and nerves.

She pulled around back, wanting to leave the front spaces for customers. What if no one showed up? Oh, please! She couldn't even go there. Pulling her dress shoes off the backseat, she ran up the stairs. Once inside, she hit the power button on her CD player. The sound of pan pipes and wind flutes filled the small space and soothed her.

Was Jenni Beth this nervous before her events? If so, she sure didn't show it. She oozed Southern charm and calm. Not a single nerve reared its ugly head.

On the other hand, if she was this anxious and simply hid it, Cricket didn't know how the woman survived. Her own heart had to be wearing itself out it was beating so hard and so fast.

Kicking into high gear, she hurried into the back section of the building and slid the first of the hors d'oeuvres platters from the fridge. Balancing it one-handed, she grabbed the bag of coffee beans. Time to set up. Then she could start praying in earnest for at least one customer to wander in off the street.

The move from Blue Ridge along with a modest down payment on the shop and her house had been expensive.

Add in the new inventory, some minor changes to the store's physical structure, a few gallons of paint, and her living expenses, and she'd pretty well drained her meager savings.

"Please, please, let the good people of Misty Bottoms want flowers," she muttered. "Lots and lots of flowers."

Five minutes later, she had the first pot of coffee brewing. On a small table toward the back of the railroad car, she arranged a platter of finger foods and Kitty's cake, and set out sugar, creamer, and cups. Small paper plates and napkins added the final touches.

Her first inclination had been to place the table just inside the door. Then good sense came to her rescue. If she wanted customers to buy her wares, she needed to lure them farther in than that. Thus the goodies moved to the back, which would require wandering through her shop. She had to start thinking like a business woman and with her head, not her heart.

The floor-to-ceiling cooler overflowed with arrangements and loose flowers. Festive balloons bobbed up and down with the wafts of air-conditioning. A rack of greeting cards, a shelf full of fairies and fairy houses, potted plants—everything fresh and fun.

As ready as she'd ever be, she glanced at her watch. Nine o'clock sharp. It was time.

Fingers crossed, she flipped the CLOSED sign on the door to OPEN and stared out the window. Within five minutes, a car pulled up, then a second one.

She had customers!

A steady stream trickled in and out all day, individuals and people in groups, both buyers and the curious.

Beck, with his mom and dad, was among her first

well-wishers and guilt nipped at her. But, smiling, she thanked them and celebrated with them. Dee-Ann from the diner stopped by and placed a standing weekly order for a small arrangement to place by the cash register. Binnie and Duffy dropped in from the pub and bought a potted *Schefflera arboricola* since it could withstand the occasional neglect.

Darlene Dixon, her hair and makeup perfect as always, had her sister watch Quilty Pleasures, her yarn and fabric store, for half an hour so she could come by to welcome Cricket and check out the shop.

Jenni Beth even managed to find time during the shower to check in with her by phone, and Cole drove up from Savannah to wish her well on her special day. Cricket couldn't help but wonder if Jenni Beth would, indeed, grill him about young Sam. Would Jenni Beth also fight the urge to share Tansy's news with Beck?

Many of her visitors talked about Pia D'Amato, and Cricket prayed they wouldn't be saying the same about her in the next week or month.

The bell above the door jingled again. Her hands grew sweaty, and the bottom dropped out of her stomach. Sawyer Liddell. The reporter, the *only* reporter, from the *Bottoms' Daily.* He'd asked if he could drop by for an interview and a few photos. It was a great opportunity for free advertising as long as she didn't throw up or put her foot in her mouth.

Why did the man have to be so good-looking?

She couldn't help herself. Before she walked to the front to greet him, she checked her makeup in a small mirror with a whitewashed frame that hung on the wall, a price tag dangling from it. After all, she needed to look pulled together in the photos, didn't she?

Oh, and she recognized the lie and called herself out over it.

The plain truth? Sawyer was a hunk. *GQ* cheekbones, a little over six feet tall, and broad-shouldered, he must turn a lot of heads when he walked along Main Street. The women in her store certainly all took a moment to enjoy him.

But he was no dark and dangerous Sam DeLuca. Yummy to look at? Definitely. Yet he didn't make her heart stutter. Damn!

Unbidden came the memory of last night, of sitting in the dark while the fire sparked into the ebony sky. The smell of Sam, all warm and delicious. The heartache that was his.

"Ms. O'Malley? Is this a bad time?"

"No, of course not. There's so much happening that my head's in a hundred places," she said, covering quickly. "Would you like some coffee? Iced tea?"

"No, I'm good. You're busy, so I'll make this as fast as I can."

"It's okay. And, please, call me Cricket."

"Cricket. I like the name. It's full of character."

"Thanks." Because her nerves ate at her, she poured a cup of coffee and held it tightly. It kept her hands busy.

Once Sawyer got started, she calmed down. He knew his job and put her at ease. He asked all the right questions and took pictures of her in front of the shop's new sign, sitting at the little red table in her new garden area, inside the train car beside a display of flower arrangements.

And then he asked her out.

She fumbled.

"It has nothing to do with the story," he assured her with a half laugh. "This place is fantastic, and I'll write you up in a good light even if you turn me down. But I hope you won't. I hope you'll say yes."

He had kind eyes, pale blue with long, dark lashes.

Refusing him would be like kicking a puppy. Besides, she'd sworn she'd settle in here and become part of the community. This was another step toward that.

"Sure," she heard herself say. "I'd love to."

"Great." He closed his notebook and stood. "Today's gonna wear you out. Tomorrow, too. I've got a couple late meetings on Monday and Tuesday, so how about Wednesday evening?"

She nodded.

"Six thirty?"

"Fine."

"I'll pick you up, then we can drive to a new place that just opened on Route 21. I did a piece on them a couple weeks ago. It's casual. Very." His brow waggled. "I did some taste testing for them, and let me tell you, their fried chicken? It'll make you want to cry it's so good."

"Sounds perfect."

She smiled and followed him outside, watched as he pulled away with a friendly wave.

A quick memory of Sam by the fire last night, of his story, and their kiss had second thoughts flooding her. Maybe she should call Sawyer and tell him she'd changed her mind.

Cripes, at this rate she'd need a therapist before the weekend was over.

Sam puzzled her. That he'd shared so much flummoxed her, to be honest. No doubt he wished he could take it all back. But he couldn't. Once words were spoken, they took on a life of their own.

And his certainly had. She'd done a lot of tossing and turning in the wee hours, imagining what he'd gone through that night. What he, no doubt, relived every night.

He'd been shot and had nearly died. Her heart squeezed; her breathing grew ragged. And as he'd lain there in that dark alley, he'd learned that his girlfriend had betrayed him with another man and set him up to die.

Worse?

While he'd watched, helpless, the gun had fired again, and, that time, Ingrid had died.

And he blamed himself.

So he'd gone AWOL. His time in Misty Bottoms was an intermission from his own life. He'd come to a place where no one knew his history or understood how messed up he was.

Yet it was temporary. It only postponed the need to deal with life as a cop on the streets. At some point, he'd have to go back to New York City, to the danger, to carrying a badge and a gun.

Right now, though, he was doing his best to need no one.

By his own admission, he wanted solitude. He wanted no connections. She, on the other hand, wanted community and long-term.

Misty Bottoms was now home to her, but never to him.

And she was woolgathering in the middle of her very special, very busy day. While she stood out there on the sidewalk, she'd left customers inside—customers who might be waiting at the cash register for her to ring them up.

She'd just started to turn back inside when a maroon SUV, followed closely by a very familiar white Buick, pulled to the curb.

With a happy whoop, she ran to them.

Her family! They'd come despite their constant voicing of regrets and countless reasons they couldn't make it. One by one, they clambered from the vehicles. Her brother, sister-in-law, and their two kids. Her mom and dad. Noisily, and with lots of hugs and kisses, they greeted her.

Shame on her for not expecting them. She should have known they'd be here to support her.

"We took a vacation day," her brother said, an arm thrown over his wife's shoulder. "Called the kids in and excused them from school. Mom and Dad left a couple employees in charge of their store."

"And the best part?" her mom said. "We're staying till Sunday."

"Fantastic!"

Where they'd all sleep, she didn't have a clue. More important? It didn't matter. She'd missed them terribly.

After her dad took a couple pictures, she ushered them inside. Her mother let out a little cry when she stepped over the threshold.

"Look what you've done, baby." She cupped Cricket's face. "I'm so proud of you."

"Thanks, Mom."

Arms linked, a parent on either side of her, they strolled through her shop. She took care of a couple customers, then they wandered back outside. She pointed out the new paint job, the garden spot, and the incredible sign she and Sam had hung.

Sam. The only one missing.

Chapter 14

SAM ARGUED WITH HIMSELF. HE SHOULD STAY AWAY. In the light of day, he was having a hard time dealing with all he'd spilled to Cricket. He was embarrassed.

But what if no one came to support her? What if no one drank her fancy coffee or ate the cute finger sandwiches and cake she'd told him she'd ordered? Besides, he'd actually bought a new shirt for her bash, and it would be a shame to waste it.

"Come here, Hobo. If I'm doing this, so are you are." He hooked a bow tie around the dog's neck. Damned if the mutt didn't look proud. "Let's go."

He spotted her the minute he turned the corner. His window down, he heard Cricket say, "My neighbor Sam helped me hang this, Dad."

Her family had come. Good for them, and that meant it was time for him to skedaddle. He'd just drive on by.

Cricket nixed that by stepping in front of the old truck, her hands in the air.

He hit the brakes. "Jeez, you could get killed pulling a stunt like that."

"Nah, your reflexes are too good." She walked to the passenger side and leaned in the window. "Hey, pretty boy, don't you look handsome, huh? Snazzy bow tie and all."

Then she turned her attention back to Sam. "Why weren't you stayin'?"

"Seems you have company enough."

"It's my family."

"I figured that out."

"You're avoidin' me again, aren't you?"

"I came, didn't I?"

"That's up for debate." She met his gaze with an unflinching one of her own. "You weren't going to stay. In order to actually say you were at my grand opening, you have to get out of this heap and come inside. Come on. I want you to meet my *people*." Her saucy grin dared him to back down even as she opened the passenger side to let out Hobo, who made his way to the shade of an oak tree.

Sam took a few seconds to study her. She looked good. That breezy little dress, rather than hiding her body, promised at all sorts of goodies hidden beneath. And the charcoal-gray color? It set off those eyes of hers perfectly. The lady knew how to dress.

The throw-me-down-and-take-me-now heels? He'd hate like hell to have to put in any miles wearing them, but they just about stopped his heart.

Opening his door, he said, "I'm not staying."

"Fine."

But he did. He liked her family; her people were good people.

The phone rang.

"Jenni Beth?" Her eyes shifted to a spot in her cooler, and she went quiet, her expression crestfallen. "I have it here, all ready to go. I am so sorry. In all the excitement—" Her frown deepened. "It wasn't your place to remember it. It was mine." She listened again, then said, "I don't know. Maybe Beck can do it if he's not out on a job." Sighing, she ran her fingers through her hair.

Sam couldn't help but grin. He loved that about her,

that whole lack of self-consciousness, that lack of concern over her looks.

When she hung up, he asked, “Problem?”

“I did the flowers for Jenni Beth’s bridal shower today.” She nodded toward the refrigerated unit. “I took them out this mornin’, but with the opening and everything, my head was in a thousand places. I forgot the nosegay for the top of the cake. Her mom and dad are out of town, and I don’t dare leave. I could send my parents and pray they make it, but… Ugh.”

“If you can pack it up so it’ll get there safely in the back of the truck, I’ll deliver it. Hobo’s likely to eat it if I put it in the cab. Darned dog eats everything.”

“You’d do that?”

“Of course.” He felt somewhat affronted she’d doubt him.

While she readied the nosegay, he wandered outside.

Two elderly women, pocketbooks swinging on their arms, came up the walk talking excitedly.

When he smiled at them, one of them said, “We saw Carter Scott today!”

Sam froze. “Where?”

“Getting gas at Tommy’s,” the second woman said. “What a handsome devil! I’ve read every single one of his books.”

“Me too.” The first woman giggled.

With a wave, they hurried inside, eager to share their news.

Sam dialed Jimmy Don. “Another Carter Scott sighting,” he said without preamble.

“He’s kind of like that damned yeti or sasquatch. People keep seein’ them, too.”

"Yeah, you're right. But Carter Scott is real, and he's got something up his sleeve."

"You see him again, you let me know."

"Will do." Sam hung up, knowing Jimmy Don would worry the news the way Hobo did his big, old bones.

Sam had meant to visit Magnolia House before this, but he'd been so darned busy.

A little uncertain, he clicked on his turn signal and started down what he hoped was the right drive. Then he saw the house and hit the brakes so hard Hobo's feet windmilled for purchase, his claws making a skittering sound on the old vinyl.

"Sorry, boy." Sam reached over and steadied him, then gave a low, heartfelt whistle. "Okay. So I've fallen into a time warp. The Old South lives again." What a Hollywood movie producer wouldn't give for the use of this place as a backdrop!

As he started moving again, Jenni Beth appeared in the doorway of an old brick carriage house. "Hey, Sam."

"Hey, yourself, Jenni Beth."

"Cricket called. She said you're playing the white knight today."

The white knight. He shook his head. If she only knew.

He threw the truck in park and hopped out. Reaching into the bed, he snagged the white cardboard box that held the needed nosegay, whatever the hell that was.

Jenni Beth took it with a wide smile and cracked the lid to look inside. "Oh my gosh, this is so beautiful."

He peeked around her at the pink, green, and purple flowers. "Hmmm. It is, isn't it?"

"I can't tell you how much I appreciate this, Sam."

"It was nothing." He tucked his hands in his jeans pockets. "This is some place you've got here."

She smiled, looking across the span of yard to the newly painted and face-lifted house. "She looks good, doesn't she? A few months ago? She was literally imploding." She checked her watch. "Want a quick tour?"

"Do you have time?"

"I do. Just."

A redhead shot out the door. "Can I come, too?"

"Sure." Jenni Beth nodded her head in the other woman's direction. "Tansy Calhoun." She shook her head. "I did it again. Sorry. Tansy *Forbes*, this is Sam DeLuca."

"Pleasure to meet you." Sam shook her hand.

A mysterious little smile crept across Tansy's lips. "So you're Cricket's neighbor."

Uneasy, he answered, "I am."

"Interestin'. You're obviously not from around here."

"No, I'm not. No drawl."

"And no animosity."

"Excuse me?"

Tansy smiled. "Never mind. You'll hear the story soon enough. I'm sorry about Gertie, Sam. She was an incredible lady."

"Yes, she was." *And so was Tansy*, he thought, *in an entirely different way*. Those eyes. He didn't think he'd ever seen eyes that deep turquoise. It was like looking into the Caribbean. And the wild mass of shoulder-length red curls. Too thin for his liking, but the woman was gorgeous.

She didn't hold a candle to his across-the-street neighbor, though.

Tansy turned to Jenni Beth. "We're all finished here, and you need to get those flowers inside, so let the tour begin."

The place was amazing. When they hit the second floor, she opened the door to the bride's room, and he grinned. Whimsical to the max, the room reminded him of Cricket. He imagined what she'd look like spread across the chaise.

Oh boy.

"Nice," he managed.

"It's pretty feminine, but when it comes right down to it, the wedding's about the bride, right?"

"Absolutely."

Nothing had been overlooked in the renovation, and Sam found himself impressed. Big time. When he thought of the hours and hours of hard labor he'd put into Gertie's house already and what still needed done there, he appreciated this house all the more.

All the wedding paraphernalia, though, made him more than a little claustrophobic.

Charlotte, the Beaumonts' housekeeper, was an absolute delight, and handed him a container of still-warm brownies. The smell alone nearly drove him to distraction. They'd ride back to Misty Bottoms in the truck bed, too, because he sure didn't plan on sharing them with Hobo.

Jenni Beth, Tansy, Charlotte, and he were talking in the foyer when the first carload of women pulled into the drive. "Think it's time I excuse myself and run for higher ground. Bridal showers aren't my thing."

"And you'd know that how?" Tansy asked.

"Four sisters. Adriana, Beatrice, Sally, and Ysabelle."

She laughed. "Enough said. You've earned your stripes. You're dismissed."

"Nice meeting you, Tansy." He tipped his head toward Jenni Beth. "See you later."

"Thanks again, Sam. You're a sweetheart." Jenni Beth kissed his cheek.

A second car slid in behind the first.

Sam skirted the edges of the melee, ignoring the questioning looks sent his way. He gave a quick over-the-shoulder wave, crawled behind the wheel of his truck, and shot down the drive. He'd escaped in the nick of time.

~

Pulling out of the lane, he noticed a car off to the side of the road and wondered if someone needed help.

"Hold on, Hobo." Using the wide berm, he executed a U-turn. Before he reached the car, though, the driver edged onto the road and headed toward town. A cap was tugged low on his head.

Carter Scott. Sam stepped on the gas and drove up practically on his bumper, then laid on the horn and jerked his thumb, indicating for the man to pull over.

Half a mile later, he did.

Unwilling to chance him bolting, Sam pulled the old truck in front of him. Close.

Hopping out, he opened Scott's door. "Out."

"I don't think so. What are you doing here?"

"That's my question," Sam said.

Scott remained silent.

"You've been following me. Took me a bit, but I finally remembered where I first saw you. Outside my parents'. In New York City."

When Carter still said nothing, Sam warned, "Leave them alone, you hear? My family's off-limits."

"That include Cricket O'Malley?"

Sam stiffened.

"You two had yourselves quite a chat last night, didn't you?"

"You were outside my house last night?" His hands fisted at his sides.

He shrugged.

A red haze clouded Sam's vision. "You son of a bitch! If I hear one word, read anything in print—"

"Freedom of the press, my friend. And unless you were feeding your girl a line, that was quite the story."

Sam felt physically sick. He'd finally shared, and they'd had an audience. He'd been in some tight spots on the job, but this was personal.

"I'm going to ask one more time. What are you doing here?"

"Actually, I was planning to leave tonight. You're boring as hell, you know that?"

"Exactly the way I like it," Sam bit out. "Answer my question."

Carter's face turned hard. "I want info on what you're working on. I want to know why you really came to Misty Bottoms. My guess? You've got a new lead."

"For a book you're writing?"

Carter Scott nodded. "The book's about Federoff, not you."

"But it's me you're tailing."

"For info."

"Here's some info." Sam rammed a finger in Carter's chest and found a small amount of pleasure as he drew away. "Stalking and trespassing are both illegal. You're guilty on both counts."

"So sue me."

Sam's temper had passed boil long ago, and this jerk didn't have the good sense to understand that. But since he, himself, didn't care to go to jail today, he pulled out his cell, hit 9–1-1, and watched an uneasy expression fill Scott's eyes.

Jimmy Don answered.

"Don't you have an emergency operator?" Sam bit out.

"She's at lunch. You got an emergency?"

"I do. Remember our talk about Carter Scott? Well, he's stalking me, and he's trespassed on my property. I want him arrested, or I want permission to shoot him. Either option is fine with me."

"Now, wait a minute," Carter blurted.

Sam smiled as a line of perspiration popped up on the guy's forehead.

"That's Carter Scott the writer, correct?" Jimmy Don asked.

"One and the same."

"Hang up," Scott said. "We'll talk."

"Hey, Jimmy Don, I'll get back to you. The jerk wants to talk." Sam ended the call. "So talk, Mr. Scott."

"I wasn't stalking. You're a resource."

"Not what I want to hear." Sam palmed his phone.

Scott swiped at his forehead. "Okay, look, I can't keep your name out of the book." When Sam leaned closer, he hurried on. "It's public record. You're the one who brought Federoff and his boys down. When you left town, it made sense to follow you, see if I could learn something."

Sam made a growling sound.

"But everything here's off the record. I promise."

"Including last night's conversation."

Scott hesitated. Another glance at Sam, and he nodded.

"I want that in writing."

"In writing?"

"That's what I said. It's that or jail." A muscle ticked in Sam's jaw.

"My tax man's not going to be happy about this. All these expenses and nothing to show for it."

Sam mimicked playing a mini-violin. "Get in the truck."

"What?"

"Get in the truck. Kemper Dobson, my aunt's attorney, will draw up a legally binding document."

"My car—"

"Will be safe. We're in Misty Bottoms. Only problem we have here is with crime writers who think they're above the law."

It turned out Mr. Scott wasn't a dog lover. Hobo, picking up on that, made a big production about having to share his seat. He whined and mumbled as Scott slid into the truck, then turned his back on the famous author and passed gas.

"Oh, for—" Scott rolled down the window and hung his head out.

Sam put down his window, too, but he couldn't hide the smile. He leaned toward his dog. "Good boy," he whispered. "Extra kibbles tonight."

Hobo grinned and laid a paw on Sam's leg.

"Will you at least give me a blurb when the book comes out?"

Sam's jaw dropped. Carter Scott was either a hell of a lot braver than Sam had thought or a complete idiot.

Chapter 15

NEARLY OUT THE DOOR WHEN THE PHONE RANG, Cricket considered ignoring it. Her feet hurt, her family waited on the sidewalk, and she wanted to shut down for the day.

Instead, she grabbed the phone. "Hello, Enchanted Florist. How may I help you?"

"How'd the rest of today go?" Jenni Beth's soft drawl greeted her over the line.

"Oh my gosh. You know how you daydream about things, imagine a best-case scenario even though you know it won't happen?"

"I sure do."

"Well, today blew my dream scene out of the water. The place was packed all day long, and people carted plants and flowers and doodads out the door like I was giving them away."

"Fantastic!"

"I've got orders, actual orders. And my family came," she squealed. "My mom and dad, my brother, his wife, and their two kids. They're stayin' for the weekend."

"I heard."

"You did?"

"Cole told me."

"Oh, of course."

For an instant, her heart pinched. Her mom and dad. Her brother Rogan and his wife. Jenni Beth and

Cole. It would be nice to be half of a couple. To have someone to share life with. To be that other half for somebody else.

Her rogue mind flashed to Sam. No, he definitely wasn't a sharer.

He was last night, her good angel whispered.

Her bad angel reared up. *Don't count on it ever happening again.*

"You okay?" Jenni Beth asked.

"Yes. Absolutely." Cricket shrugged off thoughts of Sam and the longing for someone special in her life. She made a feeble attempt at a laugh. "Cole was here when the family arrived, and I turned into a crazy woman."

Jenni Beth chuckled. "That's not quite how he put it, but he did say you were incredibly happy and that you've got a great family."

"I do. I'm so lucky. What did Susan think of the pink purse bouquets?"

"I almost had to tranq her!" Jenni Beth laughed. "And when we announced we were giving them away as game prizes, the competition became cutthroat."

Cricket breathed a huge sigh of relief.

"Speaking of flowers, I have a new client for you." Jenni Beth paused. "One of Susan's newly engaged friends would like you to handle everything. The wedding, rehearsal dinner, the whole shebang."

"Seriously?"

"Yes. I'll fill you in later, though. Go enjoy that family—and get off your feet."

"I will. Again, thanks so much."

When she closed the door behind her this time, her feet no longer hurt.

Hands on his hips, Sam stepped back and eyed the front of the house. Better but not there yet. The steps, no longer rickety, were lined with potted plants Cricket helped him salvage from the yard. Working off the afternoon's leftover anger and adrenaline, he'd anchored a tall, white post in the side yard and attached a birdhouse to the top of it. The house looked like a big old cat, its mouth wide-open. Sam doubted any self-respecting bird would roost in it, but who knew. It added a touch of whimsy to the yard, and he liked it. The piece looked like something Cricket would choose.

Speaking of Cricket, he still hadn't decided how much he'd tell her about what had gone down with Carter Scott. All of it or none of it? Whichever, it could wait. He wouldn't spoil today for her.

He heard the O'Malleys coming before he saw them. The motorcade turned the corner with Cricket's SUV in the lead. As they spilled out of the vehicles, everyone talked at once.

Sam shook his head. It sounded like dinner at his folks'.

Speaking of dinner, from the looks of things, they'd cleaned out Bi-Lo's deli. Good. Cricket had been working damn hard for weeks and been on her feet all day. Even though she'd do it without a single complaint, she shouldn't have to come home and cook for the army that had descended on her.

No business of his, though. He reached for his clippers and, a few minutes later, was busy hacking at one of the wild rosebushes, intent on taming it. It was a beautiful bush, and he didn't want to lose it, but every time he went up or down the stairs, the thing snagged him. And it wasn't particular. Skin or cotton T-shirt, either worked for the evil bush.

Cricket dashed across the street in short denims, a tank top, and flip-flops. "Hey, Sam, want to join us? We're having an impromptu celebration."

He wiped the back of a hand over his forehead. "Nah, you guys do your thing. Me, I'm up to my elbows in sweat and thorns. But, hey, thanks."

"Okay."

Her smile slipped a little, and he felt like a heel.

Tucking her hands in the back pockets of that scrap of denim she wore, Cricket started back toward her house. "If you change your mind, you know where I live," she tossed over her shoulder. "You're more than welcome."

"Gotcha. Thanks again."

He had no intentions of intruding on her family time. Besides, he needed to step back a little. Last night, he'd let himself be vulnerable, and it had nearly cost him the ranch. Fortunately, he'd nailed Carter Scott's ass to the wall. If there was a positive to that whole mess, it was in finding out someone had actually been following him, that he hadn't been paranoid.

Cricket—well, hell, Cricket bothered him. In good ways, which made it bad. His shoulder was on the mend. His head? Some days he thought he might be coming around. Other days? He didn't do so well.

Which was exactly why he'd come to Misty Bottoms. To be alone. To deal with the ramifications of his bad judgment.

Cricket muddied the waters.

He needed to spend tonight alone.

Hobo, however, had different ideas. Drawn by the activity across the street and the sound of children's excited laughter, he decided to pay a visit. A game of soccer was underway, and he wanted to play.

Cricket saw him when she carried a bowl of potato salad outside.

"That's Hobo," she told Mindy and Andy. "He lives next door."

"Did he come from New York City, too?" Mindy asked.

"Nope. He was a half-starved stray who came knockin' at Sam's kitchen door one day."

"So he's Sam's dog now?"

"I hope so," Cricket said half under her breath.

Ten minutes later, her family sat down at her cobbled-together outside dining area. Her dad and Rogan had carried a couple of her small tables outside.

When she looked up, she spotted Sam, a dark expression on his face, cross over to retrieve the dog, who now stretched out between Mindy's and Andy's feet. Seeing Sam, he grinned his doggy grin, tail thumping happily.

Optimistic little thing, Cricket thought. Then she crossed her fingers, hoping he wouldn't start howling. Now wouldn't be a good time for that.

"I'm sorry," Sam said. "Hobo's not very good at staying home."

"Guess his name fits, then, doesn't it?" Mr. O'Malley said.

"It does. Might be time for an electric fence."

"You stayin' that long?" Cricket asked.

"No," he said quickly. "I didn't actually mean it."

"That's what I thought."

"Sit down and have a bite with us. I insist," Mrs. O'Malley said. "You look like you could use a good meal. Not that any of this is homemade." She waved a hand toward the planting bench turned buffet bar. It practically groaned under the weight of the food.

"I—"

"Come on." Cricket's mom threaded her arm through his. "We won't hold you prisoner. The minute you're done eatin', you're free to go."

He laughed. "I can see where Cricket gets her stubbornness."

"Her persistence," Mrs. O'Malley corrected.

The whole family laughed.

"You won't win," Rogan assured him. "Not against her…persistence. You might as well fill a plate." He handed one to Sam.

"I hate to intrude on your family get-together."

"Don't be silly," Cricket's mother said. "It gives us a chance to say thank you. It's so nice you're here to help our daughter and keep an eye on her. This house is lovely, but I worry. For a single woman, it's rather remote."

"I'm not in Misty Bottoms permanently."

"Cricket explained that," Mr. O'Malley said. "That's okay. You're here now."

A prickle of unease chased down Sam's spine. They wanted their daughter to settle down with some nice, safe guy. That wasn't him. This afternoon offered proof of that, didn't it? A stalker! Even under the guise of research, that's exactly what Carter Scott had been.

Sam wasn't a bed jumper. That wasn't his style. When he was with a woman, he was with her, but it was always short-term. He definitely wasn't settle-down ready. And his life, his job? In New York City. He wasn't what they'd want for their daughter.

Sam found himself drawn in, though, and stayed longer than he'd intended. The O'Malleys were warm and generous—with just enough eccentricity tossed in to keep them interesting. The sun dipped below the treetops as he strolled over to his own house, Hobo trotting beside him.

Maybe tonight would be nightmare free.

"I'm not arguing with you about this. You and Dad will sleep in my bed. Period."

"But—"

"Mom." Cricket raised her brows.

"There's that perseverance you were braggin' about," Rogan said.

"Don't you get smart with me, young man."

"You tell him, Grandma," Andy said with a giggle.

"Where will you sleep?"

"On the living room sofa. I've done it before."

"Oh, honey, you have to work tomorrow."

"I'll be fine."

Her brother had packed three air mattresses—a double and two singles—and was busy filling them with air.

"Don't bother with that double. You and Shelley take the extra bedroom. I'll bunk out here with the kids."

"You sure?"

"Totally. I've missed Mindy and Andy. We can tell ghost stories after all you scaredy-cats go to bed."

"Yeah," Andy said. "Aunt Cricket tells the best!"

They moved her teal trunk against a wall and crammed the kids' air mattresses into the tight floor space. Then she tucked a sheet around her sofa cushions.

Rogan still looked skeptical.

"We'll manage just fine, big brother." Cricket gathered extra quilts and blankets from the linen closet and passed them out.

Her dad took her hand. "Come sit on the porch with me a minute before we call it a day. I know you're tired, so I won't keep you long."

"Sure." Her nerves skittered. Was something wrong?

A thousand stars twinkled in the night sky and the scent of jasmine, sweet and light, teased her olfactories as she sank into her chair.

For a while, her dad made small talk about friends from Blue Ridge, activities Mindy and Andy were involved in, day-to-day stuff about him and Cricket's mom. Finally, he got down to the real reason for the stolen minutes.

He took her hand. "Little girl, you need any money, you give me a call. Your mom and I know how hard it is to get a business off the ground."

"I'm good, Dad."

"I know, but the offer's there if you need it."

"Thank you." She leaned across the chair and gave him a kiss.

He patted her cheek. "Guess we'd best get off to bed. Morning'll come real soon."

Inside, teeth were still being brushed, final drinks of water taken, and good nights said. It was late before the house quieted and everyone fell asleep.

Cricket lay awake, enjoying the sound of her family in the little house, thankful for them and their support. What a day it had been.

~

The next day was every bit as busy. After breakfast at Kitty's, her family decided they'd do some sightseeing.

Cricket called Jenni Beth. "If my family stops by, can they get a quick tour of Magnolia House?"

"You bet. I'd love to meet them."

The day passed in a blur with her mom and dad and the kids stopping by with lunch. Later in the afternoon, Rogan and Shelley came in bearing Dairy Queen milkshakes.

Business was brisk, and, in between customers, she placed a new stock order. She'd need more flowers, more everything, and wasn't that a blessing?

That night, Rogan and her dad grilled burgers. Her mom made baked beans, and Shelley and the kids picked up chips and ice cream to round out the meal. Sam declined the invitation to join them, and, unlike last night, he meant it. He never showed, and neither did Hobo. She'd heard the dog barking at one point from inside the house. Apparently, Sam wasn't taking any chances.

Cricket tried not to let it dampen her spirits, but she was appalled by how badly she wanted him there. Later, after everyone had called it a night and she was tucked in on her sofa, she gave herself a harsh lecture about wishing for the impossible.

Sam was who he was.

The next day at noon, Sam stood outside his rickety shed and watched the entire crew, minus Cricket, bundle into their vehicles. After a lot of last-minute hugs and kisses, tons of waves and good-byes and promises to call more often, the family left.

Cricket's smile faded as they caravanned down Frog Pond Road and disappeared from sight. He had an overwhelming urge to chase after them and order them back.

Then her gaze turned in his direction.

Before he could duck out of sight, she crossed to him. Hobo raced to greet her. After she gave him the anticipated rubdown, she dropped onto the grass, pulling her knees close to her chest. The dog plopped beside her, one paw resting on her left foot.

"Why didn't you come over last night, Sam?"

"Too many people. It makes me itchy."

"Bull. What do you do when those four sisters of yours show up?"

"Truth? I get itchy then, too. All those rug rats." He shivered. "You think your family's chaotic? Compared to mine, yours is like being with a group of nuns who've taken a vow of silence."

She laughed out loud.

"Seriously." He tried to keep a straight face, but a smile tickled the corners of his mouth. "And they're nonstop…and touchy."

"They love you."

"I've never once doubted that."

"You don't think they're worried about you? You've missed a Sunday dinner or two."

He shook his head. "They'll figure I'm back on the job and undercover."

"And they'll worry more because of it."

Her words caught him flat-footed. He'd never really given it a lot of thought, but she was probably right. They didn't talk about it, but his job must cause his family grief. Maybe he did owe them a quick call. He'd think about that.

"Your folks aren't puttin' on the pressure for any little DeLucas?"

"Nah. My three oldest sisters are married and populating the world, thank you very much. They're providing the requisite grandkids."

"But they're not DeLucas. They don't carry on the family name."

He shrugged. "Too bad about that. I'm really not the white picket fence, baby bottle, and burping cloth kind of guy. My life is uncluttered. It's good."

"What a bunch of BS."

"Excuse me?" His tone frosty, his brow lifted.

"Are you lyin' to me or to yourself, Sam?"

Anger rushed through him, followed by—what? He couldn't put his finger on the emotions that barreled through him. She'd called him out and nailed him.

And it pissed him off.

"You're pushing me."

"You're hidin'. Runnin' away's not the answer."

"I'm not running anywhere."

"Keep tellin' yourself that."

Chapter 16

Time to visit Gertie. Sam had meant to do it sooner, but somehow the days had gotten away from him.

He'd dreamed about her last night, a nice diversion from his usual nightmares, and a pleasant surprise after his argument with Cricket. He and Gertie had been riding their bikes into town, the day sunny and full of hope and excitement. It felt good to be ten years old again. Damned good.

"Want to go for a ride, mutt?"

The old dog, for all that he had a hitch in his stride, beat Sam to the truck.

"Want the windows open?"

Hobo barked once, and Sam rolled them down as they pulled out of the drive. The dog hung his head out, his long ears flapping in the breeze.

They passed a farmer in his fields and Sam grinned. This visit to Misty Bottoms might be a time out of time for him, but darned if he wasn't starting to enjoy it, especially now that the mysterious stranger had been dealt with. He'd thought he might tell Cricket about him last night, but that hadn't worked out. Maybe he'd just keep it to himself. He didn't want to spook her, didn't want her to know someone had been spying on them, following him around.

He pulled into the nearly empty Bi-Lo parking lot. It was Monday morning, and everybody but him was back at work.

"Stay here. I'll be right back." He leaned across the dog and rolled up the window partway.

Once inside the store, standing in front of the flowers, he had second thoughts. Shouldn't he be buying these from Cricket?

The problem? He didn't care to explain why he needed them. Here in the grocery store, nobody would ask him. He reached for the cellophane-bundled roses but pulled his hand back. He couldn't. Cricket deserved his patronage. After all, who'd pitched in to help clean up years of neglect at Gertie's? Who'd given him breakfast and clean sheets to sleep on?

Who else looked as good in those little shorts and halter tops? Had all that silky smooth skin? A belly button jewel?

Okay, enough.

No Bi-Lo roses for Gertie today. As long as he was in the store, he hustled over to the dog food aisle to grab a rawhide bone.

When he got to the truck, he pulled the bone out of the plastic bag and tossed it toward Hobo. "Here you go. Now leave my boots the hell alone."

The dog caught it with a snap of his jaws and immediately hunkered down on the truck's floor and went to work on it.

"You're welcome," Sam growled.

He drove to Old Church Street. A car sat at a slight angle to the curb in front of Cricket's. Good. She had a customer. He pulled his own rust bucket under the shade of a large oak and hopped out, holding the door for the dog, who settled on the ground, rawhide bone secure between his paws.

"Won't be but a minute, Hobo."

Intent on demolishing his new treasure, the dog ignored him.

Cricket, busy helping a middle-aged woman, glanced up when he walked in. He saw the change in her eyes. Despite their argument last night, he read happiness… and heat. His body responded, and he willed it to behave.

"Hey, neighbor." That quiet Southern drawl drew him in, wrapped around him, and made him want to do things he'd surely regret.

"Hey, right back at ya." He kept his greeting light, then jammed his hands deep into his pockets and strolled around the small space while she made her sale.

Once the woman, phone already at her ear, left the store with a dozen peach-colored roses cradled in one arm, he asked, "You got a nice, simple bouquet?"

"Sure. What's it for?"

"Ah…"

She held up a hand and laughed. "It's okay. You don't have to tell me."

"It's no big secret. It's just…" He felt the bloom spread up his neck. *Shit.* "I thought I'd take some to the cemetery. To Gertie."

Her face changed, became softer. Were those tears in her eyes?

"Hey." He ran a thumb over her cheek, caught one as it spilled over. "You okay?"

"Yes. I never met your aunt, but I wish I had. After dusting all those photos, I feel I know her. She'll enjoy a visit from you. The flowers, too. Considering the plantings in her yard, she must have loved them. You're a good man, Sam."

He pulled his hand away. Touching her caused too many emotions, strong and unwanted, to hurtle through him. Because they did, he said, "No, I'm not. Trust me on that. You don't know the real me, Cricket O'Malley. You wouldn't like him at all."

She made a noncommittal sound and moved to the refrigerated unit where she kept a few premade arrangements. Reaching into the back, she withdrew a happy bouquet of sunflowers mixed with simple white daisies. She'd grouped them in a squat green vase tied with a purple bow.

"I don't know how much you want to spend, but—"

"That's perfect." And it was. The bouquet hit exactly the right note. As far as money went, it really didn't matter. Wasn't he sinking his savings into the old house on Frog Pond Road faster than Dale Junior made it around the track at Daytona?

Why? Not for the first time, he asked himself that question. He could have sold it as is. What difference did it make?

A lot. A lot of happy memories lived in that house, and he was fairly certain it would have fallen to the wrecking ball if sold in the condition he'd found it when he'd first arrived in town. Rather than preserve, far simpler for the new owner to knock it down and rebuild from the ground up, some new, generic house. Sam didn't want that.

"Sam?"

"Yeah?" He reached into his pocket.

"You okay?"

"You bet I am."

"Is Hobo with you?"

"He's out in the side yard playing one-dog destruction team on a piece of rawhide."

She laughed. "That's good."

He paid for the flowers and took them from her, their hands brushing even as their eyes met.

He looked away first and called himself a coward. Undercover, he'd squared off with drug dealers and hit men. When had he started running away from what he wanted?

"Thanks." He held up the flowers. "They really are perfect." At the door, he hesitated. "See you later?"

She nodded.

Despite the sorrow they witnessed day after day, year after year, cemeteries exuded a sense of quiet and peace. A final resting place. They made those who wandered within their confines ponder their own existence, the transiency of life.

The Forrest Lawn Cemetery two miles outside of town was no different. He'd stopped at the diner, and Dee-Ann had given him directions to both the cemetery itself and to Gertie's grave.

After he'd finished his undercover assignment, he'd called to order a stone for her, only to find Gertie had taken care of that and all the other arrangements. He should have known. Until now, there'd been nothing he could do for her. While he lived in her house, he could at least see that she had fresh flowers every week.

Needing the walk, he parked near the front of the

cemetery and rolled down the windows. He left Hobo in the truck. It didn't seem right for the dog to rip around among the stones, to maybe lift his leg on one of them.

Dee-Ann said he'd find Gertie under the shade of an oak tree, so he made his way slowly toward the oaks at the back. The cemetery was old. With the settling of the ground, more than a few stones tilted precariously, and the engraving on some had worn off over the years. Whole sections marked the graves of the very young and very old who'd passed away during short periods of time, probably due to flu or measles epidemics. Thank God for modern medicine.

Crepe myrtles and Southern sugar maples provided shade for the inhabitants and visitors alike. Huge azalea bushes added a riot of color. There was nothing ostentatious here, no giant mausoleums.

A bird sang high up in one of the trees, and a few wispy clouds floated in the blue, blue sky. He hadn't been sure he should come to the cemetery. Now, he wondered why he'd stayed away so long.

He stopped in the center, near a very large stone. The Beaumont family. Jenni Beth's ancestors. The newest grave, well-tended and overflowing with flowers, marked the spot where Jenni Beth's brother Wes had been laid to rest after dying for his country. Sam thought of the portrait that hung at Magnolia House, said a quick prayer, and moved on.

A little farther back, Sam found his aunt. An overwhelming sense of loss caught him off guard, like a sharp kick in the gut. He dropped onto the grass and pulled at some weeds that had grown up by her simple stone. Unshed tears clogged his throat.

Working the vase of sunflowers down into the soft dirt, he cleared his throat. "These are for you, Gertie. Have you been keeping an eye on the house? What I'm doing there? I apologize for letting it go so long, get so bad. You must be ashamed of me. I have no excuses, but I'm trying to make it right. I'm trying to make everything right."

Everything. Too much.

He found himself going under. Emotions ripped through him, and a sob tore loose. Tears he'd held back for months rolled down his face.

Tough, macho cop Sam DeLuca. A stinking, lousy facade. Inside? He was a mess, a damned category 5 hurricane.

What was he doing here in this graveyard? In Misty Bottoms, Georgia?

What was he doing, period?

He'd thought he'd started to get a handle on the resentment and rage. Carter Scott had proved him wrong. He'd simply been snugging a lid on the jumble, while beneath it, the regret and bitterness, the sense of betrayal swirled and churned.

Since that night in the alley, he barely recognized himself. Still on disability, he chafed at not being able to work, yet he couldn't argue the point. He wasn't fit to be back on the streets. Not yet.

Physically, his shoulder still gave him trouble. The yard work might be helping it, might be hurting it. He didn't know and didn't really care.

And there lay the biggest problem. His head. The memories and depression.

He sat in the sun-warmed grass, one hand on his aunt's stone, and poured out his heart.

"God, Gertie, I wish you were here right now. I need someone to talk to. Someone to help me get my head on straight. The department's shrink tried, but…"

More tears formed, and he blinked them back, thumbed away a couple that escaped.

"I can't sleep and I don't know who to trust anymore. I'm slipping up big time. How did I let myself be followed all the way from New York?" He took a ragged breath. "It's hard to put on a front all the time. Big, strong New York City detective. Hell. Oops. Sorry. I didn't mean to swear, Gertie."

He sighed and raked his fingers through his hair. "I can't talk to Mom. She worries enough as it is. Dad? He wouldn't understand. He's always been strong and sure of himself."

He flopped onto his back. "The woman I thought loved me? No, not love. Neither of us loved. But I thought she had my back—until she set me up to be killed. How do I trust again?" he whispered.

White, fluffy clouds drifted overhead. A flock of birds streaked by. Seconds turned to minutes, minutes to half an hour.

If the groundskeeper came, he'd probably call Jimmy Don to investigate a dead body, Sam thought. Why *wasn't* he dead?

A huge cloud that looked like a big, old castle floated leisurely overhead, blocking the sun and casting its shadow over him.

Why had he lived? The question was relentless. The easy answer? Rico found him in time and got help. But in a bigger sense, why had he survived? He shouldn't have. The bullet should have hit his heart and taken him out. Was there a reason he'd been spared. Why?

The question kept him awake at night.

Along with thoughts of Cricket.

"You have a new neighbor. An eccentric florist." He laughed. "You'd like her, I think. She makes incredible pancakes and has a house decorated in neon green, teals, and reds. It's not like anything I've ever seen, but it works. For her. And she has flowers everywhere. This bouquet is one of hers.

"Cricket has blond hair—well, she must have hacked it off with rusty scissors or something. No hairdresser would ever have sent her out the door like that, yet it fits her to a T. And the woman's driving me nuts."

Sam felt his equilibrium shift, return closer to normal. He propped himself up on one elbow. "Thanks, Gertie," he whispered. "I needed this visit. Maybe I'll bring Cricket to meet you when I come next time."

Rising, he kissed his fingertips and laid them on her stone. Then, without another look, he walked away.

Next on his agenda was a second trip to town. If he was lucky, he'd catch Jeremy-the-miscreant working today.

On his way, he stopped by Tommy's.

"Didn't you just fill up?"

"I did. I don't need gas today. I'm looking for a couple bottles of cold water."

"Got that right inside."

Sam grinned. "Figured you would." He grabbed them out of the cooler, paid for them, and tossed them in the back, away from the dog. Maybe he should just toss the dog back there. It might be a heck of a lot easier.

"Want to ride in the back, Hobo?"

The dog threw him a sad-eyed look and lowered himself, whining, spread-eagle on the seat.

"You do that well." Sam ground the truck into first gear and pulled onto the two-lane road. With not another car in sight, it was so unlike the crowded streets of New York. "Hobo, we're not in Kansas anymore."

The dog made a low woofing sound.

Late last night, Sam had decided he needed to come clean with Cricket about Carter Scott. Exactly when and how he'd do that eluded him.

He'd also decided it was past time for another pair of hands—young, healthy hands—and a strong back. The how of that problem, he knew. The district's school calendar had been abbreviated by cutting a few vacation days here and there, and the kids had been sprung. Jeremy should be free.

Sure enough, Sam spotted the boy weeding the town square garden, bright flowers rioting around him. Grabbing the waters from the back, he opened Hobo's door. "Stay right beside me," he warned. "Otherwise you and I will stop at Beck's for a leash. Understood?"

Hobo huffed a bark and head-butted Sam's leg.

"Okay." This whole dog-ownership thing had turned out to be far easier than he'd initially imagined, but he attributed that to Hobo, who seemed to know the ropes. It was actually kind of nice having a companion—one who didn't argue with him and expected nothing more than room and board. The shaggy-haired mutt had become family fast.

Sam would miss him when he headed back up north.

Hands in his pockets, he strolled over to where the teen yanked weeds.

"Thirsty?" Sam stopped beside the boy, the dog sitting quietly beside him. "You were here last weekend."

"Only doin' it 'cause it's court ordered, not 'cause I want to."

Sam handed him a bottle of water.

"Mom says I'm not supposed to take water from strangers."

For a fraction of a second, Sam's eyes widened; then he squinted and saw the mischief in the kid's eyes.

"Just pullin' your leg." Jeremy took the water, cracked the top, and took a long drink. "Thanks."

"Name's Sam DeLuca."

He held out a hand and the boy started to reach for it, then made a face. "I'm filthy."

"That's okay." Sam shook the proffered hand. "Honest dirt."

"Jeremy Stuckey. You're the guy livin' in Gertie's house."

"Yeah. Actually, the house is mine now. She left it to me."

Jeremy shrugged. "That your dog?"

"Maybe. He showed up the other day and won't go away."

"Could be because you're feedin' him."

"Yeah, he's pretty fond of my peanut butter sandwiches."

The look on the teen's face was priceless. "Peanut butter sandwiches?"

"Yep. I make a darned good one if I do say so

myself." Sam knelt beside the boy, plucking some of the weeds.

"What are you doin'?" the kid growled. "I've gotta do this myself. I screwed up."

"Don't we all?" He continued to pull at the weeds that had dared raise their heads in the Ladies' Garden Club's meticulously kept garden.

No doubt Cricket would be a proud member of that group soon, unless she lost points because her family had lived here, then moved away. Maybe this was one of those Southern points of honor. Born and bred Misty Bottomers might be the only members.

"You do good work."

Jeremy shrugged. "I help my mom with her garden—now that my no-good dad ran off with his arm candy. She's young enough to be my sister."

Sam's brows rose, but he said nothing, just made a noncommittal grunt.

"You're new in town, aren't you?"

Sam nodded.

"Piece of advice," Jeremy said. "You don't want to get mixed up with me. I'm bad news."

"Oh, yeah? I've heard that about myself a time or two. What makes you so big and bad?"

The kid swallowed hard, then took a sip from the water bottle. "I destroyed Ms. Jenni Beth's rose garden."

Sam decided to play dumb. "For the hell of it?"

The teen shook his head.

"You mad at her?"

"No. Somebody paid me to."

"An adult?"

"Yep."

"Sounds to me like he used you, kid."

"Maybe I used him," Jeremy muttered.

"Yeah right, and maybe the Earth really is flat." He cracked his own water bottle and took a drink. "Would you do it again?"

"No, sir. And not just 'cause I have to do this." He nodded toward the pile of weeds at his feet. "I hurt Ms. Jenni Beth, and I hurt my mom."

Sam rocked back on his heels and studied the boy. "You want to help out at my place? I could use another pair of hands and a strong back."

"Even after what I just told you?"

"Even after." Sam studied the kid as he wiped his hands on his grubby shorts. "I can't go more than the minimum wage."

"You'd pay me?" Jeremy pushed a strand of hair out of his eyes, swiping red clay across his cheek and forehead.

"Yes, I will, but you'll work hard for that money. You've seen the house. I could really use your help."

"Yeah, you could. That place is bad, man. Ain't nobody done anything there since old Ms. Gertie died."

Sam nodded. "She was my great-aunt."

"She was a nice lady, not one of those grumpy old women, you know?"

"I do."

"You really from New York City?"

"Yep."

"You really a cop?"

"A detective. Narcotics."

"No shit?"

Sam grinned. "No shit."

"What are you doin' here, Yankee?"

Sam decided to go with the truth. "I got shot."

The kid's eyes went the size of saucers. "No kiddin'?"

Sam rolled his shoulder. Felt the pain. "No kidding."

"Wow!"

"Wow?"

"I mean, bet it hurt, huh?"

"Hurt like a mother. Still does. So, you want the job?"

"Hell yeah." His ears reddened. "I mean, heck yeah."

"Okay then." Sam tipped his chin toward the flower bed. "You have to do this again tomorrow?"

Jeremy shook his shaggy head. "Nope. Only one day a week."

"Good. I have something I need to see to in the morning, so why don't you come to my place at one? Be on time."

"I don't need no keeper."

"No? I tend to agree. How about we simply call you an employee? I'm the employer, not your keeper. But I do expect you there on time."

The boy's expression turned suspicious. "Why are you doin' this?"

"Let's just say somebody helped me out once. Consider it payback or paying it forward. Whatever works for you."

Jeremy threw him a sullen look, but instead of seeing a rebellious teen, Sam saw a reflection of himself. They were both wounded souls; he understood the kid's pain.

"Your mom's been paid back, don't you think? Between you and your dad?"

"She didn't do nothin' to get paid back for."

"Then don't you think it's about time to cut her a break? My guess is she worries about you."

"Yes, sir, guess she does."

"You can call me Sam, Jeremy. You need a ride tomorrow?"

The boy shook his head and held out his dirt-smeared hand again. "I'll be on time."

Sam shook his hand and walked away, Hobo at his side. He whistled a silly little tune for the first time in months. And damned if he didn't actually feel hungry, really hungry—for the first time in a long time.

He headed toward Dee-Ann's little red-and-white diner. When he passed Quilty Pleasures, he waved at Darlene. Halfway up the block, he worried it was all beginning to feel too comfortable, too familiar.

It didn't matter. He was hungry, and Dee-Ann would feed him. Simple as that. If he said hello to a few people on the way, no big deal.

The few times Gertie had taken him to the diner had been a real treat. This time around, the diner simply made life easier. Dee-Ann's food was good enough that he hadn't bothered to stock his pantry with more than a few boxes of Pop-Tarts and some mac and cheese.

Maybe he'd pick up some angel hair pasta and the makings for his spaghetti sauce, along with a loaf of fresh, crusty bread. He might even invite his snoopy neighbor over to share, talk her into hanging around till after dark. Till he could make some night moves.

His pulse sped up. Yep. She seemed to be able to do that to him—without being anywhere around.

Was she thinking about him today? He could only hope.

And tonight he'd tell her he'd been followed, and they'd been spied on, their private moment not so private. His stomach lurched. It would be like opening a vein.

When they reached the diner, Sam pointed to a pretty, shaded bench. "Stay, boy. Behave yourself, understand?"

Hobo licked his hand, and Sam took that for a yes. He swung through the diner's door, setting the little bell to tinkling.

Beck Elliot sat at the counter, and Sam slid onto the seat beside him.

"Morning."

"Hey, Sam." He grinned. "I'm supposed to be on a delivery run."

"But?"

"I needed a break before I finish up."

"Since you're the boss," Sam said, "I don't imagine anyone will fire you."

"Yeah, there is that. What are you doin' in town?"

Uncomfortable talking about either the trip to the cemetery or his chat with Jeremy, he shrugged. "I had a couple errands to run." He picked up a menu. "And now I'm hungry."

Dee-Ann sidled up to the two men, coffeepot in hand. She refilled Beck's, held it up to Sam. "Need a cup?"

"I do, but could I have it to go?" He nodded toward the window. "I brought the dog along, and I don't want to leave him out there too long."

"I didn't know you had a dog." Beck frowned. "Thought you drove into Misty Bottoms on your hog."

"I did come on my hog, and I didn't have a dog. Jeez, that sounds like Dr. Seuss." He shook his head. "This one found me the other day. He was half-starved, so…" He held out his hands, palms up, in a what-could-I-do gesture.

Hobo, seeming to realize he was the topic of conversation, stood, and put his face to the window.

Dee-Ann laughed. "He's a character."

"He is that. Either of you know who he might belong to?"

"Never seen him before." Dee-Ann reached for a to-go cup.

"Me, either." Beck took a sip of his coffee.

"Hmmm." Sam studied Hobo for a few seconds. "Well, we're getting along okay for now. I'd like two of your he-man breakfasts, Dee-Ann. Eggs scrambled, sausage patties, biscuits with gravy, and grits."

Her penciled-in brows rose. "Somebody's hungry. Home fries or hash browns?"

"Home fries for me." He glanced out the window. "I don't know which Hobo prefers."

"You're buyin' a breakfast for that dog?"

"Yep." He grinned at her.

"My guess is home fries will work fine for him, too."

"You're probably right."

"You shouldn't be feedin' him people food, you know." Beck used his toast to swipe some yolk from his plate.

"Yeah, I know, but this morning I really don't care."

And he didn't. He felt good, better than he'd felt in a long time, and he wanted to share the feeling. Even if it was with his dog. *The* dog, not *his* dog.

Ten minutes later, he and the dog were back in the truck. From Main he turned onto Old Church Street, on the off chance he'd catch sight of Cricket.

He sighed. Oh yeah. He had it high-school bad.

She was nowhere in sight, so he headed to the banks of the Savannah River, where he and Hobo sat in the grass, staring out at the water and enjoying their breakfast.

Chapter 17

Sam stopped to catch his breath, and his stomach issued a low rumble. Breakfast had been a long time ago, and he'd worked almost nonstop since he and Hobo had returned. A few more minutes and he'd call it a day, see what he could rustle up in the kitchen. He wished now he'd made that stop at the grocer's. Spaghetti would have tasted good.

He glanced toward the road when he heard Cricket wheel into her drive. Where had the day gone?

"Had dinner yet?" she called to him.

"Nope, and I was just thinking that if I didn't get something to eat soon, I'd be too weak to manage it."

She smiled, and his stomach flipped again, but not because of an appetite for food this time.

"Well, you're in luck, DeLuca. I happen to have a ton of leftovers. My mom cooked enough to feed an army—and then the army pulled stakes and deserted. Think you can survive a few more minutes while I change and throw it together?"

"You bet."

"Why don't you wash up, then come over? We'll eat on my front porch where it's shady." She held a hand above her eyes like a visor. "This sun's brutal."

"Sounds like a gift." He watched her walk inside. Today she wore a white lace dress and sparkly sandals. She was a vision, and he wished like heck he could be the one to peel that dress off her. Kiss the shoulders he bared. Travel lower…

He said a quick prayer that he'd survive sitting on the porch on this beautiful spring night with her. His self-control when it came to Cricket O'Malley was fraying something awful.

Picking up the shovel, he carried it to the shed and, Hobo at his heels, went inside to take a quick shower. He scrubbed every inch of his body and shampooed with his own shampoo that smelled of sandalwood rather than wildflowers.

He threw on his clean jeans and a new T-shirt. Should he shave? Nah. Not enough time. Running a comb through his hair, he promised to get into the barber's.

Whistling, he strode across the street. "You can go with me, Hobo, but if Bug doesn't want you there, you have to come back. Understood?"

Hobo wagged his tail and gave a little bark.

"Okay, as long as you understand. And no arguing with the lady." He rapped on the jamb, then opened Cricket's screen door and stuck his head inside. "Anything I can do to help?"

"Grab our drinks. You can carry them outside. Everything that needs to be is warmed up. Why don't I set everything out on the counter, and we can fill our plates?"

"Sounds good to me." It looked good, too, and she was right about the amount. The kitchen counter held a veritable feast.

"Cake, too." She pointed her fork at a foil-wrapped plate. "Of course, it's leftover from my open house, so it's a couple days old. Still…"

"Works for me," Sam said. "I had a piece at your shop Friday. Good stuff."

They carried their food outside where Cricket set a paper plate of shredded chicken on the floor for the dog.

"You're spoiling him," Sam said.

"Maybe. I think you're doin' a pretty good job of that yourself, though. Heard you and Hobo had breakfast this mornin'. At the diner."

"We didn't actually eat there."

"Did you or did you not buy that dog"—she pointed at Hobo—"breakfast at Dee-Ann's today?"

"I did." His face flooded with heat.

She patted his cheek, and the quick jolt from her touch traveled straight to his groin.

"And you and Jimmy Don had breakfast together Saturday."

He scowled. "How do you know all this…and why do you care?"

"I don't care." She slid a bite of sweet potatoes between those full lips.

He blinked and breathed deeply.

"You could have breakfast with Blake Shelton and I wouldn't care. Well, that's not true." She rolled her eyes. "If it was Blake, I'd crash your party, but that's not the point. The thing is you're my neighbor."

"And?" His brow rose.

"And so the Misty Bottom grapevine keeps me informed."

"Of course they do."

She shrugged, and her swingy little pink top slid off one shoulder, baring smooth, creamy skin. "It is what it is, Sam. But don't worry. They'll keep you up-to-date on my comings and goings, too."

"No." He shook his head and scooped up the last of the corn pudding. "They won't."

"Sure they will."

"Nope, I'm a Yankee."

She had no comeback.

"See? Even you can't argue that point."

"There *is* talk about me," Cricket insisted. "A lot of curiosity. I'm the woman who's steppin' into the mobster moll's exquisite Jimmy Choos, but I'm also Beck's cousin. For that reason alone, they're willin' to cut me some slack. And they know my mama and daddy, so I've got one up there. Still, they wonder who is Cricket O'Malley? That's what they're all askin'."

Sam digested that while he took another bite. "Tell me the story of the mobster moll. Is that the same mess young Jeremy got involved in?"

"Yes. Not much to tell, though. Jenni Beth or Cole can fill you in better than me since I wasn't here. The whole thing started because of Jenni Beth's bottomland and some people who wanted it. The moll was planted in Misty Bottoms to keep an eye on things. Now she's not—and the Enchanted Florist is mine."

He narrowed his eyes. "Being in law enforcement, I know there's a heck of a lot more to that story, but it'll do for now."

"Good."

"Before we tear into that cake, come see what I did today." He led her across the road and around the side of his house. He pointed to the old live oak. A tire swing hung from a thick branch.

"Oh, Sam! It's just like in the picture on your aunt's dresser."

"It is." He stuffed his hands into worn jeans pockets. "Tommy at the Texaco station had the old tire out back in a pile. I stopped by Beck's for the rope." He tugged on it. "Gertie and I hung the other one. She had some tires in her shed and thought I might like a swing."

"And you did."

"I did." He spun it around. "Go ahead. Try it out."

"You sit on it first," she said. "I don't want to land facedown in the grass."

"Don't think it'll be your face that hits first. More likely you'll land on that beautiful butt."

She blushed, and he laughed.

"It's safe. I already took it for a test-drive."

Dubiously, she gave in. Once she was safely ensconced on the swing, Sam gave her a push, and when she squealed, he laughed again.

This was exactly what he needed. He glanced toward the sky and gave a thumbs-up. *This swing, Gertie? Still a great idea.*

An excited Hobo jumped in the air, running back and forth with the swing.

"That dog's gonna get dizzy." Cricket dragged her feet to stop.

"Probably."

Sam took hold of the rope and leaned in. He was going to kiss her. Cricket saw it in the glint of his eyes, the set of his jaw. She felt it in the thrum of her pulse.

He did.

That first touch, that first taste, and she was lost to

it. To him. When he wrapped his arms around her, she went willingly.

After another heated kiss, they ended up on the newly mown lawn, Sam's back against the trunk of the live oak, her head in his lap. The early evening sun filtered through the leaves and spread dappled light across his dark-archangel face.

As usual, he kept his sunglasses on. She missed seeing his eyes, reading his emotions, and was certain that was exactly why he constantly wore them. One more barrier to hide behind.

He plucked a fuzzy-headed dandelion and blew on it, scattering the seeds.

"You're gonna regret that," she warned.

"Nah. They give the place a nice, lived-in look."

"Really?"

"You betcha."

Here was a much more relaxed, lighter side to this dark man. A man with demons that chased him through the night.

And if she wasn't careful, he'd find a spot in her heart and hunker down. She couldn't allow that. Right now, she had way too much going on. She had a brand-new business to get up and running in a new town.

More important? Sam DeLuca was temporary. Very. He was city; she was country. Yes, there was chemistry between them, explosive enough to blow up the whole lab. She couldn't deny that.

But chemistry wasn't enough, and she wouldn't get more from Sam. He'd surrounded himself with impossibly high walls. The night in the alley when he'd nearly died because of Ingrid's betrayal had damaged him. As much as Cricket would love to heal this beautiful man, she couldn't. She couldn't risk being hurt herself—and she would be if she gave her heart to him.

"It's been fun, Sam, but I've got to go. My work day's not finished. I've been sellin' out of stock almost as fast as it comes in, and because I'm so busy, I haven't had time to reorder. Thought I'd take care of that tonight."

"Want me to give you a hand with the dinner mess we left?"

"I've got it covered." She stood. "Have a good evenin', Sam. Sleep tight tonight."

"You do know where that saying comes from, don't you?"

She frowned. "I never thought about it, to tell you the truth."

"There're a couple theories. The first is that it goes back to the days when beds were rope strung. You had to make sure the ropes were tight or your straw mattress would sag. And the straw, of course, makes for the rest of the saying about the bed bugs."

"Oooh." She made a face. "What's the second?"

"Sleep tight just means sleep well. Soundly."

"That's boring."

He chuckled. "It is."

"I like the first."

"Me too." A shadow crossed his face. "Before you go, I have something to tell you."

"You're leaving."

"No, not yet." He tugged at her hand, pulled her back to the grass. "Sit. Please."

"What's wrong?"

One big sigh, and he slit open that vein and let the story of Carter Scott spill out.

"He's been here in Misty Bottoms all along?"

"Yes, he followed me from New York, and I was too preoccupied to notice. Some detective I am."

She shook her head. "You didn't expect it."

"I should have been on guard. If it had been one of Federoff's men, I'd be dead."

"But it wasn't." Her brain scrambled to come to terms with this. To fully understand the danger he lived with as a detective.

Her voice dropped to almost a whisper. "He trespassed onto your land and spied on you."

"Yes, and on you."

She gazed across the yard, her eyes searching the tree line.

"There's no one else out there."

"I know that. It makes me jumpy and creeped out, though, to think of him hiding and watching us. He saw me kiss you."

"He did, yes. I'm sorry, Cricket."

"Me too. You should have told me sooner that you suspected something. I wish you'd trusted me."

"I do trust you."

"I wonder." She stood and walked home.

~

She didn't sleep tight. At one a.m., Cricket peeked through the blinds and saw Sam on his front steps, bathed in moonlight. Apparently he wasn't sleeping tight, either.

Instead of crawling back under the covers, she

reached for her robe. Without giving herself time to second-guess, she slipped her feet into a pair of flip-flops and headed out the door and across the street.

He stiffened the instant he spotted her.

"What are you doing? You ought to have more sense than to come over here in the middle of the night."

"Why?"

"Why?" His laugh was mirthless. "Inhibitions are lower at night, honey. Things that shouldn't happen do." His dark eyes glinted in the moonlight. "You're liable to hate yourself in the morning."

"I don't think so." She sat down beside him, their hips touching. He fairly radiated heat. Resting her head on his shoulder, she sat quietly, staring into the star-strewn sky. "We never did eat our cake."

"I know."

He smelled so good. And that hair. Of its own volition, her hand lifted, and she ran her fingers through the dark, thick mass.

He started to jerk away, then stopped. Taking her other hand in his, he kissed the palm. His lips moved up her arm, to her neck, then found her mouth.

A small sound of gratitude escaped her. She loved the taste of this man. Loved the gentle touch of his hands. One kiss led to another and another. Before she quite understood what was happening, she found herself sitting on his lap, his reaction to her closeness, to their kisses, very apparent through the thin fabric of her baby doll pajamas and robe.

He buried his face in her hair. "You tempt me, Cricket. You tempt me to forget why I'm here. That I'm a civilized man."

His hand moved inside her robe, undid the buttons on her pajama top. When he found her bare skin, Cricket thought she might die of pure pleasure.

With a ragged cry, his mouth dropped to one breast, then the other, creating an intense tug in her core.

"Oh, Sam." Her lips moved against his neck.

"I want you, damn it," Sam whispered. Breathing hard, he sat up, pulled her top together, and redid the buttons with clumsy fingers.

"What are you doing?" She stared at him wide-eyed. "Sam?"

"In the morning, you'll thank me." He dropped a kiss on the top of her head, stood her on her feet, then walked inside.

For a few seconds, Cricket actually considered pounding on his door or racing inside and simply having her way with him.

Every cell in her body screamed foul.

Chapter 18

Tuesday. Time for another garbage run with Lem. Sam had seen the movie *Groundhog Day* and knew how this worked, understood the loop that played over and over ad nauseam, the routine and the boredom that came with it.

Yet last night sure as heck hadn't been business as usual. He'd shared dinner with an intelligent, beautiful woman. One full of surprises.

Her biggest surprise to date? That late-night visit. If she'd had any idea how badly he'd wanted to take her, right there on the rickety old porch… God, her kisses. All that sweet, sweet skin, and those soft, breathy sighs. Just thinking about it nearly did him in.

It had to stop.

He'd figured it would the minute he told her about Carter Scott. She'd been upset but had handled it well enough. The sense of violation, though, showed in her eyes, along with the fact that she'd been pissed he hadn't shared it sooner.

Yet, still, she'd come over in the wee hours of the morning—and he'd turned her away.

Life could stink.

He swung his legs over the side of the bed, careful not to step on Hobo. "Come on, mutt. Time to rise and shine."

In the kitchen, he ran his fingers lovingly over his new single-serve coffeemaker and hit the power button.

Within seconds, the welcome scent of coffee, rich and dark, filled the small room, the room that still had blue-teapot paper parading around its walls.

Part of the problem was that he was leapfrogging. Instead of finishing one project, he'd start one, then before he had it finished, move on to something else. Maybe he needed to tackle the house differently. Do all the floors? All the walls? Or he could start in one room, totally finish it, then move on to the next.

A headache brewed behind his eyes.

He picked up his soup cans and started his exercises. While he did his bicep curls, he assessed the house. How the heck would he ever get it all done?

He'd focused first on the outside because that's what the neighbors had to put up with, and he'd made a healthy dent there. But inside? Still god-awful. It made him want to keep the lights off and the shades drawn.

Lem wanted to have breakfast. Why wasn't he surprised?

Jimmy Don sat with them again.

"Do you ever actually patrol?" Sam asked.

The sheriff tipped back his head and chuckled. "Darn tootin' I do. But to be real honest? When I need to catch up on what's goin' down in this town, this is the place to do it." He tapped a finger on the worn, red countertop.

Sam glanced around Dee-Ann's and realized the truth in those words. "I offered Jeremy Stuckey a job."

"That's mighty nice of you," Jimmy Don said. "Be good for the kid. And that'll get you a cup of coffee. Dee-Ann," he called. "Put Sam's coffee on my bill."

A little later, Sam wondered what difference the

price of one cup of coffee made. He stole another peek at the check, then at Lem. The man could eat. He'd ordered what amounted to two full breakfasts and finished every scrap.

Catching his eye, Lem patted his stomach. "Good feelin' to be full."

"Yes, it is." Sam pulled out his wallet.

"Mind if I get a piece of Dee-Ann's coffee cake for the missus?"

"Not at all. Why don't you make that two? One for each of you." *Were they going hungry?* he wondered. "Why don't you add an order of ham to that to-go order, Dee-Ann."

"Sure thing." The diner's owner threw him a speculative look Sam couldn't quite decipher.

When she carried the bag to the register, Lem stood at the counter, arguing with Jimmy Don about the price of parking on Main Street.

Dee-Ann tipped her head toward the old man. "When you get back to Lem's, why don't you take a minute to walk this inside to Lyda Mae? Say hello to her for me. Then have Lem take you out to that old barn of his, show you what he keeps inside."

"Something I should know?"

She studied him. "Maybe. But you won't learn about it from me. Some things are best straight from the horse's mouth." She grinned and walked away.

"You ready?" he called to Lem.

"Yep. Jimmy Don's as stubborn as any mule my daddy ever had on our farm."

"Lem, for the last time, I don't set the parking meter prices. Therefore, I can't change them."

"You're the sheriff, ain't ya?"

"Last time I looked."

"Then you're the law. What you say goes."

"If only." Jimmy Don sighed. "You two have a good day."

"We will." Sam shepherded Lem outside, his mind racing with possibilities. Darn Dee-Ann and her cryptic comments.

As he and Lem strolled down the street to the truck, his mind turned from the old man to the boy. Sam figured he had a pretty good idea about the demons that chased Jeremy Stuckey.

He might actually be on a first-name basis with a few of them himself.

"Mind if I say hello to your wife?"

"Heck no. Lyda Mae'd love the company. She'll put the coffeepot on if you want another cup."

"No, I'm good, thanks."

He turned off the old truck and followed Lem up the walkway, more than a little uneasy. He had no idea what he might be stepping into. For sure no danger. Still, his palms grew damp.

And didn't that tell it all? If he'd needed proof he wasn't ready to hit the streets yet, here it was. Anxiety, always present low grade in a good cop, still rode too close to the surface with him. He wasn't in a hostile environment and had nothing to worry about. Yet his stress-o-meter? Its needle was spiking well into the red zone.

The outside of the old farmhouse could have used a good scraping and a fresh coat of paint.

Lem pushed open the front door and stuck his head inside. "You decent, Lyda Mae?"

"Of course I am."

"We got company. Sam DeLuca. He brought you somethin'." Lem handed the Styrofoam containers to Sam. "Here. You give them to her."

"Let me start the coffee." Her soft voice, heavy with Southern charm, came from another room.

"No need, Mrs. Gilmore. I've had too much already."

And then he stepped inside. Reflex had him stopping to take another look outside. Okay, he'd heard the old "don't judge a book by its cover," but seriously?

He might as well have stepped into the pages of *House Beautiful* or one of the HGTV magazines his mom read. Dark, shining hardwood floors and soft lighting. From what he could see, the kitchen was incredible. Granite and stainless steel mixed with a farmhouse sink and a worn-brick backsplash, both striking and comfortable. And the living room? Plush carpet covered the floor, and amazing pottery pieces decorated built-in bookcases on either side of a huge stone fireplace. A sofa and two chairs made for relaxing and reading around a huge, distressed-looking coffee table. Everything in the house shouted quality—and a big price tag.

"Boy, you might ought to close that mouth of yours before it gathers flies."

"There are no flies in my house, Lem Gilmore." Lyda Mae, trim and youthful looking, appeared very bohemian in sandals and a long paisley skirt and white drawstring blouse. She stood in the wide opening between the kitchen and the living room. "You boys have a good morning?"

Sam simply nodded, afraid speech had deserted him.

Did everybody in town know about this but him? He turned narrowed eyes on Lem.

Expression contrite, he said, "Don't bother with the outside. It keeps my taxes lower."

"You have to be kidding me."

"Nope."

Lyda Mae shook her head, her long, white hair swinging. "I can't tell the old coot a thing. What our neighbors must think, God only knows. Personally, I'd like to fix it up and plant some of those pretty flowers Cricket has at the new shop." Lyda Mae arched a brow. "Don't suppose you made it to her grand opening?"

"Yes, actually, I did. She's my neighbor." Ack, why did he feel he had to add that?

"That's right. She bought Adele Michael's little house. She's done a bang-up job fixin' the mess that Northerner made of Brenda Sue's place."

Sam didn't have the least idea who Brenda Sue was, but he nodded anyway because, whatever it had looked like before, the Enchanted Florist shone like a star. Cricket *had* done a bang-up job.

He handed Lyda Mae the Styrofoam containers. "A couple pieces of Dee-Ann's coffee cake."

"Well, thank you, Sam. You sure you don't want some coffee?"

"Positive. I'll take a rain check, though, if that's okay."

"You bet."

"Lem, why don't you walk out to our truck with me?"

He let out a guffaw. "Hah! Our truck. Kind of is, isn't it?"

"Yes, it is." Sam tipped his head to Lyda Mae. "You have a nice day."

"Thank you, sweetie." She gave him a pat on the cheek and rose on tiptoe to whisper, "Did he make you take him to breakfast again?"

"He did," Sam whispered back, "but I enjoy it."

"You're a nice boy, Sam."

Lem followed him out the door, closing it behind them.

"How about you show me what's in that old barn of yours?"

"You sound like a cop."

"I am a cop."

"Heard that." Lem started across the lawn. "Come on, then. Let's satisfy that curiosity of yours."

He rolled back the door.

The place was amazing. So was the brand-new, totally loaded, white-diamond Cadillac Escalade.

Sam's jaw dropped. "Why haven't I ever seen this in town?"

Lem rubbed a gnarled hand over his cheek. "We drive the old Buick to run errands." He winked. "We take this to Savannah every Saturday night. Date night, if you know what I mean."

"Okay." Sam walked the barn's interior perimeter. The old man had a workshop that would make any grown man envious. He must have bought out an entire Home Depot.

"What do you do here?"

"Oh, I tinker a bit. Mess with this and that." Lem jammed his hands in his back pockets. "You mad at me?"

"Should I be?"

"Probably." Then he turned the conversation to Sam. "Don't rightly understand why a New York City detective would be hidin' out here in Misty Bottoms."

"Don't rightly know why you'd be pretending to be a pauper while you've got something this sweet in your barn. What did you do? Rob a bank?"

"Nah. I invented a food-processin' technique that most all the big companies are usin'. Made a nice little profit off it. We still get checks in the mail every month." He smiled. "It's allowed Lyda Mae and me to retire and fix up the place. Buy some new furniture and the Cadillac. With plenty left over, I might add. Can't see givin' those government boys any more of my money, though. Big brother already takes enough in income taxes. I figure they can do without raisin' my property taxes on top of that."

A grin tipped up the corner of Sam's mouth. "I'm sure they can."

He had to give it to Lem. He'd pulled a fast one on him. He'd handed him a good lesson, too. If there was one thing Sam should have known by now, it was to not take things at face value.

He had, and he'd undoubtedly given the citizens of Misty Bottoms a good laugh—at his expense.

Next Tuesday? He intended to order the most expensive breakfast on the diner's menu…and when Dee-Ann brought the check? Lem would be picking up that tab.

At ten minutes till one, a well-used, badly-in-need-of-paint Chevy Cavalier pulled up in front of Sam's. Wiping his hands on an old dish towel, he opened the screen door and stepped out.

"Hey, Jeremy. Good to see you."

"Yeah, I'm here, and I'm on time."

"Yes, you are."

The kid was way too thin and looked unhappy. Summer vacation should be celebrated, but Sam doubted there was much celebration of any kind in this kid's life.

"Why don't you come on in? I was just sitting down to lunch. Pizza. There's plenty for two. Got to warn you, though, it's straight out of a box from the freezer, but I've tasted worse."

Without a word, Jeremy followed him inside, then stopped. "Dude, this place is like old. Like Aunt Bee's house in *The Andy Griffith Show* on TV Land."

Sam laughed. "Yeah, it is. I want to change that." He pointed at Jeremy. "And you're going to help me."

"Thought I was pullin' weeds."

"Nope. Bigger and better things, my friend."

"I'm not your friend."

Okay. So this might be harder than Sam had initially anticipated. The chip on the kid's shoulder was more the size of a fence post than the stub of a number-two pencil.

"Guess not."

"I don't have friends. I don't want any."

"I'm okay with that. I'm kind of a loner right now, too." The timer went off on the oven, and Sam slid the pizza out, the cheese bubbling and slightly brown. "You like pepperoni?"

"Yeah."

Sam went to the fridge, took out the milk carton, and poured two glasses. When he set one down in front of Jeremy, the teen made a face.

"I don't drink milk."

"You should." He cut the pizza, plated it, and set one down in front of Jeremy, one on his side.

"What kind of glass is this?" Jeremy tapped the shiny blue.

"It's aluminum. My aunt has a whole set of them in the cupboard. Blue, green, gold, and red. Cricket, who lives across the street, said I could sell them on eBay, but then I'd just have to buy new ones." He picked up his own red one. "Guess they used to be all the rage."

"Pretty dumb, if you ask me." He picked it up. "Is it safe to drink from? I mean, am I gonna get lead poisoning or somethin' from it?"

"You get lead poisoning from lead, not aluminum."

"I know that." He scooped up a slice of pie and took a bite, then set it back on his plate. "This stuff is hot," he mumbled.

"Tends to be when it's right out of the oven." A little more carefully, Sam took a bite out of his own, then explained to Jeremy that he thought they'd tackle the wallpaper today.

He ignored the pieces of pizza and pepperoni disappearing under the table and pretended he didn't hear the happy thumping of the tail on the worn-out flooring.

"Thought we'd start upstairs, though, in case we make a mess of it."

"I stripped wallpaper for my grandma last year. I know how to do it."

Sam stared at him. "Really?"

"Yep. I'm pretty good at it." A hint of pride suffused Jeremy's face.

"All right, then. You're the wallpaper king. So glad one of us knows what he's doing."

The teen actually laughed, and Sam grinned back at him. They spent the rest of lunch talking baseball, arguing the merits of Jeremy's Atlanta Braves versus Sam's New York Yankees.

As they tossed their paper plates in the trash can, Jeremy said, "I don't think I'd let anybody else know you're a Yankee fan."

The upstairs was hotter than Hades. Sam dragged every fan he could lay hands on into the small room, and still they sweltered. Who in his right mind would live in Misty Bottoms, Georgia, without air-conditioning?

If he planned to stay here, he'd have one installed, cost be screwed. Since he didn't, the new owners could cover the cost of it.

"We'll do Gertie's room first. I cleared it last night of all the little stuff and moved the furniture to the center. I've got the drop cloths down and the power and outlet covers off."

At the bedroom door, Jeremy stopped. "This is the ugliest room I've ever seen."

Hands on his hips, Sam studied the space. "Yeah, it is. But you and me? We're going to change that."

"If you say so."

"Beck told me this is what we'd need." He pointed to the supplies. "We've got a ladder, some putty knives, a spray bottle, and remover solution."

"You could have saved your money on that." He kicked at the can of remover. "Fabric softener and water works every bit as good. Smells better, too. And it's a whole lot cheaper."

"Really?"

"Yep."

"How do you know that?"

"You said it yourself. I'm the wallpaper king."

Before he could stop himself, Sam reached out and tousled the kid's hair.

Jeremy took a step back, his eyes taking on a guarded, wary expression. Then it disappeared, and the cocky teen returned.

"We need to be careful," Sam said. "We don't want to damage the walls or ourselves."

"Biggest thing is to be patient," Jeremy told him. "Score the paper first so the gook goes clear through, and then keep it wet. You have to do a little bit at a time, so don't spray the whole wall at once."

"Okay."

Jeremy had been telling the truth about his skills. The kid knew how to strip wallpaper and was a damn hard worker.

Unfortunately, nobody before them had worried about removing old before putting on new, so they ended up with four layers to scrape off. Sam had been the one to groan and whine like a baby when they'd found blue under the pink, then yellow under the blue, and green beneath the yellow. But hiding beneath the green? Beautiful plaster walls.

So they had one swath down and acres to go.

It turned out that Jeremy was a rock music aficionado, too. Radio blaring, both of them added their voices to Kiss. They moved on to Ozzy Osbourne with a little Bruce Springsteen, U2, and Aerosmith thrown in. An eclectic mix.

Jeremy turned to Sam, scraper in hand. "For a cop, you're not too bad."

"The highest of praises, kid. Keep it up and I might give you a raise."

The teen actually smiled, full-out, and Sam felt as though he had won a coveted award.

"Bet I can strip my walls before you."

"Oh really?" Sam studied him. "What's the bet?"

"We'll take two walls each. These two are mine."

"You've got a window," Sam argued.

"So? You've got a door."

"Okay," Sam said. "What are you going to do for me when I win?"

Jeremy snorted. "I want a pizza from Mama's."

"Fine. Since you're not legal to buy beer, I'll skip the six-pack I'd like and settle for a hot fudge sundae at the Dairy Queen."

And the competition was on.

By five, they'd both had it. Bits of wallpaper clung to their hair, their faces, and their clothes. The smell of stripper and old glue hung in the air.

They'd washed down the newly bared walls with water and a sponge.

Jeremy beat Sam by three minutes.

"Now you need to let it dry."

"Good deal. You coming back tomorrow?"

"Yep."

"You want me to pay you for today?" Sam reached in his pocket.

"Nah. Why don't you wait and pay me on Friday? That way I'll have some jing for the weekend. And the pizza? I'll let you know what night's good."

"I bet you will."

The kid climbed in his car, hung an arm out the

window, and chugged down the street, smoke belching behind him. Bushed, Sam stood on the sidewalk and watched him go. Every muscle in his body ached from the scraping and climbing up and down the ladder. Damn. He'd have thought after all that yard work, he'd be in better shape.

Not so, buddy boy!

First order of business? A shower. He set the fans up in the bathroom, shed his clothes, which probably should have been burned, and stepped under the water. He sighed and closed his eyes.

Hobo lay on the rug directly in front of one of the fans, intent on mangling a squeaky toy Sam had picked up at the grocery store.

All in all, it had been a good day. His shoulder ached but it was an ache he could live with. A couple aspirins would level it out. He'd used muscles today that hadn't seen a workout in far too long.

After he cleaned up, he wanted to see Cricket, to talk about her day and tell her about his. Hopefully, she'd have gotten over her anger and hurt and be ready to forgive him—again. He couldn't wait to show her the tile he'd bought for the downstairs bath. Beck had given him some pointers on how to lay it. He ought to start upstairs, where nobody'd see it if he botched the job, but what the heck? In for a penny…

He also wanted Cricket's input on the kitchen sink. Should he replace it or not? Or did he wait till he decided what to do about counters?

Again, maybe he'd leave all those decisions for the new owners.

What would Gertie want?

He knew the answer to that, but he couldn't stay. His life wasn't here. For years, he'd worked to earn his position on the New York force. A dream come true, right?

* * *

Through the open window, he heard Cricket's car up the road.

He finished drying off and stepped into fresh clothes. Gertie's washer had definitely seen better days, so he'd visited the Laundromat this morning. On his way to the dump, he'd tossed a load in the washer. Before he and Lem went for breakfast, he'd stopped and thrown his clothes into the dryer, then picked them up before he'd driven Lem home.

Downstairs, he opened the fridge and grabbed the huge piece of red velvet cake he'd caved to before leaving Dee-Ann's with Lem and Lyda Mae's coffee cake.

He and Cricket could share it. Maybe they could feed each other.

His jeans grew tight. He'd best get going while he could still walk.

Cricket O'Malley. Dynamite. In a very small package.

Chapter 19

Sam made sure he was standing on the sidewalk in front of his house when Cricket stepped from her car. He'd keep it light. He wouldn't let her see how much her late-night visit had rattled him.

He swore he wouldn't mention it.

"Hey, neighbor, the Yankees play tonight. You got cable?" He crossed the street.

"I do," she said. "But you know Yankee is a bad word around here."

"Yeah, Jeremy explained that to me while we stripped wallpaper in the front bedroom."

"He did, did he?"

"Yep. Didn't change my mind—or my loyalty—though."

"How's the room look?"

"You didn't answer me."

"Yes, I did. You asked if I had cable, and I said yes."

"So?"

"So what?" She frowned.

"Aren't you going to be a Good Samaritan and invite me over to watch?"

"Who are they playin'?"

"Kansas City."

She hesitated.

"Did you eat yet?"

"No."

"Have dessert?"

She shook her head.

"Good because I brought a bribe." He held up the plastic-wrapped wedge of cake. "And—" He raised a finger. "I called Fat Baby's Barbecue earlier for an order of ribs and slaw. Thought I'd run over and pick it up. There's plenty for two, and I can be back for the first pitch if I leave now."

"Did you get sweet potato fries?"

"Are you kidding? Of course I did."

"Then you're on."

"What's that?" He nodded at a sketch pad she was carrying.

"Some ideas I'm playing around with for a new bride we signed on." Cricket flipped opened the pad. "She's wearing this phenomenal gown in pale, pale blue and white stripes. It might be the most gorgeous thing I've ever seen."

"Not very traditional."

"That's why I'm fussing with the flowers." She flipped several pages. "This is the one I think we'll go with. Pale blue ranunculus mixed with some white ones will give the same feel as her dress. Then I'll add some peonies, roses, gardenias, and hydrangeas—all in white. I'll wrap the stems with the same striped fabric as her dress, and it should be spectacular."

"You're good."

She grinned. "Yes, I am."

They ate in front of the TV.

Sam screamed at the first baseman and called the

umpire an idiot. He jumped up and did an air pump when the Yankees' pitcher struck out three batters in a row. Cricket rooted for Kansas City's runners and cried foul on a call that left two stranded at the end of the sixth inning.

When the game ended and the dust settled, it was New York Yankees, seven, Kansas City Royals, five.

Sam started gathering up their dinner debris.

"To show what a good sport I am," Cricket said, "the losing team will share her s'mores with the winning team. *If* the head cheerleader for those damn Yankees will start a fire out back."

"We already had cake."

"I know. Who says you can't have dessert twice in one night?"

Sam's eyes darkened, and Cricket found herself growing warm, remembering last night's kisses…delicious. Until he stopped. Until he sent her home, wanting.

"Cricket?" His voice had gone husky.

"Yes?" She chewed on her bottom lip, and the heat smoldering in his black, black eyes set her aflame.

"You want s'mores?"

"What?"

"S'mores."

She swallowed. "Oh, yes."

"Did you have something else in mind?"

"No." She shook her head vehemently.

"Liar."

She opened her mouth, then closed it. When he stepped closer, she thought he'd kiss her.

Instead, he asked, "Everything I need for the fire out back?"

"Except these." Her hand trembled only slightly when she handed him a box of long matches. When he disappeared into the night, she waited a beat, took a long, deep breath, then walked out behind him to plug in her fairy lights.

"Nice place you've got here." A bit of wistfulness crept into his voice.

"Yours will look every bit as nice. Give it time."

"Time's what got it in the shape it's in now. A lot of sweat and hard work is what it'll take to transform it, along with a little design help from an expert in plants. Know any?"

She grinned and started back inside for the crackers, chocolate, and marshmallows. "I might."

The fire crackled and popped, sending sparks into the night sky. The pungent odor of burning wood filled the air. Fireflies twinkled on and off, and a band of insects kept time to the music on Cricket's iPod. Sam decided that maybe country life had some pros after all. Relaxing was easier here.

Since they had such different tastes, they'd compromised on an eclectic mix of her songs. The Emerson Drive song "She's My Kind of Crazy" came on.

"Hey, isn't that our song?" Sam asked.

"Our song?" Cricket's head shot up. "We don't have a song. There's no *we*! Period."

"Oh, that's right. You don't like me. I'm rude and… What was the rest?"

"Sam." She fidgeted and blew out the fire that blazed on her marshmallow. "I'm sorry. I—"

"No." He held up a hand. "Don't apologize. I appreciate honesty."

"It wasn't honest, though. Well." She shrugged. "I guess it was. At the time. But since then, I mean, the dog and Lem and Jeremy. Gertie's house."

He arched his brows and waited.

"I might have misjudged you." At his fast grin, she added, "Maybe. A little. It's possible I was a bit hasty in my assessment of you."

"In your assessment, huh?"

"On second thought…"

"Nope. We'll go with that." He withdrew his own perfectly toasted marshmallow from the fire and slid it between two graham crackers. The chocolate melted, and, smiling, he took a bite. Then his eyes moved back to hers. "I accept your apology, Bug."

She gave an outraged gasp. "I really have nothing to apologize for. Besides, you're the one who suggested *I* was arrogant."

"I never said that."

"You said I was too good for you."

"Those are two very different concepts, sweetheart."

Her tone sarcastic, she said, "Sweetheart?"

"It's just a word. Don't get excited."

"Humph. Hardly."

He swallowed the chuckle and fought to keep things light. But her lips. Her eyes. They destroyed him.

He ate the rest of his s'more, then caught her hand in his, pulled her to her feet, and drew her into him. Under the moonlight, right there in her backyard full of the scent of her flowers and twinkling with fairy lights and fireflies, they shared their first dance.

Holding her was a piece of heaven. Her skin was soft and warm, and she smelled far better than the flowers. How had he turned her away last night?

His mouth close to her ear, he whispered, "They say dancing is like making love standing up. After one slow dance, you can tell how it'll be with a woman."

She shivered, and he drew her closer still, felt her curves against his body. *Oh yeah, with this woman? It would be great.* He rested his hands on her hips, felt their soft sway, and wished there were no clothes between them.

When the song ended, he led her back to the bench. Thank God he didn't respect her private space, Cricket thought. Instead, they sat side by side, knees and hips touching, arms brushing, listening to the quiet night sounds. If he hadn't sent her home alone last night, what would they be doing right now?

Cricket wasn't sure, but she did know she didn't want this evening to end. She and Sam hadn't done anything special, but tonight would go down as one of her best nights ever. They'd fought over almost every call the umpire made while they'd shared a great meal from Fat Baby's. With anyone else, it would have been unremarkable.

With Sam? Memorable.

Maybe it was the starry night sky or the soft Southern breeze mixed with the scent of wisteria and angel's trumpet. The shared dance.

She turned her head, and Sam kissed her.

He cradled her head in those big, work-callused hands, then those long, skillful fingers of his trailed over her cheek, down her neck. The first soft, tentative kiss became more insistent, deeper till she could no longer think.

It didn't matter because she no longer wanted to think, only feel. She wanted to tear off his clothes. Tear off *her* clothes.

"You know, you probably shouldn't look at me like that."

"Like what?" she whispered.

"Close your eyes, Cricket."

She did. Everything intensified. His touch, his breath, her hammering heart. Then, her little voice of reason worked its way into her head.

She pulled away, and Sam's hands dropped to his sides.

"What's wrong?"

"What do you want, Sam?"

"You. I want you, Cricket."

He studied her in the dim light, then kissed her again. Hot, hungry, and deep, their tongues touched, tasted, danced.

Drawing away, he raised her hand to his lips. "What do you want, Cricket?"

"You." When he moved in, she laid a hand on his chest. "Has anything changed? Since last night?"

He closed his eyes and shook his head. "Not really. I'm still short-term in Misty Bottoms, and you're here for the long haul. I'm still a mess, Cricket."

"That's what I thought. Once we do this"—she circled her finger—"everything changes. For me, at least."

"I can't give you what you want. Can't promise you anything beyond tonight."

She needed more and knew he saw that on her face.

"I'm going to go home now."

She nodded.

"Thanks for sharing your TV and s'mores."

"You're welcome."

He kissed the tip of her nose and walked away, disappearing into the night. She sat beside the fire as it died down and became glowing embers. Amazing how it mirrored her encounter with her new neighbor.

All that heat, then just like that…gone.

The man baffled her. He was so stern, so short in speech and temper. But his kisses? Gentle yet electrifying. He was nothing, though, if not honest. Carter Scott came to mind, and she amended that judgment. Okay, so sometimes it took a while for the honesty to surface.

All things considered, calling a halt tonight had been the right thing to do. She and Sam were all wrong for each other. He wanted solitude; she wanted community. He wanted temporary; she wanted forever.

There was no middle of the road here.

Sam stepped inside his house, Hobo at his heels. Without bothering to turn on a light, he dropped onto the sofa, welcoming the dog's warm body beside him.

When Hobo laid his head on Sam's lap, Sam absently scratched his ears.

He wanted Cricket, but he wanted her without any commitment, and somehow that didn't seem fair. There couldn't be any regret for either party when he went back to New York. For the first time in his life, a quick tumble didn't appeal. She meant too much to him.

He was out of his depth here. Frustrated, he dropped

his head to the back of the sofa and covered his eyes with a throw pillow. Hobo's warm tongue flicked at his forearm.

"You're a good pal, boy." Sam roused himself enough to toe off his shoes. "You got a minute?"

The dog barked.

"I'll take that as a yes. So, let me run this thing with Cricket past you. See if it makes any sense to you."

And he did. He sat there in the dark and spilled all his thoughts, all his emotions to the dog, leaving out nothing. Every once in a while, Hobo made a whining sound or licked Sam's hand. He barked a couple times.

When Sam ran out of steam, the ticking of the wall clock and the hum of the refrigerator made the only sounds in the house. He'd hoped he'd feel better, but even after talking it out, none of it was any clearer.

He found himself wishing his mom could meet Cricket. Weird. He hadn't taken a girl home to meet his mother since Susie Bradberry in high school.

Why Cricket?

Because one smile from her cut him off at the knees, and he didn't know what to do about it. Maybe his mom would. Didn't moms know everything?

Or maybe he needed to call his shrink in New York. It might be residue from the shooting. Or maybe it was as simple as the fact that he'd never before in his life met someone like Cricket.

One thing he knew with certainty. When he saw her silhouette on the shade tonight, he'd know exactly how she felt in his arms, how she tasted, how she smelled.

And he would suffer.

Chapter 20

CRICKET FELT LIKE A HEEL.

Was she really going to dinner with Sawyer Liddell? After those kisses she'd shared last night with Sam? The ones that came right before he'd walked away, right before he'd told her they had no future.

Hell yes, she was.

Besides, she'd given her word to Sawyer, and he'd made plans. She felt duty bound to go. If last night had happened before Sawyer had asked her out, her answer would have been an unequivocal no. But it hadn't, so she'd seen no reason not to have dinner with the handsome reporter. And no doubt about it, Sawyer Liddell was gorgeous. Yet one look from him and she didn't go all tingly. She didn't daydream about his kisses or his touch.

Sam? Oh yeah.

But Sam was off the table. He'd made himself pretty darned clear last night. There was no future there. Not that she wanted one with him. The man was messed up.

He'd come to town to straighten out his head with hard work and solitude. He didn't need or want anyone in his life.

Or so he said.

His actions, his eyes, sometimes told a different story. That wasn't her problem, though, was it? She had enough on her plate right now with starting her business, keeping up with the flowers for Jenni Beth's functions, and settling into her new home and community.

Tonight she and Sawyer might very well find that missing chemistry. Maybe she'd been too busy, too stressed before. He'd obviously felt something or he wouldn't have asked her out. She'd try harder.

Instead of anticipating the date with eagerness, though, Cricket was dreading it. She'd rather stay home, and how sad was that? Despite Sawyer being movie-star gorgeous and personable and intelligent—jeez, wasn't there anything wrong with the guy?—she didn't want to go.

Moving to her kitchen window, she rested her hands on the lip of the farmer's sink and stared across at Sam's house, wishing, despite everything, that tonight's date was with him.

The screen door banged, and she jumped. Then, with a laugh, she opened it.

"Hey, boy. Come on in."

Hobo sauntered into the kitchen, gave her a leg bump, then sprawled on the rug.

"Did you come to help? Provide some moral support? Hmmm?" She dropped onto the floor beside the dog and ran a hand over his back. His tongue flicked out and gave her a quick kiss.

She cupped his shaggy muzzle between her hands and looked into his unblinking eyes. "What do you think I should do? Should I call Sawyer? Cancel? Maybe I could tell him I'm expecting my cousin or my aunt."

Her gaze traveled to the spotless, empty sink. "Or I could say I have two days' worth of dishes to do—or that I have chicken pox or the Bubonic plague."

Hobo whined and sent her one of those soulful, blue-eyed stares.

"I know, I know. I can't lie." With a sigh, she got to her feet. "Okay, then, if I have to go, what should I wear?"

As one, she and the dog turned and headed for her bedroom.

Twenty minutes later, she studied herself in the mirror. It would do, she supposed. Sawyer had said casual, so she'd taken him at his word. After discarding more clothes than she'd realized she owned, she and Hobo had eventually decided on a pair of khaki capris, an off-the-shoulder white top, and strappy white sandals.

When a knock sounded on the door, she started, her gaze flying to the clock on her nightstand. If that was Sawyer, he was early.

Still trying to hook the turquoise necklace she'd chosen, she walked to the front of the house.

Sam stood framed in the doorway.

"Sam? Hey."

"Hey, yourself." His eyes roamed over her, took in her hair, makeup, and clothes, then returned to her face. He gave a low whistle. "You look good."

His husky voice set off a tingling in her stomach.

"Thanks. Do you need something?"

"Yeah. My dog. You seen him?"

Woof! Hobo bounded down the hall and made a leap as Cricket opened the screen.

"Slow down, boy." He rubbed the dog's ears. "You're the one who left home without telling me where you were off to."

"Sorry. Guess I should have sent him back across

the street, but, well—" She waved a hand. "He's been helpin' me pick out an outfit."

"Seriously?" Sam's eyes met hers.

She bit her lip and nodded.

"Well, you did a good job, mutt. The lady looks terrific." Jokingly, he asked, "You got a hot date tonight?"

When she said yes, the laughter died in his eyes.

Her own slitted. Did he care?

No, of course not. He'd made that abundantly clear.

"In that case, I'll get out of your hair," he said, "and let you finish up. I'll take this guy with me."

He grabbed the dog's collar, and the two started home.

Halfway across the porch, he stopped abruptly, let go of the dog, turned, and walked back to her. Curling a finger in the scoop of her top, he drew her to him and kissed her till her toes curled.

"Keep that in mind tonight." Without another word, he left, the screen door slamming behind him.

She licked her lips, her heart rate through the roof, and watched man and dog walk away. What the heck had just happened?

If he could have, Sam would have kicked his own sorry ass from here to Alaska. What the hell had he been thinking? What an absolute idiot.

Not bad enough that he went barging in to retrieve his missing mongrel. Oh no. Not for Sam DeLuca. He'd had to kiss her. Kiss her like—what? Like he had the right to. Like he needed to.

Shit!

After that little speech last night? Cricket must think he'd lost his mind.

He scowled at the dog. "It's your fault."

Hobo hung his head.

"I'm serious. It's all cause and effect. Action, reaction. Like those damn dominoes everybody's always talking about falling. If you hadn't wandered off, I wouldn't have gone looking for you. I wouldn't have seen Bug all dolled up and sexy as hell waiting for—"

He stopped. Who *was* she waiting for?

Whoever he was, Sam might have to do him some serious bodily harm. If the guy knew what was good for him, he'd treat Cricket well. But not *too* well. And he'd keep his hands to himself.

With a sigh, he rubbed his thumb and index finger up and down between his eyes.

"What's happening, Hobo? Why does it matter who she dates? Another week or two and I'll be gone. Back to the Big Apple, to life as I knew it." He stalked to the fridge. "But if she's dating somebody else, why'd she kiss me last night? And the night before?" He ripped open the door and scanned the shelves. "Want some dinner?"

The dog's tail whipped a frenzied tune on the old linoleum floor.

Damned if he'd sit around feeling sorry for himself. He'd make a big old antipasto salad, cut up some leftover steak for Hobo, and the two of them would eat outside under the stars. Dinner al fresco.

The evening couldn't be more beautiful. It would be a shame to stay inside.

Rummaging in the fridge, he found what he needed, dropped everything on the counter, then pulled out the cutting board and a knife. If his neighbor wanted to date some local country bumpkin, more power to her.

He set to work chopping salami, provolone, and mozzarella. The tomatoes he'd bought yesterday were perfect, and he cut them into bite-sized pieces. Some roasted red peppers, some olives, and a few artichokes. Nice.

When a car pulled into the drive across the street, he nearly chopped off the tip of his finger. He swore a blue streak. It didn't matter who she saw, and he damned well wasn't about to peek like some nosy old neighbor.

Like hell he wasn't!

Tossing the knife onto the counter, he hurried into the living room. Hobo's nails clicked on the worn floor as he hustled behind Sam.

Standing off to one side of the window, Sam watched as an athletic-looking guy slid from the car, flowers in hand. A wonder he could fit with those shoulders. But the man was vampire pale. Didn't he ever get out in the sun? He probably sat in some stuffy office pushing papers all day. And that hair? It had to have hairspray on it to keep it that perfect.

Then he remembered where he'd seen him before.

Sawyer Liddell, the guy from the newspaper. He'd interviewed Cricket the day of her grand opening. He'd written a good piece, put an interesting spin on things, and really played up the shop's unique design, its history.

Still, Liddell was all wrong for Cricket O'Malley. She needed someone more vital. More spontaneous.

Yeah, like he'd know anything about that.

He stopped short. Actually, he did know spontaneous. That he was here was proof. On the spur of the moment, hadn't he packed his saddlebags and headed south, out of the city and into small-town, rural Georgia?

Still, that didn't exactly make him Mr. Spontaneity.

Liddell wouldn't make that cut either, though, and Sam was honest enough to admit he'd read his newspaper piece a second time with an eye toward what it revealed about Sawyer's feelings for Cricket. He'd seen the way the guy looked at her that day.

Liddell switched the bouquet to his other hand and knocked at the door.

"Come on! Flowers? Really?" Sam smirked. Glancing down at his dog, he said, "Cricket won't fall for those flowers, Hobo. You watch. They're too trite. Besides, she has a whole damn store full of them. The woman's surrounded by flowers day in and day out. For Pete's sake, use a little creativity."

He would. If he ever took Cricket to dinner, he'd think of something more her. More him.

But she did fall for the flowers. Meeting Liddell at the door, Cricket took the bouquet and gave Mr. Newsman a peck on the cheek.

When Sam felt his hands fisting, he consciously worked to relax them.

There was nothing he could do about any of it. Time to dress his salad. He left the two smoochers across the street and headed back to the kitchen.

The antipasto salad was a work of art. He added a drizzle of extra-virgin olive oil, some red wine vinegar, a little black pepper, and some shredded basil. Good to go.

He hit the on button for the radio and grabbed Hobo's meal. The back porch was shaded at this time of day, and the temperature a good five to six degrees cooler than earlier. It felt good.

Hobo plopped down beside him and inhaled his steak. Sam stabbed a bite of his salad and angrily chewed it. While he ate, the idea of what Cricket and Sawyer were doing gnawed at him.

Last night he'd admitted that he and Cricket simply wouldn't work. That didn't change a thing. He wanted her, and if he said anything different, well, he'd just be lying through his teeth.

How could he top the flowers the boy wonder had brought tonight? The competitive streak in him wouldn't let it go. All night he ruminated on it. There had to be something for her house—or her shop. He could give her Hobo. Nope, he'd already tried that and she wouldn't take him. Besides, Sam wasn't ready to be rid of the dog yet. He kind of liked having him around.

Maybe he'd get her a cat. No, that might not work, either. Any animal would be a lot to care for with her new business eating up so much of her time.

Well, the perfect token was out there. He just had to come up with it.

And he would.

Dinner was a bust.

Sawyer had been spot-on about the restaurant, a great place with delicious food. The fried chicken? As good as promised.

But the man across from her? The wrong one.

The chemistry she'd hoped for? A no-show.

Sawyer tried. He really did. She had to give him an

A for effort. He was interesting and had traveled to so many of the places she'd always dreamed of. His stories about them made her laugh.

But she didn't want to touch him, to kiss him. To tear off his clothes.

Worse? She'd spent the entire night comparing him to Sam. And that wasn't fair, not to any of them.

Over dessert, Sawyer shared his dreams. "Eventually, I want to work for a big city newspaper. I've managed to get my foot in the door with a couple of the larger ones by doing some freelancing."

"That's good. They'll know your name."

"Exactly what I'm counting on. I've written both fiction and nonfiction pieces for some magazines, too."

"Which ones?"

He gave her a synopsis of his work. "Anyway, piece by piece, I'm accumulating experience and jazzing up my résumé. I'm getting my name in front of the editors."

She nodded.

"What about you, Cricket? I got some of your background when I interviewed you, but what did you do before you started working with flowers? Before you decided to come to Misty Bottoms?"

"Oh, now there's boring for you," she said with a smile. "Thing is, I've always wanted to become a florist. I waitressed a couple summers and even tried goin' the secretarial route. That last ended after one week. It definitely wasn't for me."

"No, I don't guess it would be. I can't see you sitting at a desk all day."

"Too ADD?"

"No, it's just not you."

They talked about Jenni Beth's venture, about the need to spruce up the town and bring in new businesses.

Sawyer amazed her with his insight, yet it was all she could do not to peek at her watch. Not to wonder what Sam was up to. Did he care that she'd come out tonight with another man?

When their waiter finally brought the check, Cricket fought the urge to cheer.

On the ride home, neither spoke much, but the silence was comfortable. Sawyer enjoyed country music, too, and they listened to a Savannah station playing the latest.

He insisted on walking her to her door. When they reached her porch, he took her hands in his and leaned in to kiss her. At the last second, she turned her head so his lips brushed her cheek rather than her mouth. As nice as he was, as handsome, as intelligent, he wasn't for her.

She'd felt nothing when he took her hand, and she sure as heck hadn't gone all tingly when their legs had brushed under the table.

It was all Sam's fault. Damn the man anyway!

Sam stood at the window acknowledging that, yes, he had, indeed, become a voyeur.

When Cricket and the slimeball left earlier, he'd wanted to drag the guy out of that snazzy little car and bludgeon him to within an inch of his life. Since Jimmy Don wouldn't have appreciated being called away from dinner, he'd decided against it.

Instead, after he and Hobo ate, they listened to a Yankee game on the radio. Sam had spent the rest of the evening moping around the house, listening for Mr. Liddell in his fancy Camaro to bring Cricket home.

A single girl out with someone she didn't really know. It was only natural to worry.

Yeah, right.

Headlights appeared at the end of the road, and Sam let out a huge breath. She was back. He could rest easy.

When wonder boy made to kiss Cricket, Sam saw red. He was almost ashamed of the glee that filled him when Bug turned her head, presenting her cheek instead of her lips. Yes! Then she actually shook Liddell's hand, the death knell to a romance.

He couldn't make out what they said but was fairly certain after that handshake there'd be no repeats of tonight.

He sure as hell hoped not; he didn't think he could stand spending another night like this.

Only last night, Cricket had kissed him. Then she'd gone out with another man. It didn't matter that she'd probably agreed days ago. It didn't even matter that Sam had acted like an ass last night—or tonight, for that matter, did it? He'd thought she was different. Yet, just like Ingrid, who'd slept with him then left his bed for Federoff's, Cricket, too, had betrayed him in a sense.

When he finally dragged himself to bed, the nightmare hit hard. But instead of Ingrid, he found Cricket at the end of that alley.

He woke shaking and covered in sweat. Turning on every light on the second floor, he practically crawled into the shower.

Dawn broke before he managed to fall back into a troubled sleep.

Chapter 21

Cricket couldn't shake the guilt.

Intellectually, she understood she'd broken no moral code by having dinner with Sawyer last night. She and Sam...

She stopped right there. There was no she and Sam. He'd made that crystal clear.

Emotionally? Her naggy little good angel would not shut up. She insisted Sam was dealing with a whole heap of trouble and he needed understanding, not some other man thrown in his face.

But Cricket hadn't been trying to be mean. Sam had insisted he wanted to be left alone. He wanted to...heal.

Oh boy. She'd made a serious mistake.

The date hadn't helped Sam. And Sawyer? After that cheek kiss and handshake, she doubted he was ecstatic. Her? Miserable.

The UPS truck pulled up outside her shop, and Cricket met the driver at the door. By now, the two of them had become practically best buds.

"Think I'll bring the wife in to look around this Saturday. We live in the next town over, about fifteen miles from here. She'll like what you've done with the place."

"Thanks, Dave. Hold on a minute." She flew to the cooler and withdrew a peach-colored rose. "What's your wife's name?"

"Lou. Well, Louise."

Attaching a water tube to the end of the stem, she handed him the rose. "Here you go. Surprise her with this tonight."

Dave grinned. "Thanks! Beautiful color."

"It is, isn't it? And you're very welcome. You've toted a lot of boxes for me." She patted the new arrival. "And thanks for this one. It's my wind chimes."

The plants she and Sam had potted hadn't bloomed yet, so she chose a wind chime made of bits of bright blue and green glass and set it aside, along with a pretty red geranium. She'd carry them out to her car later. Both would be perfect on Sam's front porch. They'd give the two-story that touch of color it needed.

The day flew by with people stopping in for a plant or flowers, then staying to chat a bit. She'd invested in a jar of lollipops for treats for the little ones who came in with their moms.

When she got home, she debated on whether to run her housewarming gifts over right away or wait. She decided to do it before she lost her courage. The splash of color on his porch might assuage some of her guilt.

They'd left things rather awkwardly last night when he'd come over to fetch Hobo. That kiss had about knocked her off her feet! And then she'd gone to dinner with Sawyer.

She rapped at his open front door. No one answered. Sticking her head inside the screen door, she called, "You home?"

Still no answer. Strange. With all the harping he did about locking up, she couldn't imagine him leaving his house wide-open.

Rumor was that he and Lem had made their weekly dump run and breakfast this morning. But he'd have taken the truck, and both it and the motorcycle were here.

Hobo sauntered around the house, alerted that someone was on his master's property and ready, no doubt, to lick the intruder to death. Spotting Cricket, he bounded to her for a quick rub.

"Where's Sam, huh? Where's the grouch?"

Hobo turned and headed around the back. Cricket set down the plant and wind chime and followed. There was Sam, sound asleep in the back porch rocker.

She put a finger to her lips. "Shhh. We don't want to wake him, Hobo. He doesn't get nearly enough sleep."

The dog leaned into her leg, tongue hanging out, and stared up at her.

The man…so male. One hand on the dog's head, she studied Sam. It was a rare treat, as he wasn't often still. His long, spiky lashes fanned across his chiseled cheeks. Stubble darkened his jaw.

He'd had the barber trim his thick, wavy, black hair, but it still touched the neck of his T-shirt in the back. It begged to be touched, all but pleaded with her to run her fingers through it.

And his mouth? Those lips? She knew what they were capable of.

Her stomach fluttered.

As she watched, he mumbled something, and she thought he'd woken. She'd just taken a step forward when he started thrashing in the old rocker. A nightmare? Unsure what to do, she laid a hand on his shoulder. "Sam?"

He jerked away and, in a movement so fast she didn't see it coming, threw her to the porch floor.

She let out a yowl as the impact rattled her teeth.

When he landed on her, fist raised, the yowl turned into a scream.

"Sam, no! Wake up!"

Hobo started to bark, circling them.

"Stop! It's me. Cricket!"

His fist lowered. "Oh God. Cricket. God, I'm sorry." For one second he dropped his forehead to hers, then pulled away. "I—"

"Shhh. It's okay. You can trust me. I'll help."

"I can't trust anyone, most of all myself."

He took her hand, pulled her to her feet before walking inside. The door slapped shut behind him.

She stood unmoving, staring at the empty doorway. What should she do?

Hobo whimpered, visibly upset. Kneeling, she assured him everything was okay. But it wasn't. Sam was hurting far more than she'd realized.

PTSD? After what happened to him in New York, she wouldn't be surprised. Actually, she should have suspected it. Her detective needed help.

He wouldn't take it from her, though. Especially not now.

Barely daring to breathe, she tiptoed across the porch. Opening the screen, she crooked a finger at Hobo. The dog understood. He walked into the kitchen, turned to meet Cricket's gaze, then left to find his master.

A master who needed his comfort.

Cricket hurried across the street. She needed to talk to Beck. He always knew what to do.

Sam threw himself down on the ugly, old sofa. He'd thought he could handle it. Thought things were getting better. He'd been fooling himself.

When Hobo slunk into the room, Sam snapped his fingers. "Come here, boy. It's okay."

Hobo crawled onto the tired couch and wedged himself in beside Sam.

"I screwed up, didn't I?" He ran a hand over the dog's head. "Cricket's bound to run fast and far from here on in. I must have scared the hell out of her. I scared the hell out of myself!"

He thought of how pale she'd gone, how big those gray eyes had been, and he tossed an arm across his forehead. "What if I'd hurt her, Hobo?" he whispered. "What if I'd actually hit her?"

The dog whimpered and slid closer.

Cricket would have more than one bruise from being body slammed to the wood floor. It had to have hurt like hell. Yet he'd seen no reproach in her eyes, only sympathy.

Well, he didn't want her sympathy or her pity, damn it all to hell. He'd had a gut full of that while he'd been in the hospital—friends, family, other cops stopping by to see him, all wearing that same expression.

It was bullshit, and he didn't need it.

Five, ten minutes went by and his breathing evened out. His hammering heart slowed to somewhere in the vicinity of normal. As much as he hated to, he had to call Dr. Phelps, his shrink. He needed help.

The doctor's receptionist patched him right through.

"Sam?"

"I thought I was getting better. I'm not."

"What happened? Where are you?"

A ragged cry came from deep inside, one he barely recognized as his own. "I—"

"Are the nightmares still bothering you?"

"Yeah, but, oh God, it's worse than that."

"You didn't hurt yourself, did you?"

"Me? No."

"Somebody else?"

"Give me a minute." He went into the kitchen, dug a bottle of water from the fridge, and took a deep pull. Then he slipped out back and settled into the rocker, the same one he'd fallen asleep in earlier.

He breathed deeply and stared out over the green backyard. The peace here usually settled him, but it wasn't working its magic today.

His gaze caught on the tire swing, and he pictured Cricket on the swing, laughing. Then he saw her on this floor, his fist raised to her. If he lived to be a hundred, he'd never get that image out of his mind. Even on the job, he'd never raised his hand to a woman.

On a shaky breath, he said, "Doc?"

"I'm here."

Sam spilled his guts, starting from when he'd left New York City right up to the crisis that led to this call, grateful Dr. Phelps didn't interrupt.

"So you're in Georgia."

"Yes."

"Does your family know?"

"Not exactly."

"You don't think they're worried?"

"Maybe."

"All right. We'll leave that for now," Phelps said. "Any idea why these problems should intensify now?"

"No."

"You're in a new place, around new people. My guess is you're confronted with new situations every day."

He thought of the other morning with Lem, of Cricket's date with wonder boy. "You've got that right."

"We talked about the symptoms of PTSD."

"I don't have post-traumatic stress disorder," he insisted. His jaw ached from clenching his teeth.

"You do, Sam. A mild case fortunately, but still... We've been through this."

Sam shook his head, fully aware the New York doctor couldn't see him. "Look, over the years, I've seen some pretty horrific things. I've been in a tight spot more times than I can count. None of them affected me like this."

"Understood."

Damn, he hated this quiet compliance. He, himself, was full of rage, sorrow, and confusion. His shrink? Calm and collected. In control.

Sam had always been in control. Before. He wanted to be again.

"So why?" he asked.

"Why what?"

"Come on, Doc, you're the expert. Why do *you* think this is happening?"

"It might be an accumulation of everything you've been through over the years. On the other hand, this last event with Ingrid and Federoff was very personal. You didn't watch it happen to someone else. Didn't arrive after the situation ended. Didn't write an impersonal incident report."

Sam grunted.

"It happened to you, Sam, and to someone close to you. It was violent, and it was deadly."

"Still…"

Hobo dropped a stick at his feet, and, by rote, Sam gave it a toss across the yard and watched as the dog tore off after it.

"Your nightmares are back. Are you bothered with this only at night, or do you find yourself dwelling on what happened other times during the day, too?"

"It's worse at night, but it's pretty much on and off anytime. It doesn't run by the clock."

"Sleeping?"

"Not much."

"How about your relationships down there?"

He stiffened. "What do you mean?"

"We've talked about that emotional wall you've erected between yourself and others. Anything change?"

Silence filled the air. A bird sang in the top of the crepe myrtle. Hobo returned with the stick, and Sam threw it again.

"I went to the cemetery."

"Who's there?"

"My aunt Gertie. She's the one who left me this house. I—" He hesitated. "It was a long time ago. I was only twelve."

"What happened when you were twelve?"

"Jeez, what is this? A game of twenty questions?"

"Sam…"

"Yeah, yeah. It was the last time I actually saw Gertie face-to-face. Between the ages of eight and twelve, I spent a few weeks here every summer. Gertie was a special lady. My visit here's bringing back a lot of feelings."

"Good?"

"Yes. Very."

"Anyone else?"

He debated, but the good doctor wasn't having it.

"What else is going on, Sam? Or should I say *who* else?"

"My neighbor. Cricket. She's the one I took down today."

"You two close?"

He thought of their shared kisses and his response to her. Thought how much he ached for her. To touch and be touched by her.

"Yes."

"That could be why you've had this flare-up."

"Because of Cricket?"

"Because you're closing that gap. Because you're letting someone into your emotional space."

"Well, hell."

"Are you taking your anti-anxiety meds, Sam?"

"No."

"Maybe you should."

"No."

They talked for a while longer, Doctor Shrink telling him to call anytime he needed.

"Thanks." Sam ended the call.

So he'd gotten too close. Guess he needed to put a little distance in there.

He didn't want to.

But he already had, hadn't he? Both intentionally and unintentionally.

After today? Cricket was out of his life. It would take a fool to come near him again, and his Cricket was nobody's fool.

Chapter 22

"This place is disgustin'." Cricket picked up a pile of catalogs from the love seat and stashed them on the floor. She gathered up three soda cans and a pizza box and tossed them in the trash. "You need a cleaning lady or a janitor in here."

"I know," Beck growled. "Jenni Beth gave me the same lecture. I can find everything, so don't be movin' it around."

"Fine." Cricket dropped onto the seat. She'd been at the lumberyard quite a few times but had never actually come back to Beck's lair.

Settled into his desk chair, he propped his work-boot-covered feet on an open drawer. "What's wrong, Cricket?"

Her head snapped up. Had he heard rumors about Tansy? No. She put a hand over her racing heart and pulled herself back to the here and now.

"Who said anything was wrong? Can't I just stop by to say hello?"

"You can, yes. Anytime. But the look on your face tells me that's not why you're here today."

She rested her head on the seat back. "No, it isn't. You're gonna be mad."

"What did you do?" His voice held a guarded tone.

"Nothin'. Nothin' at all." She chewed on her lower lip.

"Then why would I be angry?"

"Because—oh boy. I don't even know how to start."

"You havin' trouble with somebody?"

"It's Sam DeLuca."

In one fluid move, Beck came out of his chair. "If he's laid a hand on you, so help me God, he's roadkill."

"No!" She held out her palm. "No. Well, not really."

"What the hell does that mean? Did he or didn't he?"

"Sit down. Let me start over." She did. Ignoring the murderous expression in her cousin's eyes, she explained what had happened that afternoon. "And before you get yourself all worked up, I need to tell you somethin' else."

"It had better be good, 'cause from where I'm standin', it's lookin' like Detective DeLuca's expiration date is comin' up."

"Oh, stop it. You men and your machismo. I can't share everything because it's, well, private and confidential, but Sam… Oh jeez. Look, this goes no further than this office, right?"

Beck nodded.

"He had some really bad stuff happen on the job. He was nearly killed." She plucked at a piece of lint on her shirt. "Which is why he's here. To be honest, I think he's sufferin' from PTSD."

"PTSD?"

She nodded.

"You need to stay the hell away from him!"

"I can't do that. He needs help, Beck, not censure."

"He needs a shrink. Meds."

"Probably, but I think he needs friends more."

Cricket stopped at the Dairy Queen and treated herself to a burger and an ice cream cone.

Times like this she missed her brother, Rogan. But Beck had finally cooled down enough to talk about options. What was it with men, anyway? Between their fists and, well, other parts, they sure didn't think much with their brains.

It didn't help that she couldn't share Sam's story, but it simply wasn't hers to tell. Too many secrets.

Beck had agreed to see what he could do, though.

Sam wasn't in the yard when she got home. Tempted to check on him, she fought back the urge. He needed time to lick his wounds, and she had to give him that.

Speaking of, she'd need to remember in the morning to wear a long-sleeved top. A couple bruises already showed from her contact with the porch. The last thing she needed was a bunch of questions she couldn't answer.

She'd shared some of the most pertinent facts with Beck because she'd needed to. Still, it hadn't sat well. No one else would hear a peep about Sam from her.

Once inside, she changed, then picked up the book she'd tried to read the other night. A glass of iced tea in one hand, the book in her other, she took herself out to the front porch. From there, she could keep an eye on Sam's place. And if he decided he wanted to talk, she'd be right there and available.

He didn't show. Neither did Hobo.

Twilight deepened, and Cricket moved indoors.

Several times through the night, she woke and moved to the window to stare across the street, but Sam's house, like her heart, remained dark and desolate.

As much as she loved her new business, Cricket couldn't wait for the day to end. She was tired and worried. She'd spent most of last night and all of today thinking about Sam, about what she should do, could do for him.

Driving down Frog Pond Road, she spotted him and Jeremy in the side yard cleaning out gutters. Relief flooded her.

When she pulled into her drive, Jeremy waved. "Hi, Cricket."

"Hey, Jeremy. Looks like you guys have been workin' hard today."

"We sure have. The boss has been a slave driver."

Sam, halfway up the ladder, didn't respond and didn't look her way.

Fine, she thought. *He's embarrassed, not rude. Hurt and embarrassed.* Plucking her iced coffee from the cup holder, she closed her car door and went inside.

Sam wiped the sweat from his eyes and descended. Jeremy had been right. He'd really pushed them both today in a vain attempt to outrun yesterday's guilt. Cricket wanted to fix him. He didn't know if he could be fixed or that he even wanted to be fixed.

"Let's call it a day, Jeremy."

"I can stay awhile longer."

"Nah, it's time to quit. I've got a couple other things to take care of."

The teen grinned and looked across the street to Cricket's house. "Bet you do."

Sam jokingly boxed the boy's ears. "Watch yourself there, partner."

"Guess I'll have to, 'cause now that she's home, you're sure not gonna be watchin' me."

"Ha-ha. You've got a real smart mouth."

"Thanks."

Sam couldn't help himself. He chuckled. Cricket had been on his mind all day, and seeing her lightened his mood. He'd been afraid he might have seriously hurt her, but she seemed okay.

"Thought we were gonna haul the rest of these branches to the back. You too tired, old man?" Jeremy needled in jest.

"Old man? I'll show you old man!" In a flash he had Jeremy in a headlock and gave him a Dutch rub.

The giggling teen squirmed away. "Okay, okay. So you're a *strong* old man."

Sam took one step toward him, and Jeremy backed up quickly, Hobo joining in, circling the two and barking.

"You don't want to finish?"

"Tomorrow. Besides, it's a never-ending job. For every tree branch we haul, two more watch us, laugh at us, and dare us to come get them," Sam said.

"You got that right."

"Go in and grab a cold water to take with you."

~

After a long shower, Sam cut the legs off a pair of worn jeans. Why hadn't he done this before? It was too damn hot for long pants. He grabbed a white T-shirt from the closet and pulled it over his head.

From the front bedroom window, he watched Cricket watering the flowers in her front yard. Laying a hand on the window frame, he sighed, knowing he couldn't put it off any longer.

Hair still damp, he thundered down the stairs and outside. The screen slapped shut behind him. When Cricket turned, he stopped at the edge of his walk and held up a hand.

"I come in peace."

She stood, swiping at a stray strand of hair. "I sure hope so."

What should he say? "Sorry I almost pummeled you"? "Sorry I scared you half to death"? "I'm not as crazy as I probably seem"?

Hell, maybe he was, though.

Instead, he cleared his throat and simply said, "Thanks."

"For what?"

Okay. So she didn't intend to make it easy on him. He got that. Well, then, he'd start small. "For the flower."

He waved toward his porch where the geranium sat proudly on the top step, a nice pop of color. "And for the wind chime. The old porch needed a little extra pizzazz."

She nodded. "They look good, don't they?"

"Yeah." He wanted to add *so do you*, but what few survival instincts he retained warned against it. She still might want to wipe the sidewalk with his sorry butt.

Sam swiped a foot over a dandelion that had sprouted overnight. "Thanks, too, for talking me down yesterday."

"It was nothin'."

"Nothing?" His voice rose despite all the warnings the saner part of his brain shot out. Heat rushed up his neck and flushed his face. "Nothing? I raised my hand to you. My fist."

"No. That wasn't you, Sam. You'd never hurt me."

"And you know that how?"

"I've watched you with Jeremy. With Lem. With Hobo and Dee-Ann. With me."

He opened his mouth, but she shushed him.

"No, it's my turn to talk, yours to listen. You're a protector, Sam. It's what you do. But more, it's who you are, both on the job and off. You can't help it. Right now you're upset with yourself and with the world because you've been hurt."

"You don't know what you're talking about."

"Oh, I think I do."

By now, both had raised their voices, practically shouting across the road at each other.

In angry strides, he crossed to her side. "Stay away from me, Cricket," he warned. "I'm bad news."

"You're a moron if you think I'll turn my back on you. You need help."

"Bullshit! What I need is some time alone. Time without a nosy neighbor poking in my business. You're crowding me, Cricket!"

"Crowding you? I'll show you crowding." She crawled right up into his face, her flip-flops toe-to-toe with his sneakers, her body practically glued to his.

He growled. "What are you doing?"

"Tryin' to show you what an idiot you are. There's nothin' wrong with you as a person."

"Like hell there isn't." He winced when he saw the bruise on her arm. "I did that."

"Sam—"

"You need to stay far away from me."

"Would you turn your back on a friend because he had cancer?"

He frowned, his brow creasing. "No!"

"How about if your best friend had a car accident and lost an arm or a leg? Came back from the war with head injuries? Would you walk away from him?"

"Hell no! But that's different!"

"It's not. You were injured in battle, Sam, the battle that's your job. I won't turn my back or walk away, either."

"You're the crazy one, Cricket." He made the mistake of touching her cheek. "Go away."

She shook her head, rose to her tiptoes, and kissed him.

All that heat and anger fused in the touch of their lips, their tongues. His hands raced over her face and down her sides. He touched bare skin where her little top ended inches from her waistband. His fingers slipped beneath it where more glorious, silky smooth skin waited.

Somehow, with ragged breath and halting steps, they made it onto her porch and inside her house. Sam dropped hot kisses up her neck, along her ear, all the while his hands busy on that sweet body.

Cricket's hands were busy, too. She tugged his T-shirt over his head and ran her beautiful, competent hands, her delicate fingers over his chest.

He groaned. "Cricket, we need to stop."

"No, I want you, Sam."

"Don't."

"It's true. Please. Now." She nipped his lip.

"You were right. This *will* change everything."

"I know."

He shouldn't, but he knew he would. What they'd started the other night wouldn't lie dormant. Hell, maybe this had been brewing since she'd first come banging on his door.

Her fingers moved to his zipper.

He tore his mouth from hers. "Not here, sweetheart." He could barely breathe. "I'm not taking you on the living room floor like some randy teenager."

"No?"

"No." He drew away to hold her at arm's length. God, the woman was gorgeous, her mouth red from his kisses, hair tousled from his hands, stormy eyes filled with passion.

Then it hit him. "Are you laughing?"

"No."

"Yes, you are."

He gave her credit. She tried to stifle the laugh but finally gave up and let it out. "Is there a difference between a randy teen and a randy thirty-year-old?"

"You'd better believe it. Years of experience. I think you'll like the difference."

When he moved to kiss her again, she laid a hand on his chest. "I'm not on anything, Sam. Any birth control." Her tongue flicked out, wet her lips. "I don't…I don't make a habit of this."

"Me, either," he said. "But in case of an emergency, and damned if this doesn't constitute one, I have something." He reached into his back pocket, withdrew his wallet, and flipped it open. Nothing.

He remembered he'd emptied it out while he was in the hospital. He figured he wouldn't be needing anything for quite some time and didn't want his sisters snooping and asking questions.

And he'd been right. He hadn't needed anything. Until tonight. Now.

"Wait! My shaving kit. It's across the street." He narrowed his eyes. "Will you still—"

She nodded, and he tore outside and across the road. If there were any snakes in the grass tonight, they'd better get out of his way.

Racing upstairs, he found his leather shaving kit and dumped it out on the counter. Stuff skittered across the surface, but there, in the middle of the mess, he struck gold.

When he hurried back to Cricket's, she stood just inside the screen door, her hair all mussed.

"Tell me you found somethin'."

"I did." He held up the foil-wrapped package. "You haven't changed your mind?"

She shook her head and opened the door.

He scooped her up in his arms and carried her into the bedroom, his mouth on hers.

One look at the bed, though, and he set her on her feet, his jaw dropping. Clothes littered the entire surface.

"Jeez, Cricket, you ever heard of a hanger?"

"Really? That's what you want to talk about now? My organizational skills?"

Her hands moved to the waistband of his cutoffs, undid the snap, again slid to his zipper. He groaned and, with one quick swipe, scattered clothing across the room. They tumbled onto the bed.

Her finger traced the scar on his bare back, and she dropped tiny kisses along his shoulder.

"Cricket—"

"Shhh. I wish I could fix what's in here." She kissed his chest over his heart. "And here." She placed a tender kiss on his forehead.

"Not now. Don't worry about that now." His tongue dipped into her belly button and flicked at the jewel there. "I love this. I've been dreaming about it since you showed it off in your driveway."

"Really?"

"Yep."

He laved it with his tongue.

"Oh, Sam, I feel that clear to my core."

Their remaining clothes flew off, joined the rest scattered across the room.

"You're beautiful," he whispered. Resting on his elbows, he took in the toned body, the perfect breasts, the flare of her hips. He'd told her the truth. After this, nothing could be the same between them. Making love with her would change everything.

Heated flesh met heated flesh, and when he entered her, he could have wept with joy. This hot little neighbor touched him like no other ever had.

Afterward, Cricket cuddled against him, her head resting on his chest. He felt her deep breaths and knew she'd been as affected as he had.

Absolute silence filled the room. A clock somewhere in the house rang the hour.

"My grandmother's," Cricket said. "She sent it with me so I wouldn't be alone."

He wrapped a short strand of her hair around his finger. "I'm glad."

"Me too. Thank you, Sam."

He came up on one elbow and stared down at her. "Are you serious?"

"Yes. Absolutely."

"You're thanking *me*? Oh, sweetheart, I think you've got it backward. *I* thank *you*."

Another few minutes passed. He had to leave, had to risk her hating him for it. He'd wanted Cricket O'Malley more than air. Now that he'd had her, he realized he'd totally underestimated her power, her pull. This one taste had only made him want her more.

Cursing Ingrid, Federoff, and his job, Sam worked his arm free of Cricket and slid toward the side of the bed.

She sent him a dreamy smile. "Where you goin'?"

"Home."

"What?" She sat up, drawing the sheet over her to cover that siren body. "Why?"

"I can't stay."

"Sure you can." She paused. "If you want to."

He said nothing.

"But you don't, do you?" she whispered. "Hit and run? Is that your style?"

"I don't do sleepovers, Cricket. I don't cuddle."

"Understood." She plucked at the sheet. "Is this because of yesterday?"

"I can't stay. Let's leave it at that."

"Yes, why don't we? You know where the door is."

He wanted more than anything to climb back into bed with her. To kiss her and ask her forgiveness. To stay the night with her and make love with her again and again. But he couldn't risk it. He couldn't take the chance he'd have another nightmare, that he might hurt her.

Still, he wet his lips. He wanted her to understand. "Cricket?"

"Go away, Sam. I get it. You're emotionally

unavailable, and you obviously like it that way because you won't let anyone help you."

Without another word, he left the room and showed himself the door.

This time, he thought as he stepped out into the night air, *she was wrong*. He wasn't emotionally unavailable. The problem? He was *too* emotionally vulnerable.

Once home, Sam tossed and turned, unable to sleep. Hobo whined on his bedside rug, then gave up and padded downstairs.

Jeez, even the dog had had enough of him.

The night shouldn't have ended this way. He should be across the street right now, tucked up beside Cricket. But he wasn't. He couldn't risk another nightmare, couldn't risk hurting her again.

Except he had hurt her. By leaving. They probably should have kept their distance, kept their hands off each other. But, again, they hadn't.

The sex? It had been incredible. So why was he here, alone?

He stepped into his jeans and headed downstairs. If he couldn't sleep, he might as well make use of his time. Spreading newspapers on the floor, he took out the new sander he'd bought from Beck and went to work on the back door.

The thing had to have ten layers of paint on it. Well, come daybreak it would be down to bare wood, he guaran-damn-teed it. Maybe the physical exertion would tire him out and bring him down from the high he'd experienced with Cricket.

His mind, though, refused to quiet. Before he went any further with this…thing…with Cricket, he had to decide why he was here. Why he was with her.

Because it felt good? Felt right?

Or because he was trying to forget?

He'd never been a user. That had been Ingrid's thing. Damned if he'd start now.

Chapter 23

In the middle of teaching Jeremy how to take up the old floor tile in the upstairs bathroom, Sam swore when his cell rang.

Jeremy grinned.

"Don't do anything stupid, kid. Hold on a minute." Into the phone, Sam snapped, "Yeah?"

"Guess I caught you at a bad time," Beck said. "Want me to call back?"

"Nah. It's okay. Jeremy and I are up to our eyeballs in cracked and chipped bathroom tile."

"Tacklin' that today, huh? That might make my call even sweeter. Cole and I are gettin' together tonight at his place for a game of poker. There'll be pizza, cold beer, and no women."

"What could be better than that?" His mind went to Cricket. He'd like to spend the night with her, but he wouldn't be welcome. "What can I bring?"

"Yourself and as much money as you feel comfortable losin'. I'm the man when it comes to Texas Hold'em."

Sam laughed. "Sounds like a challenge."

"Nope, just the simple, unadulterated truth. We'll start around seven, seven thirty." Beck gave him directions to Cole's house. "Now go finish up that tile job."

"Can I go with you?" Jeremy asked when Sam clicked off.

"That would be a definite no. I think you're a little

too young for poker and beer. And if you're going to tell me differently, don't. Remember, I carry a badge."

"You can be a real hard-ass sometimes, Sam."

His brow shot up. "Language."

"Yeah, yeah."

They went back to destroying the floor.

Sam, though, had a slightly sick feeling in his stomach. He figured he had a pretty good idea what tonight was actually about. Cards were going to be laid out on the table—both literally and figuratively!

Somehow, Beck had learned about what had happened the last couple days, either about him taking down Cricket or about the sex. Neither would win him favor in cousin Beck's book. And Cole? Beck's lifelong friend would be there to knock him down if he got up after Beck finished wiping the floor with him.

Well, whatever happened, he had it coming.

After Jeremy left, Sam grabbed a water and wolfed down a banana-nut muffin, then showered and changed. The weather was incredible, maybe the nicest since he'd arrived. It would be a good night for a motorcycle ride. The more he saw of this area, the more he loved it.

Following the directions Beck had given him, Sam turned onto Whiskey Road and there was the Bryson farm. Cole and Beck sat outside Cole's home.

He parked the bike and studied the old barn-turned-house. "Great place."

"I like it," Cole said. "My mom and dad live in the farmhouse, and I live in the barn. That way, we all have our own space and privacy."

Beck checked out Sam's Harley while Sam and Cole swapped motorcycle stories. When Beck handed him a beer, Sam thanked him. He'd have one, then cut himself off. For two reasons. First, he had to get back on his beast and drive home. Second, after his chat with Dr. Phelps, he'd started his anti-anxiety meds again. Time to be proactive.

"I'll start the pizza," Cole said. "Why don't you come on in, grab some chips, and I'll let you guys hand me your money."

"Ha! In your dreams," Beck said. "I'm the one endin' up richer tonight."

Both of them looked at Sam.

"Talk's cheap," he said. "Why don't we let the night tell the story?"

"Oh, pretty cocky, huh?"

"Nope. Confident. Mind if I take a look around your house? Don't think I've ever seen anything quite like it."

Cole grinned. "Jenni Beth's gonna move in here after the wedding."

Sam eyed him. "No misgivings?"

"Not a single one. I consider myself the luckiest man on the face of this earth."

Sam pointed a finger at him. "Lou Gehrig."

"Yep, in his farewell speech."

"One of the best Yankees ever."

"He was that. Not that we're Yankee fans around here." Cole grinned at Sam's hat. "No accountin' for taste. Beck, give our man here the fifty-cent tour."

Sam stuffed his hands in his pockets. "A lot of this from your salvage business?"

"Most of it." Cole set the oven to preheat.

Old washtubs, turned into lights, hung over the kitchen island. White kitchen cabinets with glass doors gave the room an open, airy feeling. And the floor tiles? Blue. It made Sam think of the sky on one of Misty Bottoms' perfect days.

The living and dining rooms both held all kinds of vintage goodies, from globes to toys to clocks. Cole's coffee table was a flaking red door on legs. He'd even left the knob on it. Cole Bryson was an interesting guy.

"Come upstairs," Beck said. "You've got to see this."

For a split second, Sam hesitated. Was Cole, in that easygoing way of his, intentionally sending Sam off alone with Beck?

It didn't matter. Sometime during this evening, the shoe would drop. He had come knowing that. Expecting it.

But Beck said nothing about his cousin, gave not a clue that anything was wrong. He simply gave Sam that fifty-cent tour. In the master bath was an honest-to-God water trough that Cole had turned into a double vanity with a granite top and funky faucets.

"What'd he do? Weld legs on this?" Sam peered at the bottom half.

"He did. Quite the contraption, isn't it?"

"Yeah. I don't think Gertie's house would like it, but this baby's perfect here."

Because the no-see-ums were out in force, they decided to play inside.

"Pizza's done, so why don't we eat first?" Cole cleared off the dining table.

"Heck yeah," Beck said. "I'm starvin'. And I hate it when you get pizza sauce and cheese on the cards."

"I don't do that."

"Yeah, you do. Think you use it to mark your cards."

"Whatever."

They gathered around the table as he placed the steaming pie in the center. Munching on pizza and chips, nursing his beer, Sam started to relax. He'd missed this, missed time with the guys.

He let his guard down, and Beck pounced.

"Heard you had a problem at your place the other day."

Sam stared at him with cop's eyes. "Guess you could say that."

Cole shifted uneasily in his chair. So he knew, too. Okay. Tense as a boy waiting for his prom date beside her father Sam said nothing.

"I liked you," Beck said. "Right from the beginnin'. A city boy and a Yankee to boot, but you gave everything a shot. Then I heard what happened with Cricket and figured you for a jerk."

Anger flashed through Sam, and his hand tightened on his bottle.

"Cricket disagrees," Beck went on. "Says you've been through some tough shit."

Before Sam could respond, Beck held up a hand.

"No details. She won't break a confidence, but she said I should cut you some slack."

Sam's anger disappeared. "Sounds like her."

Cole emptied more chips into the bowl in the center of the table. His gaze slid from Beck to Sam and back to Beck. Sam recognized the signs. Cole was judging the lay of the land and preparing for whatever came next.

Beck sipped his beer. "Yeah, well, all I'm sayin' is that if, you know, you need somebody to talk to—"

Relieved, Sam laughed. "You couldn't look more uncomfortable if you'd been asked to talk about birth control to a group of senior citizens. All female."

Beck grimaced. "Not much of a therapist, huh?"

"Nope. And no subtlety whatsoever."

"Wasn't aimin' for subtle."

"I hope not 'cause you missed by a mile." He took a much-needed drink. "Seriously, though, I'm okay. I need to clear my head, and that's why I'm here. Cricket's concerned I have PTSD. She kind of caught me at a bad time."

"That's what she said."

"I don't." At the skepticism on Beck's face, he repeated himself. "I don't. After the…shooting—and I was the one shot, just so you know—I debriefed with the department's shrink, who tends to agree with Cricket, but then, what does he know? I called him after…" He waved his hand. "After the episode at my house. I'm good."

"Offer to talk stands," Beck said.

"I've got a pair of ears, too," Cole added. "We can shoot the breeze anytime you need. Cops see some pretty bad stuff."

"I appreciate it. And, Beck, I appreciate your concern for Cricket. It won't happen again."

"Can you guarantee that?"

How in the hell did he answer that? "No, probably not. But I'm on guard now, I'm more aware. I started my meds again, too, and that should help."

Beck nodded, and the talk turned to sports and the price of oil.

After they cleared dinner, Cole brought out the cards

and poker chips. "Get your money ready, gentlemen. I've got a weddin' to pay for."

"Ha!" Beck rubbed his hands together. "Bring it on."

Sam hadn't won big, but he'd held his own. Beck and Cole hadn't taken him to the cleaners, and he'd had a heck of a good time. Add in that he'd made it through Beck's version of the Inquisition and he considered it a better-than-decent night.

As he drove slowly down Frog Pond Road, he thought he saw movement on his steps. It was so damn dark, though, he couldn't be sure. He'd shut Hobo in the house before he left.

If it was Carter Scott again, he was having him locked up.

Cautious, he pulled into the drive.

"Sam—"

"Cricket?"

They spoke in unison.

Slowly, he swung his leg over the bike and hung his helmet on the handlebars. Then, unsure, he simply stood there.

"I overreacted, Sam, and I'm sorry." Her voice floated to him in the darkness.

He shook his head. "I was a jerk."

"You were afraid to stay, weren't you?"

A humbling thing for a man to have to admit, but he did. "Yes, and too proud to explain."

He climbed the stairs, then dropped down beside her, circling her waist with an arm. She rested her head on his shoulder. His left shoulder.

Instantly, she snapped upright.

"What?"

"Did I hurt your shoulder?" she asked.

"No, it's better every day. Physically, I'm doing well."

"You need to cut yourself some slack, you know."

A heavy silence hung between them.

"I didn't protect her. I didn't protect Ingrid."

"But—"

"I know. You're going to remind me that Ingrid was in bed with the devil. Hell, when you come right down to it, though, so was I."

Cricket touched his hand hesitantly. He wanted her back—his lover, his friend, his neighbor. Slowly, he turned his own hand, laced their fingers. She had pianist's hands, he thought irrelevantly, long and slender and graceful.

She steadied him.

Still, there were things he needed to say.

"She didn't deserve to die like that, Cricket. Trussed up with no chance to defend herself. Federoff executed her right in front of me, and I did nothing."

"*Could* do nothing, Sam. There's a difference. You'd been shot—because she lured you there."

"It doesn't matter. I swore to protect and serve, and I did neither that night."

"I beg to differ, Detective DeLuca. You did your job. You served *and* you protected. You served all the mothers and fathers whose children might have been lost to the drugs Federoff would have continued to bring into this country. You protected those young people. They might not know it, but that doesn't make it any less real, any less important."

In the dim light from the living room lamp he'd left on for Hobo, he met her eyes. For just an instant, he dropped his forehead to hers. "Sure you don't have a degree in psychology? Psychiatry?" He raised her hand and dropped a kiss in the palm. "You're a good person, Cricket O'Malley."

"I might say the same of you, Sam DeLuca."

"You don't know me, Bug."

"Oh, I think I do. Far better than you imagine. Far better than you'd be comfortable with."

"I talked to my shrink, and I've restarted my meds, but I can't promise that what happened won't happen again." His chest tightened with the uncertainty.

"We'll deal with it if and when."

"I want to get better." His voice broke. "I want to stop blaming myself. Stop living in the web of that one night." A sound, low and primitive, came from deep inside him. "Cricket, Beck was right, though, to tell you to stay away from me. Far, far away."

"Again, I beg to differ. Were you with him tonight?"

Sam nodded.

"I didn't tell him any details, Sam. I didn't share your secrets. I thought talking to him might help me make sense out of what happened."

"I'm glad you went to him."

"Kiss me, Sam."

He hesitated, his lips inches from hers. "One won't be enough," he whispered.

"Good."

His good sense deserted him. "Let's take it inside. I made a stop at the drugstore today, just in case."

"Thank you!"

He practically dragged her up the stairs and into his bedroom. The old bed creaked as their combined weight hit it.

Sam heard Hobo grunting his way down the hall and rose up enough to bat the door shut. He didn't need an audience, not even a four-legged one.

She tasted like ambrosia and smelled like wild roses. No matter how much he kissed her, ran his hands over her, he wanted more.

Cricket made quick work of his shirt, her touch on his bare skin sending goose bumps along his arms. He tossed her top to the floor. The lacy bra followed.

His fingers dipped lower, tugged at her shorts and the tiny scrap of lace beneath them even as she unzipped his jeans and slid them down.

Tonight he vowed he wouldn't leave an inch unexplored. She must have made the same promise because her hands kept as busy as his own; her lips traveled over his already heated, sensitized skin.

The first time with this woman had been incredible. But this? It went beyond anything he'd ever known. It left him drained and gasping for breath.

Afterward, Cricket rolled toward him, throwing one of those shapely legs over his. "Let me stay, Sam. Don't send me home."

"Cricket—"

"I trust you, Sam."

He swore he heard the huge chasm in his heart grinding, shifting, narrowing. He drew her closer, tapped a finger on her butt cheek. "Tell me about this."

She chuckled. "A twenty-first birthday dare."

"Jiminy Cricket?"

"Tattooed permanently on my behind."

"What did your friend end up with? Or was it just you who got inked?"

"No, she did it, too." Cricket paused. "Her name's Lily."

"Ahh, say no more." He slid his body along the length of hers, turned her, and kissed the cricket. One kiss led to another, the sparks between them instantaneous and hot.

Half an hour later, listening to her soft breathing, Sam fell asleep, a smile on his lips.

Chapter 24

THE MORNING AFTER TURNED OUT TO BE A SLICE OF heaven itself. They woke still wrapped around each other and hungry for each other.

As the early sun streamed through the window, they made slow, languorous love, taking their time, finding all those sensitive spots on each other's bodies that sent pleasure spiking.

After a long, steamy shower in his newly tiled upstairs bath, they went into town with Hobo for breakfast. Since Cricket had to open the shop, they'd driven in separately. Sam figured he was dead meat if anybody reported back to Beck because one look and everybody in Dee-Ann's had to know how they'd spent the night.

Cricket's face and neck were whisker burned. She had a grin from ear to ear, one that no doubt matched his own.

Hobo's breakfast was delivered to him near the outside bench, then Sam and Cricket devoured theirs like they'd been refused food for a week.

After they finished eating, he followed her to the shop and left her with a very thorough kiss he hoped would last him through the day.

Then he and Hobo took a side trip down by the river, spent a few minutes playing fetch, and headed for home. He still had lots to do.

The phone rang.

Sam jumped at the sudden sound in the quiet house and swore.

The house had gone dark around him while he'd read, and rather than turn on the light, he'd given up and simply laid the book in his lap. Cricket had dinner plans with Jenni Beth tonight, then they were working on an upcoming wedding.

As he pulled his phone from his pocket, he fumbled for the lamp switch. The wall clock read ten thirty.

Cricket! Had she run into trouble? Had car problems? An accident?

His folks? Was one of them sick?

Heart pounding, he swallowed the nervous fear. "Hello?"

"Mr. DeLuca? I know it's late, but—"

"What's wrong, Arlene?"

"Is Jeremy there with you?" Mrs. Stuckey's panic-laden voice sounded shrill.

"No, ma'am. I thought he'd be here today, but he didn't show. I assumed something had come up." He hesitated. "What's happened?"

She started to cry. "He wasn't in his room this mornin'. His bed hadn't been slept in."

"Shit! Sorry, sorry." The cop kicked in. "Do you have any idea where he might be? Somewhere he likes to hang? Friends?"

"His dad showed up last night, and we had some trouble."

"He didn't get physical, did he?"

"No, nothin' like that."

"He's not there now?"

"No. He left. Right after he told Jeremy he was gonna have a new brother or sister."

"Oh boy." Sam closed his eyes and rubbed at them with his free hand. He knew all too well how Jeremy felt about his father. This piece of news would have sent him over the edge. He wouldn't hang around if there was even a chance his dad would show up again. Where would a sixteen-year-old hide out in Misty Bottoms? Not having grown up here, he hadn't a clue. Maybe Beck would know.

"Let me make a few calls."

"Please don't call Jimmy Don."

"I won't. At least not yet. I'll take a ride around town. Maybe I'll get lucky."

"I did that all day. I asked around a bit, so maybe Jimmy Don already knows." She sniffled. "I was so sure he'd come home."

"He might still. Jeremy will be easier to spot at night when it's quiet and everyone's in bed. I'm going to go now, but I'll call if I find him. You do the same."

"Yes."

"We'll find him, Arlene. Jeremy's a smart kid. He'll be fine." Then he asked, "Where does his dad live?"

"Rincon."

"Have you checked there?"

"Yes. Nothin'."

"Okay. I'm on it. We'll find him," he repeated. They talked a few more minutes before Sam hung up.

Yesterday, the kid had left happy, teasing Sam about Cricket. Everybody liked Jeremy and held no hard feelings for what he'd done out at Magnolia House. Too bad he had such a jerk for a father.

Sam placed a call to Beck and explained the situation. Cricket's cousin had a couple ideas and said he'd check them himself. While they talked, Sam wandered into the kitchen for the shoes he'd left by the door.

A soft light toward the back of the yard caught his attention.

"Beck? Don't go anywhere just yet. I may have found our fugitive."

Sam shut Hobo in the bathroom and crept through the yard. Reaching the shed, he threw open the door, the beam of his flashlight illuminating the youngster who sat with his back to the wall, a small light in his hand.

Jeremy let out a squeal. "Jeez, Sam, you scared me!"

"Yeah?" The beam never wavered, and the teen raised a hand to shield his eyes. "How do you think your mom's feeling about now? She's scared silly, too. She's spent most of the day riding around looking for you! What's going on here?"

Jeremy squinted. "She called you?"

He nodded. "She thought maybe you were here. Guess I was wrong when I told her you weren't." Sam directed the beam toward the ground and motioned for the boy to stand. "Let's give her a call."

Jeremy shook his head. "I don't want to."

"Would you rather she calls the sheriff?"

Jeremy's eyes went huge. "No! Why would she do that?"

"Because you're a missing minor."

"No, I'm not. I'm right here."

"You know that, and so do I—now. She doesn't, and she's worried sick." He held up a hand. "She said your dad paid a visit last night."

Hobo, who'd somehow managed to sneak out of the bathroom, squirmed past Sam and went to Jeremy. The boy hugged the dog.

"I hate him."

"That may be, but your mom's having a tough time, too. Both you and your dad have really shoveled it on. She can't handle much more."

Guilt suffused his face. "You call her."

"Okay, I will."

She answered on the first ring.

After explaining where he'd found Jeremy, he said, "Mrs. Stuckey, if it's okay, your son's going to bunk here tonight. He'll be safe, and in the morning, I'll bring him home to you."

"He's so upset."

"I know. This will give us time to talk, and Jeremy looks like he could use some sleep. I don't know where he spent last night."

"Thank you, Sam. I owed you before for taking my son under your wing. After this…" Quiet sobs rent the air. "I don't know why you picked now to come to Misty Bottoms, Mr. DeLuca, but we sure are glad you're here."

"Try to get some sleep, Arlene." He didn't know what else to say, so he simply hung up and dialed Beck. He told him Jeremy was with him.

"You need a quick shower, something to eat, and bed, son."

"I'm not your son," Jeremy snapped.

"No, you're not. It's just a figure of speech. I'm sorry."

Jeremy stood there, shoulders stooped, head down, dirty and defeated. Sam wanted more than anything to wrap his arms around the kid but was afraid to.

The decision was taken from him. In one quick move, Jeremy came to him, hid his face in Sam's T-shirt. "I'm sorry, too. I wish you were my dad."

Sam's heartbeat quickened. Dad? He wasn't ready to be anybody's dad, had never considered himself in that role. He'd always figured he'd suck at it. But he had held victims after violence, and this, really, wasn't much different—except this time, like it or not, he was emotionally involved.

"He's gonna have another kid."

Sam nodded. "Your mom told me that."

Jeremy lifted tear-filled eyes. "He doesn't want me, so why's he havin' another one?"

Oh boy, talk about a tough question.

Before he could come up with an answer that would somehow navigate the waters between truth and a kind lie, Jeremy wiped at his eyes and said, "It doesn't matter. Dad doesn't want this new baby, either. I heard him talkin' to my mom about it. He claims Harmony pulled a fast one on him. Told him she was on birth control."

Sam's mouth dropped. "What do you know about birth control?"

He snorted. "I'm sixteen. They teach it in school."

"Oh." At sixteen Sam had known his way around birth control pretty damn well, too. But Jeremy? Shoot! Surely the kid wasn't—He blanked his mind. Best to stay off that street.

"Harmony," Jeremy spit out. "She sure didn't bring any harmony to our family."

"No, don't guess she did."

"Ralph Stuckey is a dirty rotten son of a bitch!"

"He's your father, Jeremy." Sam kept his voice level.

"Sperm donor's more like it."

Yep. Kids grew up too fast these days.

"Look, Jeremy—"

"No." He shook his head. "My mom's the one who worked and kept food on the table and a roof over our heads. Dad? He worked on and off, but even when he had a job it didn't help us. He spent whatever money he made in Duffy's Pub or at one of the little joints outside of town, drinkin', playin' pool, and impressin' the girls."

Sam's mouth tightened.

"He's always had girlfriends, and Mom's put up with it. I don't know why, but my guess is she did it because of me. She shouldn't have bothered. He never helped with homework or housework, never gave her any money, never went to ball games or Scout meetings."

The tears had started again, but this time Sam doubted Jeremy was even aware of them.

"And now he's made my mom cry again. He thinks we should forgive and forget. Well, I've got news for him. I don't want nothin' to do with him." He shuffled his feet. "He asked Mom if he could come back home. He says he's sorry, that he wants to live with us, that he misses us. Bull! He just doesn't want to put up with some cryin' kid."

"That still doesn't tell me why you ran away. Why did you?"

"Because I was afraid if I stayed, Mom would take him back. For me. She thinks I need a dad. I've got news for her. I've needed one for a lot of years, but even when Ralph was around, I didn't have one. Nothin's gonna change."

"So you left for your mom?"

"That's right. Without me there, she can tell him no."

"She told him no anyway."

"Yeah?" Jeremy didn't look up. "Well, good for her. About time."

"You need to come to terms with this, or it's going to eat you up forever."

When the kid said nothing, Sam slung an easy arm over his shoulder. "How about for right now we go inside, get you fed and cleaned up, then find you a bed? Sound okay?"

Jeremy nodded. "Is my mom all right?" He sounded like a little boy again.

"Now that she knows where you are, she's fine. She loves you."

"I know. C'mon, Hobo." The kid kicked at a pebble in his path as the dog shuffled beside him. "What about your mom?"

"*My* mom?"

"Yeah. You said the other day your folks don't know where you are. I don't see how that's any different than my mom wonderin' about me. Not really." He shrugged his thin shoulders. "She might be worryin' too."

The kid had sucker punched him.

"It's different."

"Why?"

"I'm older, okay?" The kid was starting to bug him.

"I don't think that matters."

What was it with this kid? Like a dog with a bone, he wouldn't give up.

"My mom says she'll still worry about me when I'm grown with kids of my own," Jeremy said.

"And she probably will. So your little stunt—"

"Bet your mom feels the same way," Jeremy interrupted.

Sam didn't have a chance to speak to that because as they started around the front of the house, Sawyer Liddell opened his car door and stepped out.

Instinctively, Sam pushed the boy behind him. "Use the kitchen door. Help yourself to anything in the fridge, but stay inside."

"What's he want?"

"A story, but he won't get one." He gave Jeremy a nudge. "Go on. Get inside. Take Hobo with you."

"'Kay. Come on, Hobo." The pair raced toward the porch.

Sam waited till he heard the creak, the slap of the screen door opening and closing. First Carter Scott had come sniffing around for a story and now this jerk.

"Liddell. You're out late." Sam stepped around the corner of the house. "Come to see Cricket or are you just snooping?"

"I stopped at the Texaco after sitting in on the town council meeting. It ran late tonight. Tommy said Arlene's been lookin' for Jeremy. Seems he's missin'."

"That right?"

"Word is he's been workin' for you. That he spends a lot of time here helpin' you. You know anything?"

"I do," Sam said. "I know you're on my property, and you need to remove yourself."

"Or what?"

"I'll have to do it for you."

"I figured you'd be worried about the kid, but I guess not. Cold bastard, aren't you? Guess that's what makes you a good detective. Facts only."

"Get off my property."

"Or what? You gonna beat me up?"

"I'll arrest you for trespassing."

"Your badge doesn't carry any weight here."

Both men took a single step toward the other.

A loud clap had them starting.

"Boys, stop it right now." Cricket stood at the end of her drive, hands on her hips. "You're just dyin' to get your hands on each other, aren't you? Too much testosterone, if you ask me."

"Nobody did," Sam growled.

"Great. Have at it, then." She walked back inside, the screen door banging shut behind her.

When Sam finally turned back to Liddell, he saw the man watching him intently.

"What?"

"You and Cricket." The newsman spoke slowly, then slapped his forehead. "That's where this animosity is coming from. A fool could have figured it out." When Sam said nothing, Liddell said, "The way you look at her? The way a starvin' man looks at a big, juicy burger. Explains some of what went on—" He shook his head. "Or didn't go on the other night when I took her to dinner."

Sam's eyes narrowed.

"I didn't realize you had dibs on her," Sawyer said. "Figured her for a free agent."

Sam wanted to say she was, but he couldn't bring himself to do it.

An owl hooted at the far end of the street. A firefly flickered past, then a second. Twilight quickly moved to evening.

"Time for me to go."

Sam cleared his throat. "Yeah. Everything's good here."

"Answer one question for me?"

"If I can." Sam stuffed his hands into his jean pockets.

"Is Jeremy okay?"

"Yes, he is. You've got my word on that. And I've spoken with Arlene."

"Good. I like both the kid and his mother. The old man put a hurtin' on them, and I'd hate to see things slide any further downhill for them."

"They won't. Not if I have anything to say about it."

Sam stood there in the dark and watched the reporter drive away. Maybe he'd misjudged him, let other things color his perception of the guy.

Restless, Sam stared up at the ceiling. The old house was silent except for Hobo's soft snoring. Jeremy, tuckered out by the day and his emotions, had gone out like a light the instant he'd hit the bed.

Sam wished he could do the same.

Liddell had been wrong. Sam had been worried sick about Jeremy. What if, instead of hiding out in the old shed, he'd hit the road?

Anything could have happened.

And that had dumped fuel on the fire. It had been one of the reasons Sam overreacted to Liddell showing up. Good thing Cricket had interfered because who knew how that scuffle would have turned out otherwise.

On top of the worry was the all-too-fresh memory of Carter Scott tailing him, spying on his private time with Cricket, on shared secrets and kisses.

He'd blown things totally out of proportion. Even though by then he'd known Jeremy was safe, the adrenaline dump still had Sam on edge. That and the realization that Jeremy's own damn father would cause this kind of havoc in the kid's life. What in the hell had the man been thinking?

Add to that the legal ramifications of what had gone down today and they had another good reason to keep all this as down low as possible. No matter Liddell's intentions, Jeremy didn't need a story on the front page of the town's newspaper.

He'd gotten off rather lightly with the rose garden fiasco, all things considered. If Judge Ramhurst heard about today's mess, would he rethink his sentence? Stick the kid in juvy?

Good thing Ralph Stuckey hadn't shown his face because Sam wanted to beat him to a pulp for not keeping it in his pants, for getting mixed up with a barely legal gal over in Rincon.

One thing he knew for sure. He meant what he'd said. He'd do whatever he could to take care of Jeremy and his mom.

And Cricket? He needed to do some hard thinking on that one. He wanted her. Right here in bed beside him.

And because he did, he refused to get up and go to the window. He would not stare into the darkness to see if she was awake or asleep.

A glance at the clock verified it was too late to call anybody. But damned if Jeremy hadn't struck right to the heart of the issue. Sam's mom no doubt was worrying, and that wasn't right. Cricket had nailed him on it, too.

Another check of the time showed it was past midnight, but he sighed and threw back the covers. *Hell with it*. He dug his phone out of the pocket of the jeans he'd dumped on the floor, brought up his contacts, and hit call.

On the second ring, he heard her voice.

He swallowed hard.

"Mom? It's Sam."

Chapter 25

Over a second cup of coffee, Sam made a decision. One he'd probably regret. He'd come to Misty Bottoms to hide away, yet here he was, about to stick his nose into yet another person's business. And it wasn't even time for Tuesday's garbage run with Lem.

Before he could change his mind, he pulled his phone from his pocket and dialed Jeremy's mom.

Arlene answered after the second ring. Even over the line, Sam heard the exhaustion in her voice. Ralph Stuckey had destroyed good people for his little fling. Now he was adding another life to his pile because Sam knew, as well as he knew his own name, that Ralph would not be around to help raise this new child, either.

Fatherhood was about more than providing sperm. Jeremy had been right about that. Too bad Ralph Stuckey hadn't gotten that memo.

"How about I pick you up in thirty minutes, Arlene?" Sam asked. "Jeremy's awake and in the shower. He's feeling kind of awkward about the whole deal, so I thought it might be easier if the three of us have breakfast at the diner. Keep things light."

"That's very thoughtful. You sure you don't mind?"

"Not at all. Jeremy's a good kid."

"Yes, he is, and he's gotten caught up in a bad situation between his dad and me. I don't know how to thank you, Sam."

"No thanks needed. We'll see you in a bit." He hung up and poured another cup of coffee. Carrying it into the living room, he studied Cricket's little house, the welcoming aura of it with its flowering vines and bright chairs.

He wished she could be at the diner with them this morning. All three of them could use her warmth, that special brand of magic she exuded.

Behind him, Jeremy thundered down the stairs.

"You have somethin' for me to do here today, Sam?"

"Yes, I do. But before we do anything else, we're going to breakfast."

"Cool. I'm starved."

"Bet you are. That hollow leg needs filling." He turned to face the boy. "First, though, we're stopping by your place to pick up your mom."

A gamut of emotions ran over the teen's face. Relief was followed quickly by apprehension, anger, and fear.

Sam dropped a hand on his thin shoulder. "It'll be okay. She's not mad."

"Huh, that's what you say."

"That's what I know. You scared her, and if she took a switch to you for that, it would probably be fair. But she won't. She blames herself for what happened."

The boy's face fell. "Why would she do that?"

"You ran away because she and your dad have problems."

"It's Dad's fault." His face darkened. "He's supposed to love my mom." His voice dropped, and his lip trembled. "I do."

"I know that, and so does she. Run a comb through that mop of hair and let's go. I'm hungry."

On the way to town, Sam said, "I owe you one, Jeremy."

"You owe *me*?"

"Yes, you were absolutely right. My mom and dad were both worried sick about me."

"You called them?"

"I did. After you went to bed. Both of them told me to thank you."

Jeremy grinned. "See? I know what I'm talkin' about. I'm the man."

"You're the man." Sam reached across the seat and high-fived him.

"We should have brought Hobo along."

Sam slid his sunglasses down and eyed him. "Not today. The focus this morning is on you and your mom."

He didn't need to remind Jeremy of that when they pulled up to the Stuckey house. The kid almost ripped the door off the old truck in his hurry to hug his mother.

Sam smiled. This was good.

The three of them bundled into the cab, and he drove to Dee-Ann's on Main.

They'd just ordered when the diner's door swung open and a man in his mid-forties swaggered inside. One look at him, at the resemblance to Jeremy, and Sam swore under his breath. This had to be Ralph Stuckey. Of all the bad luck.

Arlene's mouth tightened, and the boy went into shut-down mode.

Yep, Sam thought, *the jerk himself.*

"Hey, look here, would you?" Ralph walked right up to their table and chucked Jeremy under the chin.

The teen jerked away from him. "Don't do that."

"You're my son. Guess I can do what I want." The man's voice took on a hard edge.

Sam stood, held out a hand. "Sam DeLuca."

Ralph didn't take it. "You sleepin' with my wife?"

Arlene gasped and shot a glance at her son, who'd gone paper white beneath his summer tan. "Ralph Stuckey, you should be ashamed of yourself!" Her eyes shot fire. "For a lot of things. But how dare you ask that? Here in the diner, in front of your son."

"Sorry," he groused. "Didn't mean anything by it."

His wife arched her brow. "I'd hope not, seein' the predicament you've gotten yourself in. A little like the pot callin' the kettle black, isn't it?"

"Said I was sorry."

"Yes, you did." Arlene stared him down. Voice low, she said, "As handsome as Sam is, he's a little young for me, but then that's a concept you wouldn't understand."

A flush colored Ralph's cheeks.

Her gaze slid to Jeremy, to Sam, then back to her husband. "You're welcome to stay if you'd like. After all, this involves you, too."

Ralph's eyes moved to the diner's big front window.

"Don't tell me you've got her out there waitin' in the car."

"No, I do not. No, ma'am. I'm not sure where Harmony is right this minute. We had ourselves quite a squabble when she delivered her news." He dropped into a chair.

"Which is why you decided to come home."

The way Ralph rubbed his head, Sam figured he had the mother of all headaches. He couldn't quite find it in himself to feel badly about it, but he did get up and move to the counter. The Stuckeys needed a few private minutes.

"Got any aspirin, Dee-Ann?"

"Have a headache?"

"No, but if I'm not mistaken, Mr. Stuckey does."

"Humph. He should have after what he's put his wife and son through." Still, she reached under the counter for the bottle she kept there. "Arlene might need a couple, too, havin' to deal with that man. He gonna eat anything?"

"I don't think so. We don't want to make him too comfortable." Back at the table, he tossed the aspirins at Stuckey. "There you go. Swallow a couple of them. Maybe you'll feel better." He slid his untouched water toward the man.

When the door opened again, everyone swiveled in his seat to stare at the newcomer.

Sam grinned.

"Well, now, ain't she a looker? New to town?" Ralph asked.

Sam's smile disappeared. "Time for you to leave."

"Excuse me?" Ralph pulled himself up to his full height. "I don't think you're in any position to—"

"Sam!" Cricket crossed to them. "Jeremy, Mrs. Stuckey." She started to speak to Ralph, a question on her lips. It died away as she got a better look. She turned her back on him. "What are you doin' in town?"

"Thought we'd grab some breakfast before we started the work day." Sam's easy words belied the anger roiling through him. "Mr. Stuckey was just leaving."

"Damned right I am." Ralph shoved the chair back so hard it nearly tipped over. "Son, you comin' with me?"

Jeremy raised startled, angry eyes. "Why?"

"Summer, ain't it? Thought you and me could do some fishin'."

"Maybe Harmony will go with you."

Ralph's hand rose. "Don't you smart mouth me, boy."

"Don't touch him." Sam kept his voice low and even.

"You're gonna stop me from disciplinin' my own son?"

"Yes, sir, I am. The boy's done nothing wrong. He simply isn't in the mood to assuage your guilty conscience. Besides, he has a job, and as soon as we finish here, we're getting to it."

Arlene had her napkin clutched so tightly, her knuckles showed white. Cricket laid a hand on her shoulder, and Sam watched the woman reach up to pat it.

"Don't come around cryin' when you change your mind, Jeremy."

"I won't. Sir," he added caustically.

Cricket dropped into the chair he'd vacated. "Everything okay here?"

"It is now," Arlene said. "Thank you, Sam. Again." Her eyes grew moist.

Dee-Ann came over with the coffeepot. "I'll add my thanks. I had my cell in my hand ready to hit Jimmy Don's number when I realized you had things under control. You handled him well. Coffee's on me this morning."

"No need for that."

"Yeah, there is." She ruffled Jeremy's hair. "Pancakes are done back there. You ready to eat?"

"You bet I am." His words were chipper, but he still looked pale.

"You want something, Cricket?"

"No, actually I stopped by to thank you. Those potatoes you sent home with my mom the other night were wonderful." She looked around the diner. "I love Misty Bottoms."

"We do, too." Dee-Ann headed to the kitchen for their breakfast.

Cricket, that short blond hair tucked behind her ears, was leaning into the monitor when Sam entered the Enchanted Florist.

She glanced up in surprise. "Hey!"

"Hey, yourself. What are you up to?"

"Surfing Pinterest. I have a wedding coming up way too fast, and I want to do something other than the tried and true garlands. My bride gave me free rein, so right now I'm trollin' for ideas. I need something to kick-start the creative part of my brain."

"Ahhh. Got you. My sisters are fans of that site. My brothers-in-law, however, are not. It usually means work on their part."

Cricket laughed. "Yeah, it probably does."

"Don't brides usually have all this worked out months and months in advance?"

"Not lately it seems, but hopefully we'll get to that point. In this case, the groom popped the question, the bride said yes, and neither wants to wait. Jenni Beth, Kitty, and I are bustin' our butts to put things together quickly."

"A lot of work."

"And worth it when that bride walks down the aisle."

"You're a romantic," Sam accused.

"A hopeless one who's not ashamed to admit it."

"Well, hopeless romantic, what time are you closing today?"

"Sometime around two. Why?"

"Yesterday and last night took a toll on everybody, so I gave Jeremy and myself a free day. The work will still be there tomorrow. I dropped him and his mom off at their house. My guess is she'll spend today fussing over him. They both need that. Ralph is on his way back to Rincon, tail between his legs, and I'm playing hooky. Want to grab a late lunch? Cole told me about a great barbecue place."

"Fat Baby's? The place you ordered from the other night?"

"A different restaurant. According to Cole, there's a nursery near there you might be interested in. Thought maybe we'd stop by and you could check it out."

"You'd do that?"

"Absolutely." Because he wanted to put his hands on her, he jammed them into the back pockets of his jeans.

Cricket apparently had no such compunction. She jumped up from her desk chair and threw her arms around him.

Caught off guard, he just managed to spread his legs and brace himself. For such a little thing, she made quite an armful. God, the woman smelled good. His face dropped to that quirky hair while her snug little body melded with his, her breasts pressed against his chest. His hand ran along the length of her arm, over silky smooth skin.

"Cricket—"

The bell over the door tinkled, warning of an incoming customer, and Sam stepped away.

Cricket cleared her throat. "Hello, Mrs. Baker. How are you today?"

While she moved toward her customer, Sam took a deep breath and centered himself. He wanted her. He couldn't, wouldn't deny that. Whether or not he should have her was another matter. It wasn't in his plans, but he'd made it abundantly clear how he felt about temporary versus permanent.

If she was okay with that, so was he. Why shouldn't two healthy, young individuals enjoy each other? For now. He'd be hitting the road for New York City soon, and that would be that.

Funny. A couple weeks ago he'd been more than good with those plans. Now? He thought of Cricket, Hobo, Jeremy and his mom, Jenni Beth and Cole, Beck, Lem and Lyda Mae, Jimmy Don, Dee-Ann, Darlene… Hell, he knew half the town and had become friends with them. He'd be—What? *Sad* to leave them.

And this *thing* with Cricket. How had it happened?

Cricket O'Malley was addictive. Once he'd had a taste, he wanted more. But he'd get over her, wouldn't he? Once he hit the interstate and headed north. Once he hit the streets of Manhattan.

Right?

And wasn't it just plain stupid to wallow in all these concerns? He'd think about them later. Maybe. Right now he intended to enjoy the afternoon.

When Mrs. Baker left, Cricket turned the sign on the door to read CLOSED.

He checked the clock on the wall.

"I know. It's nowhere near two." She shrugged. "My shop, my hours."

"Sounds good to me."

"Did you bring the motorcycle?"

"No."

Her face fell.

"You love it, don't you? Admit it."

"It grows on you."

"Yeah, it does, but I had Jeremy with me this morning. On the way to breakfast, we picked up his mom, so…"

"It had to be the truck," she finished.

"Yep. Do you have a problem with it? I mean, I know it's not much."

"It's actually pretty perfect."

"The rust bucket?"

"Yeah, I like it." As she closed down her computer, she asked, "You wouldn't actually have hit Sawyer last night would you?"

Sam rubbed his chin. "Honestly? I don't know. What with his date with you, Jeremy's problem, the whole Carter Scott thing…there was a lot coming to a head there."

"Good thing I showed up then, huh?"

"Yeah. I couldn't take you to lunch if I were sitting in the slammer."

"Can you believe Jeremy's dad dared show his face?"

"The guy's got a lot of nerve."

"He does." Holding up a finger, she said, "One minute." She grabbed her purse, then went to the cooler and pulled out a pretty bouquet. "Can we stop at Mrs. Stuckey's on the way out of town? I'd like to give her this."

"You bet."

He kissed her. He'd meant it to be quick and sweet but took it deep. If someone was snooping through the window, so be it.

Chapter 26

THEY ROLLED DOWN THE OLD TRUCK'S WINDOWS AND cranked the air full blast. Wearing the craziest purple, rhinestone-studded sunglasses he'd ever seen, Cricket settled in.

"Where are you takin' me?"

"A place called Cozy Corner Barbecue."

"Sounds good."

When he turned on the radio, she switched it to a country station. About to argue, the words died on his lips when she started singing along. Her voice, cool and husky, was pure sex. One song turned to two, then four. He was mesmerized.

"Any of these songs you don't know?"

She shook her head, and the trio of golden hoops in her ears swayed.

Traveling along the back roads with her at his side, Sam couldn't remember a time he'd felt so contented. He could have driven forever.

When they pulled into the nursery's parking lot, Cricket turned into a kid at Christmas. Covering the entire area, checking every type of plant, she tucked it all away for future reference. She and the owner hit it off and promised to keep in touch.

Back in the truck, she said, "Thank you, Sam."

"You're welcome. Cole found it when he was out hunting for roses for Jenni Beth after, you know, the, ah, incident at Magnolia House."

She nodded.

They smelled the barbecue restaurant before they saw it.

"Oh my gosh, I'm practically droolin'," Cricket said.

"You and me both."

The parking lot was crowded, but Sam managed to find a spot.

Within twenty minutes, they were seated and had placed their order.

The food was every bit as good as advertised. Between them, they practically licked the shared platter clean.

Sam had just finished wiping his fingers with the wet wipe their waitress had brought when his cell rang.

"Hello?"

"Sam? It's Jenni Beth. Are you with Cricket? I tried calling her, but she didn't answer."

He glanced at Cricket, knowing she'd overheard.

"Oh, shoot. I laid it on my desk and forgot it."

He turned his attention back to his phone. "Yes, I am, Jenni Beth. Cricket forgot her phone at the shop." He raised his brows at her. "She says she's sorry."

Cricket grimaced.

"We just finished some of the best ribs and pulled pork I've ever eaten."

"Cozy Corner?"

"Yep."

"Cole said he'd told you about it. I need to prod him into taking me there again. Soon. In the meantime, I have something I wanted to run by the two of you."

"Let me put you on speaker." He set his phone in the center of the table.

"Hey, Cricket."

"Hi, Jenni Beth. What's up?"

"Five storefronts in Misty Bottoms are empty," she said. "We're working to fill them with businesses, but in the meantime, they look bad. I've talked to the owners, and they've given me permission to turn them into a kind of billboards for other businesses in town."

Cricket grinned. "Great idea."

"I think so. If you're okay with it, I thought you and I could do two together. Darlene, Dee-Ann, and Kitty will do another two with Ms. Hattie's help." She paused. "And you're not going to believe this, but Lyda Mae, Lem's wife, will do one."

"Lyda Mae?" Sam asked.

"Surprise, huh? It turns out she's quite the potter. She's actually considering renting one of the stores to open her own shop."

"Well, knock me over," Sam said.

"Exactly how I felt."

"She must have made some of the pieces I saw in her living room."

"Nice?"

"Better than."

"Go figure. Cricket, why don't you and Sam come up with an idea for one of the windows, and Beck and I will cover the other?"

Since Sam needed a couple doorknobs, they decided to ride over to Dinky Tubbs's salvage yard. From there, they hit a small frozen custard stand. By the time they arrived at the outskirts of town, evening was falling, and they were both hungry again.

"Let me fix dinner," Cricket insisted. "Nothin' fancy. How do grilled cheese sandwiches and tomato soup sound?"

"Perfect. One of my favorite meals."

Over dinner, they discussed ideas for their shop window, then Sam turned on the TV to catch the end of a ball game. Hobo, who'd been invited to dinner, stretched out on the floor and appeared to be enjoying the game, too.

"Come here, Bug." Sam patted the spot beside him.

She curled up on the sofa, and he put an arm around her, drawing her close. He smelled like fresh air and sunshine. And man. Despite his insistence that Misty Bottoms was temporary, Cricket felt a shift. His actions lately didn't match his words.

Sam lifted her hand, kissed the back of it. Then, very slowly, he began nibbling her fingers, one by one. Every nerve ending in her body sprang to attention.

He pulled her into his lap, his hand slipping under the hem of her top. Warmth spread through her. Tongues met and danced. Buttons magically came undone.

Gasping and disoriented, she found herself horizontal on the sofa with Sam's body pressed against her. His lips chased along her bare skin.

"Not here," he whispered. "Your nosy cousin might show up, and I'd be a dead man."

She laughed.

In one fluid motion, he stood and scooped her up.

"Sam! I'm too heavy."

"Not on your life!" His lips met hers again, silencing the rest of her argument.

In the bedroom he stood her beside the bed. Slowly, he undid her bra and let it slip to the floor.

She lowered his zipper.

He hooked a finger in the band of her panties and slid them down her legs. Even as she stepped out of them, she freed Sam from his boxers.

"Oh God, Cricket. You're so beautiful."

His eyes traveled over her, took in every inch, and she fought the urge to cover herself. Instead, she focused on the gorgeous man in front of her, the six-pack he sported, the tan he'd earned under the hot Georgia sun.

"I need to touch, to taste you. All of you."

She opened her arms, and he stepped into them.

Together they fell onto the bed and were lost. Sam took it all. Everything. But he also gave everything. She'd never felt so cherished, so well loved. When he finally entered her, she knew nothing would ever again compare to that moment.

She fell asleep with Sam spooned against her, his arms around her.

"Stop! No!"

Her brain fuzzy with sleep, she fought to the surface and dragged herself from sleep. Sam thrashed beside her, hot and sweaty.

A nightmare.

She slid out of bed and turned on the lamp.

Hobo whined and scratched at the door.

"Sam! Sam, wake up! You're having a nightmare." She reached out, uncertain whether or not to touch him. "Sam?"

She laid a hand on his shoulder, and he jerked, then opened his eyes.

Unfocused and haunted, they stared past her at the ceiling.

"Sam, it's me. Cricket. You're at my house." She opened the door and Hobo bounded in. Springing onto the bed, he curled up beside his master.

"Hobo?" Sam's voice was husky. Then his gaze swung to Cricket. "Oh God, I didn't hurt you, did I?"

"No." She gave him a slow smile. "You didn't. Are you all right?"

He swiped a hand over his face. "I will be. Okay if I grab a shower?"

"Sure."

While he showered, she went to the kitchen and filled a tall glass with ice and water and carried it to Sam, who stood beneath the shower, one hand planted on the wall.

She handed it in to him, and he took a greedy gulp.

"Thank you."

"You're very welcome." Unbelting her robe, she let it fall to the floor. Beneath it, she wore nothing.

"Cricket…"

She stepped in, cupped his chin, and met him with a hot kiss.

His body, so hard, so muscled against her own, sparked needs she'd only imagined before him. With a groan, his hands, slick and soapy, moved over her skin.

He ran them down her arms, over her torso, paying very special attention to first one breast, then the other. Those hands moved lower still, his lips following. He stopped at her belly button, toying with the stud she wore today, shooting hot arrows of need through her.

By the time he'd thoroughly washed every inch of her

legs, she was nearly beside herself. When he backed her against the tile wall and took her, she cried out in joy.

Satiated, they collapsed against each other, cooling water cascading over them.

When they finally regained enough strength to stumble from the shower, Sam wrapped her in a large cotton towel and slowly dried every single inch of her.

They barely made it to the bed. Another long, sweaty bout of lovemaking drove away any lingering remnants of nightmares.

Chapter 27

Two days later, they were ready to deck out their store windows.

Sam lifted his old bike from the back of the pickup. Yesterday, Jeremy had given the decades-old bicycle a couple coats of cherry-red spray paint. He'd unearthed the old bicycle basket Gertie had used, and they'd scrubbed it up and sprayed it a shiny silver.

They'd build their vignette around the old bike. Cricket would fill the basket with bright, cheerful flowers and spread others around to reinforce the outdoor theme. Wedding items would be sprinkled throughout the display. The finishing touch? Small placards to advertise Elliot Lumber, Magnolia House, and the Enchanted Florist.

Brilliant, if he did say so himself.

Dee-Ann, Kitty, Ms. Hattie, and Darlene had finished their windows, and Lyda Mae had a good start on hers. Walking along the sidewalk, Sam knew Jenni Beth had hit a home run.

Two fewer empty store windows improved the entire street. Once they finished theirs and Lyda Mae's was done? Better still.

On top of that, some of the other business owners, catching wind of what Jenni Beth was up to, had spiffed up their own displays. Definitely a step in the right direction. If anyone could turn this town around, it was Cricket and her friends. He had faith in them.

He wheeled the bike into what had once been a sporting goods store. Empty too long, it smelled musty and desperately needed a fresh coat of paint. The bump of the bike tires and his footsteps on the worn wooden floor echoed through the lifeless building.

The others had beaten him there and huddled in the back over a small table, finalizing their designs. The old measure twice, cut once. Get it right the first time.

Cricket looked mouthwateringly sexy in a pair of denim shorts and a cropped T-shirt. Her belly button piercing taunted him when she raised her arms to demonstrate where she wanted a light hung.

He wanted those arms wrapped around the rungs on his headboard while he had his way with her…and he'd better throttle those thoughts back if he intended to get anything done here today.

He dragged his attention back to the conversation.

"I'll stop by on my way to work every couple days and give the flowers a drink. I can replace them if I need to, bring fresh," Cricket insisted. "With the tinted window, they should be fine."

"Wouldn't it be easier to use plastic ones?" Beck asked.

"Easier?" Cricket asked. "Bite your tongue! If I'm advertising my flower shop, we are not using any plastic flowers!"

The men shared a sympathetic glance.

"Guess that settles that," Sam muttered.

"Yep." Beck stuffed his hands in his pockets. "What else do you need?"

Beck and Jenni Beth went out to her car for another couple boxes, and he and Cricket found themselves alone. He couldn't help himself. He pulled her in for a smoking-hot kiss.

She wove her fingers in his hair and gave back threefold.

"That short little shirt is driving me nuts. I want you, Cricket."

"I know." She squirmed against him. "I can tell."

He let out a pained laugh. "Yeah, well—"

The front door opened, and he drew away.

"Hey, come give me a hand with this," Beck called out.

Sam sent Cricket a smoldering look. "Later."

A flirty grin was her only answer.

The girls fussed, making sure everything was set exactly so, while he and Beck were relegated to the heavy lifting. As they moved things once, twice, sometimes three times to meet the girls' critical eyes, there was a lot of talk and even more laughter.

So okay, Sam thought, this felt good.

"Where's your better half?" Beck asked Jenni Beth. "Why isn't Cole here lugging stuff with us?"

"He's in Savannah. A shipment from an estate sale was due in today, and he wanted to be there to make sure everything arrived in good condition."

"Sounds like an excuse to me. Cricket managed to drag her guy in."

Sam swiped at the bead of sweat on his forehead. "Don't know that Cricket dragged me in or that this makes me her guy."

Even as he said it, he cringed. She didn't deserve that slap. Mad at himself, he grabbed the stuffed dog and moved it closer to the bike.

Damn it!

He lifted his gaze and met Cricket's eyes. The disappointment in them was a kick to the gut. Later, he'd explain to her it wasn't personal. The memory of that shared shower rushed back, the kiss they'd enjoyed while Beck and Jenni Beth were outside. How much more personal could it possibly get?

He was such an ass. If he were Cricket, he'd give himself the brush-off, refuse himself a chance to rationalize his bad behavior. But Cricket being Cricket? She'd probably let him. And wasn't that one of the reasons he...*liked* her?

After a rather awkward silence, everybody got back to work, chattering a little faster, a little louder, to cover the gaffe.

"Doesn't it feel good to help your community?" Jenni Beth asked a little later as they spread bridal magazines and plastic tumblers around the summer scene.

"Misty Bottoms isn't my home, Jenni Beth. I'm temporary."

Cricket picked up a handful of garden pots they hadn't used and hurried off to the storeroom.

"Sam, you hurt her."

"You want me to lie?"

"Actually, I was hoping you'd finally be honest and fess up about your true feelings for her."

He sighed. "My life is in New York City. My family is there. My work is there. My home is there."

"And your heart's here, whether you'll admit it or

not." With that, she followed her friend to the store's far end.

Thank God Beck had stepped outside to make a phone call.

By the time he got home, Sam was bushed. They'd all worked hard, but along with the physical, he felt emotionally drained. Jenni Beth's comment kept whipping around in his head. She was wrong. Cricket didn't have his heart.

The sex? Yeah. Hands down, best ever. Did he enjoy spending time with her? Absolutely. But over the long haul? They wouldn't work.

Feeling more than a little cranky and a whole lot frustrated, he tried to ignore the emotions that bumped and pushed at him.

When Rico's call came in, Sam found himself in a rare mood. "Hey, pal. What's going on?"

Within minutes, he fell back into the easy camaraderie he and his partner shared. The tight ball that had taken up residence in his stomach unraveled.

Chapter 28

Cricket needed to talk to Sam. Jenni Beth and Beck had both put him on the spot today. Halfway up his front porch stairs, she heard his voice out back. He laughed, and she smiled.

Headed that way, she stopped.

"You wouldn't like Misty Bottoms, Rico. There's nothing here but a boring small town."

He went quiet, and she assumed he was listening.

"Women mess with a man's head, partner. The smart thing? Stay far away from them. Trust me. I know."

Cricket drew in a deep breath, turned, and started home. Her head roared with static. How many times had Sam alluded to exactly this? He'd tried to tell her.

Well, this time she'd received the message. She'd gotten too close, had seen him at his most vulnerable, and usurped his position as protector.

Halfway across the street, she stopped for several deep breaths. She could go home and mope or meet this head-on. Moping wasn't her style.

She marched to Sam's backyard. He sat in the old rocker, his phone on the table by his elbow now that he'd apparently finished handing out advice.

"Dear Abner closed for the day?"

His eyes flew open. "What?"

"I won't beat around the bush. I overheard part of your chat with your friend."

The guarded look in his eyes said he understood exactly which part she'd heard. "You caught one side, and that's dangerous."

"I'd call it enlightening."

"Really? Do you know Carmela? The gal my partner's cozying up with? You know her history?"

"No!" Cricket's temper spiked. "And quite frankly, it doesn't matter. What does matter is that you believe women need to be given a wide berth."

"Not all women." He started to stand.

She threw out her hand. "Don't get up. Stay right there."

He sat back down, a wary expression on his face. "See, here's part of the problem. You're jumping to conclusions."

"After your comments to Beck? To Jenni Beth? To Rico? I don't think so. I think, maybe, I'm seein' things clearly for the first time in a while." She rubbed her eyes, then dropped her hand. Her heart thumped so hard, she feared she'd have a heart attack. But she couldn't stop now. "What do you want, Sam? What do you really want?"

"I don't know."

"You're sure about that?"

"Yeah. Yeah, I am."

Her heart broke. She'd done a stupid, stupid thing. She'd fallen in love with this New York City detective, and she loved him too much to settle, to take only part of him knowing full well he'd never truly be hers.

God, she hated this, but she knew what she had to do. Like ripping off a bandage, it needed to be fast.

"You didn't lead me on, Sam." She met his gaze.

"You gave me no reason to expect more. But I do." Despite her best intentions, her voice broke. She gave herself a moment, lifted her eyes to his again. "I expect someone who will love me beyond reason. Beyond all else. I expect—no, I *deserve* that happy ever after. It won't happen with you, Sam." She leaned in, gave him a quick kiss on the cheek. "I'll never regret these weeks we've shared, but it's over."

What? Sam sat up straighter. "Nothing I can say will change your mind?"

A spark of anger flared in her eyes, turning them from soft gray to roiling thunderclouds. "Why would you want to? You should be glad I'm doin' this. It saves you the trouble." She narrowed those incredible eyes. "Or are you havin' a problem with me callin' it quits instead of you? Have I dented your male pride?"

His own temper ignited. It wasn't so much pride as… What? He couldn't say, couldn't put his finger on the emotions that coursed through him.

Well, damned if he'd sweat it. If that's what she wanted, that's what she'd have.

"Fine. If it's over, it's over. Have a good life, Cricket."

"You too, Sam."

He'd have sworn he heard tears in her voice, but when he met her eyes, they were as dry as the croutons Dee-Ann had sprinkled on his salad yesterday.

Two very long days later, Sam made another decision. It was time to leave Misty Bottoms. There was no reason whatsoever for him to stay any longer. He'd made some strides toward sanity and could finish the job in New

York. The house would never be finished. He'd put it on the market and somebody else could worry about it. Jeremy and his mom should do okay now that they'd confronted Stuckey.

And Cricket? Why in the hell had she pushed it? Why couldn't she be happy with things the way they were?

Part of him had been certain she'd come to her senses and back off a bit. Instead, she'd stayed on her side of the street and avoided him. He'd been tempted to let Hobo stray to her house so he'd have a reason to see her again. If he was really lucky, the dog would start that damned howling.

After thinking about it, though, that seemed like a bad idea.

Her house went dark early. Lucky her. He'd sat out back till nearly two, but still sleep evaded him. Sometime near dawn, he'd moved inside and caught a couple hours of uneasy sleep on the ugly couch.

Yesterday, tired after the nearly sleepless night, he'd driven into town and given his New York address to the utility companies, figuring it would be best to leave everything turned on till he could get it sold. Then the new owners could switch everything to their names.

He'd ridden his Harley down every back road he found but had still come home to another sleepless night.

Now, this morning, exhausted and feeling like hell, he poured his third cup of coffee and carried it into the living room. He stood just inside the screen door. A slight breeze set the wind chime Cricket had given him into a tinkling song. It was slowly killing him. Maybe he should take it down.

He'd considered and discarded the idea of running

into Kitty's for a bear claw. Certain that word had gotten around town by now that he and Cricket had had a spat, he'd be persona non grata. Bubbly, eccentric Cricket. Everyone in Misty Bottoms loved her. If lines were drawn and sides chosen, he hadn't a doubt he would come out on the short end of that stick.

When a vehicle turned onto Frog Pond Road, he glanced up. Surprise, then anxiety rocked through him when Cole slid his big black truck to the curb. He liked Cole and didn't want any trouble with him.

Opening the screen, he said, "How's it going?"

"Goin' pretty good. For me anyway." Cole took the front steps two at a time and walked into the cool shade of the living room. "Don't know that I can say the same for you. Heard you're leavin' us."

"Yeah, it's time. Want some coffee?"

"Nah. I've got a full schedule today, so I can't stay long."

Hobo came in from the kitchen, tail practically doing whirligigs when he recognized their visitor.

"Hey, guy." Cole knelt and sent the dog into spasms of joy with a quick but thorough rubdown. "You're the reason I stopped by." He raised his gaze quickly to Sam's. "Not that I didn't want to see you, too, pal."

"Yeah, yeah, that's what they all say." Sam smiled ruefully.

Cole stood and tugged at his ear. "Dogs in the city can be difficult, so I wanted to let you know that Hobo's more than welcome at the farm. We've already got a menagerie of spoiled animals there. One more? Just adds to the fun."

"I'll keep that in mind. We appreciate it, don't we, Hobo?"

The two men talked awhile longer about Sam's plans, things he still needed to take care of, and whether either the Yankees or the Braves had a chance at the World Series.

When Sam stood at the end of the drive with Hobo by his side and waved good-bye to Cole, he appreciated the friendship that had sprung up between them. He'd miss both Cole Bryson and his soon-to-be bride.

He didn't have long to ruminate on it, though.

Jeremy chugged up the street in his wreck of a car, and Sam sighed. He hadn't planned on him coming today. He'd figured Arlene would keep the kid close for a few more days. Maybe, though, she thought he should have a man in his life right now who wouldn't knock him down.

And yet wasn't that exactly what he'd do by leaving? Responsibility he didn't want lay heavily on Sam's shoulders. Hadn't he come here to get away? To grab some alone time? How had things gotten so complicated so quickly?

Why did his chest ache so badly every time he thought about Cricket, every time he glanced at her house?

"Hey, boss." Jeremy hopped from the car, a soda in hand. "Mom said it would be okay for me to come today." He kicked a clod of red Georgia clay. "Sorry for involvin' you in my mess."

"That's what friends do for each other, Jeremy. They help each other clear up the messes they make in their lives. Or messes others make in their lives."

"You my friend?" The teen raised his head, his long-overdue-for-a-cut hair falling in his eyes.

"I sure hope so, kid, 'cause I've still got a jumble of

trees and branches out back that I'm hoping you'll help me sort out."

Jeremy grinned. "Got my gloves right here. And my hat." He pulled them from his back pocket.

"Then let's get to it."

While they worked, Sam's mind worked feverishly. He had to find a way to break his news to Jeremy today. He couldn't take a chance on someone else spilling the beans.

He prayed Jeremy wouldn't see it as yet another man abandoning him.

Tossing a limb on the burn pile, he said, "It had to have been tough when your dad walked out on you and your mom."

"Yeah, it was, but we got through it." His jaw tightened. "Then he gets his girlfriend pregnant and comes crawlin' back. I'd have been so pissed if Mom had taken him back."

"Language," Sam chided.

The kid blushed, even his ears turning red. "Sorry."

"Your dad was a jerk. Still is. No two ways about it." Sam took a huge breath, then dove into the deep end. "Sometimes we make choices; other times, choices are made for us."

Jeremy stiffened. "You makin' excuses for him?"

Sam shook his head. "No, absolutely not. There is no excuse for what Ralph did." He peeled off his gloves and scrubbed his hands over his face. "Guess I'm trying to make one for myself."

"I don't understand." Jeremy frowned.

"I'm going back to New York the day after tomorrow."

For a few seconds, as Sam watched Jeremy's face

working, he thought the boy would cry, and panic battered at him. How would he handle that and save face for both of them?

Then Jeremy pulled himself together. "Why?"

A simple question.

It deserved a simple answer. A truthful one.

Sam went down the middle of the road. "I have to report back to work."

"Thought you could take as much time as you wanted."

"Yeah, well, like everything else, all good things come to an end. After tomorrow?" He spread his arms. "All this yard work? Hauling tree branches, trimming rosebushes, scraping wallpaper? I've got to give up all this fun."

"What are you gonna do with Hobo?"

"Cole offered to take him out to the farm."

"I could ask Mom if we could keep him."

"I'm not sure that would be fair," Sam said. "Your mom's having a hard enough time making ends meet." He'd known this would be hard, but it was turning out to be even harder than he'd suspected. He didn't want to go, and wasn't that a kick in the pants?

"How about I grab us some cold water?"

Jeremy nodded.

In the kitchen, Sam braced his hands on the sink's edge and looked out the window. Jeremy sat in the grass, hugging Hobo. The old dog licked tears from the boy's face. He was far too young to carry so much responsibility and worry on his shoulders.

As if life wasn't unfair enough, Sam had just landed another shot.

To give the teen a chance to pull himself together before he headed back outside, Sam raised the window. "I've got some cookies here. Want one?"

Hobo barked.

"Not you, idiot. I'm talking to your pal Jeremy."

The boy laughed.

Sam banged around another couple of minutes to give him time to get his face mopped up. Dignity was such an important commodity.

He tried, whenever possible, to allow the men and women he booked to keep as much of it as he could. He'd promised himself early in his career that he'd never use his position to belittle anyone.

The screen banged shut behind him.

"You know, I was thinking," he said as he loped down the back porch stairs. "Maybe next summer—if you keep your nose clean and do well in your classes so there's no summer school—I'll send you a plane ticket. You could fly up to the city and take in a Yankees game with me."

The kid tried to cover his excitement with sarcasm. "Yankees? Me?"

"Okay, okay." Sam held out a cookie and a water. "Maybe..." He hesitated. "Oh boy, it hurts to even say this, but maybe we can schedule it when the Mets are playing the Braves. I could wear a disguise so no one recognizes me."

Jeremy grinned. "You'd do that?"

"For you?" Sam's own smile faded. "Yeah, Jeremy, I would. You're okay—for a sixteen-year-old know-it-all."

Jeremy's grin grew till it covered his face. "Oh yeah? Well, for an old fart, you're not too bad, either."

Sam reached out and grabbed the kid's ball cap, tugging it down over his eyes.

Jeremy laughed, and Hobo, sensing playtime, ran in circles around the two, yipping and barking.

"Can we go to the Statue of Liberty?"

"Yep. We'll take a ferry out to it and to Ellis Island."

"Can I ride the elevator to the top of the Empire State Building?"

"You bet. And we'll eat pizza at a little place close to there. It's so good, it'll make you cry."

"Deal!" Jeremy held out his hand and Sam shook it.

That, he swore, was one promise he meant to keep.

Chapter 29

Sam tied up the last of his loose ends and locked the front door. He'd call a realtor once he hit the city.

Cricket remained elusive. More times than he cared to admit, he'd headed to her shop only to turn around and come back home. She'd made her feelings very clear. If she'd had a change of heart, she'd have let him know. She hadn't.

Hands in his pockets, he stood on the walk and analyzed the old house. She still needed work, but she was a far cry from where she'd been when he'd pulled up out front that first night. It would be nice for the house to have a family live in it. Love it.

The thought of not spending another night here, of never sitting on the back porch in that old rocker, no more fires or s'mores, saddened him. Worse, there'd be no more dancing in the moonlight with Cricket.

Hell. He hadn't meant to get attached to the place. But he had. Still, he'd survive.

Wouldn't he?

He turned to look at Cricket's house, at the wisteria trailing along the porch. The drive was empty.

And then there was Hobo.

The old dog sighed and leaned into Sam, the ice-blue eyes lifting to meet his.

The decision—if there ever had been one to make—was finalized. Even though Cole had offered him a good home, Sam couldn't leave the dog. He'd gotten used to having him around. Grown used to his quiet snoring and unquestioning loyalty.

But how in the hell would he get him back to New York City? He couldn't strap him to the back of the Harley like an old suitcase.

His shoulders sagged. Though it went against everything in him, he'd load his motorcycle into the back of the old rust bucket and drive Lem's truck from Georgia to New York. *The Grapes of Wrath* lived again.

Half an hour later, Hobo riding shotgun, the bike strapped securely in the back of the truck along with Sam's few possessions, they hit the road.

Devastated, Cricket sat in Sam's old rocker. She was probably trespassing at this point, but who cared? If Jimmy Don showed up, she'd tell him Sam had asked her to check on the old house.

He hadn't. They'd not spoken a word since she'd told him they were over. She'd put a good face on it at work, but truth? She couldn't eat, couldn't sleep. She'd never been so totally miserable in her life.

She missed Sam DeLuca.

For a short piece of time, the old house had been happy again. Now it looked as forlorn as she felt. Empty house, empty heart.

Talk around town said Sam was returning to New York. She'd left for work that morning praying he'd have a change of heart, that he wouldn't leave.

Some prayers went unanswered.

Tommy at the Texaco said he'd fueled Sam's old

truck earlier that day. He'd had the Harley in the back and Hobo in the front seat. Sam had left Misty Bottoms and taken her heart with him.

But despite what she'd expected, he'd taken Hobo along. He hadn't dropped him off at Cole's. And that, in and of itself, said something. She wondered how the sweet animal would handle city life. She'd miss having him bang on her screen door. She'd miss his visits…and his owner's.

She rose and headed to her own empty house. Maybe she'd pay her aunt and uncle a visit. It had been a while.

Behind her, the rocker continued to sway, as though Sam sat in it still.

~

A cup of hot coffee in hand, the radio on, and the miles flying by, Sam contemplated his life in Misty Bottoms for the past weeks.

He let his mind wander to New York City and the life he was heading back to.

His family, yes. But also dawn-to-well-into-the-night days. A twelve-hour shift wasn't unusual. When he worked undercover? It might be days, even weeks before he got home. It was what he loved, though, wasn't it?

A wife? Kids? No way. Neither was compatible with his job.

He took a sip of his coffee and rolled down the window. Hobo raised his head as humid, hot air poured into the cab. Sniffing, he started toward Sam.

"Nope, stay on your side, bud." The dog lay back down, staring at him. "I need some fresh air."

In truth, he felt slightly claustrophobic, like the cab

of the truck was closing in on him. He loved his job and valued the detective's shield he'd busted his butt to earn, but were they enough?

He'd always thought so. Lately, he'd begun to have doubts. Ingrid, Federoff, Gertie, Cricket—they'd all played a part in his new restlessness. They'd forced him to think about his future. About who he really was and what he wanted.

They made him think about what truly made him feel alive and happy.

Wasn't he headed there? To New York City and home.

He didn't make it.

By the time he'd passed Charleston's city limits, he understood the trip was a fool's errand.

Hobo sprawled on the seat, half-asleep. The radio played a country station of all things. One of Cricket's favorite songs, Chris Young's "Who I Am With You," came on. As Sam sang along with it, he paid close attention to the lyrics.

Well, hell. Who was he kidding? He *was* a better man when he was with Cricket, and, yeah, she was so, so good for him. He hadn't known it, but she was exactly what he'd been looking for when he'd left the city and headed south.

Why hadn't he realized it sooner?

He hadn't been able to leave Hobo behind. He sure as hell couldn't live without Bug. Something inside him, something he'd been certain had died in that alley, had reawakened because of Cricket. She'd brought him back to life.

He wanted to give her that white picket fence, those two point five kids, and…whew…her happy ever after.

Yeah, he was Yankee and she was Dixie to her toes, but he thought they had a chance.

Right there, in the middle of I-95, he pulled a U-turn, churning the old truck through the grassy median.

Not ten seconds later, he heard the siren. Glancing in his rearview mirror, he groaned, put on his turn signal, and pulled over.

Shit! Really bad timing.

"Nothing's easy, Hobo, is it?" Even as he spoke to the dog, he shifted his weight and pulled his wallet from his back pocket. Driver's license, registration, and insurance card in hand, he rolled down his window.

"Hello, Officer."

The state patrolman nodded and took his cards. "Samuel DeLuca. So what's your hurry?"

"I realized I left something really important behind in Misty Bottoms."

"And what would that be?"

"The woman I love."

The trooper's head came up. "Oh yeah?"

"Yeah." Sam shook his head. "I was a fool."

The patrolman pointed at the wallet on Sam's lap. "That a gold badge? You a detective?"

"Yeah, New York City. Narcotics."

"You're a long way from home, Detective DeLuca. You workin' the job?"

Sam sighed. "I'm on leave. Took a bullet."

The trooper's eyes widened. "No shit?"

"No shit. Take it from me, Trooper, it's not as glamorous as TV makes it out to be. Avoid flying bullets."

"My wife tells me that every time I leave for my shift. Speaking of wives, is that who you left behind?"

"Not yet, but I hope she will be."

"That where you were headed when you tore up our grass?"

"Yes."

"You're gonna pop the question?"

Sam grinned. "I am. As soon as I'm done here."

"Got a ring yet?"

"A ring?" Oh boy. "No, I don't."

"Instead of a ticket, then, I'm gonna give you some advice. You're goin' back to Misty Bottoms?"

He nodded.

"My uncle, Cappy Buchanon, has a little jewelry store there. You stop in and tell him I sent you. He'll do right by you, Detective. Drive safe now."

Chapter 30

Before he talked to Cricket, Sam had a few stops to make. The first? The small, old-fashioned police station. If Jimmy Don was there, Sam was going to be very surprised. He might be able to track him down at the diner, though, or at Kitty's.

"Stay here, boy." Sam rolled the window down a few more cranks, and the dog immediately stuck his nose out the opening. "I'll be right back."

Sam hopped from the old truck, stuck a dime in the parking meter, and hurried into the station. Now that he'd made up his mind, he was in a rush to get everything settled and get Cricket back in his arms. He could only pray she'd still have him, that he hadn't screwed things up permanently.

The door creaked when he opened it.

"Thought you left town." Jimmy Don dropped a file folder on his cluttered metal desk.

"I did. I made it as far as Charleston before I turned around." Sam stood in the doorway, staring at the pine board floor.

"Couldn't leave her, could you?"

His head jerked up sharply. "What?"

"You're crazy in love with the O'Malley girl. Anybody with half a brain could see that."

Sam shrugged. "Guess I've been operating on less than that then." His gaze met the sheriff's and held. "I didn't know."

"Didn't *want* to know would be my guess."

"Maybe." Sam hooked his thumbs in his jeans pockets. "Thing is, I need a job if I intend to support a family."

Jimmy Don's face nearly split in half with the smile. "She said yes?"

"I haven't asked her yet."

The sheriff nodded. "Gettin' those ducks in a row first, are you?"

"Yep. So that job offer you made a while back. Is it still on the table?"

"You bet. Still haven't found anyone qualified to take Tyrell's place."

"When can I start?"

Jimmy Don laughed. "You in a hurry?"

He nodded.

"Will tomorrow give you time to propose—properly—to Cricket?"

A slow smile crossed his face. "It should, but she might take some convincin'."

Jimmy Don rubbed a hand over his chin. "Why don't we say noon then. Who knows? You might not get much sleep tonight."

Sam shrugged.

"Go on. Get out of here, and get it done. See you tomorrow, Officer DeLuca."

"Thanks." He shook the sheriff's hand, then headed out the door to his future—if Cricket would have him. He'd hurt her. If he was lucky, he'd get to spend the rest of his life making it up to her.

Sliding behind the pickup's steering wheel, he said, "Check one, Hobo. I am now officially on the payroll of the Misty Bottoms, Georgia, Police Department. I'll email my resignation to my New York captain tonight."

He held out his hand, and Hobo placed his paw in it for a shake.

"We're not done yet, though. Still lots to do."

Catching Sam's excitement, the dog turned a couple circles, barking excitedly. Worn out, he dropped back onto the seat.

"You done?"

Hobo gave a small whine.

"Then let's go."

Sam pulled out and drove to Kitty's Kakes. Let Liddell give Cricket flowers. He'd give her a pecan sticky roll! Guess that showed who really knew her.

The bell over the door tinkled.

"Sam DeLuca, what are you doin' here?"

"Buying some of your pastries."

"That's not what I mean and you know it. Thought you'd headed back to the Big Apple."

"I did. Then I came to my senses and turned around."

Her face burst into a smile. "Town grows on you, doesn't it?"

"It does."

"Our florist does, too."

He grinned. "Yes, ma'am, she certainly does."

"You gonna pop the question?"

"This evening."

Kitty squealed and clapped her hands.

"Don't you say anything to anybody, you hear me? I need it to be a surprise."

She drew a finger across her lips, turned the invisible key, and tossed it away. "They're sealed."

"Great. I thought maybe you could help me. I need one of those pecan sticky rolls Cricket's so fond of."

"I just happen to have one."

"Don't suppose you could put it in a box instead of one of your little bags?"

"I could. Any special reason?"

"I plan to tuck something special in that roll before I give it to her."

Kitty's eyes sparkled. "You're usin' my pecan roll to surprise her with the ring?"

"If you put it in a box for me, I am."

She clapped her hands again. "I've got a pink, heart-shaped box in the back. It's the prettiest little thing with sparkles on it and all. One of the salespeople gave it to me thinkin' I might want to order them for Valentine's Day. Give me two shakes of a lamb's tail."

She disappeared into the storeroom.

Since Sam had no idea how long it took a lamb to shake its tail twice, he wandered behind the counter and poured himself a to-go cup of rich, black coffee.

He sniffed it. Oh yeah, he needed this. It had been a long day. He'd been up early to finish things at the house and load the Harley. Then he and Hobo had hit the road. Two hours running away and two hours scurrying back, with a little extra time tossed in there for doggy breaks at roadside rest areas.

Kitty appeared, beaming, the heart box held high in the air. "Found it. Isn't it beautiful?"

It was.

"You're dead-on with that one, Kitty. Toss a pecan roll in there and wish me luck. Hopefully, I'll have some good news to announce tomorrow."

She pulled out the tray and selected the biggest sticky roll. Lining the box with waxed paper, she positioned the roll in the center and closed the lid. "There you go. I tucked a whole lot of love inside."

He leaned across the counter and gave her a kiss smack on the lips. Her cheeks turned pinker than the box.

"You sure do smell good, Sam DeLuca."

"Thank you, Miss Kitty. And after tonight? I'll be *Officer* DeLuca. Jimmy Don hired me."

"You're gonna stay here?"

He nodded.

"Oh, thank the Lord. I was happy and all about you and Cricket, but I sure would hate to lose that girl."

"You're not going to. If—and that's still a fairly large if—I can get Cricket to say yes."

"Oh, she will. I've known Beck and his mama and daddy for as long as I can remember. Not a one of them is a dummy. Since they're Cricket's people, she's no dummy, either. No way she's gonna pass up a man like you. Smart, hard-workin', and sexy." She winked at him.

"Kitty, I do love you. Right now, though, I've got to run."

"Do this right."

"I'm sure going to try."

"Here." She reached for his cup. "Let me top that off. You look like you need it."

"Thank you, ma'am."

She snapped the lid back on and handed him the refilled coffee. "Now go. Get out of here. We both have a lot to do."

Laughing, believing he had a real shot at this, he left.

Next stop? Cappy's, to buy something he'd had no intention of ever purchasing.

He drove past the jewelry shop twice before he spotted it. The small brick storefront had an inconspicuous sign above the door, its gold lettering nearly worn off. Sweat trickled down Sam's back as he opened the door and walked in. Another of those damn tinkling bells announced his presence to the salesman.

The idea of selecting a ring proved more daunting than he'd have believed. This might be the single most important purchase of his life. If he was a lucky man, Cricket would wear it for the rest of their lives.

Of course, if she hated it, she could always exchange it, couldn't she?

For some reason, though, that kind of bothered him. Maybe he was more macho than he'd thought, but he liked the idea of his wife wearing the ring he'd chosen.

Just inside the door, he stopped, his first instinct to turn around and leave. Cappy's couldn't possibly have what he wanted.

"Hey, young fellow." The jeweler started toward him, hand extended. "I'm Cappy Buchanon, owner of this shop for the last thirty-six years."

Sam took the hand in his, surprised at the firmness of the jeweler's grasp. "Sam DeLuca."

"Ahh, yes. The detective from New York City. Gertie Taylor's nephew."

Sam nodded. Oh yeah. No secrets in small towns, he reminded himself, and no need to ask for help. Somebody would always step up before he needed to ask. This would be his life. He grinned again, feeling a little like an idiot. He'd grinned more in the last hour than he had in the last year.

"Lookin' for somethin' special?"

"I am. Trooper Buchanon suggested I come see you."

"Andy's a good kid."

"He is that."

"What can I help you with?"

"I need an engagement ring for a very special lady."

"Wonderful. Engagement rings are my favorite sales. They're so happy, aren't they?"

"I guess so. If she says yes."

Cappy looked crestfallen. "You think she might not?"

Sam shrugged. "With a woman? Who knows?"

"Oh. Well." For the space of a heartbeat, Cappy seemed at a loss. Then he put on his salesman's hat and got to work. "Do you have any idea what kind you'd like?"

He walked Sam to a small display case. Two trays of wedding and engagement rings stared up at him, glittering under bright LED lights.

"Clueless." Sam spread his hands. "Up until a few hours ago, I hadn't given a single thought to doing this."

"Honestly?"

"Honestly."

Cappy studied him and seemed to see right into his soul. "Detective DeLuca, if you don't mind my saying so, I think this will turn out to be the best decision of your life."

"I agree, Cappy. Now, what do I need to know here?"

"The most important things to keep in mind are your tastes, both yours and your future fiancée's, what the ring represents to you as a couple, and, of course, your budget. I probably should have my tongue cut out for sayin' this, but a lot of guys spend far more than they can afford in order to impress their ladies. Not a good idea."

Sam laughed. "You're right. As a jewelry store owner, that's probably not the best sales pitch, but as a person? Kudos to you."

Cappy smiled. "Thank you. Now, that said, you'll want to keep in mind the four *C*'s."

"Carat, cut, clarity, and color," Sam interjected. "I have four sisters."

"Then you've been through this before."

"Only as a bystander who tried to pay as little attention as possible."

"Let's start with color. You can actually find diamonds in nearly every color. Colored diamonds are called fancies and can be pretty pricey. I don't carry any, so I'm afraid if you want a pink or yellow or black diamond, you'll have to go to Savannah."

"Nope. I don't need a color."

"Then you want the whitest one you can afford."

"Okay. What else?"

"The carat weight."

Sam shook his head. "You know, I'll just wait till I see what I want to decide on that."

"Fair enough. You'll probably want a round brilliant cut. They sparkle more than the others. More facets equal more bling. The clarity adds to that, too."

"Got it. How about shape?"

Cappy crooked a finger. "Let me show you." He opened the case and took out both of the display boxes. One at a time, he showed the rings to Sam. "Most are pretty self-explanatory. Oval."

Sam examined it and handed it back.

"Pear. Emerald. Round brilliant. Marquise. See the smaller, straight, tapered stones around this round brilliant?"

Sam nodded.

"They're baguettes."

"Like the bread."

"Exactly," Cappy said. "Set beside a center stone, they give it a little more zip. We don't carry much stock, but I try to have at least one of every shape."

"That's smart."

"Then there's the band itself. Gold, white gold, or platinum. I don't carry any platinum, though. Too expensive for most Misty Bottomers."

"Okay." Sam blew out his breath. "Nothing's simple, is it?"

"Nope."

"I think white gold for the band."

"Good choice." Cappy slid the tray of yellow gold rings back into the display case. "So, we've narrowed it down."

Frustrated, Sam studied the remaining rings. He didn't see the one. That right *one*.

"Tell me about your intended," Cappy said. "What's she like?"

Sam closed his eyes. How did he encapsulate Cricket in mere words? "She leans toward vintage and whimsy, in her clothes, in her home, and in her shop."

"Her shop?"

"She owns the Enchanted Florist."

"Beck's cousin, Cricket O'Malley."

Sam laughed. "That's her."

"She's beautiful. And full of life and sparkle."

"She is."

"Maybe this is what you need." Cappy walked to another section and opened a new case. He reached in and withdrew a single ring.

Cricket's ring.

Sam took it almost reverently. "What is this?"

"A 2.64-carat gray sapphire. It was mined in Montana. On either side you have diamond baguettes. Nice clarity on them."

"It's her. It's Cricket with the storm-cloud-gray eyes. That touch of eccentricity." Sam lifted his gaze to the jeweler's. "Cappy, you've done it."

"You haven't heard the price yet. Gray sapphires aren't cheap."

"It doesn't matter."

Cappy glanced out the window at the old rusty truck with the dog hanging out the window, and Sam laughed.

"You know what they say, Cappy. Don't judge a book by its cover."

Cappy scratched his head. "Actually, I'd say that Harley's a pretty expensive book."

Sam nodded. "It is."

"And the truck? That's Lem Gilmore's old one, isn't it?"

"Yes, it is."

"And you're the young man I've heard Dee-Ann talkin' about. That old coot's had you runnin' him to the dump on Tuesdays."

"Every single Tuesday since I bought it."

"You're quality, Sam, and I believe Ms. Cricket knows that." The jeweler scratched his head. "Like I said, that ring's kind of expensive. The wife wasn't happy with me for buyin' it, limited customers and all. But I don't know. I almost felt compelled to bring it home."

"I can only say thank you." Sam picked up the ring again. "It's the one."

"I believe it is."

Relieved, Sam reached for his wallet and took out a credit card. He'd been afraid he wouldn't be able to pull the trigger. But he had. He'd made his choice. In both a wife and a ring.

A wife.

He'd walked into the store sweating buckets and blaming it on the hot, sticky Low Country weather. Yet when he left the store, the purchase tucked safely in his pocket, not an ounce of nerve was left. He whistled as he walked back to the well-used, weather-beaten truck.

Hobo spotted him, stood, front paws on the edge of the partially opened window, tail wagging.

Hand on the door handle, Sam waved as Beck slid his truck in behind Sam's.

"Thought you left town."

"I changed my mind." Sam braced for a battle.

"Why'd you come back?"

"For your cousin, if she'll have me." Sam pulled the jeweler's box from his pocket and opened it.

"Well, son of a..." Beck grinned. "You finally came to your senses."

"I did."

Beck slapped him on the back. "Good for you. But I'm warnin' you here and now. Do not make Cricket unhappy ever again, or you'll answer to me."

"Understood."

Beck nodded at the gray sapphire. "That's the perfect ring for Cricket."

"It is."

A short brunette hurried toward them, and Sam stuffed the ring back into his pocket.

"Hey, Beck."

"Lucinda, how are you?" Beck nodded toward Sam. "Sam DeLuca, Lucinda Worthington. Lucinda runs the preschool here in town."

"Nice to meet you."

"You too." Lucinda turned to Beck. "Guess you've heard the news by now, huh?"

Beck looked at Sam, who held his hands up in an I-know-nothing gesture.

"What news?"

"Tansy enrolled her little Gracie today. She's comin' home. Isn't that wonderful?"

"Wonderful?" Beck snarled.

"I thought, well, that maybe the two of you—"

"When hell freezes over!" Beck stalked back to his truck and jerked the door open. "Good luck, Sam."

He whipped out of the parking space and tore down the street.

"Oh my." Lucinda stared after him.

"Yeah, oh my," Sam repeated. Had he ever really thought Misty Bottoms a quiet little town?

Chapter 31

Cricket's house showed no sign of life when Sam, finished with all his stops, drove down Frog Pond Road. Good. It would give him a little more time. He parked the truck around back and unloaded the Harley.

He hoped Beck had settled down. He'd give him a call later. Right now, he needed to get ready for Cricket and pray she'd forgive him.

The first thing he did was turn on the water and hot water tank. He'd shut both off this morning before he left, but now, after today's drive and all the running around he'd done, he wanted another shower.

Checking the linen closet, he found clean sheets and made the bed. A man could always hope to get lucky. After a marriage proposal? His system went on overload, and he wondered if maybe he shouldn't take yet another shower.

Champagne chilled in the fridge and a sticky bun with an engagement ring sticking out of it sat on the counter.

Nerves set in.

He checked out the window for the umpteenth time, but she still wasn't home.

With nothing else to do, he found himself rattling around the house, upstairs, downstairs, to the kitchen, to the living room, and back. Finally, he popped the top on a soft drink and enjoyed the setting sun on the back porch. He swore he could smell Cricket, that wildflower scent that was uniquely hers.

Hobo decided it was nap time, and he joined Sam on the porch. Every once in a while, his body would jerk or his tail would thump. Doggy dreaming.

Soda gone, he looked at his watch again. She should be home soon. He checked the truck again to make sure it wasn't visible from the road.

He was inside when he heard her coming.

From the window, he watched Cricket park, gather her purse, and start toward the house. When she turned to look across the street, Sam backed up, finger across his lips to silence Hobo. He swore the dog nodded in understanding. He'd missed their neighbor, too.

It had been three days since they'd visited. Since she and Sam had talked. Since he'd held her, tasted her. It felt like a lifetime.

"Come on, come on," Sam whispered as Cricket stopped to pinch some dead blossoms off the potted plants on her porch. When she dropped onto one of the brightly painted rockers on her porch, he groaned.

He was on a mission, and she was throwing his timing off.

Finally, she opened the front door and disappeared inside. He swore. She hadn't locked up again.

He gave her ten minutes, then sat on the sofa and called the dog to him. "Okay, mutt, here's where you earn your dinner."

Fumbling in his pocket, he pulled out the note he'd written. Maybe he should copy it onto fancier paper. Except he didn't have any fancy paper, no fairies, no hearts-and-flowers paper.

He did have a heart and a ring, though, if she'd give him a chance to offer them to her.

This was the tricky part. He'd run it over and over in his mind. Dropping the note into a small paper bag, he threaded the only thing he'd been able to find, an old wire twist tie from a bread wrapper, through the bag, then secured it to the buckle on Hobo's collar.

Gently, he cupped the dog's muzzle in his hand. "You've got a little gray showing, fellow. It looks good on you."

The dog's tongue flicked out for a quick kiss.

"We talked about this. You know what you're supposed to do?"

Hobo barked in answer.

"Okay, boy, off you go."

Opening the screen door, he watched Hobo leap down the stairs and head across the street.

Now, he waited.

Cricket turned on a single lamp and curled up in a corner of her couch. She wanted to cry but had promised herself she'd finished with that. Hadn't she cried the last two nights away? Hadn't she cried this morning in the shower and again at lunch as she ate a sandwich out behind her shop?

His house was dark. No Sam, no Hobo, no rusty old truck or Harley. It should have rained today. She'd wanted it to. A nice, dreary gray day to match her mood.

No such luck. The weather had been amazing. It had been sunny and bright and really hot. She opened the window beside her and felt what could pass for a cool breeze. The light cotton of her skirt fluttered.

Moving into the kitchen, she grabbed a glass of filtered water from the fridge, then went to open the window above the sink. As she turned to go back to the living room, she thought she caught sight of something crossing the street. An animal? What lived out here? Foxes? Coyotes?

She stood on her tiptoes and peered out the window.

Hobo!

Had Sam left him behind after all? Left him here alone to starve? Could the Sam she'd come to know—and, yes, love—do that?

No, Tommy had said Hobo was with Sam.

Running to the screen door, she heard the first bang against it. Hobo's calling card.

"Baby, what are you doin' here?" She knelt and cradled the dog in her arms. "I thought you left me too." Burying her face in his fur, the tears, despite her promises to herself, started again.

As she ran her fingers through his hair, something crinkled. Pulling back, she saw the brown paper bag. "What's this, guy? Huh?" She stood and moved to the rocker. "Come here, Hobo." She patted her leg, and the dog obediently trotted over to her.

Carefully, she untwisted the tie and removed both it and the bag from the dog's collar. Something tinkled when she did, and she saw Sam had taken the time to get a license and ID tag for Hobo, one with his name inscribed on it. Owner: Sam DeLuca.

"So why are you still here? Why aren't you with him?" She swiped away a stray tear.

Opening the bag, she pulled out the scrap of paper inside.

What are you doing tonight?

Her head jerked up and she stared at the house across the street. A light switched on in the front room.

"Oh my gosh." Her hand moved to cover her racing heart. "Is he here, Hobo? Is Sam here?"

The dog barked and started prancing around the porch as though impatient to get this done.

A bubble of laughter mixed with Cricket's tears.

"I think this note deserves an answer, don't you?"

Hobo barked again and followed her inside.

Digging in her junk drawer, she found a pen. A pink pen. Oh well. She was a pink girl—and her guy had returned. She felt almost light-headed.

Flipping the note over, she wrote her reply, then stuffed it back in the bag.

"Before I send you back with this, you deserve a treat. Yes, you do."

Hobo, understanding the word *treat*, practically danced to the pantry.

She opened the door and offered him one of the biscuits he loved.

When he hesitated, she said, "Sit, boy, and enjoy your treat. After what he's put me through, Sam can wait a little longer."

The dog dropped onto the floor, the biscuit held daintily between his paws. Three gulps, though, and it was history.

"Didn't he feed you yet? Huh?" She cocked her head. "What exactly did you two do today?"

The dog's ears perked up, and he put a paw on Cricket's leg.

"Yeah, yeah, you'd tell me if you could, but your master swore you to secrecy. I understand."

Hobo rubbed against her, and she knelt to hook her return message to his collar.

What was taking so long? Sam had about worn a hole in the living room rug. He'd expected something sooner than this. But what? Had he really thought he'd look out the window to see Cricket running across the road to welcome him with open arms and no questions asked after the way he'd behaved?

He wasn't really that naive, was he?

Yes, he was. Although it shamed him to admit it, that's exactly what he'd expected. What he'd hoped for.

It hadn't happened.

But why hadn't Hobo returned? Maybe she intended to hold his dog hostage until he issued her compensation for his past sins.

Should he walk over? Show up at her door and pray she didn't kick him off the porch?

Standing by the window, he jammed his hands in his pockets and rocked back and forth on his heels. He didn't wait well, was too impatient. Too many hours spent doing surveillance, too many nights sitting in a cold car waiting for what came next had worn him down.

He didn't want that life anymore. He wanted to clock out and come home—to Cricket. To a settled life. To her love. He sighed. What would he do if she didn't want the same thing or didn't want it with him?

If it came to that, he'd pull out whatever patience he still had, and he'd wait. He'd accept Jimmy Don's job and become a small town Southern lawman and bide his time. Despite his impatience, he'd hang around till Cricket changed her mind.

Her front door opened, and Hobo stepped out. The dog turned his head back inside as though listening to directions. A small hand reached around the door frame and patted the dog's head.

"Lucky dog," Sam growled.

And then his dog made a beeline toward him. Sam did a fist pump when he saw the paper bag reattached to the collar. Yes! At least she'd answered him.

He opened the door, and the dog bounded in, yipping and yapping and dancing around Sam's feet.

"What? You're lording it over me because you got to spend time with Cricket and I didn't? Hmmm? Is that what this is?" He knelt. "Slow down. Sit, Hobo. Let me get this off you."

His fingers trembled as he undid the tie and withdrew the note from the bag. Sending up a hopeful prayer, he unfolded the now rumpled paper.

Written on the back of his scrawled *What are you doing tonight?* she'd written her answer in pink, girly ink.

Waiting for you.

Sam's reaction was instant and very physical. Wow!

He looked around, at all the work that still needed to be done in the house. He'd thought to leave it to the new owners. Now?

He'd do it himself, because he wanted to raise a family here. With Cricket.

~

She met him in the yard.

As she tucked a strand of pale silk behind her ear, he caught sight of the jewel that winked there. It reminded him of another on her body, of the last night they'd spent in bed.

He wanted her so badly he ached. But he wanted even more than that.

He ran a finger over the earring. "I've been fantasizing about seeing that belly button jewel again."

His fingers traced over her neck, her shoulder, and down her arm. "This hand. So delicate. So strong. And you have me right here in the palm of it. Tell me what you want, Cricket." His voice grew husky; his heart hammered.

Her eyes met his, yet no words came.

After what he could have sworn was several lifetimes, she said, "You. I want you."

"I'm a risky deal."

"No, you're not, Sam. You're a good man with a great heart and wonderful values."

"I'm a man who's in love with you." He remembered her words from before. "I love you beyond reason. Beyond all else."

"Oh, Sam."

"Tell me you love me back, Cricket."

"I do. I love you so much. I've missed you."

He stepped to her, and their lips met.

When Sam pulled back, he whispered, "Why don't we go see Jenni Beth about a wedding?"

"Are you—"

"Yes, I'm asking." He dropped to one knee, right there in her front yard. "Cricket O'Malley, would you do me the honor of putting up with me for the rest of my life? Of being my wife, having my babies?"

She threw her arms around his neck.

Caught off balance, he toppled back into the grass. She went with him. Sprawled over him, she laughed, then kissed him once, twice.

He cupped her face with one hand. "Stay with me forever."

She kissed him again.

He handed her the heart-shaped box he held in his free hand. "Thought you might be hungry."

"Hungry?" She frowned at him. "Now?"

"Go ahead. Open it."

She did. A smile spread over her face. "A pecan sticky bun. I love these things. Not as much as I love you, but they sure do come in a close second."

"Speaking of close," Sam said. "Look at that roll a little closer."

Her mouth dropped open, and she let out a squeal he was certain the neighbors a mile down the road must surely have heard. He'd be surprised if Jimmy Don didn't come rolling up in his squad car in the next few minutes.

"Oh my God! I've never seen anything like this. It's absolutely perfect."

"It's a gray sapphire. The baguettes, though, are diamonds. If you don't like it—"

She silenced him by kissing him silly.

When she rested her head on his chest, he said, "I hope it fits."

"Let's see." She plucked the ring out of the pastry, and Sam took a napkin from his back pocket and handed it to her.

"Might be a little sticky."

"I don't care." She thrust her left hand at him. "Put it on, please. I want you to do it."

"Does this mean you're saying yes?"

"Am I ever! You just try to get rid of me, Sam DeLuca."

The ring slid on easily, and he drew her to him and kissed her, a kiss that promised forever. Hobo danced around them, barking and sharing the moment.

For an unexpected proposal, it had gone exactly right.

Keep reading for an excerpt from the next book in the Magnolia Brides series

Picture Perfect Wedding

In a perfect world or, heck, even in a movie, music would play softly in the background. The SUV's windows would be down, her auburn hair blowing softly in the breeze. Her hero would wait at the road's end, arms open and welcoming.

They'd kiss...

Tansy Calhoun Forbes's cell rang, and, startled, she glanced in the rearview mirror. Gracie, her four-year-old daughter, slept soundly, a welcome respite from today's endless are-we-there-yets.

"Hello?" Tansy practically whispered.

"You unpacked yet?" Jenni Beth Beaumont, her best friend forever, sounded stressed.

"Still a few miles from town, but almost there."

"Good. Great. Listen, I know this has been a stressful day, heck, a stressful year, and you're tired..."

Tansy smiled. She could practically see her friend squirming. "What do you need, Jenni Beth?"

"Oh, Tanz, I have two weddings and a sixteenth birthday party coming up this week. Magnolia Brides is booked solid for the next nine months—my dream come true—but I'm dying here! I need cakes. Phenomenal cakes. Your cakes!"

"I don't have—"

"Kitty said you can use the bakery's kitchen."

Tansy sighed and ran her fingers through her already mussed hair.

"I know, I know." Jenni Beth's tension vibrated over the airwaves. "I'm putting you on the spot. Big time. I'm a horrible person. An even worse friend."

"No, you're not." Determined, Tansy sat up a little straighter. "This is exactly what I've insisted I want. Part of the reason I'm on my way home. Color me stupid, but I'm in."

Her friend let out a quiet squeal. "Kitty has all the details. Colors, design ideas, size, but if you have any questions—"

Tansy laughed. "I'll call."

As the city-limits sign loomed, she hung up and removed her dark glasses. Misty Bottoms, Georgia. The Low Country. Even slowing to a crawl didn't stop the inevitable.

Home, sweet home.

Right back at the starting gate.

Waiting for her? No music, no hero, and no kiss.

And no one but herself to blame.

Tansy pushed her sunglasses back in place and glared at the brilliant sunshine that bathed the beyond-gorgeous autumn day. The humidity had dropped, and a few white clouds drifted high in the bluebird sky. Shouldn't it be raining, the sky dark with ominous thunderheads?

Divorced for fifty-three days, five hours, and—she checked the dashboard clock—six minutes, and here she was, hell-bent on creating the cake for a bride's special day.

She'd had her own shot at the dream and lost—because the wrong groom had stood beside her at the altar.

A self-absorbed, compulsive gambler, her ex had lost their house along with all their savings and investments. She'd supported Emerson through multiple rounds of rehab because he was her daughter's father, but when two goons showed up at the front door demanding her jewelry for money owed, her first call had been to the police, the second to her attorney. At that moment, Emerson Forbes became nothing more than a footnote in her life.

In the blink of an eye, she'd gone from a forty-five-hundred-square-foot home to her SUV and the contents of a few suitcases and boxes. All without a single regret because, from her perspective, she'd drawn the Golden Ticket. She'd left the marriage with Gracie Bella, her daughter.

The wedding and engagement rings, the for-show-only anniversary necklace and earrings she'd refused to hand over to the goons? After her first-ever trip to a pawn shop, the jewelry had financed her and Gracie's move and given her some essential seed money.

For the next little bit, she and Gracie would stay with her mom. Since Tansy's dad's death almost five years ago, her mother had been lonely. She'd provide a haven for Tansy and her daughter, and they'd fill a void for her. A temporary one. Tansy intended to start searching for a place of her own right away. Till she found something and the movers delivered the few things she'd stored, she and Gracie would live out of their suitcases.

Walking out of her supersized house this morning had been confusing. She'd expected a huge weight to lift, and it had. Still, that was the house she'd brought Gracie home to when she'd been born. Where her first four birthdays had been celebrated. Christmases and Thanksgivings.

And so much unhappiness and deceit.

Tansy massaged her temples where a screaming headache had taken up residence. How long since she'd had a decent night's sleep or a good meal? Driving one-handed, she rooted around on the passenger seat with the other till she found a bag of almonds. Maybe some protein would give her a boost.

A building off to her right caught her attention and caused a hitch in her heart. Elliot Construction and Lumberyard. She tossed the almonds aside untouched, any semblance of appetite deserting her.

Beck Elliot, the groom behind door number one, the door she hadn't chosen.

Oh boy. She rested a hand on her stomach. Was she making another mistake? Should she have started over somewhere else?

Ding, ding, ding. The low-fuel indicator chimed, and the little red light blinked on. Shoot! She'd meant to get fuel a while ago, but Gracie had been sleeping so soundly she'd hesitated to take a chance on waking her. Gracie was the sweetest, easiest-going child on Earth, but one more question, no matter how innocent, might be enough to send Tansy over the edge. She felt totally wrung out. From the move, the emotions and uncertainty of the past months.

"Months?" she whispered. "Oh, Tansy Calhoun Forbes, you are still lyin'. Nothing's been right for years. At least be honest with yourself!"

Tommy's Texaco loomed.

Relieved, she flipped on her turn signal, veered into the lot, and pulled up to the gas pump.

And there it sat.

A big red truck with *Elliot Construction* written on the side.

The door to the gas station opened, and Beck Elliot, looking hotter than any man had a right to in dusty jeans, a faded T-shirt, and old work boots, stepped outside.

He tore the wrapper off a candy bar and took a bite.

Then his intense midnight-blue eyes met hers. The chill had her rubbing her arms even though the temperature read seventy-five in the shade.

As she got out, her gaze collided with Beck's again.

His eyes radiated resentment and betrayed hopes.

Hers? She figured they held remorse, hurt, and impossible-to-deny desire.

Beck nearly choked on the bite of chocolate. *What the hell?*

He tossed the bar into the trash barrel outside the door.

Months ago he'd heard rumblings that Tansy'd enrolled her daughter in the local preschool, but since no one had said anything else about it, he'd figured she'd changed her mind. That fancy SUV of hers was loaded to the roof, though—way more than she'd need for a quick visit.

His chest constricted, and he swore under his breath. Why would she return to Misty Bottoms? She looked like one of those emaciated French models in the magazines his mom read. A good strong wind off the coast would blow her from here to Atlanta.

The strong, carefree Tansy he'd known had disappeared. She'd become… He didn't know. *Ethereal* came to mind.

Not his business—and she'd be the first to tell him that.

"Hey, Beck," Tommy said. "Got your truck filled for ya."

"Thanks. I left the money on the counter. Later, pal."

Without another word, without another glance toward the woman he'd once expected to marry, Beck hopped in his truck, turned the key, and pulled out of the gas station reminding himself that Tansy Calhoun—no, make that Tansy Forbes—was history. Ancient history.

Tommy watched as first Beck, then Tansy headed down the road. He dug out his phone.

Chapter 2

Too restless to head back to work, Beck turned off the main drag and drove along one of the smaller ones that led toward the river. Spotting the sign for Whiskey Road, he made a quick right. If his pal Cole was home, he'd probably have the inside scoop since Tansy and his fiancée had been best friends since kindergarten. If Tansy was indeed moving home, Jenni Beth would know.

He'd have thought somebody would have given him a heads-up.

Beck pulled into the drive behind Jenni Beth's '65 'Vette and studied the renovated barn his friend called home. Since Cole owned a huge architectural salvaging company in Savannah, he'd filled the house with some really unique pieces, like the granite-covered trough in the master bath.

Right now, though, Beck didn't care about that trough. He had an inexplicable—and unwelcome—pain in his chest. Climbing out, he slammed the truck's door.

Cole rounded the corner. "Hey, Beck, figured you'd be at work." His eyes narrowed. "What's wrong? Your family okay?"

"Yeah, everyone's fine."

Jenni Beth stepped out of the house, a glass of iced tea in one hand, a ring of fabric swatches in the other. "Hey, Beck, maybe you can help. I'm tryin' to decide on table covering colors for my New Year's Eve bride. She can't make up her mind between blue and purple." She held up the ring. "What do you think?"

He shrugged. "No clue."

"Want some tea?"

"Yeah. No. I don't know." He jammed his hands in his pockets.

Her face clouded with concern.

Kicking his front tire, he said, "Tansy's in town."

His friends shared a look, and it wasn't one of surprise. "How long have you known she's movin' back, Cole?"

"Jenni Beth told me last night."

"And you didn't call?"

"At midnight?"

"How 'bout you, Jenni Beth?"

"She told me a couple weeks ago she was comin' today."

"Son of a—"

Not in the least intimidated by his scowl, she walked to him and threaded her arm through one of his. He didn't move a muscle, hands still tucked in his pockets.

"Sam said you were with him when Lucinda spilled the beans about preschool."

"Yeah, I was." He scuffed his booted foot over the pebbles. "But, hell, when nothin' happened, I assumed she'd come to her senses." He raised his head and met her gaze. "Why would she move back here?"

"Because she *did* finally come to her senses. Now that she's divorced the loser, she wants to start over."

"Why here?"

Jenni Beth shrugged. “Same reason I came back. Misty Bottoms is home. Did you run into her, Beck?”

A muscle worked in his jaw. “Yep. Stopped at Tommy’s for some gas and she pulled in with Gracie and a jam-packed SUV.”

Cole dropped onto a wooden chair and nodded for Beck to sit. “Thought you’d moved past all this, bud.”

“I have. It’s just—I don’t know. Damn, she looked beat—and would hate that I noticed.”

Jenni Beth sighed. “And I’ve added to her load.”

“What?” Beck looked confused.

“She hadn’t even hit the town limits when I begged her to tackle three cakes. This week.”

Cole took her hand, ran his thumb over the back of it. “Probably best she stays busy, sugar.” Turning to Beck, he changed the subject. “You still gonna be able to help me on that new Savannah project this week?

“You bet.” He checked his watch and gave Jenni Beth a quick hug. “Gotta run. Take care of Tansy. And don’t you dare tell her I said that.”

“Okay.” She hugged him back. “I know this is hard for you.”

“I’ll be fine.”

“You seemed pretty fine last week when Rachel, that hot brunette you’ve been seeing in Savannah, showed up on the job site.” Cole shot a look toward Jenni Beth. “Not that I noticed her.”

Jenni Beth just shook her head.

“I like Rachel,” Beck said.

“But?”

“I’m not sure it’s gonna work. I told her it might be time for us to start seein’ other people.”

Cole tipped his head. "Kind of like Roxy?"

"Yeah."

"And Cindy?"

Beck rolled his eyes skyward. "You sayin' there's a pattern here?"

"Nope." Cole smiled. "You did."

"Point taken."

"You don't still love her?"

"Who?"

Cole snorted. "Who?"

"No." Beck shook his head. "That's long-ago over and done with. But I *was* in love with her. She left, I mourned, and we both moved on."

"Glad to hear it."

Something in Cole's tone warned Beck his pal didn't believe him. "It's true."

Jenni Beth chimed in. "Thou dost protest—"

"Too much," Beck finished. "Yeah, yeah. I took Mrs. Fitzgibbon's English lit class, too." He tapped Jenni Beth on the top of her head. "Don't you have something to cook or clean?"

She narrowed her eyes. "Once."

"What?"

"You get a pass on a comment like that once."

He laughed. "So noted."

"Seriously, Beck—"

"I'm good. I've got this covered. Thanks for listening." He slapped his thighs. "I've got to go. It's a workday. Jobs to do, people to see."

With a single wave, Beck hopped in his truck and headed toward the Savannah River. Forcing himself to drive sanely, he acknowledged the fact that specters of days past rode with him. How many times had he and Tansy stolen off to the riverbank to snag a few kisses? Hot kisses. Kisses that ripped him up inside.

Now? Hadn't his life just turned on its ear! Tansy. So slick and polished, except for that unruly, tousled head of auburn curls. He'd teased her no end that her hair gave her away, hinted at what lay beneath her cool exterior and exposed the wild child locked away.

And that wild side had driven him nuts. Even now, memories of the two of them steaming up the windows in the old truck he drove in high school spiked his blood pressure.

Then Tansy'd given that wild side away. To Emerson Forbes.

He pulled onto the shoulder, under the shade of a weeping willow. Time he let go of the anger. She'd moved on and so had he.

Still, pinching the bridge of his nose, he tussled with the reality of a newly divorced Tansy who'd returned to Misty Bottoms. And with her? Gracie, Emerson's daughter.

Every time he saw that beautiful little girl with either Tansy or her grandma it tore him up. She should have been his, should be little Gracie Elliot, not Gracie Forbes. But she wasn't, and that was that.

He and Tansy? Past tense. Still, he'd just as soon not run into her when he turned a corner in the grocery store or walked into Dee-Ann's Diner.

Shit!

Whew! Tansy's knees went wobbly when Beck stepped out of Tommy's. Even after everything that had happened, her fingers itched to run through all that curly blond hair. But his eyes had changed. They used to be full of love—for her. One look and she felt cherished. Not anymore.

"Mama? I'm thirsty." Gracie, wide awake now and blissfully unaware of Tansy's turmoil, caught her eye in the rearview mirror.

They'd already pulled out of the Texaco station, and the drinks in their tiny cooler had gone warm after Gracie'd played around in it and left the top off.

"We'll stop at Kitty's, honey. You can get a drink there."

Since she had three cakes to create this week, she'd take a few minutes to talk to Kitty about them. She'd work up some designs after Gracie fell asleep tonight.

She also needed to pull herself together a bit before she hit her mom's. Even though she'd run into Beck occasionally when she'd visited, it felt different this time. It *was* different. She was now a single mother with no home and no job.

Jeez.

"Are we almost there, Mama? I'm hungry, too."

"Another couple minutes. Pinky promise."

Gracie grinned. "'Kay."

Driving along Main Street, Tansy noticed a change, an air of hope. Yes, the brick sidewalks still buckled in places, but no empty storefronts stared back at her. People she'd never seen before wandered along the street, shopping bags in hand. A new gourmet wine and cheese shop had opened in the old five-and-dime building. The drug store had a fresh coat of paint.

The town looked good. Vibrant. Darlene, the owner

of Quilty Pleasures, walked her pair of Cairn terriers, dressed today in jaunty green-and-blue-plaid sweaters to match hers.

Tansy slowed and lowered her driver's side window. "Hey, Darlene."

"Hey, yourself, Tansy. Welcome home!" She scooped up first Mint Julep and then Moonshine, waving their paws. Her voice raised three octaves as she slid into baby talk. "Tell Gracie we're glad to see her. Yes, we are." She kissed each of the dogs' noses.

In the backseat, Gracie Bella giggled and waved. "Can I have a doggie, Mama?"

"Maybe someday." A red Volkswagen beetle came up behind her, so with a promise to stop by Darlene's shop, she continued down the street, a smile tugging at her lips. Jenni Beth Beaumont, with her dreams and hard work, had put Misty Bottoms back on the map. Magnolia House, her renovated antebellum home, had become *the spot* for destination weddings, engagement parties, proms, reunions, birthday parties, you name it.

Tansy's heart fluttered. With this week's cakes, she'd be part of that.

Live oaks, heavy with Spanish moss, shaded the sidewalks and added an air of gentility to the street. There was a hint of fall in the air, and the little park that separated the two sides of Main Street burst with the golds and russets of autumn flowers. The Ladies' Garden Club had clustered chrysanthemums, zinnias, and pansies around an old wooden wheelbarrow. Scattered pumpkins added a festive flair.

Autumn. Her favorite season.

As she idled past Dee-Ann's Diner, the old building all

but smiled at her in its red-and-white finery. Geraniums bloomed in planters out front, and Lem sat at a table by the window. No doubt he was mooching something off Dee-Ann even though he had nearly as much money as Croesus.

Misty Bottoms. So different from the glitzy shops and malls she'd grown used to. The town felt comfortable, like slipping into a pair of favorite slippers.

The big question? Could she fit into life here again or had she been gone too long?

Only time would tell if those slippers welcomed her or pinched her feet.

She turned onto Old Church Street, past the pretty little periwinkle railroad car that boasted a florist and gardening center, and slid to the curb in front of Kitty's Kakes and Bakery with its funky pink-and-green awning. The shop's huge front window proudly displayed today's temptations and looked exactly as it had when she and Beck had stopped in for a treat before Saturday football games—another lifetime ago.

The bell above Kitty's door jingled welcomingly when Tansy pushed it open.

Gracie squeezed around her to run inside. "Ms. Kitty, we're here!" Her soft child's voice was high-pitched with excitement.

Kitty peeked around the kitchen doorway, her full face breaking into a sunny smile. "Well, you certainly are, Gracie Bella."

Wiping her hands on the batter-smeared apron that covered her girth, she stepped around the corner of the display case, arms wide to catch the grinning child. "Welcome home."

Tansy watched as Kitty kissed her child and fussed over her.

"Don't you look a picture!"

Gracie's brows drew together, and the older woman laughed.

"You're as pretty as any picture I've ever seen," she amended.

"Mama bought me a new dress for today." Twirling, she showed off the pastel-flowered smock. "I gots ribbons to match." She reached up to her long, dark hair and fingered the silky ties in her ponytail.

"You sure do." Kitty turned her gaze to Tansy. "You doin' okay?"

She nodded.

"Been to your mom's yet?"

"No." She pointed to the packed vehicle. "That's our next stop. Gracie and I decided a drink and a snack were in order first."

"Then you've come to the right place." Kitty studied Tansy. "I know this has been hard for you, sweetie, but it sure is good to have you home."

Tansy gave her a wobbly smile. "It's good to be home."

"One of these days, you'll be able to say that and mean it," Kitty said.

Tansy nodded sadly.

"It'll be okay." She patted Tansy's shoulder, then turned to her daughter. "Why don't you come over here and show me what you want, sweetheart?" Kitty took Gracie by the hand and led her to the rows of baked goodies.

"I think, as much as I'd like one of your maple-iced donuts, we should both stick with bagels," Tansy said.

"Neither of us has had much today." She glanced at her daughter. "A sugar high's probably not a great idea, so we'll save the donuts for another time."

"Smart." Her gaze ran over Tansy. "You're way too thin, though, honey. I think a few calories might be exactly what the doctor ordered."

When she opened her mouth to protest, Kitty shook her head. "But not today. Understood." Her tongs reached inside the case for a bagel. "Toasted?"

"Yes, please."

"I have some maple-flavored cream cheese." She eyed Tansy.

Laughing, Tansy said, "Why not?"

"To drink?"

"A glass of milk and a cup of coffee. Black."

"Can I have a soda, Mama?"

Tansy shook her head, and the little girl's lip stuck out in the beginning of a pout.

"Kitty has the best milk in the county," Tansy said.

"You got that right. Maybe in all the South."

"You do?" Gracie pressed her face against the display case.

"Yes, ma'am." As Kitty prepared their order, she spoke over her shoulder. "You still want to do this?"

Nerves sizzled. "Yes, I do, but the location's crucial."

"Not much to choose from. The town's booming!"

"Jenni Beth's dream has been good for Misty Bottoms, hasn't it?"

"A blessing. And Cricket? Hard worker, that girl. I liked her right off. Our new deputy's warmed up to her, too."

"So I hear." Tansy pulled a couple of napkins from a

holder. "I'll call Quinlyn Deveroux tomorrow. See if she has anything that might fit my needs. I'm really hoping to find something with living quarters above. My budget would be a whole lot happier paying one mortgage."

"Thought you were livin' with your mama." Kitty placed their drinks in front of them and went back for the bagels.

"Only till I find something." Tansy unwrapped Gracie's straw. "I need to be on my own."

"Understood." Returning with their food, Kitty dropped into a chair beside her, buttered the bagel for Gracie, and cut it into quarters.

"Jenni Beth says you're swamped."

"I am. Honey, to be honest, the only reason I'm still open is because I don't want to let her down. She needs somebody to bake her cakes and such, but I'm too old and too tired."

"You're not old!

"I am. I checked my mirror this mornin'. Above my head, the name Methuselah flashed on and off." She opened and closed her hand in a flashing gesture.

Tansy laughed. "Quit."

"That's exactly what I want to do." Kitty sipped the coffee she'd poured for herself. "This is a young person's job. Besides, Harvey's finished his treatments. He beat the Big C. Got a clean bill of health on his last visit."

Tansy squeezed her hand. "Mom told me, and I can't tell you how happy I was to hear that."

"You and me both. It's time I retire. Time somebody else takes care of this town's sweet tooth and caffeine addiction. Harv and I don't plan to leave Misty Bottoms right away, but eventually we'd like to sell that big old house we're in and downsize. We're thinkin' to move to Charleston to be close to our daughter. She and Joe have two little ones now." Kitty pulled a phone from her pocket and brought up the latest pictures of her grandchildren.

Tansy looked at them while she picked at her bagel. Gracie demolished hers, and Tansy felt a prick of guilt. She should have realized sooner how hungry Gracie'd been. But then she'd been asleep, right?

Ah, the perils of parenthood. Tansy did guilt extremely well.

Beck, stepping out of the gas station, that heated moment when their eyes met, popped into her head. Regret, stepsister to guilt, washed over her. Yep, she was an expert at guilt and all its relatives.

She yanked herself back to Kitty's conversation.

"If I owned this place, honey, I'd let you have it for a song. But, stupid me, I've leased it all these years. Made a small fortune for Howard Greene. Like I said, though, the equipment's all mine, and you're welcome to whatever you can use. You can have it for a song instead."

"I appreciate that." Tansy stacked their plates, then stood and carried their trash to the wastebasket. "So we have three cakes to make, huh?"

"*You* have three cakes," Kitty said. "Let me get the order forms, and we can go over them. And for you"—she pointed at Gracie—"I've got a *Frozen* coloring book and some crayons."

Gracie clapped her hands. "Is Olaf in it?"

"Yes, he is." She carried the book and crayons to Gracie, then held up a finger to Tansy. "I have one quick call I need to make."

"Fine. I'll get another coffee if you don't mind?"

"Help yourself. Pour me a refill, too, would you?" Kitty pulled her cell from her apron pocket and punched in a number. She moved behind her bakery case. "Hey, you out and about?"

She listened a minute, then said, "I've got some of my date-filled cookies here. Your mom's favorite. If you could stop by in the next little bit, I'll send them home with you." She nodded. "Wonderful. See you."

Walking over to a filing cabinet, she pulled out three folders.

"There you go." She set them on the table beside Tansy. "I've got a hunch you can put some magic in these."

Tansy flipped open the first. "Betsy and Clem. They want a Vegas-themed wedding?"

"Roulette table and all. Beck managed to find everything Jenni Beth is gonna need to turn the barn into a Vegas gambling hall for the day—minus the actual betting, of course. That would be against the law."

"I didn't realize she was using the old barn."

"You know Cole and old buildings. Nothin' he likes more than to get his hands on one. He and Beck have worked miracles with Jenni Beth's. It's like a blank canvas. She can turn it into anything she—or her brides—want."

"Hmmm." She flipped open a second file. "A vintage-style wedding?" She rubbed her hands together. "This will be fun! I know exactly what I want to do with this one."

Before she could take a peek at the notes for Tanya and Ray Miller's daughter's sweet sixteen party, the door opened.

"Do you know what Coralee's…up to?" Beck stopped,

one foot in, one foot out of the bakery shop as he caught sight of Tansy. He swore all the oxygen in the place had been sucked out.

"Beck." The page Tansy held fluttered, and she laid it on the table.

He nodded at her, then glanced toward a very innocent-looking Kitty.

Beaming, she hustled behind the counter, then handed him a coffee. "Here you go. On the house. Look who just got into town. Why don't you catch up with her while I get those cookies boxed up?"

"Your timing's off, Kitty."

The older woman plumped her gray hair. "I don't think so, honey. Have a seat. This won't take but a minute."

He'd rather stand. Hell, he'd rather eat Dee-Ann's liver and onions or walk barefoot over a fire ant hill. But since neither was an option, he walked stiffly to where Tansy sat, staring with those damn big blue-green eyes of hers.

Taking a deep breath, coffee in hand, he headed into enemy territory. Nodding at the empty chair beside Gracie, he asked, "You mind?"

"Not at all."

He nearly spewed the sip he'd just taken. If her voice had been any chillier, that snowman Gracie was coloring would turn to a chunk of ice.

Tapping the picture, he asked, "Whatcha doin' there, Gracie?"

"I'm drawin' a necklace for Olaf, Beck."

Raising a brow and ignoring the question in Tansy's incredible Caribbean-blue eyes, he returned his gaze to Gracie. "You do know Olaf's a guy, right?"

"Yeah, but he wants one."

"Okay." He drew out the word, then lifted his gaze to meet her mama's.

"What were you saying about Coralee?"

"Your crazy aunt's up to somethin', Tanz, and knowin' her?" He shook his head. "Could be anything."

"Well, you know what they say. Here in the South, we don't bother to hide crazy. We plop it right down in a rocker on the front porch with a big old glass of sweet tea."

"If Coralee would stay on the front porch, I'd be good with that," Beck answered. "Problem is she carries that crazy all over town."

"Don't I know it." Tansy sipped her coffee. "Remember the time she marched down to the old swimming hole where the Sunday school class was splashing around, stripped down to her skivvies, and insisted Pastor Jeremiah baptize her? I about died of embarrassment."

He laughed. "And if memory serves, you hid behind me so she couldn't see you. But she waded right over to you and pulled you along beside her, insisting you be a witness."

"I swore I'd disown her."

"But you didn't."

"No. Deep down, she's a wonderful woman."

Gracie tugged at Beck's sleeve. "She bought me a BB gun."

His mouth dropped open. "For a four-year-old?"

"Mama put it away. She said I had to be older to shoot it." She turned that beautiful smile on him. "I think I should have it now. Don't you?"

Despite himself, he grinned. "Oh no, you don't." He tapped the end of her nose. "I'm not gettin' into this. What your mama says goes."

The child's smile turned to a pout.

"And will the real Gracie Bella please stand up?" Tansy sighed.

"Why do you want me to stand up, Mama?"

Tansy looked toward the ceiling and shook her head. "It's just a saying."

"'Kay." She bent her head to her coloring, tongue slipping out between her lips as she concentrated.

Tansy studied her daughter. "Gracie, how do you know Beck?"

"He comes to see Grandma."

Tansy met Beck's midnight-blue eyes. "Seriously?"

He shrugged. "I like your mom. The problem was between you and me, Tanz. Never with me and your mom or dad." He nodded toward the papers she'd spread over the table. "What have you got there?"

"Cake orders. Jenni Beth called on my way into town. It seems our unflappable Ms. B is quite flapped."

Beck threw her a lopsided grin. "Yeah, it's that old 'be careful what you ask for.' She said she'd thrown herself on your mercy."

Kitty swiped at some powdered sugar on the counter. "Afraid that's my fault. I can't keep up with both the bakery and all the fancies for Magnolia House's events."

"Nonsense. You can still run circles around all of us," Tansy said.

"Harv's cancer took a lot out of me."

"But he's good now," Beck said.

"He is. And looking forward to my retirement. Says

he intends to chase me around the bed mornin', noon, and night." She blushed like a schoolgirl.

"You play tag?" Gracie asked.

Everybody chuckled.

"Somethin' like that," Beck answered. To Kitty, he said, "Enviable goals, you ask me."

His gaze settled on Tansy. "Chasin' is fun." He arched a brow. "Catchin' is even more fun."

She choked on her coffee. "Beck, you can't say things like that."

"Sure I can. I just did."

He looked up to see Kitty holding a white baker's box, a twinkle in her eyes. An uneasy thought slithered through his mind. Had she mistakenly called him while Tansy was here or was the old gal up to something?

Nah. Everybody knew he and Tansy were history.

About the Author

The luxury of staying home when the weather turns nasty, of working in pj's and bare feet, and the fact that daydreaming is not only permissible but encouraged are a few of the reasons middle school teacher Lynnette Austin gave up the classroom to write full-time. Lynnette grew up in Pennsylvania's Allegheny Mountains, moved to Upstate New York, then to the Rockies in Wyoming. Presently she and her husband divide their time between Southwest Florida's beaches and Georgia's Blue Ridge Mountains. A finalist in RWA's Golden Heart Contest, PASIC's Book of Your Heart Contest, and Georgia Romance Writers' Maggie Contest, she's also published five books as Lynnette Hallberg. She's currently writing as Lynnette Austin. *Every Bride Has Her Day* is the second in her sparkling new contemporary romance series, Magnolia Brides. Visit Lynnette at www.authorlynnetteaustin.com.